"A beautifully c... derness that cel... ships and the c... rich in detail, you'll feel bubbles on your tongue."
—Susan Meissner, bestselling author of *Only the Beautiful*

"Blackwell sits firmly on my list of must-read authors!"
—*New York Times* bestselling author Victoria Laurie

"Plan your trip to Provence now. In this meticulously researched novel, Juliet Blackwell deftly navigates three time periods, taking us from contemporary California to both the Belle Époque and Nazi-occupied France as she spins a story as charming as an antique carousel."
—Sally Koslow, author of *The Real Mrs. Tobias*

"With crystalline imagery, vivid characters, and lively prose, Juliet Blackwell redefines what family means in a way that will touch readers long after they've read the last page. . . . This novel should come with a warning: will cause enormous desire to travel to France."
—Stephen P. Kiernan, author of *The Glass Château*

"Blackwell seamlessly incorporates details about art, cast making, and the City of Light . . . [and] especially stuns in the aftermath of the main story by unleashing a twist that is both a complete surprise and a point that expertly ties everything together." —*Publishers Weekly*

"Bestselling author Blackwell brings us another captivating tale from the City of Light." —*Booklist*

TITLES BY JULIET BLACKWELL

ASYLUM HOTEL

THE PARIS SHOWROOM

OFF THE WILD COAST OF BRITTANY

THE VINEYARDS OF CHAMPAGNE

THE LOST CAROUSEL OF PROVENCE

LETTERS FROM PARIS

THE PARIS KEY

The Witchcraft Mystery Series

SYNCHRONIZED SORCERY

BEWITCHED AND BETROTHED

A MAGICAL MATCH

A TOXIC TROUSSEAU

SPELLCASTING IN SILK

A VISION IN VELVET

TARNISHED AND TORN

IN A WITCH'S WARDROBE

HEXES AND HEMLINES

A CAST-OFF COVEN

SECONDHAND SPIRITS

The Haunted Home Renovation Series

THE LAST CURTAIN CALL

A GHOSTLY LIGHT

GIVE UP THE GHOST

KEEPER OF THE CASTLE

A HAUNTING IS BREWING

HOME FOR THE HAUNTING

MURDER ON THE HOUSE

DEAD BOLT

IF WALLS COULD TALK

ASYLUM HOTEL

JULIET BLACKWELL

BERKLEY

NEW YORK

BERKLEY
An imprint of Penguin Random House LLC
1745 Broadway, New York, NY 10019
penguinrandomhouse.com

Book design by George Towne
Interior art: Dark Room © Rob van Hal / Shutterstock

Library of Congress Cataloging-in-Publication Data

Names: Blackwell, Juliet, author.
Title: Asylum hotel / Juliet Blackwell.
Description: First edition. | New York : Berkley, 2025.
Identifiers: LCCN 2024048368 (print) | LCCN 2024048369 (ebook) |
ISBN 9780593638248 (trade paperback) | ISBN 9780593638255 (ebook)
Subjects: LCGFT: Detective and mystery fiction. | Novels.
Classification: LCC PS3602.L32578 A88 2025 (print) |
LCC PS3602.L32578 (ebook) | DDC 813/.6—dc23/eng/20241021
LC record available at https://lccn.loc.gov/2024048368
LC ebook record available at https://lccn.loc.gov/2024048369

First Edition: July 2025

Printed in the United States of America
1st Printing

The authorized representative in the EU for product safety and compliance is
Penguin Random House Ireland, Morrison Chambers, 32 Nassau Street, Dublin
D02 YH68, Ireland, https://eu-contact.penguin.ie.

To Xe Sands
Who inspired this novel through her nuanced,
tender, loving photography—
and our shared love of all things abandoned.

ASYLUM HOTEL

PROLOGUE

Had she known about the Seabrink curse, she might not have gone. Aubrey Spencer was on the hunt for photographs, not for ghosts.

But in all her research there had been barely a mention of the old Hotel Seabrink, and only a passing reference to a few long-ago tragedies. All Aubrey knew was that the grand hotel had been built by the fabulously wealthy T. Jefferson Goffin, who had made his fortune in the unromantic field of salt mining before investing in the quixotic world of moviemaking. The Seabrink had been a lure to Hollywood's elite during the Golden Age of cinema, and its guests included movie stars such as Clark Gable and Judy Garland and Bette Davis. The presence of such celluloid luminaries attracted the wealthy and powerful to the Seabrink to mingle with their idols at glittering parties and dazzling banquets, and to stroll through its extensive, walled-in gardens far from the hoi polloi.

But it wasn't just the chance to hobnob with the rich and famous that enticed those privileged guests to this remote stretch of the Northern California coast, where the Spanish Gothic extravaganza clung, barnacle-like, to a mountainside overlooking the Pacific Ocean. The Seabrink also held out the promise of improved health, thanks to the natural mineral water that flowed into the large stone baths in the hotel's basement and was piped into every lucky guest's room. The special waters were said to cure everything from rheumatism to pneumonia to what was referred to, unironically, as simply "the crazies."

As it turned out, statins and antibiotics and mood-altering drugs did a better job of curing whatever ailed a person than the Seabrink's Miracle Water Cure. And as the health of the hotel's founder, T. Jefferson Goffin, began to fail, he was beset by scandal and his fortune dwindled. Younger movie stars began opting for weekends in Vegas and Acapulco over remote mountain resorts, and the wealthy and powerful soon followed.

When the hotel's storied guests did not return, the live-in staff began to look for work elsewhere, and the once-fine Hotel Seabrink closed its doors.

It was soon shuttered. Forsaken. Neglected.

But as with all grand, abandoned buildings, that was not the end of the story.

Not by a long shot.

And Aubrey Spencer, camera in hand, arrived to immortalize the Hotel Seabrink in all its derelict glory.

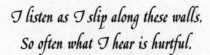

I listen as I slip along these walls.
So often what I hear is hurtful.

Perhaps we are all born maniacs.
That's what they say I am.
But they have never understood me.

ONE

A rusty, pockmarked NO TRESPASSING sign dangled from the Hotel Seabrink's massive wrought-iron gates. It *clang-clang-clang*ed against the open gates, swaying slightly in the breeze; the mournful sound echoed off the high stone walls surrounding the grounds of the former hotel.

Aubrey got out of her car and paused, breathing deeply of the damp mountain air scented with evergreen needles—redwood and Monterey pine—as well as the distinct but indefinable aroma of the decaying plants that carpeted the forest floor.

In the normal course of her life Aubrey Spencer was a rules follower, sometimes to a fault. But when she was on the hunt for photographs, all bets were off.

After another brief moment of hesitation, she slipped through the gates.

The Seabrink's once-manicured grounds were now choked with weeds and wild plants native to the Northern California coast; the forest was reclaiming its own. Leaves and pine needles blanketed the brick and stone pathways, and ivy had run wild, climbing over the walls and winding itself around lichen-encrusted statuary whose original forms were now left to the imagination. Vibrant ferns dotted old stone benches, and a thick carpeting of moss encased long-empty stone planters.

Gravel crunched underfoot as Aubrey walked up the long drive. The grounds were otherwise quiet, the only sounds those of nature: the birds flitting through the trees and the breeze rustling the oak leaves. A squirrel eyed her from the top of one high stone wall, chattering indignantly at her presence, and two hawks—or maybe turkey vultures?—glided through the air high overhead.

The drive ended in a large loop encircling a massive fountain in front of the hotel's main entrance. The pool was filled with stagnant rainwater, bright green with algae. The fountain's sculpture featured three women, their faces distorted in anger and their hair entwined with snakes, attacking a cowering young man as he attempts to flee, his head covered by his muscular arms.

"Welcome, one and all, to the Hotel Seabrink," Aubrey murmured to herself.

She snapped a few photos of the fountain and gardens but did not linger. It was the building itself that called to her.

Aubrey had first stumbled across a brief reference to the Hotel Seabrink while perusing the musty aisles of her favorite used bookstore in Oakland. In a slim, self-published volume on the history of coastal Northern California, she read:

The famous Hotel Seabrink, tucked into the hills north of Stewarts Point with a spectacular view of the mighty Pacific Ocean, was from its beginning mired in scandal and lurid rumor. The pet project of the fabulously wealthy salt miner, T. Jefferson Goffin, the lavishly decorated hotel (reminiscent of Hearst Castle much farther down the coast) was host not only to the Hollywood and financial elite from the 1920s through the 1940s, but also to several mysterious deaths. The most recent known fatalities were of a teenager murdered in the hotel's famed spa baths on her prom night by a security guard who had been hired to protect the abandoned building, and his own subsequent suicide. Perhaps overcome by guilt, he was found hanging in the hotel's main stairwell.

That's all it said. Just those four tantalizing sentences before the author turned to a discussion of the nearby coastal communities of Stewarts Point, Sea Ranch, and Gualala. Aubrey tried researching the Hotel Seabrink on the internet, but although T. Jefferson Goffin's life was otherwise well-documented, she could find only passing references to the actual hotel.

Now she studied the massive building through her camera's viewfinder and took a few shots of the exterior. The hotel was four stories tall, built in the Spanish Gothic revival style popular during the Golden Age of Hollywood. There were intricate stucco decorations surrounding the windows and doors, multiple panes of dazzling stained glass—many of them now broken—and two soaring towers. *A Hearst Castle wannabe indeed*, she thought.

Half a dozen shallow stone steps led up to the main entrance, where massive wooden doors hung on black iron hinges. A drawing in smeared yellow chalk marred the dark wood doors; the design was a stylized cross bisected by several crooked lines and circles. At the base of the door was something that looked like a line of salt. Aubrey took photos of each.

The metal doorknob was cold and slick in her hand as she tried to turn it. Locked. No surprise there.

She went back down the steps and explored the area to the right of the building, where she found the remains of an atrium, half of its glass panels smashed. Moving carefully to avoid the jagged shards at the edge of a low window, she climbed through and slipped inside, glass debris snapping underfoot. A bird's nest was lodged in one corner, atop a caryatid. The floor of the atrium was a now-mossy mosaic with an intricate design featuring a symbol surrounded by stylized snakes. Long strands of ivy hung down through the broken sunroof and still more moss blanketed the frayed remnants of a woven loveseat. Its pillows had been shredded, the stuffing no doubt long ago harvested to line the nests of birds and rodents.

Aubrey shot photos with abandon, marveling as always at how different everything appeared when viewed through the lens of her camera. She often preferred the camera's version of reality to what she saw with her bare eyes. Was it the addition of boundaries, of parameters that appealed to her? The barrier the camera created between her and the world? Without it, she often felt overwhelmed by her own feelings.

In the viewfinder there was also no smell of mildew and must and neglect. Empty buildings carried a scent, an aura of something . . . almost sacred. But also rank.

Aubrey jumped as a mouse scurried past. That explained some of the odor.

She took a small vial of Thieves oil from her backpack and rubbed a dab of the clove-scented oil under her nose. Funny to think how appropriate the name was: Thieves oil. Not that

Aubrey ever stole anything, no matter how tempting. There was a code.

A massive set of French doors connected the atrium to the building's interior. She pushed one door open, revealing a wide corridor with intricately tiled floors. A detailed frieze near the ceiling ran the length of the hallway, echoing the mosaic's design in muted colors of ochre and sienna and sap green. Half a dozen small oil paintings in gold gilt frames decorated the walls, depicting anonymous landscapes and seascapes. Several hung crookedly, as if jostled by a long-ago elbow.

Aubrey proceeded down the hall, toward the front of the building.

The massive hotel lobby was paneled in some kind of wood that she didn't recognize but that looked expensive. The high, water-stained ceiling featured a mural of cherubs frolicking in celestial clouds with an occasional star twinkling through. A fireplace with an art deco marble surround was big enough to walk into without ducking. Ferns sprouted from an old banquette, and ivy snaked in through a broken window and wrapped itself around a heavy wooden desk with carved rococo detail. Round upholstered benches made of what appeared to be tufted velvet were caked with dust and grime and splitting at the seams. A huge cloisonné vase in an arched niche held a cluster of ragged peacock feathers, furry with dust. A tall grandfather clock, its brass pendulum long since silenced, stood in one corner, its ornately wrought hands frozen at 4:07.

Aubrey took photos of a couple of old-fashioned wooden wheelchairs and a single gurney, forlorn and dusty. What was *that* about?

Holding pride of place in the precise center of the lobby stood a grand piano. It was covered in fallen paint chips and a thick layer of dust, but it otherwise appeared to be in decent condition. Aubrey tapped a couple of the piano's keys; their discordant notes echoed in the emptiness of the once-bustling lobby.

Behind a long wooden counter was a wooden grid of tiny boxes marked with room numbers, with many of the old-fashioned brass keys still in their allotted nooks.

How are those keys still here? Or the paintings, or even the wheelchairs, for that matter? How has this building not been entirely looted?

Perhaps it was due to the Hotel Seabrink's remote location and lack of presence on the internet. Still. The building had been abandoned for decades. Surely those with the soul of an intrepid scofflaw—like her—had walked these halls before. A smattering of graffiti testified that Aubrey was hardly the first trespasser.

Taking a seat on the edge of a sturdy oak chair, Aubrey closed her eyes and soaked in the profound silence unique to abandoned places. She let the history envelop her, settling on her shoulders like a soft blanket.

In her mind's eye, Aubrey could see the laborers who had built these walls; the staff who had run the hotel; the guests hustling in and out, looking forward to a pampered respite, glittering parties, and water cures. Romantic trysts and high-powered deals, secret jealousies and raucous good times. She heard jaunty piano music, and could see a beautiful, bejeweled woman perched on the bench, smiling flirtatiously as she played for the new arrivals. All those moments were now gone; the commotion of new arrivals, the dinging of the service bells, the clattering of silverware, the laughter and whispers and conversation, had been replaced by a bone-deep stillness. It was an abnormally silent void, simultaneously eerie and comforting.

Most of Aubrey's life was so . . . noisy.

The weight around her neck reminded Aubrey of why she was here. Lifting her camera, she got up, adjusted the lens, took a deep breath, and started shooting photos.

Off the main lobby, through an arched doorway, she found a library covered from floor to ceiling in bookshelves, a ladder on rails allowing access to the volumes on the high shelves. Dozens of books lay splayed on the wooden floor, but most remained on the shelves gathering dust. There was another huge fireplace, this one beige marble with a mantel carved with angels. Flakes of ceiling paint and bits of plaster were sprinkled over everything—books, furniture, the floor—giving the impression of a dusting of snow.

Above the fireplace hung an oil painting of the Hotel Seabrink in its heyday. Guests in old-fashioned garb strolled the landscaped gardens, the window boxes were filled with lush flowers, and a bellboy stood at attention at the front doors, ready to receive the hotel's elite guests. On one wall a series of framed and signed celebrity headshots captured Aubrey's attention, though she did not recognize the names. A few blank spots on the walls suggested some photos had been removed, no doubt those of the more famous movie stars.

One large, framed black-and-white photo depicted a grand costume ball. Men and women sported Venetian masks, a few young women were dressed up as French maids, and one woman wore a Cleopatra costume. Another photograph was a solo shot of a beautiful, sloe-eyed woman with a barely there smile, dressed as a fairy. She wore a band across her forehead, with a large jewel right in the middle. Apart from the actors' studio headshots, it was the only solo portrait, making Aubrey wonder who the woman was.

Aubrey froze as she smelled cigar smoke and caught a whiff of perfume. Turning around slowly, she saw no sign of anyone and heard nothing more than the pounding of her own heart and the harsh sound of her ragged breathing.

Your imagination run amok, no doubt. The people in the photos seemed so alive, so vivid, that she could practically smell them.

Aubrey took several shots of the framed photographs, then moved on to what she imagined had been a smoking room, paneled from floor to ceiling and furnished with leather club chairs. Maybe this was why she had smelled cigars? The smoking room led on to what appeared to be an executive office, dominated by a massive oak desk. Several cabinet doors stood open and empty, and in one corner sat an ornate Victrola atop an intricately decorated stand.

She startled at the sound of fluttering. Or . . . was it a whisper? A sigh? It was more a sensation than an actual noise. Aubrey reached for her can of pepper spray, again glancing over her shoulder to make sure she alone was roaming these broad corridors.

She continued down a long hallway. A swinging door creaked loudly as she pushed through and found herself in the hotel's enormous kitchen. She could practically hear the banging of pots and pans, the clatter of silverware and clink of dishes as the staff prepared gourmet meals for the lauded guests. Exploring the large space, she found a pantry with shelves still half-full of mason jars and ancient canned goods.

Aubrey spied a row of large earthen jugs emblazoned with the hotel's logo and labeled **CRAZY WATER**. She winced. Huh. It was a different time indeed.

Aubrey clicked photos freely, grateful that her digital camera enabled her to take as many images as she wanted. She was never quite able to capture the haunting yet romantic nature of an abandoned building, to evoke the smells and the sounds and the three-dimensional feel of it all, the sacredness that permeated the decay. Still, looking through the camera lens allowed her to concentrate, to sublimate her father's recent death, the disaster at work, the nightmares that ensued. When she was behind her camera, the world was reduced to nothing but what she saw through her viewfinder.

She called it her photographic fugue state, a feeling of momentarily existing out of time and space.

Focus, Aubrey. Just click.

Returning to the lobby, she snapped a few photos of the ornate metal cage encapsulating the old-fashioned elevator, then headed for the grand staircase. The stairs weren't circular but elliptical, the center opening an oval shape like a giant eye, topped by a still-intact stained-glass cupola.

Aubrey knew that stairs can be dicey in abandoned buildings, and are often among the first parts of any structure to collapse. But these steps were made of stone, which should be sturdy. Still, she placed one foot after another carefully, listening for creaks or groans. Her phone did not appear to have service, and no one knew where she was; if something were to happen to her, she wondered, how long would it take before she was found? Would she become just one more of the Hotel Seabrink's "mysterious deaths"?

As she cautiously mounted the stairs, Aubrey's mind was again filled with the low thrum of conversation, the ding of the bells from the reception desk, the bellboys lugging leather-bound suitcases and trunks up these stairs, the starlets descending in feathers and spangles accompanied by men in black-and-white tuxedos. How grand it must all have been, once upon a time.

Leaning as far as she dared over the stair railing, Aubrey tried to capture the perfect shot of the elliptical stairwell: first looking down to the mosaic floor below, and then up to the stained-glass cupola overhead. She held her camera in an outstretched arm, taking care not to lean on the balustrade in case it was not secure.

The security guard, found hanging in the stairwell . . .

She heard the fluttering again and felt a rush of . . . what? A strange, sighing hum. And then a tingle on the back of her neck. As if she were being watched.

Your imagination is running wild, Aubrey. Shake it off.

There was a sudden sound, right behind her.

TWO

Aubrey jumped back and let out something between a yelp and a squeak.

"Sorry!" said the stranger, holding his hands up in surrender. "Didn't mean to alarm you."

He stood a few steps higher than she did on the stairs. Of average height and build, he had dark hair, olive skin, and old-fashioned, romantic good looks. Had he not been wearing Levi's, a dark blue cable-knit sweater, and a black down vest, he would have fit in well with the vintage photos in the library.

"No, no, I'm..." Aubrey stammered, her heart pounding as her fingers closed on the can of pepper spray hanging from her belt. "Sorry. I thought I was the only one here."

"So did I. You scared the hell out of me, to be honest. For a moment I thought you might be an apparition." His voice was low and melodic, and he spoke with a hint of an accent, though she couldn't place it.

They stared at each other for a long moment. Aubrey berated

herself for coming alone to such a remote location, with only pepper spray for protection. Still . . . once the initial scare wore off, she felt herself relax. Was it his easy smile, or dark, seemingly kind eyes? Aubrey was not naïve; she knew very well that an attractive face did not mean a pure heart. But her gut was usually right about these things. Her fraught child-hood had made her a good judge of character.

As she studied him, realization dawned.

"Wait a minute," she said. "I know you."

"I don't believe we've met," he replied with a tilt of his head. "I rarely forget a face."

"You're the Abandoned Guy from YouTube, right? Dimitri something?"

"Dimitri Petroff." He nodded, his smile broadening. "Wow, this is a bit of a rock star moment for me, I have to say. I'm rarely recognized off camera. And you are . . . ?"

"Aubrey. Aubrey Spencer."

"Aubrey with a 'b'? As in the illustrator Aubrey Beardsley?"

"Exactly."

"Nice to meet you. What might you be doing trespassing at the Seabrink?"

Aubrey held up her camera. "Taking photographs. You?"

He held up his phone. "The same. Just a few quick snaps and videos, for a promo piece for a proper video I'll be doing later. I just landed a deal with Netflix for a new series on abandoned buildings. It's to be called 'Abandoned'—rather unimaginative, I know. But the executives came up with it, and who am I to argue?"

"Congratulations. I think it's a good name. Easy to re-member."

"Thank you. The show's a dream come true, really. And the Hotel Seabrink would be perfect for the first episode, assuming I can get permission to film here before they start the renovations."

"What renovations?"

"A developer wants to revive the old place, re-create a luxury hotel. But it seems there's an issue in the courts concerning the title to the land. Which is not uncommon. There are any number of hurdles to renovating an old place like this."

She nodded. "I get it. I'm an architect."

"Sorry," Dimitri said with a little duck of his head. "I tend to get stuck in lecturer mode. It's an occupational hazard. In any case, their legal troubles are a welcome reprieve for those of us who would like to see it stay just as it is."

"I'm really glad I stumbled upon it. How did you hear about this place? I couldn't find much about it on the internet."

"I was doing a little reading on Old Hollywood and came across a reference in a gossip magazine. It seemed odd that there was so little information available, given its formerly high profile, so I posted about it on my blog. The next day my post was gone; apparently a hacker doesn't want any mention of the Seabrink."

"That seems odd."

"Indeed."

"Why would someone do that?"

"Hard to say. I've reached out to the folks who are planning the renovation, but they're hard to pin down. So tell me, Aubrey, how did *you* find your way here? This place isn't on any map."

"I was photographing the old Haupt Ranch cemetery and stopped in at the deli counter at the general store in Stewarts Point. The young woman who made my sandwich gave me directions. Much better than Google Maps." The wrinkled napkin was still in the back pocket of her faded jeans.

He grinned. "Well done, you."

"Finding abandoned buildings is my only natural talent."

"Somehow I doubt that," he said, holding her gaze just a beat too long. "Anyway, shall we continue exploring together, then? Or would you prefer to be alone?

Aubrey hesitated. The profound loneliness of abandoned spaces was what drew her to them in the first place. Then again, knowing he was somewhere in the building would mean she wasn't alone anyway, so they might as well explore together. Maybe he could tell her more about the hotel. Still . . .

An ungodly sound ripped through the silence. Not quite a scream and not quite a moan, but definitely not human.

"What the *hell*?" Aubrey swore, her hackles up. "What was *that*?"

"Mountain lion," Dimitri said calmly, as he leaned against the stairwell wall. "You've never heard one before?"

"That didn't sound like a lion."

"You're thinking of an African lion, like the MGM mascot. Mountain lions—or cougars or pumas or panthers—sound more like a scream."

"More like a vampire, if you ask me," she muttered.

Dimitri laughed. "Can't say I've ever heard a vampire scream."

"Neither have I, but if I did, I bet it would sound like that."

"I bet it would, as a matter of fact."

"Maybe I'll accept your invitation, after all."

"Excellent! Safety in numbers." He pointed to the mezzanine at the top of the stairs. "Shall we?"

"The Seabrink would be a fabulous place to kick off your new show," said Aubrey as they climbed the stairs. "It has everything: the faded beauty, ferns growing on furniture, loads of nooks and crannies . . ."

"And ghosts." Dimitri held her gaze. "Or so they say."

"Don't tell me you're a ghost hunter, too."

"Not a fan of the supernatural, eh?"

"I don't believe in such things," she said, peering through her viewfinder at a long hallway lined with guest room doors. "And even if I did, whenever I watch those ghost-hunting videos and their manic hosts, I always think, 'If I were a spirit, those would be the last people I'd waste my energy materializing for.'"

He chuckled. "I get it. The only ghosts I hunt are those in history books. But I do believe that historic buildings have their own kind of spirits. Those who pass through leave a residue, traces of ourselves as sure as footprints in the sand. Objects have lives, walls bear witness."

"That's very poetic."

"Sorry, I tend toward the elegiac."

"You also have an impressive vocabulary," Aubrey said with a smile. She gestured toward the long hallway dotted with numbered doors. "If you're right, and there's residue of past lives here, I bet it'd be in the guest rooms. Have you checked out any of them?"

"Several. Let me show you my favorite," Dimitri said. He walked halfway down the corridor, opened a door marked 211, and waved her in. "After you."

"Yeah, no. You first, in case there's residue."

The room's windowpanes had long since been broken and ivy twined in, blocking most of the light and lending an eerie green tinge to the dim interior. Pretty, flowered wallpaper was peeling off the wall in long shreds, and the carpet was an indistinguishable shade of beige and mud. Twin beds, still made up with lace-trimmed linens, were covered in bright green moss, dead leaves, and baby ferns. On one bedside table sat a lamp, a pair of old-fashioned wire-rim glasses, and a small stack of books. All were caked in dust, frosted with moss, and topped with tiny ferns.

"Get a load of that moss," said Aubrey, focusing through her viewfinder.

"What I love about moss is that it barely has any roots," mused Dimitri. "Yet it endures in the crevices, and flourishes in the broken parts."

Absorbed by what she was seeing, Aubrey couldn't take photos fast enough.

"It's the natural cycle of decay and birth, the way new life springs from the remains of what came before," Dimitri continued. "Many ancient cultures believed that large buildings like this one were an affront to nature, and nature eventually reclaims her own. Sometimes with a vengeance."

"Sounds like you're working on sound bites."

He chuckled. "Maybe I should be taking notes as I pontificate."

"Something tells me you don't need notes. You're a natural."

"I'm going to take that as a compliment." Dimitri smiled, his eyebrows lifting as his gaze shifted to the top of her head and he reached out and plucked something from her hair. He held up a small paint chip. "It just fell from the ceiling onto your head. You've been anointed. That must be good luck."

"I hope so. Hey, what's this?"

She opened a door about the size of a dumbwaiter cabinet. It led to a small space with another door at the back.

"It's a valet pass-through," he said. "Back in the day, a lady or gentleman would place their soiled clothes or shoes in there, and the valet or lady's maid would take care of cleaning them. Or something along those lines. The door at the back opens to a central staffing area."

"Seems like a handy way to spy on the guests."

"I imagine there was a bit of that going on, as well."

They wandered up to the labyrinthine third floor, opening doors and exploring long hallways, finding closets within closets and hidden passages connecting guest rooms. Concealed behind the rows of grand guest rooms were utility areas full of cabinetry, deep sinks, and ancient mops and brooms, as well as narrow tunnels for the pipes that brought the mineral water into each guest room.

A huge ballroom was decorated with ornate crystal chandeliers and statuary and at one end a raised stage was framed by shredded velvet curtains. A balcony, edged by an ornate balustrade, ran nearly the length of the building, looking out toward the forest. The hotel sat so high on the hill it was above the level of the fogbank, obscuring the view of the ocean and making it seem as if the Hotel Seabrink were in its own world, above the clouds.

"Speaking of ghosts," said Dimitri, looking out a shattered French door. "A starlet allegedly jumped from this balcony to her death on the flagstones below."

"When was this?" Aubrey said, gazing at the place where the unfortunate woman likely landed.

"It was during the height of the hotel's popularity, so probably the 1930s? They say she was from France, and played the flute."

Aubrey recalled the photo she had seen in the library. "How sad. Any idea why she would have killed herself?"

Dimitri shook his head. "No idea. But I imagine early Hollywood was rather cutthroat."

They continued exploring the vast hotel in companionable silence, each absorbed in their thoughts. Dimitri paused occasionally to shoot a video with his phone, narrating where he was and what he was looking at, while Aubrey took photos of the numerous architectural features: the intricate crown moldings, the painted and tiled murals, the transoms and iron grates and fireplaces; as well as the ever-present decay: the dust-furred cobwebs and fallen plaster, the broken glass and moss and tattered upholstery.

At the base of the attic stairs, they came across a large marble plinth topped by an orb of quartz crystal the size of a grapefruit. Despite the dust, the crystal ball seemed to gleam in the colored lights streaming through the stained-glass cupola skylight crowning the stairwell. Aubrey stared through it, intrigued. Due to the way spherical shapes refract light, crystal balls flip the scene, so that the world looks upsidedown. The bits and bobs of the hotel appeared topsy-turvy and slightly distorted. Kneeling to get the best angle, Aubrey focused on the crystal's inverted view and photographed the hallway stretching out from the landing to an open door that revealed a cramped, dark stairway going up.

"'Beauty is a necessity, like dreams and oxygen,'" Dimitri said into the camera.

Aubrey looked up at him. "What a lovely thought."

"I stole it from Toni Morrison," he said with a little duck of his head. "Always steal from the best."

Aubrey smiled. "I make it a point not to steal. It's my trespasser's code of ethics. But if I did, I'd take . . ."

She trailed off as she felt it again. That sense of sighing, or a whisper. A fluttering. A tingling sensation at the back of her neck. Her hackles rose and her heart sped up as she studied her surroundings. Suddenly she could have sworn she heard the muffled sound of a flute emanating from somewhere in the walls. First to her right, then to her left.

She felt simultaneously drawn toward and repulsed from the dark rectangle of that doorway. In her viewfinder, through the glass orb, she could almost see a form take shape on those shadowy stairs . . .

"You'd take what?" Dimitri urged her to finish her thought.

"Um . . . this crystal ball." Blowing out a harsh breath, she stood up, lowered the camera, and searched the opening to the dark stairs with her naked eye. Nothing appeared odd or amiss. Were the shadows playing with her mind? "Do you . . . did you see something over there, on the stairs? Or hear something that sounded like . . . a flute playing?"

Dimitri shook his head. "Did you?"

She checked the last few photos in her digital camera's history, but the images revealed nothing more than darkness beyond the doorway.

"Must be my imagination."

"Easy enough to imagine things here. Or it could have been birds. I went up to the attic earlier, but part of the roof has collapsed and the wildlife has moved in. I wouldn't recommend it—I don't believe it's safe."

She nodded. Still, she stared at the dark rectangle of the doorway to the attic stairs, fighting the feeling of the walls closing in on her.

"Hey, I have a question," said Dimitri in an upbeat tone. "How many ghosts does it take to screw in a lightbulb?"

"How many?"

"Doesn't matter, they won't go toward the light."

She groaned but gave him a pity chuckle.

"If you want some amazing photos, you should see the mineral baths. Have you been to the basement yet?"

Aubrey shook her head. "I heard someone was killed down there."

"A teenager, on prom night, they say. Though that might have been embellishment."

"I'm more into abandonment than murder."

"As am I. But you really should see the ground floor. The water still runs—it's a natural mineral spring that continuously courses through the baths. According to legend, the waters will cure whatever ails you."

"They should bottle it. Or maybe they did—I noticed some jugs in the kitchens."

"Goffin tried to cash in on it. The man didn't miss a trick."

Dimitri led the way down a back servants' stairs, a series of narrow, steep steps that lacked the grandeur of the main staircase but was more direct. The stairs ended at a doorway that opened onto the kitchens.

"I love the working side of places like this," Aubrey said. "Even more than the public spaces. The meat locker, the—"

She cut herself off as she caught something out of the corner of her eye: something passing by the open kitchen door.

"The meat locker, the . . . ?" Dimitri urged.

"I . . . I thought I saw something," she said, but when she went to peer down the corridor, there was no one.

"Everything okay?" Dimitri asked.

She nodded. "I think this place is giving me 'Shining' vibes."

"Good book."

"Good movie, too."

"Made me nervous about snow, though."

"And hedge mazes."

"And Jack Nicholson."

They shared a smile.

"There's not nearly as much graffiti or signs of looting as I would have expected," said Dimitri as they left the kitchen and headed down a corridor leading to the rear of the building.

"I had that thought, as well. You know, I have to tell you: I really appreciate your YouTube videos. You explain things clearly and are so respectful of the buildings in your videos."

"Thank you, I try."

"On so many other channels, the guys are so hyper they can barely speak in full sentences, much less explain a building's history or architecture. Assuming they even know it."

"YouTube can be the Wild West sometimes—social media attracts all sorts, such as the 'bros' who don't know what a bidet is, or what a larder was for." He paused and added, "Or a valet pass-through, for that matter."

"Very funny," she said with a smile. "The worst is that guy who likes to decorate old buildings with mannequins. Have you seen his stuff? What an ass."

"Stephen Rex."

"Oops . . . Is he a friend of yours?"

Dimitri let out a bark of a laugh. "I wouldn't go that far. We have what I would call a friendly rivalry. He has a bit of a troubled past, but then, I have a theory that those of us fascinated by all things abandoned had dysfunctional childhoods."

"Really? Why would that be?

He shrugged. "No idea. That's why it's just a theory. But everyone I meet in this business seems to have come from a tough situation."

"Maybe *everyone* comes from a tough situation. I don't think childhood is as idyllic as most people would like to believe. So how about you? Was your childhood dysfunctional?"

"Of course," he said with a smile. "That's why I assume everyone else's was, too."

"Hop up there," Aubrey said as they passed an old shoeshine stand, "so I can take your photo."

He frowned. "Not to post on social media, please. It probably sounds pompous, but I curate my public image."

"I'm not much of a social media person," Aubrey said. "This will be just between us. I'll send it to you. Please? It's almost like you belong here. I can imagine you in period clothing, a stogie in your mouth . . ."

"I can hardly refuse an invitation like that," he said, and climbed up to sit in the carved oaken shoeshine chair, one leg crossed over the other, his elegant hands draped over armrests carved to resemble lion's claws. She hadn't lied: when Aubrey studied him through the viewfinder, Dimitri appeared as though he belonged to the Hotel Seabrink's glittering heyday. His romantic good looks, his semiformal way of speaking, his air of mystery . . . it was easy to imagine meeting him at the costume ball portrayed in the photos on the library walls.

"Now it's your turn," he said as he climbed down. "Tell me about your childhood."

"Count me in on the dysfunction. My mother and father divorced when I was too young to understand what was going on. All I knew was that my father disappeared, and my mother was bitter about it and had a hard time making ends meet. We moved around a lot, even lived briefly in our car, and it seemed like every time I started to settle in and make friends, we moved again. It was confusing, to say the least."

"Are you in contact with your father now?"

"He died recently. I don't suppose I'll ever know why he decided not to be a part of my life. If he even had a reason."

"So you're grieving."

Aubrey calmed herself by looking through her viewfinder, concentrating only on what she could see in that little square.

"Grieving for what never was, I suppose. I never really knew my father. At his funeral I met his new family, the one he created after he left my mom and me. His stepdaughter's about my age and was crying her eyes out, kept saying how wonderful and caring he was. My mother was furious I went to the funeral and still refuses to talk about him. Now . . . I don't suppose there will ever be closure on that relationship."

"Closure is overrated," he said quietly. "Sometimes living a life of your own invention is more real than real life."

"Interesting way to look at it. Although . . . it sounds like something my mother would say."

"Grief has a blistered, bony clutch, doesn't it?"

"I'm sorry?"

"Too florid?" He asked with a crooked grin. "I've been working on how to describe intense feelings. Emotions are so layered, so complex, so hard to describe. Virtually impossible to capture in words."

Aubrey paused to snap a few photos of a life-size marble figure festooned with dust-furred cobwebs.

"I do believe that's Thanatos, son of Nyx," said Dimitri. "He was the Greek god of death."

"Curious choice," Aubrey said. "Why would anyone decorate their hotel with sculptures of the god of death?"

"I've always thought of life and death as a bit of a courtship—a dance, if you will," mused Dimitri. "And in the end, we finally embrace our lethal lover. It's nothing to be afraid of."

Aubrey did not know how to respond to that.

"I should note that Thanatos is the god of *peaceful* death, which makes all the difference," said Dimitri. "Did you notice the fountain in front of the hotel?"

"Yeah, what's that about? It seems a strange way to welcome monied clientele to a luxury vacation."

"The classical Greeks can get away with a lot. According to

my research, Goffin brought it over from a pillaged château in France. It represents the Erinyes, who are better known as the Furies."

"Didn't the Furies go after people?"

"That's why they have the guy on the run—they're punishing him. In today's vernacular we would probably call the Furies a metaphor for a guilty conscience. They represent the guilt that won't leave a person alone." He gazed at Thanatos and added in a thoughtful tone, "In my experience, extremely wealthy people often have a lot to feel guilty about."

A moment of silence passed. Aubrey clicked a photo of Dimitri's profile as he gazed up at the sculpture.

He turned to her with a sudden grin and asked, "How many fatalists does it take to screw in a lightbulb?"

"Three?" Aubrey suggested as they continued down the hallway.

"Why three?"

"I was just taking a wild guess. How many?"

"It doesn't matter. It's just going to go out again, anyway."

"That's actually pretty good," Aubrey conceded with a chuckle. "But . . . maybe hold on to the day job."

"Such as it is," he murmured.

They reached a set of wooden double doors, above which hung a plaque with BATHS painted in florid script.

As Dimitri started to open the door, Aubrey wrinkled her nose. "Do you smell that? *Woof.* That's unpleasant."

"Sulfur. Hydrogen sulfide gas in the water makes it smell like rotten eggs."

"I always assumed mineral baths smelled nice, like lavender or something floral. I guess this isn't that kind of spa."

With the doors opened wide, the odor intensified and enveloped them. Dimitri took a large flashlight from his backpack to illuminate the dim stairwell, but the batteries must have been failing, because the flashlight's beam was weak.

"Watch your step," Dimitri said, their footsteps echoing as they descended. The stairs had two switchbacks before opening onto a huge room that was partly underground. Massive columns supported wooden rafters high above them, and in the center of the floor were ten stone troughs. The water running through the troughs sent a trickling sound bouncing off the walls. A little natural light sifted in through the narrow windows under the eaves, though several were blocked by vegetation. Aubrey used her phone's flashlight to guide her steps and took a deep breath to keep calm.

"Are you all right?" Dimitri asked.

"I'm a teensy bit claustrophobic. Best to distract myself. So, does the water come directly from the springs? It wasn't heated or filtered in any way?"

"Back then it was heated, yes, but not filtered. That was the point of partaking of the mineral spring water." Dimitri looked around. "It's a bizarre space, isn't it? So evocative, somehow. I believe it's due to the salts in the mineral water, and the way everything echoes."

"There's more graffiti down here," Aubrey said, perusing the walls. "I imagine it's a bit of a pilgrimage for the local teens to come here, where the girl was found murdered."

"I think you're right. Here's a nice one: 'Weaving spiders come not here.'"

The phrase was written in bloodred spray paint along the wall. The messy writing and dripping paint gave it a serial killer vibe, which had probably been the intention of the artist.

"'Weaving spiders, come not here'?" Aubrey read. "What do you suppose that means?"

"It's Shakespeare. 'A Midsummer's Night's Dream.' It means, essentially, to leave one's outside concerns outside."

"First Morrison, now Shakespeare? You're well-read."

"English lit major. Now doing videos. Anything for the big bucks."

"A Netflix deal sounds pretty impressive, big-bucks-wise."

"We'll see. I'm still not sure it will happen. Hollywood is notoriously fickle."

Her eyes having adjusted to the dim light, Aubrey turned off her phone's flashlight and studied the baths through her viewfinder, imagining glitzy Hollywood stars lounging in the baths. The steam rising while they lolled, servants at the ready with fluffy towels, champagne on ice, strawberries dipped in chocolate.

But then Aubrey remembered the story of the security guard and the prom girl. *She had been found down in the baths . . .*

"Where are you staying?" Dimitri asked.

She jumped at the sound of his voice. "I'm at the Driftwood Cove Inn."

"Oh, nice. I'm at the St. Ambrose, just north of Gualala. You should check it out, it has really interesting architecture."

Beyond the mineral baths, a small hallway led to storage rooms full of shelves holding dusty jars and burlap bags and more water jugs. There was a laundry area and a small chamber jammed with broken furniture, apparently awaiting repairs that had never come. The largest room was a woodshop, with hammers and saws and vises and sharp implements of various kinds scattered atop several workbenches. Half a dozen concrete steps led up to a set of flat cellar doors that opened like a hatch, secured with a rusted chain and padlock.

"And over here we have an old wine cellar," said Dimitri, opening a large door to one side of the shop. "Though why it's located off the woodshop, I have no idea. Probably the right temperature down here."

As they returned to the baths, they heard the sound of a piano playing. Muffled and mournful, the notes echoed off the basement walls.

"What is that?" Aubrey whispered.

"'Nearer My God to Thee,' if I'm not mistaken."

"But from where? And . . . is that the elevator?" They listened intently to a far-off clanking. "It couldn't be, could it? The electricity isn't on."

"And even if it is," Dimitri said, "who's *calling* the elevator?"

"The same person who's playing the piano? Please don't suggest ghosts."

"More likely addicts, or your garden-variety copper thieves," said Dimitri. "They strip the wires and pipes, looking for copper to sell in bulk."

"You think copper thieves play a few tunes on the piano before getting to work?"

"It could happen," he said with a duck of his head. "But if so, I doubt they'd choose 'Nearer My God to Thee.'"

They were silent for a few moments, then Dimitri said, "It seems to have stopped. My point is, thieves are the ones we need to worry about. Not ghosts."

"Yeah, I got that. It only now occurs to me to ask: Is there a back way out of here?"

"I—"

Their eyes met as they heard the door at the top of the bath stairs open, and the sound of footsteps descending. They heard whispering, though the words were just out of earshot.

Dimitri pulled Aubrey into a dark nook under the stairs, holding his finger to his lips.

They listened, trying to silence their harsh breathing, as the hurried footsteps neared their hiding spot.

THREE

The interloper reached the bottom of the stairs, then paused. Aubrey and Dimitri heard the clicking of the light switches being turned on and off, to no avail. The room remained dim, lit only by the small windows under the eaves.

"This is ridiculous," Dimitri murmured. "It's probably just a kid."

Before Aubrey could stop him, Dimitri jumped out and yelled: "Stop right there!"

The man shot his hands high in the air. Aubrey guessed he was in his mid- to late twenties, though he had the kind of looks that could have been anywhere from a mature eighteen to a youthful thirty-five. Tall and thin, he had dirty blond hair and bloodshot eyes and held himself awkwardly, as though not comfortable in his own skin.

"Hey, how ya doin', man?" His voice shook. "Take it easy. I'm Cameron. Peace."

"Cameron Peace?" Dimitri demanded with an air of authority, as if he owned the place.

"Huh? No, like, my name is Cameron. And I come in peace. Chill out, bro. Geez." Cameron still held his hands aloft, as though Dimitri had a gun pointed at him.

"Are you alone? I thought we heard you speaking to someone."

"Nah, dude. Just talking to myself. Bad habit, I guess."

Dimitri relaxed, lowering his flashlight, and Cameron dropped his hands. Aubrey emerged from the nook but held the pepper spray at the ready. Just in case.

"So, this is quite a place, right?" Cameron asked. "What are you guys doing here? I didn't, like, interrupt anything, did I?"

"I'm making a video, and she's taking photographs. Documenting the building as it is before the renovations begin."

"Right on," Cameron said, nodding his head. "Well, at least you're not a couple of stupid kids, out to scare each other or destroy things just for the fun of it."

"As a matter of fact, I'm surprised there's not more damage here," said Dimitri.

"I read they used to have security guards watching over the place," Aubrey said, her eyes sliding over to the baths as she remembered reading about the murdered teenager. *Is that where the victim was found?*

"That could explain it," Cameron said agreeably. "Either that, or people are afraid of the curse."

"What curse?" said Aubrey.

He looked incredulous. "'What curse'? You're telling me you came to the Hotel Seabrink and don't know about the curse?"

"Why don't you enlighten us?" Dimitri said.

"They say there's a ghost here, and if you see her image in the attic window, you'll die within twenty-four hours."

"That's a pretty specific curse," Aubrey said.

"People around here take it seriously."

"We'll be sure not to look at the attic window, then. Were you playing the piano a few minutes ago?" Aubrey asked.

Cameron cocked his head, looked confused. "Nah. My mom forced me to take piano lessons for a while, but what a waste of money that was. I'm lucky if I can manage 'Chopsticks.' You mean there's someone *else* here?"

As if on cue, they heard a thin, warbly voice singing.

"Okay, now *that* is creepy," said Aubrey.

"Sounds like the old Victrola," Dimitri said.

Suddenly there was an outburst of noise from above: the Victrola, the piano, loud footsteps running about, something crashing to the floor. The ancient elevator clanked as it ascended and descended, and the high-pitched, piping notes of a flute came from within the walls. And in the far-off distance, the vampire-like scream of a mountain lion.

"What in hell is going on up there?" Cameron said.

He sounded curious but not concerned, and Aubrey wondered if he might have friends upstairs who were causing the ruckus.

"Do you smell smoke?" Dimitri asked.

"No way, bro. Can't be."

"Smells like smoke to me," Aubrey confirmed.

Cameron lifted his head high and took a few exaggerated sniffs. "*Shit!*" He ran for the stairs, taking them two at a time.

"Should we go with him?" Aubrey asked Dimitri.

"He's on his own. I don't trust him," Dimitri said with a shake of his head. "I suggest we leave through the cellar door, at the back of the woodshop. It's the closest exit, and if this place really is on fire, the upstairs will be a death trap within minutes."

They ran through the basement to the woodshop. Dimitri

climbed up to the cellar doors and yanked and turned the padlock, with no effect.

"*Damn*," Dimitri said, rattling the doors. "Okay, that's out. Earlier I saw what looked like the entrance to an old tunnel behind the wine cellar. Not sure where it goes, but it may lead to another exit."

"I don't relish the thought of being stuck in a dead-end tunnel if this place goes up in flames."

"Good point. All right, this old lock is pretty rusty. Maybe it'll give." Dimitri grabbed an old sledgehammer from a workbench. "Stand back."

Dimitri swung the sledgehammer awkwardly, missing the padlock but putting a major dent in the cellar door.

"Just getting my bearings," he muttered. He tried again, and this time struck the padlock dead center. A few more swings, and the padlock gave way, the chain clattering as it fell on the stone floor. Dimitri shoved the hatch open, and they rushed out into the blessedly smoke-free air and ran down the long driveway to the gates.

There, they stopped to catch their breath, looking back at the Hotel Seabrink.

"Do you see any signs of fire?" Dimitri asked, searching the hotel's facade and windows for indications of a blaze. "I swear I smelled smoke."

"I did, too. We should call it in, just in case." Aubrey took her cell phone from her pocket. "Except I still don't have any service."

"Cell phones don't usually work up here, which only ups the eerie factor. They—" Dimitri cut himself off and frowned.

"What is it?" Aubrey asked. She followed his gaze to the top of the hotel but saw nothing amiss.

"I thought . . . I thought I saw something."

"Fire?"

He shook his head.

"You didn't see a face in the attic window, did you?" she teased. "That would mean you're cursed."

He looked shaken, so she softened her tone. "I thought I saw something earlier, too. This place puts spooky thoughts in a person's head. I suggest we get out of here. Where's your car?"

"Up that little logging road," said Dimitri. "I didn't want it to be obvious that I was here."

"Ah, that's smart. I didn't think of that."

"I do this sort of thing for a living. Sort of." He fixed her with a gaze. "So, what now?"

"It'll start to get dark soon," Aubrey said. "I should head back to my hotel and call the fire department, just in case."

"Any chance your hotel has a decent bar?"

"It has an excellent bar."

"Good." He smiled. "I'm buying."

FOUR

The next morning, her eyes shut tight against the bright silver light of dawn, Aubrey reached out and explored the soft mound of snow-white sheets next to her.

The linens were cold.

She opened her eyes and looked around. Dimitri was gone.

Groaning, she fell back on the pillow. Her head was spinning, the light streaming through the window hurt her eyes, and her stomach was signaling a possible revolt.

What have I done?

Her best friend, Nikki, would no doubt say something like, "It's about time, Spencer!" After all, how long had it been since Aubrey had allowed her instincts to lead her instead of her common sense? Since she had felt so energized, so alive? It had been a long time. A long, *long* time. Not since her undergraduate days at UC Berkeley.

A lifetime ago.

I'm not sorry.

The day before had been . . . bizarre, from start to finish. As Dimitri had said over drinks, when they were sharing their love of all things abandoned: *Historic buildings are snapshots in history, a time out of time. It's like stepping into another world when one passes over their thresholds.* Aubrey had allowed herself to cross over that threshold and stepped right through the looking glass. Or, perhaps more aptly, into the upside-down world of that crystal ball at the hotel.

After she and Dimitri drove to the Driftwood Cove Inn, they called 911 to report the smell of smoke at the Hotel Seabrink. Then they climbed up to see a tall peace sculpture perched on a mound behind the inn and followed a narrow trail along the cliffs to the ominously named Dead Man's Bluff, where they gazed out at the coming sunset, the cloud-shrouded sun hovering just over the Pacific and casting pink and orange hues onto the ocean. Waves smashed violently onto the rocky outcroppings at the base of the cliff far below them. The wind whipped her hair and filled her lungs with the briny scent of the sea. Aubrey had felt so *alive.*

"When I checked in the other day, the desk clerk mentioned that the whales are migrating in search of food and warmer waters," Aubrey said. "Or is it colder waters? Anyway, they're in search of something."

"Aren't we all?"

She smiled. "I keep looking for them, but they've eluded me so far. I love whales."

"I'm an octopus guy, myself."

"I love those, too. They're so smart. A lot harder to see from this distance, though."

A gust of cold wind left her shivering. Dimitri wrapped his arms around her and nuzzled her hair. She leaned back against him, letting herself absorb his warmth. After a long moment, she looked up at him over her shoulder, searching his dark eyes.

"I know we've only just met, Ms. Aubrey Spencer . . . but would it be too forward to kiss you?"

"A first kiss at Dead Man's Bluff? There's nothing inauspicious about *that*."

"Ah, but we've already braved the Seabrink curse, after all."

The kiss was long, and slow, and searching. Intoxicating.

They returned to the warmth of the inn. As they passed through the lobby on their way to the bar, the young clerk behind the front desk stopped them and said he recognized Dimitri from his YouTube channel. Blushing and stammering, his Adam's apple bobbing, the desk clerk introduced himself as Xavi and asked for an autograph.

Dimitri took a moment to chat with him and signed his name, wishing him the best.

"You see? I'm not the only one who recognizes you," Aubrey teased as they took their seats at the bar. "You really are a YouTube rock star."

"A dubious distinction," Dimitri said with a duck of his head.

They ordered Irish coffees to help them warm up and swapped tales of their experiences exploring places others shunned. The Irish coffees were followed by shots of single-malt bourbon, and their talk turned intimate. They spoke of their travels, of loves won and lost, of the lure of the abandoned. Maybe it was the booze talking, but they seemed to understand each other on a rare, profound level, and when the bartender announced, "Last call!" Dimitri asked Aubrey if it was true that the rooms at Driftwood Cove Inn had old-fashioned record players.

"They do indeed. And there's a great selection of vintage vinyl records in the lobby. We could choose a few to listen to, if you'd like."

They selected an old Donovan album, Carole King's *Tapestry*, and several by the Rolling Stones. In the privacy of Aubrey's room, they embraced and swayed to a slow dance. She kissed him, and he kissed her back, and things progressed from there . . .

And now he was gone.

Aubrey rummaged around for a note, then checked her phone, in case he had texted her. Nothing.

Had they even exchanged phone numbers? She couldn't remember. Then a chilling thought: their time together wouldn't show up in a video for his YouTube channel, would it? *No*, she thought, surely not. Dimitri would not do something like that, she was certain. Almost certain. She had watched his videos, and none had included anything personal. Besides, he hadn't even had a real camera with him, only his phone.

But just in case, she opened her laptop and checked his YouTube channel. Her stomach clenched when she realized he had uploaded a new video late last night, after she had fallen asleep. She hesitated for a long moment, her finger hovering over the touch pad. Finally, she clicked "Play."

The video was a brief promo piece about the Hotel Seabrink, showing Dimitri exploring the building and briefly explaining its history, the alleged curse, and the rumors surrounding the mysterious deaths that had taken place there. The shaky footage included a few glimpses of Aubrey on the hotel stairs as well as a brief shot of her peering down into the baths.

There was nothing remotely personal or suggestive about any of it, yet it made Aubrey uncomfortable. She hadn't realized Dimitri had been filming her. Why hadn't he mentioned it? Or asked her permission to include her in the video?

He's a stranger, Aubrey reminded herself. *You slept with a total stranger.*

Why had she been so quick to trust him? Their shared love of abandoned places had given her a sense of a kindred spirit. Their mental—and, let's face it, physical—connection was so immediate and exceptional that she had simply dived in, unheeding.

Her head ached. Aubrey reached for her purse, rooting around blindly until she found the bottle of ibuprofen. She swallowed three pills, chased by a big glass of water. She would worry later about the medicine's impact on her kidneys. Or was it the liver? She couldn't remember.

Swinging her legs out of bed, she paused, willing her head to stop swimming. Slowly she got to her feet and gazed out the window. The water was several shades of steel gray, the colors moving and swirling, hinting at the ocean's powerful depths. The skies were also gray, and though the sun was beginning to shine through, mist clung to the jagged rocks that lined the cove.

It was March on the remote Northern California coast. Blustery and wild, and very few tourists. That was the best thing about it.

The swanky Driftwood Cove Inn was a jewel of midcentury-modern architecture perched high on the cliffs above the Pacific Ocean. Aubrey could normally never have afforded to stay at such an upscale hotel. Or to be more precise, she would never have been able to justify spending so much money on a hotel room, no matter how great the view. But after her father's funeral and the disaster at work . . . Aubrey was badly in need of a break from her reality. Luckily for her, her best friend had come to the rescue: Nikki reached out to an old childhood friend, now the manager of the Driftwood Cove Inn, and finagled a "friends and off-season" discount for Aubrey.

She rubbed her temples, willing the ibuprofen to hurry up and work its magic. What she needed right now was a shower and some coffee. Heading to the bathroom, she spied Dimitri's backpack lying on the floor on the other side of the bed.

So he didn't leave without a word, after all.

He had probably just slipped out for coffee.

Aubrey brushed her teeth and hopped into the shower. As she ran the washcloth over her body, her skin tingled. Her thoughts cast back to last night. Their physical connection had been intense, almost electric. The kind of feeling she had not experienced in forever.

Correction: the kind of feeling she had *never* experienced, not really, not outside of novels.

And they would have one heck of a quirky meet-cute story: two strangers trespassing in an abandoned hotel, then sharing a first kiss at Dead Man's Bluff. No doubt their how-we-met would become more elaborate in the retelling, involving the ghostly sounds of the grand piano echoing through the halls, the Victrola, the flute, the clanking of the wrought-iron elevator ascending and descending without electricity . . .

Except she still knew almost nothing about Dimitri, other than his YouTube channel. More than likely last night really had been a one-night stand. And there was nothing wrong with an adult, single woman enjoying an occasional wild fling. At least it gave her a story to amuse her friends the next time they got together over a bottle of wine and tarot cards. Aubrey rarely had anything interesting to contribute to those conversations.

Toweling off quickly, she did her best to calm her curly chestnut hair with a dab of gel. She slipped into yesterday's jeans and a clean ivory tank top, then pulled on a warm, heather-green sweater. Part of her wished she had brought something cute to wear, maybe a sweet little dress, or a pair of shoes other than her scuffed-up boots . . .

She reached for her small bag of makeup, then hesitated. *Dimitri liked you just fine yesterday, clad in jeans and no makeup.* On the off chance their relationship developed into something more, it would not be because of how she looked but because they had found common ground, talking about real things.

It was so rare for Aubrey to meet someone with whom she clicked right away, with whom she could talk about things that mattered to her, without holding back. Without hiding. Without feeling like a freak for feeling too much, for seeing things that others didn't.

Grief has a blistered, bony clutch. How often did she meet a person who said things like that, out of the blue?

A *ping* made her glance at her phone, before she realized the sound had come from Dimitri's backpack. His phone was in a front mesh pocket, the screen facing out.

It pinged again.

Through the mesh, she read the message: **You were warned.**

That was . . . unsettling. But it could be anything, right? A joke with a friend, maybe. Probably.

On the way out of the room, Aubrey picked up the little paper envelope containing her room's key cards. They had given her two when she checked in, but only one remained. Dimitri must have taken a key card to let himself back in. Perhaps he was even now climbing the stairs, coffee and baked goods in hand . . .

She stepped out into hallway. No Dimitri.

Aubrey generally eschewed elevators, claiming she needed the exercise, though in reality she opted for the stairs because she tended toward the claustrophobic. Her mind cast back to the attic stairs, and then the baths at the Hotel Seabrink, how the walls had seemed to close in on her. And the elevator . . . had they really heard it moving? How could that be?

When she reached the lobby, Aubrey spotted a handful of guests milling about the continental breakfast station, but Dimitri was not among them. Maybe he had gone out for a brisk walk, relishing having the bluff to himself before the other tourists made their way outside and ruined the opportunities to film. He would stroll in at any moment, and they would discuss whether to get breakfast at the inn's restaurant, or maybe return to Stewarts Point for sticky buns and eat them huddled over one of their picnic tables.

Or maybe he would simply thank her for the evening, fetch his backpack and phone, and leave.

First things first: Aubrey poured herself a large mug of coffee, reveling in its warmth and aroma and the promise of caffeine.

She looked up at the sound of a commotion. Several of the hotel staff had gathered at the front desk, speaking in low voices. A few rushed outside, trailed by curious onlookers.

"Another one? *Dude*," she overheard the young man behind the front desk say.

"At Dead Man's Bluff," said another fellow.

Coffee mug in hand, Aubrey followed the others outside. The parking lot was full of rescue vehicles, their lights flashing.

She tried to ignore a whisper of foreboding. Surely not. Right? Surely . . . not.

Several hundred yards away, along the cliffs north of the hotel, a crowd had gathered to watch and speculate as a knot of first responders finished setting up rigging. A hush fell over the crowd as a sandy-haired, well-muscled man dressed in climbing gear and secured by ropes slowly began to rappel down the side of the cliff. Very near the spot where she and Dimitri had stood last night. Where they had leaned against each other. Shared a first kiss. And laughed at having survived the Seabrink curse.

Seagulls cried and swooped in the air, mocking the earthbound humans, and in the distance a squadron of pelicans flew in tight formation, skimming the surface of the ocean in search of breakfast. Last night, the tide had been high, and the waves had reached the base of the cliffs. But the tide was out now, revealing numerous craggy rocks and a small, secluded beach.

Aubrey summoned her courage and looked down at the base of the cliff.

A dark-haired man lay facedown on the sand and rocks, his legs splayed at an unnatural angle, his arms flung over his head. He wore jeans, a dark blue sweater, and a black down vest.

FIVE

---

re you all right?"

Aubrey looked up to see a paramedic standing over her. After spotting Dimitri's broken body, Aubrey's legs had given way and she had slumped to the ground. Her coffee mug lay in several pieces beside her, a dark coffee stain marring the rocks.

"Ma'am? Are you all right?" the woman repeated.

"Yes, I . . . I'm sorry. I don't know what happened."

"Don't apologize," the paramedic said, as she crouched down and looked Aubrey over, assessing her condition. "Looks like you've had a bit of a shock. It happens to the best of us. Here, drink this." She handed Aubrey a juice box.

"I can't . . ."

"Are you allergic to orange juice?"

"No, but . . ."

"Then drink it," the woman said. "It will help. What's your name?"

Aubrey cleared her throat and took a sip of the juice. "Aubrey Spencer."

"Hello, Aubrey, I'm Mia Ramirez. I'm a paramedic with the volunteer fire department. You collapsed suddenly. Do you have a medical condition I should be aware of?"

"No, nothing like that. It was just kind of a . . . shock, seeing him."

"Do you know the man on the beach?" Mia asked gently.

Aubrey nodded, then shook her head. "I mean, no. Not really. Well, sort of."

"You're not sure if you know him?" Mia asked with a smile. "Have some more juice. The vitamin C helps to lower cortisol levels. And take a few deep breaths."

Aubrey did as Mia suggested. The paramedic was right; she did feel better; more centered and able to respond.

"I met him yesterday. I don't know him well, but . . . I know him."

"I'm very sorry about your friend, Aubrey," Mia said as she stood up. "The deputy will want to speak with you, so stick around. And finish that juice."

Aubrey spent the next hour watching as the volunteer firefighters and paramedics worked carefully and methodically to recover Dimitri's body from the narrow strip of beach at the bottom of the high cliff. She wished she had her camera with her, wished she could look through the viewfinder and be separated from all of it. Watch it all from a detached perspective.

I've always thought of life and death as a bit of a courtship, a dance, if you will.

She racked her brain, trying to remember everything they had talked about. Dimitri had said so much last night, and yet she still knew so little.

When the body was finally lifted to the top of the cliff, the face was battered beyond recognition.

"No ID," she heard one of the paramedics say.

Maybe it isn't him.

Maybe there was a terrible mix-up . . . maybe some other poor dark-haired soul had been wearing the same outfit Dimitri had on last night. Jeans and black vests were hardly unique.

At long last a young, slender man in uniform approached Aubrey. He was all knees and elbows; his smooth cheeks revealed no sign of a beard.

"I'm Deputy Kenneth B. Jenkins," he said self-importantly. "So, you're the girlfriend?"

"I'm not, not really. But I . . ."

"Name?"

"Aubrey Spencer."

"Audrey Spencer," he said, making a note.

"Au-brey, with a 'b.'"

He looked up, confused.

"Not Audrey as in Hepburn, but Aubrey as in Aubrey Beardsley, the illustrator?" At the deputy's blank look, she spelled it out: "A-U, B as in boy, R-E-Y."

"I've never heard of that name."

"It originally meant 'king of the elves.'" As a thirteen-year-old, Aubrey had been thrilled to discover her odd name's etymology, but now, saying it aloud, she realized how ridiculous it sounded.

Deputy Jenkins seemed to share that opinion. He studied her for a beat, then made a show of crossing out "Audrey" and writing in her correct name. "Shouldn't that be 'queen of the elves'?"

Aubrey shrugged. "I suppose it's a sort of non-binary situation."

"Okay, Aubrey, elf royalty. So, was your boyfriend depressed? Showing signs of distress, drug use, maybe?"

"He wasn't my boyfriend. And I have no idea if he was depressed or using drugs. I wouldn't think so, but I don't know him well. We just met yesterday."

"And he spent the night with you?"

"He did."

The deputy's eyebrows rose, and he looked her up and down. She still felt shaky, the lingering effects of too much bourbon, too little sleep, and the shock of Dimitri's death. She looked around for someplace to sit down, then edged over to hitch a hip up on a nearby boulder. The deputy followed her.

"Let me get this straight: you two sleep together, and then he comes out here and flings himself off a cliff?"

"I, uh . . ." Aubrey said, trying to wrap her mind around it. "I guess that's about the size of it."

"You two have a fight? Lover's quarrel, maybe?"

"No, nothing like that. And as I said, we'd only just met."

"Smoke anything? Maybe pop some pills?"

She shook her head.

"You sure?"

"Positive."

The deputy looked skeptical. "What about booze? Had you two been drinking?"

"Yes, but—"

"Alcohol can amplify emotional problems, you know. Deepens despair, makes people impulsive."

"That's true, but—"

"So you two met yesterday, drank too much, went to bed,

and this morning he's dead at the bottom of the cliff and, well, you aren't. I mean, no offense, Aubrey, but doesn't that sound weird to you?"

"No offense, Deputy," Aubrey parroted. "But that's what happened."

She looked around to see if there were a more senior colleague with whom she might speak, someone older and more experienced in life.

"I'm just saying," said Jenkins, shaking his head. "Weird."

"Uh-huh. And I'm just saying, that's all I know."

"Let's start at the beginning. What's his name? He doesn't have ID on him."

"Dimitri Petroff. He left his backpack in my room if you want it."

"And you're very sure it's him? His face is pretty banged up."

Her stomach clenched. "I recognize his clothes, they're the same as he was wearing last night. Check his chest. He has a dragon tattoo on the . . . upper left side."

A sudden flash of memory: running her hands over that tattoo, leaning over to kiss it, to run her tongue along its lines. Their room lit only by the moonlight streaming through the window, he had reached up to stroke her hair, and murmured to her . . .

"Wait here." Deputy Jenkins went over to the ambulance and spoke with the muscular, sandy-haired firefighter, who leaned over the body and examined Dimitri's chest. Aubrey held her breath, again hoping against hope that it was all some sort of terrible mix-up. A distraught stranger who had come out to Dead Man's Bluff and—

The sandy-haired man nodded.

"It's your friend, all right," the deputy said when he returned.

He must have seen something in her face, and added, "Sorry about that. I mean, my, uh, condolences. Okay, how's about you and me go see what he left in your room."

Several onlookers stared at her, gawking and whispering. Feeling self-conscious, Aubrey knelt down and carefully picked up the pieces of the broken coffee mug, then walked on shaking legs down the trail toward the inn, where she tossed the shards into the trash. The deputy followed her into the lobby.

Deputy Jenkins headed toward the elevator, but Aubrey said, "I'll meet you up there. I prefer the stairs. It's the second floor, room 207."

The deputy raised an eyebrow. "I'll go with you. Good exercise."

As they climbed the steps, Aubrey said, "It must have been some kind of accident, right? The rocks can be slippery with all the fog."

"I guess it's possible, but people go to that spot to kill themselves, you know. Happens all the time. It's a damned shame. I mean, if you're feeling blue then ask for help, there's a national hotline and everything. Don't throw yourself off the cliff and make people risk their own lives to retrieve your body."

Aubrey bit her tongue. The flippancy of youth.

"Tell me, isn't rappelling down the cliff dangerous?" Aubrey asked. "Wouldn't a boat be a better option?"

"You would think so, wouldn't you? But we're racing against time here—we have to retrieve the body before the tide comes back in. Anyway, to me attitude is everything, know what I mean?" Jenkins continued. "Like, you think your life is in the pits but a lot of it is attitude."

Aubrey remembered having a similar outlook, back when

she was young and naïvely optimistic. Before life had dealt her a few body blows.

"Have you been a deputy long?" Aubrey asked.

"I know, I look young, right? We're shorthanded at the moment. There was a multi-car accident this morning on Highway One, and those take priority since it's the only road up or down the coast. Also, a bunch of the guys are down at the Russian River, helping to evacuate citizens on account of the wildfire near Cazadero."

"I'm just wondering what makes you so sure Dimitri's death was a suicide," Aubrey said as she used her key card to open her door. "Oh, that reminds me: I think Dimitri took a key card."

"A what, now?"

"The hotel gave me two key cards when I checked in. They were in a little paper folder, and this morning there was only one. Dimitri must have taken the other one."

"You're saying he's a thief?"

"No. I'm saying he was intending to return to my room. So he must not have killed himself."

"Kind of a leap in logic there, if you ask me," Jenkins said with a shrug. "Could be he took it out of habit, you know, just slipped it in his pocket without thinking. Or maybe he was still making up his mind about jumping. I gotta think a decision like that is a pretty big deal."

"Did they find the key card in his pocket?"

"Dunno, but not sure it matters."

"Well, couldn't someone have pushed him?"

Jenkins scoffed. "What would make you think something like that? He have any enemies?"

"I don't really know, but—"

"That's my point, you have no reason to suspect something

like that. I mean, it's a pretty big deal to push someone off a cliff."

"I imagine it is. But surely it happens. Also—he received a text message on his phone this morning that said, 'You were warned.'"

"Okay, that is weird. But it doesn't make sense that it had anything to do with what happened, right? I mean, why would someone send a message like that if they'd already pushed him off a cliff?"

Good point.

"So, let me just take a look-see," the deputy said, and made a show of nosing around the room. "Pretty nice place you got, here. Great view of the cove."

"Here's Dimitri's backpack," said Aubrey, handing the bag to him.

"Gotcha." He pawed through the backpack. "Water bottle, energy bar, phone, car keys . . ."

"Oh, that's right: What about his car?"

"What about it?"

"Maybe it will provide a clue?"

"A suicide note would be a clue. He leave you anything at all?"

She shook her head.

"Maybe a 'It was nice to meet you but farewell' note or text? Something like that?"

"No. Nothing."

"Welp, only a small minority of suicides leave notes. Depending on which study you look at, and ethnicity and all that, it could be as low as two percent, with a high around forty percent."

"I didn't know that."

Deputy Jenkins nodded and said, with a world-weary air,

"You learn a lot of things when you wear the badge. A whole lot of things that civilians such as yourself don't have to worry about."

"I can imagine," Aubrey said. "Still, it just doesn't make sense that he got up early this morning and spontaneously jumped off a cliff. Among other things, he was excited for the future. He told me he had signed a deal with Netflix for a show based on his YouTube channel."

"Maybe it was too much pressure, and he couldn't take it," the deputy suggested, and looked at her with sympathy.

Whether that sympathy was rooted in her "boyfriend's" loss, or Aubrey's doubts about how Dimitri died, was anyone's guess.

SIX

Deputy Jenkins slung Dimitri's backpack over his shoulder. "Anyhoo, I'm sorry about your boyfriend, ma'am, but these things happen."

"Shouldn't we at least ask if the desk clerk saw Dimitri talking with anyone, or, I don't know, witnessed anything?"

"S'pose it wouldn't hurt. Nothing more to see here," the deputy said, glancing around as he opened the door. "After you."

The hotel clerk who had recognized Dimitri last night was still behind the registration desk. He was young, tall, and awkward, with big blue eyes that looked perpetually startled. As they approached, he hurriedly put down his phone. His face was marked with acne scars and the nameplate pinned to his chest read, I'M XAVI! HOW MAY I HELP YOU?

"Morning, um, Ksavi, is it?" Deputy Jenkins began. "Never heard that name before. Last name?"

"Krasniewski." The clerk spelled it out slowly.

"Ksavi Krasniewski?" Jenkins wrote the name on his pad. "Heck of a moniker, there, son."

"That's why I just go by Xavi. It's pronounced Havi, like with an 'H.'"

"*Hhhh*avee?" Jenkins repeated, exaggerating the *H* sound. "I'm Deputy Kenneth B. Jenkins. Did you witness a man—Caucasian, about five-ten, dark hair, wearing jeans, a blue sweater, and a dark vest, um, how old . . . ?"

He trailed off, looking at Aubrey.

"About my age," she said. "Let's say late thirties, early forties. Maybe."

"Anyway, you see anyone of that description exit the hotel early this morning?"

"Dimitri Petroff, right? I recognized him last night when he and the, um, lady here came in. He has a great YouTube channel."

"A what, now?"

"YouTube channel? Like, with abandoned houses and stuff? It's really good, you should check it out. He's on, like, Insta and TikTok, too. All the socials."

"We in law enforcement frown on trespassing on private property," said Jenkins. "You might want to keep that in mind."

Xavi's eyes widened again, his Adam's apple bobbing.

"Anyway, what time did you see the man leave the hotel?"

"A little after four this morning."

"Was anybody with him?"

Xavi shook his head.

"All right, then. Thanks for your help."

"*I* have a question, Xavi," Aubrey said, unimpressed by the deputy's interrogation skills. "Did Dimitri say anything when he left? Anything at all?"

Xavi shook his head and let out a huge yawn. "'Scuze me," he said with a shake of his head. "No, I said hello, but he didn't say anything."

"And you're sure it was around four?"

He nodded. "I remember checking the time because I was hoping maybe I'd fallen asleep, and it was near the end of my shift. This night shift blows."

"Was anybody else in the lobby when he left?" Aubrey asked.

"At four in the morning? No, nobody. Sometimes the surfers are up and out before dawn, but never *that* early."

Jenkins rested one elbow on the counter and leaned in close to the night clerk, as if sharing a confidence. "And did you see this lady here leave the hotel at any point during the night?"

The clerk looked wide-eyed at Aubrey and shook his head. "Uh-uh. Only when they first came in."

"But sometimes you fall asleep?"

"I try not to, drink lots of Red Bull. But sometimes. Please don't tell my boss."

"Then you might not have noticed if, for instance, this particular woman here followed this Dimitri fellow outside and maybe pushed him off a cliff?"

The clerk's eyes widened, deep blue pools of doubt. "I didn't see anyone then, but I guess I might have missed her. I definitely saw her come downstairs a couple of hours ago, like at a decent hour. But . . . wait. If she went back in her room earlier this morning, it would be recorded on the key card log. You want me to check the computer?"

"If you don't mind," said Jenkins.

Xavi began tapping furiously on the keyboard. "Says here, the last time anyone went into her room was, like, ten minutes ago. Before that, it was last night, just before midnight. If you need proof, I can print this out. You, uh, want me to?"

"That would be helpful, thank you," said Jenkins. He

turned to Aubrey and said with a half smile, "Well, I guess you're off the hook, then, Aubrey. Case closed."

"Deputy Jenkins, you don't seem to be taking this very seriously."

"On the contrary. Any loss of life is tragic. I just don't think this is a case of homicide. I mean, no one even knew this Dimitri person was staying here last night, right? You said it was a one-night stand, so he wasn't an official guest here? So really, you're the only one who might have motive, and Xavi here just gave you an alibi: you were in your room all night."

He pronounced "Xavi" as "Ksavi" again.

"His name's *Xavi*, with an 'H' sound," said Aubrey, her voice sounding hollow to her own ears.

"You're really hung up on this name business," Jenkins said. "My point is that you're off the hook, so don't worry about it."

Don't worry about it. Don't worry about the fact that a man who was so alive and vibrant yesterday was now gone. No longer walking this earth, making videos about abandoned buildings, asking questions like *Do the dead leave the world, or does the world leave the dead?* Don't worry about the fact that the man to whom she had felt so strangely connected went outside at four in the morning and . . . fell or jumped or was pushed off a cliff to his death?

Don't worry about it wasn't really an option for Aubrey.

"I guess I was, like, maybe the last person to see him alive," mused Xavi, breaking into her thoughts. "That's wild to think about, you know? He was nice to me, and everything. Gave me his autograph. Wish I could have, um, helped in some way."

Aubrey gave Xavi a warm, sad smile. "Thank you, Xavi. That's kind of you to say. Hey, what about cameras?"

"What about them?" asked Jenkins.

"Do you have any CCTV cameras installed here?" Aubrey asked Xavi.

The young man's blue eyes widened as he looked away. "Not, like, not really? I mean, I don't want to say . . . you should probably ask Monica about it. She's the manager here."

"Well, that's that, then," said Jenkins, flipping his notebook closed and putting the printout of the key card log in his pocket. "Thanks to both of you for your time. Unless . . . I seen some pretty wild stunts on YouTube and TikTok. Could this have been some kind of stunt gone wrong?"

"That seems pretty far-fetched," said Aubrey. "And even if so, how would Dimitri have filmed himself? There would have to have been someone else with him."

"You got me there," said Jenkins, picking up Dimitri's backpack. "Anyhoo, if the coroner declares the death a suicide, like I imagine he will, then his effects should go to his family. You have their contact info?"

Aubrey gritted her teeth. "No. I don't know his family. I barely knew *him*. We met yesterday, and he spent the night, and that's all I know."

"Oh, that's right. Where'd you say you met this guy?"

Aubrey considered making something up, but she could not think of a reason not to tell the truth, and she didn't trust her memory to keep her lies straight. "At the old Hotel Seabrink."

"The Seabrink?" Jenkins exchanged glances with Xavi, whose wide-eyed stare fell to the papers on the desk. "What were you doing up there?"

"Just . . . looking around."

"Trespassing, you mean."

"I didn't disturb anything, just took some photos."

"And nothing strange happened when you were there?"

The elevator clanking, the old Victrola playing, the notes of the piano, the piping of the flute, shadows taking shape on that attic stairwell . . .

But Aubrey just said: "Strange, like what?"

"Nothing. It's just . . . sometimes things happen up there. But listen, we in law enforcement frown on trespassing no matter where it is." He looked at her askance. "Also, I heard someone called in the suspicion of a fire up there last night, but the firefighters didn't see anything. Not the first time it's happened."

"The Hotel Seabrink has its own mind, in a way," Xavi said, tapping his temple. "It's like it gets inside your head."

"Well now, I wouldn't say that, exactly," scoffed Deputy Jenkins. "You're not from around here, ma'am, but that old place has a bit of a reputation. Of course, Xavi here might believe in superstitions like that, but we in law enforcement don't truck with such things."

At least he pronounced Xavi correctly, Aubrey thought. *That's progress.*

"Are you suggesting that our being at the Hotel Seabrink could have had something to do with Dimitri's death?" Aubrey asked.

"Of course not," the deputy said, looking uncomfortable. "But a lot of locals think that people who go snooping around there die a mysterious death, or whatever."

"It's cursed," Xavi mumbled.

"See what I mean?" said Jenkins. "People around here are full of superstitions."

"All's I know is people go in there, and nothing good happens," Xavi said, glancing at his phone. "Anyway, my shift was over a coupla hours ago, but Monica said I had to stay in case you needed to talk with me. Can I go now?"

"Sure, son. The sheriff's office appreciates the cooperation of good citizens such as yourself," said Jenkins.

"Deputy Jenkins—" Aubrey began, but Jenkins was already dialing his phone. He held up one finger in a "just a moment" gesture. Aubrey waited impatiently.

"My boss says to tell you you're free to go and thanks for your assistance in the investigation," Jenkins said, hanging up. "Here's my card in case anything else occurs to you. Nice to meet you, ma'am."

Jenkins picked up Dimitri's backpack and turned to leave.

"Deputy Jenkins."

Jenkins sighed and turned back to her. "Ma'am?"

"You . . . you honestly don't think Dimitri's death could be anything other than a suicide?"

"Look, lady, I know you're from Oakland, and a lot of nasty things happen down there. But up here, in this area? It's different. Sometimes there's, like, domestic disputes and the occasional theft or bar fight. The last murder I can think of was when Shaun Gallon killed his brother and those campers on the beach down in Jenner. That was a very long time ago, and he's been locked up ever since. And sure, there was the deal at the Hotel Seabrink, with the security guard, way back in the nineties, but that's about it. Do you really think some Hotel Seabrink ghost followed you back here?" His smile was tainted with a sneer. "There's no evidence of anyone else being present when he died. Just your guy, alone, out on the bluff."

SEVEN

Aubrey watched as the deputy ambled away, stopping at the buffet to nab a chocolate chip cookie before heading out the main doors.

Stunned and weary, Aubrey returned to her room. She stood at the window, gazing at the crashing waves in the cove, then craned her neck to see the open ocean. Where were those damned whales when she needed them? For a long while she searched the azure depths for a dark form breaking the surface of the sea, or a spout shooting up out of the water. The midday sun had burned off the morning mist, but she saw nothing but a V of graceful pelicans skimming the water, as if pointing the way.

Had this been Dimitri's last view?

Don't be ridiculous. At four in the morning Dead Man's Bluff would have been pitch black, the only light that of last night's nearly full moon. What had he been doing out there? He had taken a key card and left his backpack and cell phone, so Aubrey felt sure he must have planned on returning. Maybe he had been feeling restless, decided to go for a walk, wandered too close to the edge of the cliff, and somehow tripped? Slipped into oblivion? She wondered if he had taken his big flashlight. It wasn't in her room, so it had probably fallen onto the rocks alongside him. Not that it mattered.

What did a person do after something like this?

Aubrey lay down on top of the fluffy comforter and surprised herself by falling into a deep but troubled sleep, marked by a familiar recurring nightmare. She was walking along a city street on a sunny, windless day, when she heard someone scream. She looked up to see broken glass raining down on her from high atop a skyscraper. She was pierced by pain as shards shredded her skin. Bright red arterial blood sprayed, staining the sidewalk in an abstract pattern.

Aubrey startled awake, heart pounding, breath ragged. She got up to splash some water on her face, then took two more ibuprofen and downed a full glass of water. Her stomach growled, but she felt too nauseated to eat.

Aubrey opened her computer and watched a few of Dimitri's videos. He was so animated, so thoughtful and funny and *alive*, that tears welled up. She brushed them away, annoyed with herself. She hardly knew the man, after all. But as she scrolled through the list of videos, she realized the one he had uploaded last night—the one she had seen earlier this morning—had disappeared.

She looked again, searching his channel for anything that included the name Seabrink, but there was nothing. That was strange.

At a loss for what else to do, Aubrey began to look through her recent photographs, beginning with those from the Haupt Ranch cemetery, where she had started out yesterday, before she found her way to the Hotel Seabrink.

The patch of ground was barely recognizable as a cemetery; it was more a small clutch of lichen-crusted headstones, listing this way and that like a set of bad teeth. Aubrey remembered how her breath had come out in clouds and mingled with the waves of fog rolling in off the ocean, making the photographs deliciously hazy and mysterious.

She started applying filters, attempting to lose herself in the editing. But she kept thinking of Dimitri. Last night she had told him how she had noticed that in the old days, most epitaphs were brief: usually just names and dates, or perhaps "Mother" or "Father." After all, stone carvers used to charge by the letter. But when her own father died, Aubrey learned that the letters are now cut by lasers, so loved ones can have as much written on a tombstone as they want, for no extra cost. Nevertheless, most people still just write the deceased's name, dates, and "Mother"/"Father"/"Sister"/ "Brother."

Grief is complex, and slippery, and hard to set down in stone, Dimitri had said. And later when they were talking about life and death and love and loss, he added: *Your grief is too precious to waste on those who are unworthy.*

They had had too much to drink last night, no doubt about that. But the real reason Aubrey had been so open with Dimitri was their rare sense of connection, of mutual understanding. The feeling of being on the same wavelength with another person, of not having to explain oneself. Recognizing a kindred spirit in someone who has known betrayal and sorrow, who has faced despair. Someone who has *lived* and is not only not afraid of death but even, occasionally, entertains it.

Not everyone is afraid of death. Had he been trying to tell her something?

Aubrey's computer signaled its battery was low. She went

to plug it in and noticed that the nightstand drawer on the side where Dimitri slept last night was ajar.

She pulled it open. Inside was a worn brown leather wallet, slightly concave, as though years of use had made the leather conform to his body. Aubrey picked it up, running her fingers over the soft leather and cradling it for a moment, as if she could somehow feel Dimitri's warmth. As if it hadn't been sitting there for hours while his broken body lay on the cold sand at the bottom of Dead Man's Bluff.

She hesitated before opening it, but really, if a person was going to take a swan dive off a cliff, their privacy was bound to be compromised.

Inside were three crisp twenty-dollar bills, a couple of singles, a AAA card, a library card, two credit cards, and a driver's license with a San Francisco address. That was it. No photos of loved ones, no receipts, no scribbled phone numbers or appointment reminders. Nothing at all personal.

The only real item of interest was a plastic hotel key card from the St. Ambrose Hotel.

Aubrey returned to the lobby, grabbed a croissant from the now-pillaged display of baked goods and treats, and poured herself another cup of coffee. It was almost three in the afternoon, but she needed a pick-me-up.

"Aubrey," called Monica, crossing the lobby to join her.

"Hi," Aubrey replied. "Hey, I broke a hotel coffee mug this morning, out on the bluff. I'm happy to pay for it."

"Don't worry about it. Cost of doing business," Monica said in a brisk tone. The hotel manager's blond hair was cut in an asymmetrical bob, and she wore a chic gray striped pantsuit and a light pink blouse. Monica appeared highly efficient and rather uptight, which Aubrey supposed were ideal qualities in the manager of an upscale boutique hotel. Still, it was difficult to imagine Monica and Nikki as childhood friends. Nikki was so easygoing, quick with a laugh and a snarky comment, while Monica seemed the type to freak out over a toilet paper roll hung the wrong way. But then again, people changed and grew apart over time. And Aubrey was extremely grateful to Monica for extending her the heavily discounted room rate.

"How are you doing?" Aubrey asked.

"I was about to ask you that. Do you have a minute?"

"Of course."

They took seats on a low banquette. Monica glanced around the bar, then leaned toward her and in a low voice said, "Having deputies and fire and rescue personnel milling around is not good for business."

"Are they still here?" Aubrey asked, setting down her coffee mug and taking a big bite of the croissant. It was stale.

Monica shook her head and pursed her lips. "But still. They *were* here, and that's never good. What the hell happened?"

"I honestly have no idea. We—Dimitri and I—met yesterday and came back here for drinks."

"I got that much from the bartender on duty last night. Sounds like you two ran up quite a tab."

Aubrey felt heat rush to her cheeks. She almost never let loose, and now, having finally done so, not only did everyone know about it but her "date" ended up at the bottom of a cliff.

"We may have overindulged on a legal substance," Aubrey said. "So sue us."

"I can't very well sue *him*, now, can I?"

Aubrey felt the blood drain from her face, and the croissant seemed to stick in her throat. She washed it down with a swig of the tepid coffee.

"No, I suppose not." Aubrey cleared her throat. "I met a man, we had drinks, we slept together, and then he left the room at four in the morning, wandered out to Dead Man's Bluff, and . . . jumped. Or so they say."

Monica's gaze softened. "Are you okay?"

"I'm . . . yes, I'm okay. I'm sort of . . . still in shock, I suppose. And to borrow Deputy Jenkins's favorite word, it's just all so weird. Dimitri seemed fine yesterday; I never would have guessed he was contemplating suicide. He was charming and relaxed and spoke about the future. We talked about some very personal things last night, and never, not once, did he seem in despair, or desperate."

"These things are hard to predict," said Monica. "Sometimes it's the person you'd least suspect who's caught up in a very private tragedy. I speak from experience."

"I'm sorry to hear that."

Monica shrugged. "My point is, you never really know what another person might be going through."

"That's true. But I can't help wondering . . . could it have been an accident?" Aubrey asked. "Dimitri went out at four in the morning for—what? A smoke? A breath of bracing ocean air? A walk in the predawn darkness? And maybe he thought he saw something, got too close to the edge, and the rocks were slippery, and he lost his footing, and . . . could that be it?"

"I suppose it's possible," Monica said. "The sheriff's deputies are considering it a presumed suicide, but I suspect that's mostly because of the location: Dead Man's Bluff. It's happened there before, you know—not as often as people seem to think, but it *has* happened, hence the name. Where did you meet this guy, anyway? You were going up to Stewarts Point yesterday, weren't you? To take photos of the old cemetery?"

Aubrey nodded. "But afterward I went up to the Hotel Seabrink."

Monica's eyebrows shot up. "*Really*. That place is . . . I mean, around here everyone says it's cursed. How did you even find it? They took down all the signs."

"The clerk at Stewarts Point Store gave me an idea of where it was, and I've got a kind of sixth sense about these things. Have you ever been?"

She shook her head. "Of course not. It's off-limits. Surely it's posted."

Aubrey remained silent as she recalled the numerous NO TRESPASSING signs she had ignored, most of which were rusted or riddled with bullet holes.

"You met him at the Hotel Seabrink, huh?" said Monica. "Maybe that explains it."

Aubrey raised an eyebrow and took another bite of the stale croissant.

"I used to be skeptical, too," Monica said. "But people around here take the Seabrink curse seriously. There's been a lot of spooky stuff happening up there, over the years. And unexplained things happening to trespassers."

"Well, I was there, too, and I haven't fallen from a cliff."

"Not yet, anyway," Monica mumbled, keeping a watchful eye on the hotel's patrons coming and going.

At Aubrey's silence, Monica turned back to her.

"Be careful, Aubrey," Monica added. "I'm serious. People seem to come to harm when they're involved with the Seabrink. I have a business to run and Dead Man's Bluff being known for suicides is better than the headline 'Driftwood Cove Guest's Suspicious Death.'"

"I suppose that's true. Hey, do you have CCTV cameras installed?"

"We have cameras . . . but they're not recording anything."

"Why not?" Aubrey said, surprised. What was the point of installing cameras if they didn't work?

"One of the owners is strongly opposed to them, believes we shouldn't have to live under constant surveillance. Besides, just the sight of the cameras themselves serves as a deterrent, or so they say."

"Do you know the St. Ambrose Hotel?"

"Sure, it's north of Gualala, up Highway One," Monica said. "About a half an hour or so."

"Is it competition for the Driftwood Cove Inn?"

"Not really. It's a nice place, but it's pretty small and it appeals to a different clientele. The Sea Ranch Lodge is more a direct competitor, or even one of the Ukiah hot springs resorts. Assuming something ever comes of the development plans, the Hotel Seabrink might pose some competition, what with their mineral baths and all. That's why my boss has been lobbying so hard against it. Still, our location on the ocean is our ace in the hole, and besides, the Seabrink has its curse to overcome." Monica glanced at the reception desk, where guests were lining up to check in. She sighed and stood. "I'd better go lend a hand. We've had trouble getting reliable help lately. But Aubrey? Maybe . . . maybe do yourself a favor and stay off the bluff, and away from the Hotel Seabrink. Nothing good has ever come from that place."

EIGHT

As Aubrey headed out to the parking lot, she saw a tow truck pulling onto the highway, trailing an olive-colored Subaru. *Dimitri's car.* She wondered if Deputy Jenkins had bothered to look inside, and wished she had thought to do so before it was towed away. She didn't know what she would have hoped to have found, but she was pretty sure Jenkins wouldn't bother to even look unless there was a suicide note explaining what Dimitri was going to do—and why.

Aubrey climbed into her gray Honda sedan and headed up the winding Highway One, which was the only route up and down the coast. The sun had burned off the morning fog, and the day was chilly but spectacular: robin's-egg-blue skies dotted with puffy white clouds, the ocean on her immediate left, lush meadows dotted with boulders and cows and tree-covered mountains on her right, small herds of deer here and there. She drove through a few towns, most little more than a small clutch of houses, with names such as Stillwater Cove and Ocean Cove, and passed a couple of small general stores advertising fresh bait and locally caught smoked salmon. Occasional highway signs indicated places of interest: Wildcat Creek, the campground at Salt Point State Park, a rhododendron reserve, and the occasional beach access point.

At last, she spied Stewarts Point Store, where everything had started yesterday. But this time, instead of turning up Asylum Point Road toward the mountains and the Hotel Seabrink, she continued north, finally approaching the Sea Ranch Lodge and the community of Sea Ranch.

Why was she going to the St. Ambrose? What did she expect to find? Deputy Jenkins, as unimpressive as he seemed, was probably right: Dimitri had been suffering with a deep, desperate dilemma of some sort, and decided to go on to . . . whatever was next. And as close as they had seemed last night, they were not true friends. Besides, she had plenty of problems of her own; why borrow those of a virtual stranger? Whatever might have developed with Dimitri no longer would. She should allow herself to grieve the loss of what might have been, bring this very short chapter of her life to an end, and get back to reality. Such as it was.

Still . . . she had his key card. She would feel better if she checked out his hotel room, just in case. Maybe there would be something obvious, such as a suicide note or a journal entry, that might explain what happened. Or at the very least she might find some family information to give to the authorities. How awful to imagine that Dimitri had loved ones who did not yet know that he was gone. Forever lost to them.

A bridge crossed over the Gualala River, a broad, shallow waterway that led out to the sea, with a large stretch of sandy beach to the left. In a small lot by the side of the highway were several tents with signs extolling handmade jewelry and fresh-caught fish. Downtown Gualala boasted two grocery stores, several small gift shops, vacation rental agencies, a café called Trinks, and a bookstore called Four-Eyed Frog Books. A historic hotel with a sign proclaiming it had been established in 1903 held pride of place on the main drag; sadly, it was closed for business. Her stomach growled at the aroma of ribs being barbecued in a parking lot, but then she thought again of Dimitri and lost her appetite. The croissant still sat heavily in her belly.

A few minutes later, she spotted the sign for the St. Ambrose Hotel. Dimitri was right about the architecture: it was quirky and eye-catching, with Russian-style onion domes, multipaned windows, wood shingles, stained glass, and extensive decks.

Over the years, Aubrey had become disillusioned with her chosen profession. Being an architect involved much less designing and creativity and much more checking of local building codes and pushing documents through permit offices, conforming to electrical and plumbing and earthquake safety regulations. All essential tasks, but boring. Tedious. Mind-numbing. And when they're ignored . . . potentially catastrophic.

In contrast, whoever had designed the St. Ambrose Hotel had clearly had a blast. She could only describe the architecture as joyful, exultant, with an aura of funky artistry melding with seaside luxury. Several of the outdoor posts were decorated with little glass and amethyst knobs that reminded her of the quartz crystal orb she had seen at the Seabrink. Good thing she hadn't been able to see her own immediate future in its depths.

Beauty is a necessity, like dreams and oxygen, Dimitri had said, quoting Toni Morrison.

A wood-planked deck led to the main door, with a stairwell

to the immediate right. Inside the lobby, to the left, a roaring
fire in a large stone fireplace warmed a sitting area, where
several guests were chatting and enjoying drinks. A sign for a
restaurant led to the other side of the lobby.

A pixieish, dark-haired woman was entertaining the customers at the hotel's bar, laughing and mixing drinks with
enthusiasm. It was a jocular crowd, and though it was still
early the bar was busy, with several customers dressed casually in T-shirts and jeans, others in fishing gear, in addition to
a smattering of well-dressed tourists.

Aubrey was surprised to recognize two of the patrons. Mia,
the paramedic who had helped her that morning, was sitting
at a small, high table. Beside her was the sandy-haired man
who had rappelled down the cliff to retrieve Dimitri's body.

Aubrey's first impulse was to hide.

But they spotted her before she could leave.

Mia waved and called out, "Hi! From earlier, right? Aubrey?"
"Good memory," Aubrey said, forcing a smile. Why did
she feel like running away? Was it guilt? Or was she just feeling awkward, not wanting to be reminded of the morning's
events?

"And this is Jasper," Mia said. "Jasper, this is Aubrey. She
knew this morning's victim, identified him."

The sandy-haired man nodded, his hazel eyes steady and
kind. When he spoke, his voice was sincere. "Nice to meet you,
Aubrey. I'm very sorry about your friend."

"Thank you."

"So how are you doing?" Mia asked. "You had quite a shock
this morning."

"I'm . . . I'm okay. Sort of thrown for a loop."

"Why don't you join us?" Mia offered. "I think you need a drink. And I say that as a medical professional."

"Oh, thanks, but . . . it's a little early."

Jasper checked his phone. "It's four thirty. That's close enough to five to count."

"You know, I think you're right, I could use something," Aubrey said, giving in to the inevitable and taking a seat.

Mia waved at the bartender, who came to their table and in a lilting Mexican accent introduced herself as Lucia.

"I have a special drink on tonight's menu, an herbal martini," she said. "The owner grows the herbs herself, everything organic."

"It's a house specialty," said Jasper. "You should try it."

"I'm game," Aubrey said.

"Two of your special martinis, and a club soda with lime for me," Jasper said, and Lucia nodded.

"You're both paramedics, then?" Aubrey asked.

"In a manner of speaking," Jasper said.

"We're *volunteer* paramedics," Mia clarified.

"Seriously? You do all that as volunteers?"

"Somebody has to. There's a small medical clinic here in Gualala, but we're about it when it comes to emergency services, especially when the sheriff's department is busy with other things," said Mia.

"We both also work for a living," Jasper said. "I run my family's hardware store here in town, and Mia has a consignment shop."

"Uh-oh, sounds like trouble. I love consignment shops," said Aubrey. "A little too much."

"What about hardware stores?" teased Jasper.

"Do you sell cool clothing, too?"

"We've got some pretty spiffy rubber boots."

Aubrey smiled. "So, Mia, where's your store?"

"In the Cypress Village shops, not far from the bookstore. Come by anytime."

"I love that Gualala has a real bookstore."

"It almost closed a few years ago, but the folks in town stepped in to save it," Mia said. "None of us wanted to live in a town without a bookstore."

"Sounds like a close-knit community," said Aubrey.

"It is," said Mia. "There are a lot of tourists in the season, of course, but those of us who live here year-round are pretty public-spirited. Where are you from?"

"Oakland. It has its charms, but not nearly enough bookstores."

"How long are you in town for?"

"Another week. I got a special deal at the Driftwood Cove Inn."

"Nice place," Jasper commented.

Lucia arrived with their drinks.

"Here's looking at both of you," Jasper said, and they clinked glasses.

The martini was ice-cold and delicious, but Lucia had been generous with the pour and the alcohol went straight to Aubrey's head.

As if reading her mind, Jasper ordered fried calamari and garlic bread for the table. "That should soak up the alcohol."

"You read my mind," Mia said.

Aubrey took another sip of her martini and felt herself beginning to relax. They chatted easily for a while, Mia and Jasper describing what it was like to live in such a remote coastal town, especially during the offseason.

Aubrey nodded and smiled, but her mind kept wandering

back to that awful moment this morning, when realization dawned that the dead man was, in fact, Dimitri.

Mia reached out and put her hand over Aubrey's. "I'm very sorry for your loss, Aubrey. I hope his memory is a blessing."

"I . . ." Aubrey was growing weary of explaining that she was not, in fact, Dimitri's girlfriend. "To tell you the truth, I hardly knew him. We just met yesterday. We hit it off, and he has a YouTube channel I'm familiar with, where he posts videos of abandoned buildings, so in a way I felt like I knew him already."

"How did you two meet?" Jasper asked.

"We ran into each other at the old Hotel Seabrink."

"The Seabrink?" Mia said, as she and Jasper exchanged glances. "Really?"

"I take it you know about the curse?" said Aubrey.

"I don't believe in curses," said Jasper.

"Neither do I," said Mia with a firm shake of her head. "But I do believe in bad people. And bad places."

"There's a curse, all right," said Lucia as she set a plate of glistening fried calamari and a basket of fragrant garlic bread on their table. "I can't believe there are plans to redevelop it as a hotel. How many people have to die up there before they burn it to the ground, like they should do?"

"The Quiet Girl tried that already, long time ago," said a sixtyish man nursing a beer at the bar.

"Time to finish the job," said Lucia.

"We don't need any more wildfires, now," said an elderly woman sitting in the corner. "Best to let nature reclaim it in her own time."

"A new hotel could be a real boon to the local economy," another bar patron said. "More jobs, bigger tax base. Win-win."

"Not if they're afflicted by the Seabrink Curse," Lucia replied.

"Who's the Quiet Girl?" Aubrey asked.

"Don't ask," muttered Jasper.

"Someone who lived there a long time ago. She's called the Quiet Girl because she was mute," said the elderly man. "They say she haunts the place, and if you look up and see her in the attic window then you'll soon meet your own death."

"It's just a popular ghost story in these parts," Jasper said. "Pay it no mind."

Soon, everyone in the bar was chiming in on the wisdom of developing the Hotel Seabrink, the ghost of the Quiet Girl, the Hollywood starlet who jumped from the hotel balcony, and the teenager killed on the night of her prom by a security guard who then either hung himself or escaped into the woods, depending on which version of the story one believed.

Aubrey listened and sipped her martini. She was an outsider in this bar full of regulars. Still, she had been new to established groups before and had never felt quite like this. Was it because of what had happened with Dimitri? C. S. Lewis wrote that grief felt a lot like fear, or being slightly drunk, creating an invisible barrier between the grief-stricken and the rest of the world. But . . . had she really known Dimitri well enough to mourn him?

Aubrey felt like an imposter with everyone assuming that she and Dimitri were together. And yet, if she could get some answers as to what had happened to him, maybe she could put some of these feelings to rest.

"Here's the one thing that's true," pronounced a grizzled old man in a Greek fishing cap, standing and speaking loudly to the entire bar, as if claiming the last word on the subject: "Doesn't really matter which one she is. If you look up and see the ashen, haunting visage of a young woman in the high attic window of the Seabrink, it foretells your imminent death.

That fellow who died at Dead Man's Bluff early this morning? He must have seen her face. Poor sod."

There were several murmurs of agreement, and the bar patrons returned to their private conversations.

"Well, now that you're up to date on our local legends, I guess it's time for me to go home and feed my kids," said Mia, as she got up from the table and held out some cash for her drinks.

"It's on me," Jasper said, refusing the money. "You can pick it up next time."

"Thanks." Mia lingered for a moment, her hand resting on her purse strap, as though she wanted to say something more. "It was nice to see you, Aubrey, though again, I'm sorry about the circumstances. Come by the store if you have time."

"I'll do that, thanks. And thank you again for this morning. It's amazing what you do for perfect strangers."

"I'm glad to help."

On her way out, Mia stopped to greet several people in the bar. Everyone, it seemed, knew each other.

"I should get going, myself," Aubrey said to Jasper. "Thank you as well for all you do. It was quite something to see you rappelling down that cliff. That must take courage. It scared the hell out of me just watching you."

"You get used to it," Jasper said, and met her gaze. "Tell me something, Aubrey: Did you come to the St. Ambrose Hotel because your friend was staying here?"

"How did you know he was staying here?"

"I made a few phone calls to local hotels. It didn't take long to track him down."

"Why were you trying to track him down?"

"You say you didn't know him well?" Jasper asked.

Aubrey shook her head. "We just met yesterday. We sort of bonded over a shared love of abandoned places, and then . . ."

"He spent the night with you at Driftwood Cove."

"He did."

"And he went out to the bluff in the predawn hours and wound up on the rocks at the bottom of Dead Man's Bluff."

Aubrey nodded and downed the last swallow of her martini. "That's pretty much the size of it. And . . . I'm not sure what I thought I'd find coming here, but I happened upon his key card and thought, I don't know, maybe something in his room could tell me something."

"I see. In that case . . ." Jasper stood, greeted several new arrivals at the bar, then said to Aubrey, "Let's settle up our bill and go."

"Go where?"

"Upstairs. To check out his room."

You didn't answer my question," Aubrey said to Jasper's back as he strode toward the main door, then turned into the stairwell. "Why did you track Dimitri down, and why do you want to see his room?"

"Let's just say I'm curious." Stretching across the bottom of the stairs was a velvet cordon, from which hung a sign: GUESTS ONLY. Jasper unlatched the cordon, waved her through, then reattached it behind him.

"About what?" Aubrey asked as they quickly climbed the stairs.

"About who your mystery man was and his manner of death." Jasper looked at her. "As are you, I imagine, or you wouldn't be here."

At the top of the stairs was a hallway, lined by a half a dozen closed doors.

"Which room was his?" Jasper asked quietly.

"I have no idea. I planned to see which door lock lights up when we hold the card next to it."

Number six was the charm. The light turned green and beeped quietly.

Aubrey glanced down the hall, checking for witnesses. They were, after all, trespassing. Her second time in two days. This was becoming a habit.

"After you," Jasper whispered.

They slipped into the room. It wasn't as spacious or as luxurious as Aubrey's room at the Driftwood Cove Inn, and it lacked her room's spectacular ocean view. But it was comfortable and charming, and the bed was neatly made.

"Any idea what we should be looking for?" Jasper asked.

"I'm hoping we'll know it when we see it." Aubrey didn't know what she wanted to find. Maybe something to explain why he might have died so suddenly, or at the very least a way to contact Dimitri's family. She felt a duty to speak with them, to tell them that their son, brother—husband, father?—had made an impression on her. Surely a man like Dimitri, so charming and intelligent and considerate, had people who cared about him. Who loved him.

"Let's get started, then. I'll search the closet and the bathroom, you take the bedside table and the desk," Jasper suggested. "Divide and conquer."

Aubrey started with the bedside table, on which were two novels: Toni Morrison's *Beloved*, and Gabriel García Márquez's *Love in the Time of Cholera*, classics she remembered from her college years. Both had bookplates that declared: *Stolen from Roger Harmon*. There was nothing in the table's drawer, so she turned to the bed itself, running her hands under the mattress and the covers. Again, nothing. Nor was anything stuffed into the pillows. She heard Jasper moving around in the bathroom and called out, "Any luck?"

"A toiletries kit. No clues there, unless toothpaste, dental floss, and a high-quality razor mean something to you."

Aubrey turned to the only other piece of furniture in the room, the desk. She took a seat in the chair and pulled the drawer open. There, tucked beneath a handful of tourist brochures and take-out menus from local restaurants, was a canvas bag.

Inside was a bound journal labeled *Seabrink*. Detailed notes about the building and its history were scrawled in a cramped, messy handwriting, presumably Dimitri's. She flipped through it briefly then set it aside to read later. She reached back into the bag and retrieved a thumb drive, presumably also Dimitri's, and set that on the desk alongside the journal.

Next, she found two notes composed of words torn from a magazine and glued onto plain white pieces of paper. They read: **answer me!** And **you can't ignore me.**

"Find anything?" Jasper asked.

"You could say that."

Jasper joined her at the desk and peered over her shoulder. "Get a load of the old-fashioned threatening notes. I didn't know criminals still cut up magazines anymore. Whoever sent these is a traditionalist. That's something."

"This morning, a text popped up on Dimitri's phone, saying 'You were warned.'"

"That sounds ominous. But—the text was sent *after* he was killed?"

She nodded. "I mentioned it to Deputy Jenkins, but he didn't think it was relevant because of the timing."

"Kenny Jenkins is . . . well, he tries his best," Jasper murmured. "Still, that is strange. Either the message had nothing to do with your friend's death, or whoever sent it killed him and was trying to throw the investigation off track. Little did he know he had no reason to worry, not with Kenny Boy Jenkins on the case."

"Or Dimitri's death really was a suicide or an accident."

"Or maybe the text was delayed. That happens—phone service can be a bit wonky up here on the coast."

"In other words, there's really no way to know what it might mean."

"Sounds about right. And given the limited resources for law enforcement around here, and the fact that those in charge of the investigation seem convinced your friend died by his own hand, I doubt they'll be calling in a technical expert to parse that text."

Aubrey sighed and looked into the canvas bag once more. "Get a load of this," she said, holding up a US passport.

"Is that significant?"

"The photograph is of Dimitri—a younger Dimitri," Aubrey said, looking through the passport. "But check out the name: Roger Harmon. At the back is an aka, also known as: Dimitri Petroff. That name, Roger Harmon, is inscribed on his books, as well. Why would he be using two names?"

"Hard to say. He's dodging child support? On the run from the law?"

"He has a YouTube channel. That's not exactly keeping a low profile."

"Maybe Dimitri Petroff is his professional name. What else is in the bag?"

This time Aubrey pulled out an ancient-looking, yellowed

letter, extracting the pages from their envelope. A sound from the hallway startled her, and she spilled the papers onto the floor.

She bent over to pick them up, and when she straightened, she found Jasper's eyes on her. "I guess I'm a little jumpy."

"Don't worry, this place isn't haunted. Not yet, anyway. It looks historic, but it's only from the 1970s."

"I imagine fifty years is more than enough time to acquire a couple of ghosts."

"You've got me there."

Aubrey startled again when the door swung open.

NINE

A short, stout woman with a salt-and-pepper pixie cut and a clipboard stood in the doorway, frowning. "This room was supposed to be vacated hours ago. We have another guest coming in, and it needs to be cleaned."

"Oh, I—" Aubrey said, but Jasper interrupted.

"Hi, Miriam," he said.

"Jasper? What are you doing here? And who's she?"

"This is Aubrey. Aubrey, Miriam's the manager here. I don't know if you heard, Miriam, but there was a tragedy this morning and—"

"Out at Dead Man's Bluff."

"Small town, news travels fast," said Jasper. "The thing is, your guest here was the victim."

"No."

"I'm afraid so."

After a beat, she said, "Who's going to pay his bill?"

"Really, Miriam?"

"Sorry, but our profit margin's thin enough already, not to

mention he ate in the restaurant two nights in a row. Somebody needs to pay for that. But . . . I guess I can just run his
credit card. Unless his death has already been reported to his
bank."

"Do you recall the name on his credit card?" Aubrey asked.

She frowned. "Roger Harmon checked into this room.
What other name would he have?"

"It's not important. Oh, I have some cash," Aubrey said,
taking Dimitri's wallet from her bag. "It belonged to Dimitri.
I mean Roger. Sixty-three dollars. I don't suppose that's
enough to cover his bill."

"Nowhere near," Miriam said. "But it's a start." She took
the money from Aubrey. "Are you staying here as well?"

Aubrey shook her head. "No, I'm at the Driftwood Cove Inn."

Miriam snorted. "Of course you are. What are you doing
here, then?"

"Just . . ."

"Collecting his things," Jasper intervened smoothly. "For
the family. Deputy Jenkins suggested it."

Miriam snorted. "Kenny Boy?" Her phone pinged and she
read a text, frowned, and slipped the phone back into her
pocket. "I have to go. Laundry crisis. I . . . I don't know what
to say. I'm sorry for your loss. And . . . the room still needs to
be cleaned, so at the risk of sounding insensitive: please don't
linger. I've got a paying guest arriving shortly."

After Miriam left, Jasper turned to Aubrey. "Let's gather
up his things and go somewhere to talk."

They packed Dimitri's few clothes, the canvas bag, the toiletries, and the books into the small rolling suitcase in the
corner. There was nothing else.

Outside, evening had fallen. Except for the occasional
passing car on the nearby highway, all was quiet, the air red-

olent of redwood trees and sea brine. Pulling the suitcase, Jasper led the way down a discreetly lit forest path, through a small canyon, and up crooked wooden stairs to a clearing where a clutch of small cabins encircled a central building with a pool. Mist rose from the water, and rippling underwater lighting reflected off the building and the surrounding patio, giving the area an otherworldly, ethereal feel amid the dark canopy of the trees.

"What is this place?" Aubrey asked.

"The St. Ambrose Hotel was built on the site of an old fishing village. The main inn doesn't have that many rooms, so they refurbished several of the fisherman shacks."

"It's charming. And it's okay for us to be here?"

He nodded. "I went to school with the hotel's current owner, and she lets me use the pool. Like Mia said, we all pretty much know each other 'round here."

As Aubrey took a seat on one of the comfortable Adirondack chairs by the pool, Jasper opened a nearby cabinet and retrieved several clean pool towels to use as blankets to ward off the chilly evening air. Although the afternoon had been sunny, the temperature plummeted as soon as the sun went down. He draped a fresh-smelling towel around her shoulders like a shawl, and she snuggled into it, grateful for its warmth.

Aubrey leaned over and unzipped Dimitri's suitcase, extracting his journal and thumbing through it. "The journal seems to be mostly about his research on the hotel, but it's pretty hard to read in this light. Do you want to try?"

She held it out to him, but he shook his head.

"I'm not interested in the Seabrink. I wanted to talk to you about our victim," Jasper said, settling into the chair next to Aubrey. "Dimitri, aka Roger."

"You keep calling him a victim," Aubrey replied. "Does

that mean you have reason to believe he didn't commit suicide?"

"Let's just say I have my doubts. And by the way, I've been taught by bereaved family members not to say 'committed' suicide. The only things that are 'committed' are crimes."

"I've never thought about that. What do you say instead?"

"I say 'killed themselves,' or 'took their own lives,' or 'died by suicide'—or even 'suicided,' though that sounds awkward to my ear. Anyway." Jasper gazed up at the sky, as if picturing something in his mind. "I've participated in several recoveries of people who've taken their own lives. More than I care to count. I don't think Dimitri was one of them."

"Why is that?" Aubrey said.

"When folks jump off a cliff, they usually, you know, *jump* off the cliff. Your guy didn't."

"What makes you think he didn't jump?"

"His hands. His fingers on both hands were crushed and bloodied, the fingernails dirty and torn. I don't see that in the cases of suicide jumpers. I do see it, though, when people fall and are trying to save themselves. You ask me, he was holding on to the side of the cliff, until . . ."

"Until . . . ?"

"Until he couldn't. Or until someone made sure he couldn't."

"Did you mention this to Deputy Jenkins?"

"I did. But . . . does Jenkins strike you as an especially insightful kind of guy? Or more as someone who prefers to wrap things up easily and quickly? I'm guessing Kenny Boy has already typed up and filed his official incident report."

Aubrey sighed.

"Normally Sam would have handled this—he's the head deputy sheriff for that stretch of the coast. But things were busy this morning, what with the highway crash and a wild-fire. We'll have to wait on the coroner's office in Santa Rosa for the official determination of death, but . . . I imagine they'll go with suicide."

"The coroner's office is in Santa Rosa? That's quite a ways from here."

He nodded. "Driftwood Cove and Dead Man's Bluff are in Sonoma County. The river marks the county line, so here in Gualala we're in Mendocino County. Locals call the area Mendonoma, since it's really our own little stretch of the coast, straddling two counties. It makes policing a little complicated."

"I see. And you don't think the coroner will find the wounds on Dimitri's hands suspicious?"

Jasper shrugged. "Maybe, but I wouldn't hold my breath. Unlike medical examiners, coroners aren't required to have much specific medical training or expertise. Usually that doesn't matter because around here most sudden deaths are due to heart attacks, car crashes, drug overdoses, the occasional drowning. Suspicious deaths are few and far between."

"Deputy Jenkins mentioned a double homicide on the beach in Jenner a while ago."

"Yes, that's a famous case, in part because it's so rare. Let me ask you: Why were you trespassing in an abandoned hotel?"

"I was taking photographs."

"That wasn't my question. Why the old Hotel Seabrink?"

"It's sort of hard to describe. I find the emptiness and the decay . . . fascinating. And strangely peaceful. I've photo-graphed all kinds of abandoned places: loads of old houses, of course, but also a 1950s motel on old Highway Sixty-Six, an auto plant in Michigan that closed in the 1970s, and an empty trailer park in Alabama. That one was interesting because all the trailers were still there, just no people."

"What, no zombies?"

She smiled. "Luckily, no."

He held her gaze. "Not to sound patronizing, but is it safe to wander around abandoned places on your own?"

"I'm an architect. I know not to go into areas that aren't structurally sound."

"Rotting wood isn't the only potential danger in an abandoned building."

"I also carry pepper spray."

"Oh, well, that's a whole different story, then."

"Listen, I'd like your take on something," Aubrey said, and tried to open the YouTube app on her phone to show Jasper some of Dimitri's YouTube videos. "Huh. It's not loading."

"Phone reception in this area can depend on your service provider, or which cell tower might have been taken out by fire or wind, that sort of thing. Mother Nature is a challenge up here."

Frustrated, Aubrey tucked her phone back in her pocket. "Okay, the thing is, when I woke up this morning, before I found out what happened to Dimitri, I saw that he had posted a new video to his YouTube channel, time-stamped at eleven thirty last night. Just a little teaser, he said, for a 'coming soon' video about the Hotel Seabrink: the building, the mineral baths, the history. But when I went to watch it again this afternoon, it was gone. It had been deleted."

Jasper nodded. "I'm not surprised. The internet appears to be regularly scrubbed of any and all references to the Hotel Seabrink and its past."

"Dimitri mentioned that as well. Is that sort of thing legal? I mean, how would you even accomplish something like that?"

"Don't ask me. Not exactly a techie."

"Okay, so: *Why* would someone do that?"

"If I had to guess, I'd say it was through the intervention of the heirs to the hotel. Not long after the original Goffin closed the hotel, the family leased it out to be used as a nursing home. But they refused to permit the building to be altered in any significant way to accommodate the new residents, so that iteration didn't last long."

"That explains the wheelchairs and gurney," Aubrey murmured to herself with a shudder, remembering the forlorn, old-fashioned medical equipment she had photographed in the lobby.

He nodded. "With the Seabrink's reputation for murder and mayhem, it's not an easy sale. At least, not at the price they're asking. Maybe that's why they try to keep it out of the news."

"Who are the heirs?"

"The greater Goffin family, I would imagine. The Hotel Seabrink was the creation of T. Jefferson Goffin, a newspaper and salt mining magnate who amassed a fortune."

"I read about that. Who knew there was so much money in salt?"

"Sure was, back in the day. Goffin initially built the Seabrink for his young son, who he hoped would be cured by the Seabrink's mineral water, but no luck."

"Sounds like you know a lot about it."

"My grandmother grew up in Gualala, and she used to tell me stories about the glamorous Hollywood stars who came to the hotel to relax, refresh, and 'take the waters.' In fact, my grandmother says that when she was a girl, she was on a church hike and witnessed something tragic there, a starlet falling from a balcony. That story was covered up, as well. But some locals claim her restless spirit is still there, wandering the halls."

"Is that the Quiet Girl? The one associated with the curse?"

He shook his head. "Different ghost. The Quiet Girl supposedly stands at one of the attic windows, looking out toward the gates. If you look up and see her, you'll die within a day or so. The exact details change, depending on who's telling the story."

Their gaze met and held for a long moment.

"I didn't see her," said Aubrey softly. *Did Dimitri?* Was that what he was staring at right before they left?

"Good thing," Jasper said with a crooked smile. "Sounds like you had quite enough drama, as it was."

"We did meet someone there, but he wasn't a ghost. Some guy named Cameron."

"Cameron Meroni?"

"He didn't mention a last name."

"There's a guy named Cameron Meroni—white, youngish, kind of nondescript—who's a rep for the people buying the Seabrink."

"Sounds like him. He didn't tell us he was working with the developer, though," Aubrey said, recalling the scene in the baths, the music, the footsteps. A shiver passed over her. "We thought he was just another trespasser."

"Imagine that. No honor among trespassers, eh?"

"So, what does any of this tell us?" Aubrey asked. "Dimitri Petroff, aka Roger Harmon, trespassed at the Hotel Seabrink yesterday, where I met him. He sure didn't strike me as a Roger, by the way."

"What does a Roger look like?"

"I don't know, but 'Dimitri' seemed much more apt. Anyway, we hit it off and he spent the night with me—actually, if we're going to be precise, it was only a few hours—before going out to the bluff and winding up at the bottom of the cliff. That reminds me: Did you find a flashlight with him? Or my key card? Or, I don't know, anything else that might have been a clue?"

Jasper shook his head. "I checked for a phone or other source of identifying information, but otherwise I was focused on retrieving the body. Why?"

She shook her head. "I was just wondering why he would go out in the middle of the night without a phone or a flashlight. When we were exploring the Seabrink he carried a big, heavy flashlight, the kind that can be used as a weapon."

"It was nearly a full moon last night," said Jasper. "Bright enough to walk without a light, maybe."

Aubrey gazed up at the brilliant night sky. True darkness had fallen, revealing an astonishing canopy of stars. The Adirondack chairs were relaxing; one could lay one's head back and take in the celestial view as it was meant to be seen, far from urban light pollution. So many stars crowded the darkness that the black sky looked murky, the sky dusted with misty clouds and sprinkled with sparkling glitter.

Exhaustion started creeping up, and Aubrey's eyes grew heavy.

"Sleepy?" Jasper asked, his deep voice rousing her.

Aubrey sat up with a start. "I guess I am. I should be getting back to my hotel."

"You sure you're okay to drive?" Jasper asked. "You can crash on my couch if you're not up to it."

"Thanks, I'm fine, but I really should get going."

Jasper walked her back to the St. Ambrose parking lot, where they stashed Dimitri's suitcase in the trunk of her car and traded contact information.

"I'll let you know what the head deputy sheriff says," he said. "Or when the coroner makes his assessment."

"And if the coroner and sheriff agree it was a suicide?"

Jasper waved at a couple going to their car.

"I'm no detective," said Jasper, turning back to Aubrey. "I hadn't really thought past checking out where this guy was staying and seeing if anyone could tell me anything."

"But you didn't learn anything pertinent?"

He shook his head. "The hotel desk clerk and the restaurant staff said he was polite and kept to himself. Checked in alone and ate alone."

"I guess that's that, then," said Aubrey. "I'm no detective, either. Maybe this will remain one of life's unsolved mysteries."

"You never know. Maybe his journal will tell you something."

"From what I've seen so far, it seemed to be mostly about the history of the building. But you're right, you never know."

He nodded. "Listen, if you need anything, you can find me most days at Stillman's Hardware and Lumber. We're right off the highway, just north of Gualala."

"You're very kind."

"Here to serve, as they say."

She smiled and opened her car door. "Thanks, Jasper. Good night."

"Sure you're okay to drive?"

"I am. Tired, but okay. The garlic bread did the trick."

"Garlic bread usually does."

Aubrey had started her car when Jasper leaned in through the open door. "Hey, Aubrey? I don't believe in ghosts or curses, either . . . but if I were you, I'd stay away from any more explorations of the Hotel Seabrink. And maybe stay off the bluff, as well."

"You're the second person to tell me that today."

"Then it must be advice worth listening to."

The true curse of small coastal towns was that while they were charming as all get-out, they were severely lacking in twenty-four-hour convenience stores. Aubrey had hoped to stop somewhere for a cup of coffee to go, but except for a small take-out pizzeria and an upscale restaurant overlooking the ocean, everything in town was closed up tight.

Tonight's full moon was bright and silvery, reflecting off the water. Jasper was right: the moon had been almost full last night, so maybe it had been bright enough for Dimitri to take a walk without a flashlight or his phone. Still . . . was he just taking a walk, or meeting someone? Could it be connected to the strange cut-and-paste notes she had found among his things?

The drive back to Driftwood Cove seemed to take much longer than the drive to Gualala had that afternoon. The road along the coast was dark and lonely; there was almost no traffic, and few signs of life in homes or businesses. But she continued, and at long last spotted the cheerful lights of the Driftwood Cove Inn.

As she crossed the lobby, Dimitri's suitcase rolling along behind her, Aubrey spotted the night clerk, Xavi, with his head bent over his phone. Not for the first time, Aubrey wondered whether an entire generation would develop crooked necks from the incessant hunching. That, and arthritis in their thumbs from overuse.

"Oh, Ms. Spencer? Something came for you," Xavi said, and handed her a manila envelope with a printed label on the front: AUBREY SPENCER.

Curious, she tore open the envelope as she stepped away from the front desk. Inside was a note, written in letters cut from a magazine:

Back Off Now Or the Sea Brink curse will take YOU next.

TEN

———

"Xavi, who left this for me?" Aubrey turned back to ask, her heart pounding.

He shook his head and blushed. "I'm sorry. I was in the bathroom. When I came back, I found it on the counter, with your name on it. Is everything all right?"

"Yeah, it's fine. Thanks. Just—maybe don't give out my room number to anyone, okay?"

"Of course not," he said, his eyes widening and his Adam's apple bobbing. "Company policy, discretion at all times."

Now wide awake and senses heightened, Aubrey returned to her room, glancing over her shoulder as she let herself in. She flipped on the lights, then quickly shut and double locked the door with the security bolt. She checked out the closet and the bathroom, peering behind the shower curtain, just in case. The big window only opened a few inches and looked out to the ocean. Unless someone could levitate, there was no way to access her room from there.

She slumped down on the side of the bed and rooted

around in her bag for her phone and the business card with Deputy Jenkins's number.

"What have you been doing to be warned *against*?" asked Jenkins after Aubrey told him about the threatening note.

"Nothing. That's my point."

"Nothing at all?"

"Well, I . . ." Given the way people gossiped around here, Jenkins would probably hear about it anyway, so there was no point in beating around the bush. "I did go check out Dimitri's hotel room at the St. Ambrose."

"Did you find anything? A suicide note, maybe?"

"No, nothing like that. I was looking for information to contact his family. I thought they might want to talk to me, since I seem to be among the last to have spoken with him."

Silence.

"Hello?" Aubrey urged. "Are you still there?"

"Yes, I'm here," said Deputy Jenkins. "Listen, ma'am, it's late. Let's sleep on this. I really don't think there's anything to worry about."

Maybe not for you, buddy. "Let me ask you: Have you found any information about the family? Any personal contacts, maybe in his phone?"

"Nothing so far. I've been busy; this isn't my only case, you know."

"I found a few more things in Dimitri's room, and the manager there asked me to clean everything out. Should I turn them over to you?"

"You said there was nothing pertaining to the suicide, right? I mean, as his girlfriend you might as well keep his stuff."

"I'm not—"

"Have a good evening, ma'am," Jenkins said and hung up.

"—*his girlfriend*," Aubrey muttered, glaring at the phone. Ol' Kenny Boy was a real piece of work. Jasper had mentioned he would talk to his friend, Sam, the head deputy sheriff; with luck, he would be more helpful.

And in the meantime? She studied the menacing note and examined the manila envelope but found no clues as to its origin.

For some reason she kept thinking about her father's funeral, and her fraught childhood, and the disaster at work. Aubrey had read that trauma responses were connected, one trauma reviving past ordeals, which then rose zombielike from the dead.

Aubrey had come to Driftwood Cove in search of rest and relaxation, not another nightmare.

Had someone sent the note because she was asking questions at the St. Ambrose Hotel? That would mean she was being followed, or perhaps someone in the bar recognized her and knew where she was staying. Assuming Dimitri's death was intentional, did the murderer suspect Dimitri had told her something incriminating during their time together? And if he had been killed to silence him, did it follow that her life could also be in danger?

Dimitri had spouted more poetry than anything remotely suspicious.

Or . . . could the alleged "Seabrink curse" truly be to blame?

She scoffed at herself. There was no such thing as curses, or ghosts. *Only our own regrets and fears and memories haunt us.*

Aubrey took several deep, calming breaths. Someone clearly thought she posed a danger of some sort, and since she didn't know why or to whom, she couldn't very well stop doing whatever it was they felt threatened by. She did know that

Dimitri had apparently posed a similar threat. So that left only one option: to see if she could learn what Dimitri might have known.

Or she could pack up her things and go home. Ending up a corpse at the bottom of a cliff would benefit no one, least of all herself. And the last thing she needed just now was to be drawn into investigating a violent death, much less incurring anonymous threats. Aubrey didn't even know what she was supposed to be backing off *from*.

Kicking off her shoes, Aubrey sat back against the headboard and unzipped Dimitri's suitcase to go through everything again, just in case. There wasn't much there: two pairs of jeans, four long-sleeved dress shirts, four T-shirts, socks, and underwear. Nothing in the side pockets. All in all, a perfectly innocuous suitcase.

Still, she held one of his T-shirts up to her nose and inhaled. It smelled very slightly of him, and again she flashed on last night, their closeness, the intimate meeting of bodies and minds in tune, on the same wavelength.

Aubrey flipped through Dimitri's copy of *Beloved*, then opened *Love in the Time of Cholera* and read its famous first line, which Dimitri—or someone—had underlined in blue ink:

It was inevitable: the scent of bitter almonds always reminded him of the fate of unrequited love.

She set the novels on her side table; it had been too long since she had read either of them.

Next, she opened the canvas bag she had found in the desk in Dimitri's hotel room and spread everything out in front of her: the old letter, the journal, the thumb drive.

She plugged the thumb drive into her computer, but the files were password protected. She took a couple of stabs at guessing what the password might be: Abandoned; Seabrink; Netflix. ThisIsDrivingMeNuts. No luck. Also no surprise; computer sleuthing was not her strong suit.

And speaking of sleuthing . . . she googled "Roger Harmon" and found a famous English cricket player as well as several references to people around the country. They were all the wrong age, and none lived in San Francisco, or even close to it. How did police and private investigators find people? There must be official databases a person could check . . . maybe tax rolls, or birth certificates, or Social Security numbers? But how would she access any of those?

The real question, though, was why Dimitri would be using two different names.

Aubrey sent a text message to her friend Nikki. Nikki was a production manager, not an IT professional, but she was a decade younger than Aubrey and seemed to understand computers on an almost instinctual level. Maybe she could dig up something.

Defeated for the moment by modern technology, Aubrey paged through the journal and tried deciphering Dimitri's messy, detailed notes on the Seabrink. Most of the entries were thoughts on what his video should focus on, but there was also mention of the Kashia band of Pomo Indians referring to the mineral springs as a "cursed portal," as well as a rundown of the Goffin family and a cryptic list of deaths associated with the Seabrink:

The Dead: multiple previously; Grange? Young woman, balcony, 1934; Quiet Girl death date unknown; Timothy Goffin, age 7;

multiple from convalescent home period; apparent accidental death of male trespasser on the stairs; teenager murdered in baths by security guard 1987; security guard suicide by hanging.

That was a lot of dead. Not that Aubrey believed in ghosts . . . but there was something to some places. A frisson of . . . what? What had Mia said? Bad places.

Finally, Aubrey turned to the old letter, only then realizing that she must have dropped its outer envelope in the St. Ambrose Hotel room. Mindful of the age of the paper, Aubrey carefully unfolded the pages. It was dated April 12, 1932, and signed "Effie Mae." The old-fashioned handwriting, combined with the faded ink and occasional tears and stains, made the reading as slow going as interpreting Dimitri's scrawled journal.

My dear Auntie Gwen,

I am pitiful sorry to say I cannot get to you this holiday after all and so I shall not have the pleasure of seeing my dear Victoria. How it pains me that we are so far away. I beg you to write and tell me all about my little angel; is she yet walking, or speaking?

It rained so hard here the other day, the winds rattled the windows, we worked by candlelight and no one could leave, the roads were blocked by felled trees so that even the most emminnent guest could not escape. There were several tantrums! Perhaps you heared that lately many movie stars come to stay. It is ever so exciting but at present I can see or think about nothing but the beastly work, from dawn to well after sundown.

I live in the attics with the other maids—that's where I found the envelope for this missive, there with the old stationery! The youn-

gest among us is called Dummy, for she does not speak at all, though she works hard, and she loves music ever so much. Once, a beautiful guest—who come all the way from France!—gave her a strange little flute and tought her to play which she does now, night and day.

Little Victoria's father says he will marry me as soon as he can make arangements so we can stop this sharade. I must believe he tells me the truth, though I do despare at times. I toled him we must marry before I let him meet our little angel.

I hope to hear of you soon and if your cold has left you.

Your affectionate and ever-grateful niece,
Effie Mae

Aubrey's eyes were beginning to lose focus. Time to pack it in. She was heading to the bathroom to brush her teeth and take a shower when her cell phone rang.

Nikki.

"Who's this Roger guy and why do you want me to track him down?" Nikki demanded without preamble.

"It's . . . kind of a long story," Aubrey said, loath to get into it at this late hour. She gazed longingly at the bed's plush white linens, the comfy duvet, the fluffy pillows. Suddenly the thought of sleep was enticing in the extreme.

"What's going on? Something's wrong, I hear it in your voice."

Aubrey surrendered to the inevitable and gave Nikki an abbreviated version of the past two days, including the unsettling note warning her away from . . . some unspecified something.

Nikki was quiet for a moment, then said, "I'll be there first thing in the morning."

"That's not necessary," protested Aubrey. "I'm fine. Truly."

"You're always fine. It's, what? A two-hour drive? Two and a half?"

"More like three, and it can take longer with traffic," Aubrey said. "There's only one road in and out, you know."

"You think there'll be a lot of traffic up there first thing in the morning?" Nikki said. "I'll be there by nine. Maybe earlier."

"Don't you have to work tomorrow?"

"Let me worry about that."

"Nikki, honestly, I'm okay."

"I know you are. But . . . what makes you so sure the nasty note wasn't from Ty?"

"That never occurred to me. How would he even know I was here?"

"I . . . it's possible I mentioned something on social media. Nothing about you, just an endorsement of the Driftwood Cove Inn—I was promoting it on my Instagram, to thank Monica for giving you a deal on the room rate. I didn't mention your name, of course, just that it was a great place with a wonderful staff, that sort of thing. It didn't occur to me that Ty might put two and two together."

"It seems a stretch, but then again, Ty's not stupid. All he would have to do is call the inn and ask for you or me."

Ty was a tech support professional Nikki had met through work. When Nikki first told Aubrey about Ty, she said his only fault was that he had a wicked nicotine habit—unfiltered Pall Malls—and that he had promised her he'd quit. But otherwise, she referred to him as a unicorn: a mythical creature who was handsome and straight and single and employed—really, too good to be true. Which, it turned out, he was. As Ty became increasingly controlling, Nikki began to understand why "the unicorn" was still single, and when she broke up with him, he became enraged. He had fixated on her and the idea of the two of them together, forever—and he saw Aubrey, who had intervened more than once, as an impediment to his imagined future with Nikki.

After weeks of increasingly unhinged harassment, Nikki had filed a police report and gotten a protective order, as a result of which their employer had fired him. The court order appeared to succeed in getting Ty to back off, and they had not seen or heard from him lately, but Nikki remained vigilant. And angry. It wasn't easy living in a constant state of anxiety, waiting for the other shoe to drop.

Nikki swore then let out a long breath. "Okay, clearly, I screwed up. My bad. I'll skip the useless albeit heartfelt apology and get down to brass tacks: promise me you won't go anywhere alone and will keep your pepper spray handy at all times. I'll do some snooping, see if I can find anything that might suggest Ty's in your vicinity. I'll be there bright and early in the morning, and we'll figure this thing out."

"Thanks, Nikki. What would I do without you?"

"Without me Ty would never even know who you are, remember? That's on me."

"No, it isn't. It's on Ty, and no one else."

"Maybe," Nikki said, and Aubrey could envision her friend's face, chewing her lip, feeling worried. Guilty. Enraged.

"Have a safe trip," said Aubrey after a beat. "I'm in room 207. The door's double locked, and I have my pepper spray. I'll be waiting. Take care of you."

"Take care of *you*," Nikki replied, and hung up.

Aubrey had her recurring nightmare. This time she was leaning out the window from high up in the skyscraper, watching helplessly as shards of glass rained down on innocent passersby. She awoke with a start and could have sworn Dimitri was lying in bed with her, spooning her from behind. Still in a muddled semi-sleep, she whirled around, but the bed was empty.

Her heart pounding, she took several breaths, trying to calm herself.

The glowing red numbers of the bedside clock read a bit past four in the morning. It was around this time that Dimitri had headed out to the cold, blustery Dead Man's Bluff last night. *His* last night. Had he truly been in despair, feeling the need to bring an end to this existence? Unwilling, or unable, to wake her, a near stranger, to ask for help or solace or support? And how had she not picked up on his pain?

Or was his death simply a stupid accident, the result of getting too near the slippery edge of the cliff and losing his balance?

Or . . . had someone met him out on the bluff? Far from witnesses, far from cameras, far from help?

Dimitri's violent death was connected to the Seabrink—she felt it in her gut. Had he discovered something about the land title, something crucial enough for someone to silence him forever? Nikki's suspicions would naturally go to her stalker ex-boyfriend, Ty, but after giving it some thought, Aubrey decided that was unlikely. Ty was menacing, but he was an in-your-face danger. Also, he was a techie who used to bombard Nikki and Aubrey with threatening texts and emails from various addresses. It was hard to imagine Ty taking the time and making the effort to compose a threatening note by cutting letters out of a magazine and pasting them onto a sheet of paper.

Now wide awake, she got out of bed, slipped into a pair of sweatpants and a T-shirt, and made herself a cup of coffee in the room's small coffee maker. It was not great, as java went, but it had a nice aroma, and it was caffeinated.

Aubrey flipped through Dimitri's journal for a while, but nothing jumped out at her. A lot of the notes were cryptic and would make sense only to him. There were lists of dates and names, but as far as she could tell they weren't obviously associated with anything.

She gave up, opened her laptop, and started to review the photographs she had taken at the Seabrink. There was a good one of Dimitri in front of the ornate elevator, and after playing around with Photoshop she was able to bring his partially shadowed face into focus. Then she opened the shot of Dimitri sitting on the shoeshine stand and took in the steady, searing look in his eyes as he gazed directly into the camera. She recalled that when she took the image, he had seemed so . . . different. A man out of time, in both senses of the phrase.

A few lights appeared in the background of the photo, dust motes floating this way and that. She started to erase them but changed her mind. She rather liked the ethereal background they created.

According to many ghost chasers, orbs such as these were not technical flaws but indications of the presence of spirits. *Perhaps we really did pick up something at the Seabrink*, Aubrey thought with a rueful smile.

Seriously, though: when—and *if*—she tracked down Dimitri's family, they would want these photos. Wouldn't they? Aubrey was again awash in sadness. She knew almost nothing

about the man, but their meeting was one of those rare en-
counters when you look into someone's eyes and see a bit of
their soul, and they see yours, and somehow the twain mesh.
Twin flames, she had heard it called. Spirits in tune.

*Ugh. Don't be maudlin, Aubrey. You barely knew him; he
probably would have turned out to be as self-obsessed and
dreary as other men you've dated.*

Twin flames or not, Dimitri's shocking death was sad.
Even the rather oblivious Deputy Jenkins had remarked that
any loss of life was tragic.

Aubrey flipped through more photos, losing herself in the
work, deleting duplicates and the less inspired tableaus, marking and sorting her favorites: the stained-glass transoms; the
creepy valet pass-throughs; the guest room filled with moss
and ferns; the atrium with its broken panes of glass littering
the floor and glinting in the afternoon sun, the vines creeping
in and hanging down through the broken ceiling panels.

To those, she started applying colored filters, marveling as
always at how the different filters could change the mood of a
vignette entirely, highlighting features she would not otherwise have noticed.

Aubrey came to the series of photographs she had taken
through the crystal ball on the plinth in front of the attic
stairs. When she applied the yellow filter, she saw something
that had not been obvious to the naked eye: a message
scrawled on the wall. The image was inverted by the crystal,
so she flipped it.

The message read: BREATHE ME IN BEFORE TAKING
ME OUT.

And standing on the shadowed stairs was what looked
like . . . a young teenage girl? She was wearing a dark dress
and a stained, old-fashioned apron, some kind of headband

around her forehead, and in one hand held what looked like a small wooden flute. Her face appeared distorted, the edges blurring and melting into the darkness behind her.

She held a finger up to her lips, as if shushing someone, and she was smiling.

Straight into the camera.

As I felt the breath,
mon pneuma,
leave me,
I vowed I would never leave the Seabrink.

ELEVEN

A t the sharp rap of a knock on the door, Aubrey jumped and
let out an undignified yelp. Morning sun streamed in
through the window. She had lost track of time.

"It's me!" Nikki's voice called out.

Nikki Politis was athletic, snarky, and a fan of true crime
and truth-telling tarot cards. A full-figured, curvy woman,
she wore her long black hair in a messy knot on the top of her
head, was dressed in black leggings and an oversize sweater,
and clutched a travel mug in one hand and an overnight bag
in the other.

They shared a long hug.

Nikki stood back, holding Aubrey at arm's distance. "Are
you okay? You look as if you've seen a ghost."

"As a matter of fact, I just saw . . . something. Something
really odd."

"Where?" Nikki glanced around the room.

"Not in here," said Aubrey. "I was reviewing the photos I
took up at the Hotel Seabrink, and I saw something."

"Oooh, *was* it a ghost?" Nikki said with a smile. "I love ghosts."

Aubrey didn't answer.

"You're shitting me," said Nikki. "I thought you didn't believe in ghosts."

"I don't. I mean, only the metaphorical kind."

"Could I see?"

Aubrey opened the photos on her laptop, but the spot where the girl had been now looked like an amorphous black splotch merging into the darkness behind. The message on the wall had disappeared, as well.

"That's weird," Aubrey said. "Maybe the filter's turned off." But no matter which filter she applied, the image did not reappear.

"I swear it was there . . . There was a girl, she looked maybe fourteen or fifteen, wearing an apron, and there was a message on the wall: 'Breathe me in before taking me out.'"

"Is it possible you fell asleep and dreamed it?" said Nikki. "Or misinterpreted that black splotch, somehow?"

"How could I misinterpret a black splotch?"

"No idea. You're the one who saw something that isn't there."

"I could have sworn . . . but maybe you're right. I am tired. Wow. It was so creepy. Her face was sort of distorted, but she was looking at the camera and smiling . . ."

Nikki looked skeptical.

"Okay, sorry. You're right, I must have nodded off and dreamed her. Too much talk about the Quiet Girl."

"The who, now?"

"Never mind. I'll shake it off," said Aubrey. "What time did you leave home? I didn't expect you *this* early."

"Couldn't sleep. Aubrey, you sure you're okay?"

"I told you, I'm fine."

"You're always fine. Until you're not."

"Kettle, meet pot."

"Fair point," Nikki said, exploring the room. "Wow, get a load of that view! And a fireplace! No wonder this place is so expensive. The bedside clock's broken, though. It's blinking at 4:07."

Aubrey stared at it.

"No worries. It's just a cheap clock," Nikki said. "I'm sure Monica will replace it."

"It's not that. Dimitri left the hotel around that time. And I remember . . . the grandfather clock at the Seabrink was frozen at 4:07."

Nikki frowned. "And you think they're all connected somehow? As in, you're being haunted?"

"Of course not," Aubrey shook her head. "Just a weird coincidence. I'm a little on edge lately. Anyway, this hotel room is really something, isn't it? I could get used to this."

"Is that a record player? An honest-to-God record player?"

"It is indeed. There's an extensive collection of vintage vinyl in the lobby. And a bunch of old-fashioned board games. Not to mention the funky furniture in the lobby. It's sort of like being at your grandma's house."

"Not *my* grandma's house, but maybe if your grandma were rich and exceedingly cool."

"True. My grandma's house smelled like stale cigarette smoke and Diet Dr Pepper. And there was nothing remotely fun to do. Anyway, how about I buy you breakfast? They say the restaurant in the lobby is really good."

"Great idea. I'm running on pure caffeine at the moment, which means I need to eat something soon or I'm likely to become unpleasant to be around. Or so I've been told."

"I'm aware," Aubrey teased, as she exchanged her sweat-pants and T-shirt for jeans and a sweater. Nikki stashed her bag, and they proceeded downstairs to the Starfish Cafe, off the lobby. The restaurant was only half full, so they nabbed a small table near the bank of large windows overlooking the ocean.

"I always forget how gorgeous it is up here," said Nikki, gazing out at the foggy morning. Seagulls swooped around the vacant picnic tables on the bluff, searching for scraps left by yesterday's picnickers. "I should have come with you in the first place."

"Speaking of which, you're sure it's okay to miss a few days of work?" Aubrey asked as the waiter brought them coffee and menus.

Nikki waved her hand. "I work remotely, remember? Be-sides, we just finished a major project and I'm owed some se-rious comp time. My boss won't mind if I take a few days." Nikki looked toward the lobby. "I haven't seen Monica yet. How's she been?"

"A little stressed, what with a death nearby, and law en-forcement hanging around."

"I can imagine."

"But otherwise, she seems fine. I really appreciate the room discount; this is such an amazing place. And thank you for pushing me to get out of town."

"Next time, I'll cover your tracks better," Nikki said, then announced to the waiter that she had decided on the avocado toast, a mango smoothie, and coffee. Aubrey considered the smoked salmon plate for the sake of bodily health but then went with waffles with extra butter and maple syrup for the sake of her mental health.

"You really *are* on vacation," Nikki commented approv-ingly.

"I am in desperate need of comfort food this morning," said Aubrey, handing the menus to the server.

"So, now, tell me everything, in detail," said Nikki. "Last night was the edited version, I could tell."

Aubrey gave Nikki a full account of recent events, emphasizing how connected she had felt to Dimitri, even though they didn't really know each other.

"I think that's the odd thing about people we see on social media or television," said Nikki, after the server set their breakfasts in front of them with a flourish. "Especially when they're not playing a part, but just being themselves. We, the audience, feel like we have a relationship with them because, in a real way, we do. It's just that it's an entirely one-sided relationship and by its very nature incomplete. So, while *Dimitri* slept with a near stranger, you slept with someone you've known for a while."

She took a huge bite of her avocado toast.

"Wow, you're good," said Aubrey with a smile. "Really, that's a great way to justify my uncharacteristic, and quite possibly unwise, decision to sleep with a perfect stranger."

Nikki snorted. "If you're waiting for me to slut-shame you, you've got a long wait. It's about time you let loose and celebrated your sexuality. When's the last time you slept with anyone?"

"A very long while. Not since my ex."

"You see? At the very least, you now have a story."

"I had the same thought yesterday morning, before . . ." Aubrey trailed off and stared at her plate with distaste. Despite her earlier desire for comfort food, her stomach clenched, and she pushed the food away.

Nikki followed her gaze. "Too sweet? Order something else. When's the last time you ate?"

"I had fried calamari and garlic bread last night. And an herbal martini."

"A nutritious meal, if ever I heard one," Nikki said dryly.

"I know, I know. I think I'm swearing off alcohol for a while, anyway."

"So, you were saying? You had a similar thought before what? Before you found out what had happened to Dimitri?"

Aubrey nodded. "You know . . . I should probably just drop the whole thing, pack my bags, and get back to real life."

"That's one option. You want to know what I think?"

"Since when do you have to ask?"

Nikki took a gulp of her smoothie and cleared her throat. "Okay, here it is: your 'real life' hasn't been so great recently," she said, then added in a gentler voice, "Aubrey, you really should try to eat something."

"You *know* it's serious when I'm off my feed, right?"

They shared a smile. They had met years ago at a Thai cooking class, bonding over their mutual enthusiasm for a huge mound of savory pad thai and rather sad-looking, but delectable, pad see ew.

"The thing is," Aubrey said, considering her words, "I slept with a man, and then that man went and jumped off a cliff. I'm still trying to process that."

"Understandably. That's not the way first dates typically end," Nikki said. "But listen, Aubrey: if this guy was set on taking his own life, it had nothing to do with you. As you keep saying, you know almost nothing about him, or his life, much less the reasons he might have had to *exit* this life. Think of it this way: you made it possible for him go out on a high note."

Aubrey cast a side-eyed glare at her.

"I think what's bothering you is that you're not convinced

he killed himself," said Nikki. "You suspect there was foul play, and you think you need to find out if that was the case or not."

"According to one of the paramedics, Dimitri had bloodied hands and broken fingernails, as if he had been trying to hold on."

"That sounds pretty gruesome."

"Or maybe it was a freak accident," Aubrey added. "He slipped and tried to keep himself from falling."

"Both would explain the injuries to his hands. But for the moment, at least, you have no way of determining what happened. You do have some of his things, right? Anything that might provide a clue?"

She nodded. "Maybe. There's a journal and a thumb drive that's password protected. I tried to access the files but had no luck."

"Let me try. I probably won't have any luck, either, but I know someone who might, a wunderkind who works in the animation department. In his free time, he excels at hacking and as far as I can tell he isn't particularly worried about the ethics involved. And as for the driver's license, I found a birth record for a Roger Harmon born in 1979."

"You did? You have a lead on his family?"

"Sort of. Turns out, Roger was adopted as a baby by the Harmons. It was a closed adoption, so I couldn't find out anything more about his birth parents. He graduated from Washington High School in Bakersfield, then got a degree in English Lit at UCLA. And then he sort of disappeared."

"What do you mean, disappeared?"

"As far as I could tell, he seems to have been largely replaced by Dimitri Petroff."

"Wait—when did you have time to do all that? We spoke late last night, and you must have left at the crack of dawn to get here so early."

"Couldn't sleep." Nikki shrugged. "You know how I am, ever since the whole deal with Ty."

"Speaking of whom, I really don't think Ty sent the threatening note. It was made up of letters cut from a magazine, which doesn't sound at all like him, does it? Besides, if Ty had followed me here, he probably wouldn't warn me. He'd just jump out from behind a pillar and try to push me down the stairs."

"Cheerful thought," Nikki said and signaled to the server to bring them refills of coffee. "I don't need more caffeine this morning, but it's just not civilized to end a breakfast without it. Anyway, as for Ty: I suspect you're right. But I couldn't find anything about his recent whereabouts. I even reached out to his mother."

"Was that wise?"

"She's been trying to get him help. She loves her son, but she's no fool. She's afraid he'll eventually hurt someone and end up in prison."

"Whereas I'm praying he'll end up in prison. Just without hurting someone."

"Oh, here's something else that's interesting: I heard a detective on a true crime podcast say cut-and-paste notes like the one you received are more likely to have been composed by women than by men."

"Really? What'd he base that on?"

"Probably a sexist assumption that women are more into crafts than men," said Nikki. "But that doesn't mean it's not true. Still, you're right: Ty isn't the scrapbooking sort."

The server returned with the coffee. As Nikki stirred cream into hers, Aubrey watched the white clouds blooming on the coffee's dark surface and was tempted to take a photo. But then Nikki's spoon clattered against the ceramic mug, ruining the effect.

"I gave scrapbooking a try once but never really got into it," mused Nikki. "All those tiny pieces of paper wind up on the floor, and it doesn't matter how much you vacuum, you're still finding them weeks later. And don't get me started on glitter . . ."

"*That's* the reason you quit?" Aubrey smiled over the lip of her steaming mug of coffee.

Nikki shrugged. "That, and the fact that I stunk at it. Never been any good at arts and crafts. My parents still display some of my horrid childhood art projects. It's a shame I'll never live down."

Aubrey chuckled and gazed out at the ocean. There were plenty of whitecaps; must be windy out. Wisps of fog still clung to the jagged outcroppings, muting everything, softening the edges. All shades of gray, one hue bleeding into the next.

"This may sound strange," said Aubrey. "But I need to go back to the Seabrink."

"This is the place you explored with Dimitri the afternoon before he was possibly murdered? And from which it has been strongly suggested that you stay away?"

"That would be the one."

"Why?"

"I can't shake the sense that it's all related." Aubrey paused. "Remember the girl and the inscription I thought I saw in the photograph? 'Breathe me in before taking me out.' Have you ever heard anything like that?"

Nikki shook her head. "Could be a poem or a song lyric. You think it's significant in some way?"

"I should look it up. And . . . I could be wrong, but I'm wondering if Dimitri was leading me away from the stairs that led up to the attic. As if he didn't want me to go up there."

"Why would he do that?"

"I don't know, but that's where I thought I saw the teenage girl in the photo. She was standing on those stairs."

"You think Dimitri was trying to keep the ghost to himself?"

"I don't believe in ghosts, but maybe there was something special up there he wanted to put in his show, or something . . ." She trailed off with a shrug. "I don't know."

"I think it'd be *awesome* to see a ghost," Nikki murmured.

Their server came by with the check, which Aubrey charged to her room and left a generous tip.

"After we spoke last night, I tried looking up 'Hotel Seabrink' but couldn't find much of anything," said Nikki. "Nothing more than a couple of passing references, as a matter of fact, which is odd, given just how much useless information is on the internet."

"According to Dimitri, and Jasper, too, the web is regularly scrubbed for any reference to the hotel."

"Who's Jasper?"

"He's a member of the volunteer fire department," Aubrey said. "He recovered Dimitri's body. I ran into him and another paramedic, Mia, at the bar at the St. Ambrose Hotel yesterday. They're nice people."

"Huh. There's scrubbing, and then there's scrubbing. If it involves actually hacking into blogs and such, that's expensive. Not to mention against the law. Does this Jasper person have any theories as to who is going through such trouble, or why?"

"He suggested it might be the family that owns the hotel. Apparently they're trying to sell, and the fact that there have been several mysterious deaths on the premises is not attractive to prospective buyers."

"Imagine that," Nikki said, downing the last of her coffee. "Well, I signed up for whatever you need. Waffles, moral support, trespassing in creepy abandoned buildings . . ."

"I hate to say it, but if we go back, I think we need backup. A strong, brave, gentlemanly sort who is willing to jump in front of danger to save our—"

Just then Monica walked up to the table. "Nikki! I didn't know you were coming!"

"Last minute decision." Nikki stood, and they hugged. "Nice place you got here."

"Do you need a room?" Monica asked. "There's a small convention coming in tomorrow, so things are a bit tight."

"Thought I'd crash with Aubrey, if that's okay."

"Of course. I'll let the front desk know," Monica said, adding, "You'll be needing more bath towels. No extra charge."

"Thank you, that's very generous. By the way, would you ask the desk staff to be sure not to give out our names to anyone?"

Monica frowned. "You're worried about the ex-boyfriend? The stalker?"

"Not worried, just cautious," Nikki said smoothly. "Better safe than sorry."

"I'll remind the staff of our policy not to give out that information, but we're a little shorthanded and some of the employees are a bit . . ." Monica trailed off with a shrug. "Well, I guess it's enough to say that a lot of them spend their time surfing the web or on their phones, when they should be working. Anyway, how was breakfast?" Monica's blue eyes zeroed in on Aubrey's plate. "Something wrong with the waffles? That's real maple syrup, you know."

"It's delicious," Aubrey said. "I'm just not terribly hungry this morning."

"I'll have your server wrap it up for you. You can keep it in your mini fridge."

"Thanks," said Aubrey, though the thought of cold, soggy waffles wasn't particularly alluring as a midnight snack.

"Anything else you two need, just let me know," Monica offered.

"The clock in Aubrey's room stopped, but it's no big deal," Nikki said.

Monica made a note on her phone. "Anything else?"

"We were just saying we're in the market for a strong, brave, gentlemanly sort to act as backup."

Monica's eyes widened and she glanced around the restaurant and lobby, as though she might spot an imminent threat. "You really *are* worried about your stalker following you here?"

"Actually, we were talking about going to—" Nikki stopped when Aubrey kicked her lightly under the table. "Um, yeah, we were thinking it couldn't hurt to have someone to watch our backs, just in case."

"I'll have housekeeping swap out the clock. But someone who's 'strong, brave, and gentlemanly'? I'm afraid I don't know anyone local who fits that description," said Monica with a sigh. "More's the pity."

"I might know someone," says Aubrey.

"How would you know someone?" demanded Nikki. "You're not even *from* here."

"It's amazing what a person can pick up at the local hardware store."

TWELVE

Y ou work fast, Spencer, I'll give you that," said Nikki as Aubrey drove them north on Highway One toward Gualala. "In less than a week, you've what? Already found—and lost—a boyfriend, and met a brave, strong hardware man?"

"Not to mention gentlemanly. I told you, he was one of the volunteer paramedics. Jasper, the guy who rappelled down the cliff to get Dim—" Aubrey cut herself off. "To retrieve the body."

"He *rappelled* down a *cliff*? Wouldn't a boat have been easier?"

"I wondered about that, too," Aubrey replied, trying to clamp down on her frustration at the slow-moving car ahead of them, its brake lights flashing constantly. Highway One was only one lane in each direction, and because of the myriad twists and turns there was no way to pass another car safely. If a person found themselves behind a nervous tourist painstakingly navigating the curves atop the dramatic cliffs, and that tourist refused to pull over at a turnout to allow cars to pass, there was nothing for it but to practice one's patience and enjoy the view.

Aubrey reminded herself to relax and looked out over the ocean. No whales that she could see, but a squadron of pelicans was flying along at the height of the cliffs. She had seen a similar gaggle yesterday, while she was standing on Dead Man's Bluff, before looking to the rocks below and seeing Dimitri's body.

"And . . . ?" Nikki urged. "Why didn't they use a boat?"

"Sorry," Aubrey said. "My mind wandered. Something about the tides, and the rocks, and wanting to preserve evidence."

"What kind of evidence?"

"I don't think there was any, as it turns out."

"And why would this hardware guy want to risk his life to escort you to an abandoned building?"

"I wouldn't say he's 'risking his life,'" said Aubrey, glancing at Nikki. "I mean, yesterday's tragedy aside, hardly anyone who goes to the Seabrink dies."

"Uh-huh," Nikki grunted, unconvinced. "But I say again: Why would this Jasper be willing to accompany us? You barely know him."

Aubrey shrugged. "He'll probably say no. It's just that he's sort of . . . gentlemanly. Probably has a neurotic savior complex of some sort. Maybe I'm wrong, but I'm usually good at reading people. Anyway, it's worth a shot."

There was a pause, each lost in thought.

"It really is gorgeous here," Nikki said with a sigh as she gazed at meadows dotted with oak trees and sprinkled with lichen-covered boulders. A dozen cows grazed on lush green grass, apparently ignoring the spectacular view of the ocean.

Crooked wooden rail fences, bleached by age and the salt in the air, separated one rancher's fields from another's. "It's been ages since I've been this far north. I went to Mendocino once, years ago, and up through the big trees to see the giant sequoias. But not to this area."

"It's pretty remote," said Aubrey. "I think that's what the locals like about it. Too far north for a day trip from the Bay Area, and not a whole lot of civilization once you get here. Mostly just trees, seashore, and wildlife."

"Paradise."

"That's the historic cemetery I came to photograph." Aubrey gestured as they neared Stewarts Point. The slow driver turned into the general store parking lot, and Aubrey sped up with relief. "I stopped in at that little store for a sandwich, and that's where I got directions to the Hotel Seabrink. It's not easy to find."

"It's up there, then?" Nikki craned her neck as if she might be able to spy it in the mountains.

Aubrey nodded. "A ways up there, yes. I don't think you can see it from here."

"Why is it called Asylum Point Road?" Nikki asked as they passed the road sign.

"I'm not sure. They say the road goes all the way to Cazadero if you stay on it long enough. If the road to the hotel is any indication, though, it's pretty treacherous. Narrow and windy, and not the best if you're prone to carsickness. Right now we'll stay on the highway, and pass by Sea Ranch next, and then Gualala. That's where the hardware store is."

"Once more for those in the cheap seats: *Why* go back to the Seabrink? I mean, I've got my Mace, and I'm not afraid to use it. But if everyone is telling you the place is cursed, and it's, you know, illegal to trespass, *and* the last time you were there you met someone who died not long after under questionable circumstances . . . what's the attraction?"

"It's hard to explain. It's . . ." How could Aubrey describe the pull she felt toward abandoned places? The certainty that such buildings had stories to tell, if only she had the patience to listen. The traces of lives lived, of dreams dreamed and loves loved. The profound silence. The peace. She hadn't needed to explain it to Dimitri; he had understood it at a visceral level. And now how could she explain her conviction that the hotel held secrets related to Dimitri's demise? She shrugged and gave up. "I just do."

"All righty, then," Nikki said with a little nod. "That's good enough for me."

Aubrey slowed from sixty to twenty-five once they crossed the river and entered Gualala town limits.

"Cute town," Nikki said. "And look! A bookstore! I love that such a small town still has a bookstore."

"That's what *I* said. Stillman's Hardware and Lumber should be coming up soon, on our left."

The store was large, with a separate lumber section and even an automotive area, a veritable one-stop shop for getting things done. A hardware store like this was a lifeline for those who lived along the coast. Without it, locals would have to drive to Fort Bragg or Santa Rosa, each about two hours away—or more, depending on weather and slow drivers.

"Busy place," Nikki remarked as they parked alongside several pickup trucks packed with construction equipment. Once inside the store, they asked for Jasper, and a young woman at the register pointed them toward the paint department.

"Oh, hey, Aubrey," Jasper said, looking surprised at their approach. He measured liquid pigment into a gallon of paint, placed the lid back on, tapped it with a rubber mallet, and set it in a machine that began vigorously shaking the can. "Nice to see you again."

Aubrey introduced Nikki to Jasper.

"Good to meet you, Nikki. So, you realized you *do* have some hardware needs?" he asked Aubrey with a crooked smile. "Or perhaps you're in the market for some really stylish rubber boots?"

"Tempting as that sounds, I'm more in the market for a favor."

"Personal or professional?"

"A bit of both," Nikki said.

Jasper raised an eyebrow, and Aubrey hurriedly explained. "I was hoping you might be willing to go with us to the Hotel Seabrink."

"The Seabrink." He leaned against the paint counter and crossed his arms, his eyes shifting as he studied the women, one after the other. "Why would you want to go back there?"

"I suspect the hotel can shed some light on what happened to Dimitri. And yes, I do know how that sounds and that it doesn't make any sense, but . . . let's just say I have a strong hunch."

"A hunch."

"According to my extensive study of true crime podcasts," Nikki said, "a hunch is a valid investigative technique. It's the result of your subconscious analyzing facts and evidence and reaching a conclusion."

"Uh-huh," Jasper grunted. He removed the gallon can of paint from the mixer, wrote something on top of the lid in black Sharpie, and set it aside.

"Have you ever been up there?" Aubrey realized she hadn't asked him.

"Not since I was a stupid teenager. I don't recommend it."
Jasper ran a hand through his sandy hair, making it stick up
this way and that. "You two are going to go, whether I accompany you or not, aren't you?"

"Yes."

Nikki added, "I told Aubrey we needed someone brave and
strong and gentlemanly to come with us, and she immediately
thought of you."

"Nice try." He blew out a loud breath and glanced at a large
clock on the wall. "And, gentleman that I am, an effective one.
Okay, I can meet you there on my lunch break. Give me a couple of hours and I'll join you outside the gates, one o'clock."

So, what does a person do in Gualala to kill time?" Nikki
asked as they exited the hardware store.

Their eyes met and they said in unison: "*Bookstore.*"

Cypress Village was a brightly painted complex of multi-
story, vaguely Victorian wooden buildings that included a restaurant and sports bar, a few cute boutiques selling handmade
knickknacks, a gym, and the bookstore. Four-Eyed Frog
Books was packed floor to ceiling with hardcover and paper-
back books as well as miscellaneous items crafted by local
artisans: hand-knitted socks and scarves, leather notebooks
and bookmarks, greeting cards and fountain pens.

They browsed the shelves, Nikki in the mystery section
and Aubrey in local history.

"Can I help you find anything?" offered the sixtyish
woman behind the counter. She wore her gray hair in a stylish
bob and was dressed in a coral-colored cardigan and match-
ing lipstick.

"I'm interested in the Hotel Seabrink," said Aubrey.

The bookseller's eyebrows rose. "*Really*. Were you wondering about the renovation? I hear it's been delayed, problems with the land title, or some such."

"I'm actually more interested in the history of the place."

"I'm afraid I don't know much about that," the woman said. "I'm from L.A., Hank and I retired up here to Sea Ranch a few years ago. I just help out here from time to time."

"Is there a local historical society, or something like that?"

She frowned in concentration. "The Point Arena Lighthouse museum has some information about the area, but I doubt it would include anything about the Seabrink. And Sea Ranch has an archive devoted to its development, but that's pretty specific to its own story. There's an historical society in Mendocino, or perhaps Ukiah . . . but then again, Seabrink is in Sonoma County, not Mendocino County. Maybe try the public library in Santa Rosa?"

"Okay, thanks."

As Aubrey joined Nikki in the mystery section, a petite, white-haired woman approached.

"I couldn't help but overhear you're interested in the Hotel Seabrink," she said. "I am Mrs. Sheila Harrison, and I'm an Episcopalian."

"I, um, hi," Aubrey stammered, hoping Mrs. Harrison was not going to try to convert them. Or might this be a small-town thing, to announce your religion when you introduce yourself?

"I overheard you asking about local history. You should talk to Deborah Goldman," Mrs. Harrison continued. "She lives just down the way, in Sea Ranch. She'll be able to tell you much more than any dusty old museum."

"Is that right?"

"Before Deb retired, she was an archivist at Sonoma State, specializing in genealogy. She's spent years talking to elderly locals, collecting their oral histories. I daresay she knows more about this area and its people than anyone." Mrs. Harrison paused and lowered her voice. "Best of all, she knows things that don't make it into museums or history books. If you catch my drift."

"Sounds like my kind of historian," Nikki said.

"Do you think she'd be willing to speak with us?" Aubrey asked.

"Honey, the only problem with living here is that there is absolutely nothing to do, and no one new to talk to. Once you get your fill of ocean vistas and hikes through the redwoods, things can become a bit . . . quiet."

"Meaning she might enjoy the company," suggested Nikki.

"That she would. Bring some snacks and it'll be a party. She might even invite the neighbors." Mrs. Harrison took out a smartphone and started scrolling through her contacts. "I'll give you her number. She won't mind, we go way back."

"Just be wary of Gideon," suggested the woman behind the counter.

Mrs. Harrison cast the bookseller an annoyed glance. "Gideon won't be there. Why would Gideon be there?"

"Because it's about the Hotel Seabrink," said the saleswoman. "And Gideon has his ways . . ."

The older woman shrugged and turned back to Aubrey. "Pay her no mind, that's just local folderol. You give Deb a call, and tell her Shelley Harrison sent you."

Aubrey took down Deborah Goldman's information and thanked Mrs. Harrison for her help. The bell on the door tinkled cheerily as she left the shop.

"Who's this Gideon you two were talking about?" Aubrey

asked the saleswoman as they approached the counter with their goodies. Aubrey and Nikki had each selected several books, and Nikki added a pair of hand-knitted socks while Aubrey bought a calendar—on sale since it was already mid-March—with photographs of the area.

The bookseller leaned forward and whispered, "He's an unrepentant conspiracy theorist. Bit of a nut, you ask me."

"Is there some sort of conspiracy involving the Hotel Seabrink?" Aubrey asked.

The saleswoman straightened and took a deep breath. "In Gideon's mind, *everything* is a conspiracy. He's filed suit against the Seabrink's potential developers and made a huge fuss over the original land deed. If memory serves, it's connected to the founders of Sea Ranch—or maybe it was the Bohemian Grove? And, I dunno, probably the Illuminati or something. I'm just saying, take what he says with a grain of salt."

"I love salt," said Nikki. "Thanks for the tip."

"Shelley's right, though, that Deborah Goldman is a font of information," the saleswoman continued, handing them their bagged purchases. "She's a good person to talk to if you're interested in local history."

They thanked her again and gathered up their loot.

"I think I'm going to start introducing myself to strangers as 'Ms. Nikki Politis, Unrepentant Sinner,'" Nikki told Aubrey as they left the shop.

Aubrey laughed. "Yeah, what was that all about?"

"Probably just establishing her social bona fides. It's kind of sweet and old-fashioned if you think about it."

"Let me give Deborah Goldman a call," Aubrey said.

"Good idea," Nikki said. "But if Gideon answers, hang up."

Deborah Goldman's voicemail picked up, so Aubrey left a

message explaining that Shelley Harrison had suggested they meet to discuss local history in general, and the Seabrink in particular.

"Where to now?" asked Nikki once Aubrey put away her phone.

"We still have a long while before we need to leave to meet Jasper," Aubrey said. "Oh, look: a consignment shop. That must be Mia's place. Let's check it out."

"And who's Mia?"

"The other paramedic I met yesterday."

"Gotta hand it to you, Spencer," Nikki said. "For someone who calls herself an introvert, you sure have gotten around. You spend another week in town, and you just might be elected mayor."

"It's been a strange couple of days."

The small consignment shop was full of clothes neatly hanging on metal racks, jewelry in glass cases, and the scent of fresh laundry and potpourri. An old-fashioned pastry rack held dozens of pretty little jars with handwritten labels containing oils, herbs, and salves.

Mia was behind the counter, her dark-haired head bent low over a stack of receipts. She looked up as they walked in.

"Aubrey! You found me!"

Aubrey introduced Mia to Nikki. "We were at the bookstore, and I remembered you said your shop was nearby."

"I'm so glad you stopped in. Tell me: How are you doing? For real."

"I'm . . . okay."

"She always says that," said Nikki. "She's shaken."

"Of course she is," said Mia, then met Aubrey's eyes. "Any sensible person would be. Have you found out anything more about your mystery man?"

"Not much." Aubrey started looking through some gauzy blouses hanging on a nearby rod, fighting the sudden burn of tears at the back of her eyes. Why did she feel so emotional about a man she hardly knew? Was it simply the shock of it all? Or was it true loss? Loss of a possibility, at least. Of a potential future with someone who seemed to understand her.

"Nice town you got here," Nikki said to Mia.

"It is sweet, right?" said Mia. "I love it. But, like any small town, we've got our issues."

"Do tell. What kinds of issues?" Nikki said, leaning on the counter.

Mia chuckled. "Nothing too salacious, I assure you. It's just that here in 'Mendonoma,' we're a bit isolated. A lot of locals struggle to get by, working at construction gigs and fishing, cleaning houses and working at the hotels, that sort of thing. It's hard to make a decent living, and a lot of our young people leave. We also have folks coming up from Mexico and Central America looking for work, like my grandparents did. A lot of the residents of Sea Ranch, on the other hand, are wealthy out-of-towners. Many use their places as vacation homes, and there are a lot of short-term rentals, but ever since Sea Ranch put in high-speed internet, a lot of folks in the tech industry now live there full-time and work from home. By and large they're good neighbors, and they spend a lot of money locally, including in my store. But . . . it can get awkward."

"Sounds like a recipe for tension between the folks at Sea Ranch and the locals," said Nikki.

"Sometimes," Mia said with a shrug. "People have different experiences and assumptions about the world and how it works. Still, the Sea Ranch folks are a great source of clothes for my shop and for a charity called Goodbye Clothes that benefits local folks in need."

Aubrey pointed to a series of old sepia-toned photographs hanging on one wall. "These are great. Are they your family?"

"Afraid not," Mia said with a shake of her head. "I can't trace my family back more than two generations. Too much was lost on my grandparents' journey north. I found these in a junk store in Mendocino. My antiquing friends call them instant ancestors. But they create a nice ambience, don't you think?"

"They do." Aubrey took note of one in particular, a beautiful dark-eyed woman with a bejeweled headband, holding a small musical instrument. "I swear I saw a photo of the same woman, dressed as a fairy, in a photograph at the Seabrink."

"I wouldn't be surprised," said Mia. "The woman was an actress in early movies, originally from France. Named Colette, like the author . . . though I can never remember her last name. She was known for playing the piano, as well as an instrument called a flageolet."

"Isn't a flageolet a kind of bean?" said Nikki.

"It is. It's also the name of a simplified kind of wooden flute, sort of like a recorder. And the headband is called a ferronnière; they were popular in the Renaissance, and are featured in several famous paintings, one by da Vinci, I think. Ferronnières enjoyed a brief resurgence during the 1920s and '30s, which is when I suppose these photos were taken."

"Fashions were at their best back then," said Nikki.

"I love that time period, as well," Mia agreed. "As you can see, though, my vintage isn't *that* vintage."

"Do you know Deborah Goldman, from Sea Ranch?" Aubrey said. "I heard she's the one to talk to about local history, and the Hotel Seabrink."

"She's definitely worth talking to," said Mia.

"What's she like?"

"She's very vocal at community meetings," Mia said with a shake of her head. "She's involved with the historical preservationists who are trying to stop the Seabrink development plans, so she'll have a decided opinion. But she seems very knowledgeable about local history ... especially if you're looking into rumors of haunted houses."

Aubrey and Nikki exchanged a glance.

"I love woo-woo stuff; I'm studying tarot reading right now," said Nikki. "Is Deborah into the paranormal?"

"You'd have to ask her about that," Mia said, looking uncomfortable. "I don't have much interest in that sort of thing. My *abuela*—my grandmother—makes salves and balms using natural botanicals." Mia gestured to the bottles lined up on the repurposed pastry shelf. "But I'm more about used clothes. Speaking of which, can I help you find anything?"

"I love those earrings," Nikki said, pointing to a pair of dangling Victorian crystal earrings in a mahogany-and-glass display case.

"Good choice! These just came in yesterday."

Aubrey found a hand-knit sweater in shades of heather gray and forest green that was perfect for the chilly seaside mornings. As they were paying for their items, Aubrey's cell phone rang: it was Deborah Goldman, inviting them to her house for "coffee and conversation" the following morning at nine.

"Oh, by the way," Nikki asked Mia. "I noticed there's a Mexican restaurant on the highway. Is it any good?"

"It's not bad, but I prefer the bakery next to Gualala Supermarket—it doesn't look like much, but the burritos are amazing and as big as my head. It's popular with working folks, which is always a good sign."

Nikki said, "We've got lunch handled, then."

As they carried their purchases to her car, Aubrey noticed the lanky young man she and Dimitri had met in the basement baths at the Hotel Seabrink: Cameron "I Come in Peace" Meroni. He was ducking into a sports bar with another man who looked familiar, though Aubrey couldn't quite place him. Well-built, tall, and blond, the man's regal Viking look was spoiled by a slouchy knit cap, threadbare jeans, and a faded long-sleeved polo.

"I know that guy," Aubrey said to Nikki.

"*Another* new acquaintance? Seriously, Aubrey. Just how many people could you have possibly met in your time here?"

"His name's Cameron. I ran into him when I was exploring with Dimitri. The other guy looks familiar, too . . . I don't know. Maybe I saw him at the St. Ambrose last night; there were a lot of people there. Not that it matters, I suppose."

"Do you want to talk with him? Or them?"

"I wouldn't have any idea what to say. Besides, I want to find that burrito place before we meet up with Jasper. My stomach's growling."

"*Vamanos*," Nikki said. "I'm not one to say no to a burrito."

When they returned to Aubrey's car, they found an envelope tucked under a windshield wiper.

"What's that?" Nikki asked. "Surely not a ticket?"

Aubrey opened the envelope with a sense of trepidation. Inside was yet another note written in magazine cutouts:

YOU wiLL BE t#e next tO DiE, Ritc#!

THIRTEEN

et me see that." Nikki took the note and studied it, her lips pressed together. "Short and succinct. Points on style, at least."

Aubrey scanned the parking lot but there was not a soul in sight.

"How did they even know it was my car?"

"You do have that distinctive bumper sticker on it: 'My Coffee, My Life.'"

"Not my fault. It was on it when I bought it."

"I'm just saying, I doubt anyone else around here has the same sticker. I have to say, the idea of cut-out notes seemed a little comical at first, but now . . ." Nikki trailed off and shook her head. "How do you want to proceed?"

"I don't know about you, but this pisses me off," Aubrey said. "Okay, *now* I want to go talk to those guys in the bar."

"Are you sure?"

"It's a public place, seems safe enough." Aubrey waved the

note in the air. "Let's see if they have anything to do with this."

"After you. I'm your backup, after all."

"I'd say you're more like my sidekick. Either way, we make quite the intimidating pair," said Aubrey with a wry smile.

"You're right about that, girlfriend: armed with Mace and a kick-ass attitude, you and I could do some real damage."

The bar smelled of stale beer and French fries. Several wall-mounted TV screens displayed muted games of soccer and tennis, and a regulation-size pool table took up most of the floor space. A hallway on the right led to a sit-down restaurant specializing in burgers and fish and chips.

Cameron and his friend were leaning on the stained wooden bar, nursing mugs of beer.

"What the hell is this?" Aubrey demanded, waving the note in Cameron's face.

He reared back, looking not at the note, but at her. "Oh, hey! I know you. From the Seabrink, right? Yesterday, down in the creepy baths . . . ?"

Aubrey flapped the note at him again. "You have something to say to me, use the phone, like a normal person. And watch your language."

"What are you talking about?" Cameron said, looking confused. He took the note from her and read it. "*Whoa*, that's . . . disconcerting, am I right? Where did you find it?"

"On the windshield of my car a few minutes ago."

"Gotta tell you, that seems worrying." He met her eyes and his concern ratcheted up. "Wait, you think *I* put it there? Why would I do something like that?"

Aubrey studied him for another moment. "You tell me. You had the means and the opportunity."

"Me and everybody else in town," Cameron said. "But I didn't do it. I'm not a craftsy kind of guy, much less someone who leaves nasty notes on women's windshields."

Aubrey believed him, leaving her both relieved and deflated. If not Cameron, then who?

"Hello," said Cameron, his gaze fixed on Nikki. "I'm Cameron Meroni. And this is Stephen."

"I'm Nikki, Unrepentant Sinner."

Cameron's grin widened. "*Very* nice to meet you, Nikki."

"You look familiar," Aubrey said to Stephen. "Have we met?"

Stephen ducked his head, took a swig of his beer, and stared straight ahead, focusing on the bottles lining the back of the bar. "I don't think so. I'm not from here."

"Neither am I," said Aubrey, focused on his profile. Something about it nagged at her.

"And yet she already knows half the town," added Nikki.

Cameron chuckled. "How about you, Nikki? Just in town for a visit?"

The bartender, a tall, tattooed young woman with long black hair, came over to them. "Get you something?"

Cameron turned to the bartender. "Lauren, put whatever they want on my tab."

Stephen blew out an audible breath, apparently annoyed.

"Thanks, but we have someplace to be," said Aubrey.

"And burritos to buy," said Nikki.

"Burritos? I know the best place in town," said Cameron, blatantly staring at Nikki. "My treat."

Nikki chuckled. "That's sweet, but I'm not looking for a date."

"Why not?"

"Oh, darlin', I would squash you like a bug," said Nikki. "I've got forty pounds on you. And anyway, Aubrey and I have places to go, people to see."

"Oh, hey, Cameron, is it true you're working with the folks who want to renovate the Seabrink?" Aubrey asked.

He looked surprised. "Where'd you hear that?"

"I'm learning there aren't many secrets in small towns," said Aubrey.

"I'll tell you what I tell everybody who asks me about the hotel redevelopment plan: I'm just an underling. Talk to Obi."

"As in Obi-Wan Kenobi from 'Star Wars'?" asked Nikki. "He lives around here?"

Cameron winked at Nikki, pulled a business card out of his jeans pocket, and handed it to Aubrey. On heavy stock paper, engraved with a phone number and an email address, was a name: AADARSHINI OBEYESEKERE.

"We go with Obi for short. She's heading up the development project. You got questions, talk to her."

"Why didn't you say anything when we saw you at the Seabrink?" asked Aubrey. "I mean, if you were working there, and Dimitri and I were—"

"Trespassing, I know." Cameron shrugged. "It happens. You weren't bothering anything and didn't seem likely to graffiti the walls or steal stuff. Trespassers of a certain age, if you get my drift. And then . . . the thing happened, so it seemed like a moot point."

"The fire?"

He shrugged. "Never did figure out why it smelled like smoke—the fire department showed up and checked everything out. No problem. Anyway, I'm more of a lover than a fighter, if you know what I mean . . ."

Again he made googly eyes at Nikki, who ignored him.

"I don't know if you heard, but the man I was with, Dimitri—" Aubrey's voice caught. "He died."

Cameron froze, his beer halfway to his mouth. "*What?* At the Seabrink? What happened?"

"Not at the Seabrink. At Dead Man's Bluff. I'm surprised you haven't heard about it."

"I'm not from here, so nobody tells me nothin'—unlike you, I guess. You're not gonna try to blame this on the Seabrink curse, are you?"

"I'm not, but others have mentioned it."

He swore under his breath and took a big gulp of beer. "Feels like we'll never get past this. Everyone thinks the place is cursed, and then people go and die and it's like a self-fulfilling prophecy. Or whatever."

"Who else died?" asked Nikki.

"Recently?" He shrugged. "The only confirmed murder was the one by the security guard, back in the eighties or nineties. And some kid fell down the stairs at one point, but it was declared an accident. But people love ghost stories, am I right? It's all a moot point; I'm just trying to help the developer get the project off the ground, and talk of curses doesn't help."

"Mia mentioned there's an historical preservation movement?" said Nikki.

Cameron shook his head in disgust. "They're loud, but they're no threat. Those whack jobs don't have any serious financial backing and think they can waltz in with money from hot dog fundraisers and that sort of thing. You've seen the Seabrink, Aubrey. We're talking some serious money to buy the place and to fix it up. What are they gonna do, let it sit and rot? You ask me, it's better to preserve it as a profit-making enterprise."

Aubrey was in no mood to debate the pros and cons of historical preservation versus commercial development, ethical and practical arguments she was only too familiar with from her days as an architect. There were good arguments to be made on both sides, and ultimately the outcome had to do more with how the winners dealt with the building than who won.

"Cameron, is the electricity on at the Seabrink? We thought we heard the elevator moving."

"That's what I was doing there. We turned it on for a day, mostly to see what's still working. When I smelled the smoke, I was afraid maybe we had started an electrical fire, that's why I ran. And afterward I couldn't find you guys, but I take it you got out through the woodshop hatch. I had to put a new padlock on it, by the way. And, I mean, *geez*, thanks for having my back."

"Sorry about that; it was a strange situation, and we weren't sure what was going on. Anyway, Nikki and I better get going. Thanks for the developer's contact info. Nice meeting you, Stephen," Aubrey said to the blond man as they turned to leave. He held up a single finger in acknowledgment, but kept his gaze averted.

"Let's avail ourselves of the restroom first," said Nikki.

"Good idea," said Aubrey, and they followed the signs through the restaurant to the women's room.

As they were leaving, they encountered Lauren the bartender in the narrow hallway.

"Listen," Lauren said to Nikki in a low voice. "It's none of my business, but are you really interested in that Cameron guy?"

"Are you two an item . . . ?" Nikki asked.

"Not hardly," Lauren replied with a snort.

"I mean, he's cute in his own way, but sort of weaselly, right?" Nikki said. "Anyway, I'm here with my friend, not looking for a date. Why?"

"I don't mean to tell tales out of school or anything," Lauren said, glancing over her shoulder as if worried someone might be listening. "But I bartend over at the Garcia River Casino on weekends. Cameron ran up so many gambling debts that he was barred from the place."

"And here he seemed so promising," Nikki murmured.

"All's I know is," Lauren continued, "when Cameron came in today, he was asking for the nearest pawn shop or antique store that might be buying."

"Don't tell me little Gualala has a pawn shop," said Nikki.

Lauren shook her head. "Nah, we don't even have a proper drugstore. Nearest pawn shop I know of is in Santa Rosa, and the best antique stores are up in Mendocino. Anyway, I gotta pee and get back to work, just thought I'd poke my nose in where it doesn't belong. Cameron seems like the kind of guy who, if you let him buy you a drink, the next thing you know he's moving in. You know the type?"

"Sadly, I do," said Nikki with a nod.

"Thanks for the heads-up," said Aubrey. "One last thing: Did Cameron mention what he was hoping to pawn?"

"Some kind of antique he said he 'found,'" Lauren said, pausing before pushing open the bathroom door. "You believe that, and I've got some beachfront property to sell you on the cheap."

"Found" at the Seabrink, no doubt. Aubrey wondered if she should confront him. She and Dimitri had admittedly been trespassing at the hotel, but there was a line an ethical person who loved abandoned buildings did not cross—and that included theft. Then again, if Cameron was working for the

Seabrink's developer, perhaps he had permission to take things. For all she knew it was his job to gather valuables from the building, though it wouldn't explain why he was trying to pawn what he found. Still, it wouldn't hurt to ask him.

But when they returned to the bar, the men were gone, their half-finished pint glasses abandoned on the counter.

"And here I thought the little weasel really cared," said Nikki with a dramatic sigh. "I was sure he'd wait for me."

"Easy come, easy go. C'mon, I'll assuage your broken heart with a burrito the size of your head, and then we'll see if we can't stir you up some ghosts at the Hotel Seabrink."

FOURTEEN

This time the tall iron gates of the Hotel Seabrink were wide open, so Aubrey drove up the long drive to the loop and parked right in front. She and Nikki got out but paused by the car, staring up at the once-grand building.

"This must have been quite the destination, back in the day," said Nikki. "You can practically see the Hollywood stars arriving in their expensive cars and fashionable clothes, can't you?"

Aubrey nodded. "I had the same reaction. Not only is it a beautiful, dramatic setting, but natural mineral springs supply the old baths in the basement. The water was originally piped into every guest room and also bottled for sale. The hotel's mineral water was said to cure what ails you, from infections to lung disease to what they used to call 'the crazies.'"

"They were certainly blunt back then, weren't they?" Nikki said. "But how would mineral water cure mental illness?"

"Maybe they thought it had to do with an imbalance of minerals, or something? I was reading up on it, and apparently with the development of antibiotics during World War Two, and modern psychology, mineral water 'cures' were largely abandoned. Hey, speaking of magic water: we still have fifteen minutes before Jasper said he'd meet us. What say we go find the source?"

"The source of what?"

"The miracle mineral water, of course."

"Why would we want to do that?"

Aubrey shrugged. "Curiosity. Maybe it'll cure whatever ails us. Or . . . apparently the original inhabitants thought it might be a portal."

"Portals are never a good thing. Have you noticed? They never lead to the land of pretty fairies and guardian angels and fluffy puppies. Always to demons and suchlike."

Aubrey stared at her friend. "Is that a yes or a no?"

Nikki looked around. "How far is it?"

"It can't be too far. The mineral water in the hotel baths was delivered via a gravity pump, which is usually located at the rear of a building. Let's check it out."

They exited through the front gates, then followed a rough dirt road that skirted the outside of the tall stone walls, a thick forest on the other side. Halfway down the road they spotted a metal hatch set into the ground, similar to the one Aubrey and Dimitri had used to escape from the woodshop. Curious, Nikki tried to open it, but it was locked.

At the rear of the grounds, the road turned and followed the walls around to the right, and they spied a large set of gates, not nearly so grand as those in front. A heavy chain was wrapped around the massive metal bars and secured with a huge lock.

"Funny how careful they were to lock up everything else,

but left the front gates wide open," said Nikki, weighing the heavy padlock in her hand.

"Maybe Cameron has left the front gates unlocked, since he's been coming and going."

"Those gardens must have been truly impressive, back in the day," Nikki said, peering through the gates.

They both took a moment to imagine the formal gardens in the hotel's heyday: paths led to hidden patios and gazebos, elaborate fountains, and a large rectangular basin full of algae that must once have been a reflecting pool. A decrepit barn stood in one corner of the property, as well as a partially collapsed chicken coop and several other small outbuildings. An ancient greenhouse had most of its glass panes broken, just like the atrium's. Aubrey took several photos, including the gates in the foreground, which gave the Seabrink's grounds a "secret garden" panache.

"So, now that the road's run out, how are we supposed to find this magic spring?" asked Nikki.

"It can't be far, right? A gravity pump needs to be up high to work. Oh, look, there's a path up the hill, see it?"

"That looks more like a deer trail than a people path. But I suppose I need to work off that burrito. Besides, never let it be said Nikki Politis was not an intrepid explorer. Lead on, O Fair One."

They followed the path uphill through the forest.

"Not sure what we're looking for, exactly," said Aubrey after several minutes of climbing.

"What about that pipe?" Nikki said, pointing to a section of corrugated metal that peeked out from the layer of leaves and pine needles on the forest floor, a few feet off the path.

"Oh! You're a genius. We'll just follow it to the end."

The farther they climbed, the wetter the path became, the mud increasingly sucking at their boots.

"This is really fun," Nikki said, struggling to wrench one booted foot free from the muck. "Seriously. I'm enjoying this."

"Let's keep going," Aubrey said, trying not to slip and fall. "Can't be far now."

"Oh, I'm not about to quit. In fact, I'm thinking we'll be encountering a spot of quicksand soon. Fortunately, I know how to escape from quicksand thanks to many hours spent watching old westerns late at night."

"I thought you preferred horror movies and true crime documentaries?" Aubrey asked, stopping to catch her breath.

"A girl can only watch so much gore before it starts getting weird."

"Hold on," Aubrey said as they emerged at a plateau. "What's that?"

"Looks like a swamp to me. That's not how natural springs look in the beer commercials."

"And look, there's an overgrown road just ahead. This way."

They reached the road and followed it, lured by the sound of water flowing into a small pond. Wild irises, lupines, and ferns lined the lush banks, and at their approach half a dozen frogs jumped into the water with a splash. They paused, panting from the exertion, Nikki scraping mud off the soles of her boots.

"It's beautiful," said Nikki, wrinkling her nose. "But I think someone laid a dookie."

"It's the minerals in the water. Sulfur, I think. But look over there—the water is coming straight out of the rocks," Aubrey whispered, awed by the natural beauty of the place. "I swear, it's a grotto. An actual grotto."

"Okay, now *this* is what a spring is supposed to look like,"

Nikki conceded. "Where a troll might live, or an exiled princess."

As Aubrey snapped photos of the grotto, she noticed the detritus of several tea candles, as well as a drawing scratched onto the surface of the face of one large rock. It looked like the symbol she had seen on the front door of the Hotel Seabrink the first time she had come: a stylized cross bisected by crooked lines and circles. She zoomed in.

"Any idea what that's about?" Aubrey asked Nikki, gesturing to the drawing.

Nikki shrugged. "Graffiti signatures are notoriously hard to interpret."

"It doesn't look like graffiti, though, does it? I mean, it's not initials, and it doesn't look like a tag—"

A scream split the air.

"What in the actual *fuck* was that?" Nikki demanded, jumping next to Aubrey and grabbing her arm. "A rabid raccoon?"

"I'm pretty sure it's a mountain lion."

"Aren't mountain lions nocturnal?"

"I'm not up on the sleeping habits of wildcats. All I know about them is that they want to kill and eat me."

"Correction: they want to kill and eat *us*."

"Seriously, they're usually shy, I think," Aubrey said. "The hotel clerk actually mentioned this to me upon check-in, because so many of their guests are hikers: never run away, and try to look big."

"I'm very happy to be a woman of size right about now," Nikki said.

"We should go back arm in arm, and hold your coat out to the side, like this." Arms linked, jackets held out at their sides, they started down the road, walking as quickly as they could.

Once they hit the muddy hillside, however, Aubrey stumbled and fell, pulling Nikki down with her.

"Smooth, Aubrey," Nikki said, gaining her footing. "Here, take my hand."

Aubrey struggled to her feet. "See? Easy as—"

Nikki's foot slipped in the mud, Aubrey tripped over her, and the two fell again, this time rolling several feet down the hill in the mud, shrieking and laughing.

"Teamwork!" Nikki said, as they lay on their backs for a brief moment, staring up at the tall trees and blue sky overhead. "You know, if we weren't in imminent danger of being eaten by a large cat and looking forward to an afternoon in a haunted house, I would remark upon the beauty of our surroundings."

Muddied and bruised, they managed to regain their footing and scurried down the path, through the trees, the meadow, then more trees, until at last they reached the road that skirted the Hotel Seabrink's grounds. They hurried along the service road to the front gates and down the drive to the car, where they halted, looked at each other, and burst into laughter.

"We sure showed *that* mountain lion," Nikki said. "I— *Ahhhh!*"

Footsteps crunched in the gravel behind them, and they whirled around.

"I thought we agreed to meet *outside* the gates," growled Jasper.

"This is closer," said Aubrey.

"I realize that. Still . . ." He took a deep breath and looked around, taking in the hotel, the algae-filled fountain, the formal grounds now swallowed up by ivy, small trees, and weeds. "Seems safer outside the stone walls, somehow."

"Not necessarily," Nikki muttered, batting at mud on her pants.

"Go for a nature walk, did you?" Jasper said, his eyes raking over them and taking in their disheveled appearance.

"We were looking for the source of the mineral water."

"Find anything?"

"Found the spring, all right," said Aubrey.

"And a mountain lion," added Nikki.

"You found a *mountain lion*?"

"*Possibly* a mountain lion," said Aubrey. "We might have been wrong."

"It could have been Sasquatch," said Nikki with a sage nod. "Whatever was screaming at us sounded more like a monster than a cat, if you ask me."

"We didn't actually see Sasquatch, or a mountain lion, for that matter," Aubrey clarified.

"You rarely see a mountain lion," said Jasper in an ominous tone. "Until it's too late."

"Now, that's a thought that's going to fester," Aubrey mumbled. She reached into the car and handed Jasper a foil-wrapped bundle. "Here, we brought you a burrito."

"I risk my neck escorting you into an abandoned hotel and you pay me with a burrito?"

"It's a really good burrito," said Aubrey.

"That there's carne asada with extra guac, my friend," said Nikki. "I'd say that's a pretty fair deal."

Jasper smiled, leaned back against Aubrey's car, and took a huge bite. They gazed at the hotel, no one in an apparent hurry to enter.

"By the way, I was told not to look up at that attic window," Aubrey said, pointing.

"Do I want to know why?" Nikki asked.

"Rumor has it a ghost lives up there," Aubrey said.

"What's wrong with that?" said Nikki.

"If you see this particular ghost, it's a harbinger of your own death," Jasper explained. "Which, again, makes me ask myself why I agreed to come with you."

"Maybe because you don't believe in such things?" Aubrey suggested.

"Now that you've told me not to look, I desperately want to," said Nikki, exaggeratedly staring at the ground. "Of course, if it's a true harbinger, then you won't see anything unless you're about to die, isn't that how it works? I mean, a harbinger doesn't cause your death, just warns you of your impending death, right?"

"Not really sure if this ghost is a harbinger, or if she curses you somehow," Jasper said. "What do you think, Aubrey?"

"I'd rather not think about it, that's what I think," Aubrey said. "Jasper, what happened with the security guard? Various people have mentioned him."

"Yeah, the security guard story," he said around a mouthful of burrito. "The hotel's owners hired folks to watch over the place and guard against trespassers like us. But this one guy . . . he was really just a kid, right out of high school. Used to bring high school girls here, give them the tour. The girls found him a little odd, but harmless. And he was. Until he wasn't."

"What happened?" Aubrey asked.

"He brought two teenage girls here on prom night, according to legend. The one who escaped said he told them he heard the police coming, so they hid in the baths in the basement."

"Terrible idea," said Nikki. "Never hide in the basement. It's almost as lethal as hiding in the attic. Does no one learn from scary movies?"

"I'm sorry to say the story gets worse. After he sexually assaulted them, one girl managed to escape, but he murdered the one who couldn't get away. When the cops arrived, they found him in the grand stairwell. He had hung himself."

"Good riddance," Nikki muttered.

"That wasn't the worst of it."

"There's more?" Aubrey asked.

"The emergency responders were so focused on the murdered girl in the basement baths that no one paid attention to him at first. By the time they did, he was gone."

"You mean dead," Aubrey said.

"Nope. Gone. As in no longer there." Jasper shrugged. "Maybe an unnamed someone cut him down and, I don't know, threw the body down a well or something. Or maybe he wasn't actually dead and managed to escape."

"Sure, that makes sense," Nikki said. "Lots of folks who hang themselves manage to cut themselves down and walk away, no problem. Happens all the time."

"As kids, we used to taunt each other with tales of a homicidal security guard roaming these woods, sometimes with a broken neck, sometimes without, depending on the storyteller."

"*Okaaaaay*," said Nikki, her eyes scanning the grounds. "That's not creepy at all."

"One other thing," Jasper said, ominously. "The first responders swore they heard music from the 1930s playing when they arrived."

"Change of plans," Nikki announced. "How's about you kooky kids go in while I wait out here and keep the engine running for a quick getaway."

Jasper chuckled. "Pretty sure the part about the music was made up."

Or not. Aubrey and Dimitri had also heard the music. But surely that had been Cameron's friends screwing around. It must have been.

"All right, no use procrastinating. Let's get this over with," Nikki suggested.

"Thought you wanted to wait in the car?" Jasper asked.

"Changed my mind. The person who goes off by themselves is the first to die. Everybody knows that. I've got a better chance if we stick together."

"Plus, you want to see a ghost," teased Aubrey.

"A ghost, yes. Not a homicidal security guard. Let's be reasonable."

"I'd say that's a good rule of thumb," said Jasper: "Ghosts, not murderers. Way to set boundaries. But just in case, let's stick together. Deal?"

"Deal. Follow me," Aubrey said, circling the building and showing them how she had climbed in through the broken atrium window.

"This must have been beautiful, back in the day," Nikki whispered, their footsteps crunching on glass shards and fallen plaster.

"You don't have to whisper, you know," Aubrey said, snapping photos of the bird's nest. "It's not a church."

"It sort of has that feel, though, doesn't it? Sepulchral."

Jasper appeared uninterested in the architecture, but continuously scanned their surroundings, bodyguard-style. He poked his head into the corridor, looked in one direction and then the next, before nodding to Nikki and Aubrey.

They passed into the hallway and headed toward the lobby.

"You ever hear of the Blackburn Cult?" asked Nikki. "They kept a body under the floor, hoping to resurrect it."

"What made you think of that?" asked Aubrey.

"It's pretty rank in here."

"I think that's just the smell of abandonment. Try this, it'll help," said Aubrey as she took out her vial of Thieves oil and shared it with Nikki and Jasper. "Or are you suggesting there are bodies concealed in these walls?"

"I'm saying this would make a great cult headquarters, wouldn't it?"

As they entered the lobby, Aubrey watched Nikki and Jasper take it all in: the faded grandeur of the murals, the beautiful stained glass, the rich wood paneling. The tufted chairs sprouting ferns, the mossy reception desk with the brass keys in their nooks. The peacock feathers, furry with dust.

"What's with the stuff that looks like snow everywhere?" Nikki asked.

"Bits of paint and plaster that fall from the walls and ceilings," said Aubrey, remembering Dimitri reaching out and plucking a piece from her hair. It seemed like years ago, not the day before yesterday. "They say if a paint chip lands on your head, it's good luck."

"Not if it's lead paint, it isn't," said Jasper.

"How is it that all this stuff is still here, after all these years?" Nikki asked.

"I've been wondering that, too," said Aubrey. "I imagine it helps that the hotel isn't well-known nowadays and isn't on any map."

"And there's the curse," suggested Jasper.

"That, too." Aubrey noticed the grand piano was now listing to the side, one front leg broken. "Look, the piano has been damaged. That's new. It wasn't like that before."

"Maybe it finally just broke," Nikki said. "That would be a weirdly random act of vandalism. Teenage trespassers would focus on tagging, or random graffiti."

"Hate to be a spoilsport, ladies, but I'm expected back at the store before too long," Jasper said. "Is there something you especially wanted to see?"

"I want to go upstairs," said Aubrey. "Unless you two want to check out the mineral baths?"

"The basement baths in which that poor girl was murdered?" asked Nikki. "I'll pass."

"I'm just the strong, gentlemanly backup here to protect and to serve," said Jasper. "I don't especially want to see *anything* while we're here."

"Wait—what was that?" Aubrey asked, breathless. She could have sworn she saw a woman walking at the end of the hall, dressed in flowy, 1930s-style garb. "Did you see that?"

"See what?" Jasper asked, his eyes searching the perimeter, his hands balled into fists.

"I thought I saw . . ."

"What?" Nikki urged.

"It looked like . . . nothing. Sorry, eyes playing tricks on me, I guess. Up to the attic, then."

"I feel duty bound to point out that liminal spaces, such as basements or attics, are the most likely to be—or to *seem*—haunted," said Nikki as they started up the grand staircase.

"Why is that?" Aubrey asked.

"Don't know, but every movie and horror story I'm familiar with makes that clear. Never go into the basement or the attic—especially at the suggestion of a killer."

"Good safety tip," said Jasper.

They mounted the magnificent stairway to the second-floor mezzanine, then continued on up to the third floor.

"It's a melancholy place, isn't it?" said Nikki, gazing up at the stained-glass cupola as they climbed the stairs, nearing the third-floor landing. "I mean, once you get past the smell, it just seems sad, like it's asking for help. Oh! A crystal ball! How cool. I wish I knew how to read these. Maybe after I master the tarot..."

"If you look through it the world appears upside down, see?" Aubrey said, as she and Nikki leaned over to gaze into the ball.

"*Boo*," Jasper said suddenly from behind them, and they both jumped.

"Very funny," said Aubrey.

Jasper grinned. "Again, I don't mean to rush you, but..."

"Right," said Aubrey, and headed for the door to the attic stairs. "It's up here."

"Are you sure?" Nikki paused and stared at the dark doorway. "Like I said, I don't like attics. And there's ... isn't there something creepy about this doorway? Or is it just me?"

"It's not just you," Aubrey said under her breath. As soon as she stepped into the dim stairwell, Aubrey sensed, more than heard, the sensation of fluttering, like wind moving through feathers, followed by the horrifying sensation of the walls closing in on her. True, cramped spaces triggered her claustrophobia. But it was more than that.

She gazed at the top of the staircase. It seemed darker than it should be, given that the day was bright enough, and there were windows in the attic. But the darkness seemed somehow... slippery. As if it were moving, sinewy, snakelike ... the inky tendrils coming together and forming an image ...

"You okay, Spencer?" Nikki asked.

"What? Oh, yeah, I'm ... did you see anything up there?"

"Just looks like a dark, spooky stairwell to me."

"Maybe I should go first," Jasper suggested from the lower doorway.

"No, I'm fine," said Aubrey, holding her phone's light up to the wall. "So, this is where I thought I saw that phrase written: 'Breathe me in before taking me out.'"

"I don't see anything," said Nikki. "Do you see it now?"

"No, but . . ." Aubrey went higher on the stairs and ran her hands along the old plaster. Her fingertips sensed what her eyes could not: there were slight, subtle indentations.

"It *is* there!" Aubrey exclaimed. "I didn't dream it. Feel it? Something was carved into the plaster, but the wall was repaired and painted over so you can't see it with the naked eye."

Nikki reached out and followed Aubrey's hands with her own. "Okay. And that tells us what, exactly?"

"That what I saw in my photograph wasn't a dream. It's real."

"Does that include the girl you saw in your photograph . . . ?"

"I . . . I don't know. Maybe I dreamed that part." As she reached the top of the stairs, a bird suddenly flew into the air, and Aubrey yelped in surprise.

"You okay?" Jasper asked.

"I'm fine. Just a bird."

Aubrey trod carefully, remembering Dimitri's warning that the attic might not be safe. There was a broad central space with small chambers on both sides, presumably the bedrooms of the hotel's live-in staff, as well as numerous built-in cupboards and shelves for storage, several large armoires, and stacks and stacks of boxes and crates. The rafters were uneven, slanted, and in spots Jasper had to duck to avoid hitting his head on the eaves. Several dormer windows let in the afternoon sun, which painted bright squares on the wooden floor.

In the far corner a portion of the roof had caved in, and there was ample evidence of avian occupation: feathers and bird droppings everywhere.

Aubrey paused. "Do you smell that?"

"Bird poop," Nikki said with a sage nod. "Nasty stuff when it's en masse like this."

"Not that." Aubrey sniffed again. "Almonds. It smells like almonds."

"I don't smell anything but vermin," said Nikki. "And cloves from the oil you gave us."

Aubrey looked at Jasper. "Do you smell almonds?"

He shook his head. "But I have Thieves oil under my nose, as well." He put his hands on his hips and looked around. "Was this what you wanted to see?"

"Yes, though I'm not sure why. I guess I thought something would jump out at us. Figuratively speaking, of course."

"I was gonna say," said Nikki. "I don't need anything jumping out at me, thank you very much. Though these huge old wardrobes do look like they might lead to other worlds, don't they?"

"A secret passage, maybe?" Aubrey said with a smile. "Or an opening to Narnia?"

Jasper walked over to the large, central multipaned window. "I presume this is the window out of which the alleged ghost allegedly looks down upon her alleged victims."

"Allegedly," repeated Aubrey with a nod, snapping photos of their surrounds. Now that they were all up in the attic together, chatting casually about the alleged Seabrink curse, it all seemed so . . . banal. Silly, even.

Aubrey was reminding herself of the inane videos she had seen of ghost hunters, thinking they heard something—*What was that?*—but in actuality, finding nothing. Had her mind been playing tricks on her, making her think she saw something taking shape in the darkness? Was it simply the memory of the girl she thought she had seen in her photograph? The one who had looked straight at her, held her finger to her lips, as if to say *Shhhhh* . . .

"Hey, get a load of this," Nikki said. "A box marked '1938 Receipts/Logbooks.'"

"Let me see." Aubrey tried to shake off the image of the ghostly girl, and knelt down next to Nikki. "Looks like records from the old hotel—pay stubs, and receipts of all sorts. How cool is that?"

"Why is it that I loathe my own paperwork, but I love historical paperwork?" asked Nikki. "Here's a receipt for laundry broken down by guest rooms and dining room, a list of live-in staff . . . general accounting."

"A wholesale order of crackers from Portland Cracker Company. Look how pretty it is, with all the elaborate scrolls and whatnot. They just don't make receipts like this anymore," said Aubrey.

"They paid $5.48 for what looks like a hell of a lot of crackers."

"Only the best for Hollywood's best," said Jasper, looking over their shoulders.

"And ten dollars for a barrel of beer. So interesting. Look at this," said Nikki, handing a menu to Aubrey. "A prix fixe meal from the hotel restaurant. Nine courses for two dollars and seventy-five cents. Are you kidding me?"

"Sweet pickles and olives," Aubrey read aloud. "Waldorf salad or something called shrimp mayonnaise—which scares me a little—"

"Not a big mayo fan," Nikki explained to Jasper.

"Then there's a soup course, and fish, veggies, and a choice of leg of lamb or beef tenderloin."

"And your choice of peach pie or apple pie for dessert. À la mode, of course. And then coffee or tea."

"All for two dollars and seventy-five cents?" said Jasper. "I wonder what people earned in a typical job back then."

"Here's a receipt for meat, lard, vanilla, and baking soda for $1.27," said Nikki, her butt up in the air as she started rooting around in an old wooden crate. "Campbell's tomato soup was ten cents a can, which actually sounds like a lot next to a nine-course meal for two dollars and seventy-five cents."

"Right?"

"And hey, look at these old leather-bound ledgers," said Nikki. "Okay, this is weird . . ."

"What is it?"

"This one's titled 'The Seabrink Poor Farm and Asylum.'" She handed a heavy red leather tome to Aubrey. "I thought the Seabrink was a luxury hotel?"

"It was," said Aubrey, looking at Jasper. "Wasn't it?"

He shrugged. "I've always heard of it as a hotel. But until you came to town, I didn't spend a whole lot of time thinking about this place. You should talk with my nana if you want to know more about it."

"So, if I'm understanding this ledger, before the Seabrink was a hotel, this building was a 'poor farm and asylum'?" said Aubrey, studying the logbook and taking photographs of it. "Wow. I wonder if that tells us anything . . ."

"What's a poor farm, exactly?" asked Nikki.

"Sort of like a pauper's prison, I think?" said Aubrey. "I remember my grandmother used to warn us that if we spent all our money on candy, we'd be sent to the poor farm. It didn't sound like a fun kind of farm."

"Here's a record of the deaths at the poor farm," said Nikki, her voice subdued. "There were a lot of them, poor souls."

Aubrey came over to look at the book. "And look at the

map: they buried their dead right here on the property. They were numbered; here's a little schema with names attached."

"I didn't notice a cemetery on the grounds, did you?" asked Nikki.

Aubrey shook her head. "The hotel probably landscaped right over it. I wonder if they bothered to move the bodies."

"Not only is that so disrespectful," Nikki said, looking appalled, "but have these people never seen 'Poltergeist'?"

"I think the movie was a little after their time. More likely 'Poltergeist' was inspired by a place like this."

"It was a Native American cemetery in the film, though, wasn't it?" said Nikki. "At least *that's* not an issue here . . . or is it?"

"I've heard that the reason so many of American ghost stories are centered around Native American graveyards is because of our collective guilt," said Jasper.

They both looked up from the book and stared at him.

"You know, because of the genocide," said Jasper. "One of my childhood friends is a member of the Kashia band of Pomo Indians, who are from this area originally. He tells me things. But I seriously doubt they had a cemetery here. There were legends about this place, long before anything was built. They say that the place where the waters emerge from the rock is a portal."

"It looked like a regular spring to us," Aubrey said. "Though it's true that there was something about it, something sort of . . . mystical."

Suddenly, from far off behind the walls, Aubrey thought she heard a flute playing. First from one side, and then the other. The scent of almonds intensified.

"Do you hear that? Smell that?"

Jasper shook his head.

"As before, I smell only cloves, and bird poop," said Nikki. "And all I can hear is my own heart pounding."

Aubrey tilted her head and listened carefully. The flute seemed to be emanating from the other side of the wall, behind the massive armoire. Aubrey cast her phone's light inside. The wardrobe was empty of boxes and clothing, but she thought she spotted something at the back—something similar to the valet's pass-throughs she had seen in the guest rooms. Crouching over, she climbed in to investigate.

"So, tell me more about this portal theory," Aubrey heard Nikki asking Jasper. "I mean, what are we talking? 'Portal' as in 'demon portal,' or a door for cute little fairies?"

"I'm just saying, my friend would never come up here, to the Seabrink. He—"

"*Um, guys?*" Aubrey said, her voice muffled from within the cupboard.

"Find something?" Nikki called out. "How far back does it go?"

"There's an opening. To a *secret chamber.*"

FIFTEEN

The windowless chamber was small, about ten feet by twelve. In one corner, rotting blankets and pillows seemed to form a makeshift bed. Ancient jars of canned fruits and vegetables were lined up on one wall, along with boxes of crackers, a mishmash of candles, and stacks of old books. Everything was caked with mold and grime and swathed with spiderwebs.

Aubrey stopped in her tracks and took photographs of the bizarre tableau.

"What *is* this place?" Nikki whispered, joining Aubrey.

"I think someone must have lived here," Aubrey said.

"Given the size of this hotel, why would anyone live here, hidden in the attic walls?"

"Now, that is a very good question. And look, there's another way out." Aubrey pointed to a small door in one corner. She tried opening it, but the door was stuck. After several tries she finally yanked it open. It led to a very narrow interior passage full of pipes. "Looks like a plumber's access point."

"Could a person even fit in there?" asked Nikki.

"I don't think *I* could, but maybe plumber's assistants were small, back in the day . . ."

"Everything okay in there?" Jasper called from the outer wardrobe.

"We're fine!" called Aubrey. She passed her phone's beam again over the blankets and the books, the jars and the candles, and snapped a few more photos.

"Am I the one who's going to have to say it?" said Nikki. "Didn't you see that movie with the guy who lived in the attic and spied on people?"

"You think that's what this is?" Aubrey asked.

"Maybe," said Nikki. "Or there could be a much more prosaic explanation: maybe they ran out of rooms for the maids, and someone drew the short stick and got stuck in here. Employees weren't treated very well, back in the day."

"That wouldn't explain all the food, though." Aubrey approached the messy pile of blankets. Was it her imagination or was there something beneath . . . ?

Cautiously, she lifted one corner of the top cover.

Nikki screamed.

It was a body. A small, skeletonized body, with bits of leathery skin and hair attached, still wearing a dark dress, stained apron, and black boots.

"Shit!" Nikki cried out, jumping back and fleeing the chamber. Jasper caught her as she stumbled out of the wardrobe.

"What is it? What happened?" Jasper said, and called out: "Aubrey? Are you okay in there?"

"I'm fine!" she replied, taking photographs of the poor creature.

"I am *out* of here," Nikki said and started for the stairs.

"Nikki, *wait!*" Jasper yelled after her. "We stay together, remember? Aubrey, will you get out here, please?"

Aubrey emerged from the wardrobe to see Nikki heading down the stairs.

"*Shit shit shit shit shit,*" Nikki muttered, repeating the word once for each step in a staccato, gasping chant. "*Shit!*"

"Let's go," Jasper said to Aubrey. "Now."

Breaking her own rule about taking things from abandoned houses, Aubrey shoved the red leather Seabrink Poor Farm and Asylum ledger in her backpack, then hurried after Nikki, with Jasper taking up the rear.

Nikki continued swearing as she flew down two more flights of stairs, ran through the lobby, and burst out the front door. Jasper and Aubrey weren't far behind. She skittered to a halt on the top step, looking toward the exit. "Who closed the gates?"

"Not I," Jasper said with a shake of his head. "The gates were wide open. And now they're not just shut, but it looks like they're chained."

"No *way,*" said Nikki. She ran down the drive, Aubrey and Jasper right behind her.

"They're locked, all right," Nikki said, pulling ineffectually on the chain. "Someone locked us in? *Shit!*"

"And here I thought you were keen on seeing a ghost," said Aubrey.

"I was very specific: I said a ghost, not a *body*! And how are we going to get out of here? Is there another exit? *Who the hell locked the gates?*"

"We saw a service gate at the back of the property, but it's also chained," Aubrey said to Jasper. "So now what?"

"We need bolt cutters," said Jasper, inspecting the thick-gauge chain. "The real question is who the hell locked the gates? They must have seen your car parked in front of the hotel. So why did they want to keep us in here?"

"There are some tools in a basement workroom," Aubrey said. "I saw them the other day."

"I gotta say," Jasper said, scanning the hotel grounds. "If someone locked us in here on purpose—and it's hard to see how it could have happened by accident—then going back inside where they might be lurking seems like a rotten idea."

"Especially going down into the murder baths," Nikki added.

"Then what do we do?" Aubrey asked. "I mean, if someone is after us then being trapped inside these stone walls isn't much of an improvement."

"Maybe we can climb out," said Jasper.

"Not a chance," Nikki said, as the three of them gazed up at the high walls. "There's nothing to hang on to."

"The ivy?"

"More likely we'll break our necks."

Aubrey checked her phone again, hoping for a miracle. Still no service.

Jasper let out a forceful breath. "Here's the deal: You two lock yourself in Aubrey's car and wait here. I'll go back inside and look for tools. You said they were in the basement?"

"If you go in, we all go in," said Aubrey, shaking her head. "I agree with Nikki. Nothing good ever comes of splitting up in these ghost/killer situations."

"You'd be safer in the car. Probably," said Jasper.

"Nope. We're sticking together. Right, Nikki?"

A wide-eyed Nikki let out a loud sigh and nodded.

Moving as silently as possible, they crept back in through the atrium window. As they moved into the corridor, they could hear the clanking of the elevator, and warbly 1930s era music emanating from the Victrola.

"What is going *on*?" Nikki demanded in a fierce whisper.

"You wanted a haunted house, didn't you?" snapped Aubrey. They were all on edge.

"Or whoever trapped us is playing with our minds," said Jasper in a grim tone. "Let's make this fast."

Aubrey led the way, hustling down the barrel-vaulted corridor—past the sculpture of Thanatos—to the doors labeled BATHS. Jasper went first, carefully opening the doors to check the stairwell, and then they all proceeded down the dim stairs. Aubrey cringed at the sound of their footsteps in the echo chamber of the basement.

The baths appeared to be empty. As before, the water trickled as it flowed through the tubs, but otherwise it was eerily silent.

Aubrey guided them toward the back, past the storage rooms, to the woodworking shop she had seen with Dimitri. Nikki stood watch at the door to the narrow hallway while Jasper and Aubrey searched through the scattered tools. There were no bolt cutters, but there were crowbars and the sledgehammer that Dimitri had used to defeat the lock on the cellar doors. Those doors now sported a shiny new padlocked chain, no doubt due to Cameron.

"This may work, but I can't promise anything," said Jasper as he hoisted the sledgehammer. "I really think—"

Nikki ran into the workshop, flapping her hands and mouthing, "I heard something! I think someone's coming! And I smell smoke—do you smell smoke?"

Jasper went to the door that led to the corridor, peeked out, listened for a brief moment, then closed the door as quietly as he could. Nikki and Aubrey each picked up a side of the heavy workbench, and Jasper helped to position it in front of the door.

"Now what?" whispered Nikki.

"Dimitri was able to get those hatch doors open with the sledgehammer," said Aubrey. "But they lead out to the grounds, so we'd still be trapped inside the walls. But Dimitri thought there was a tunnel leading out the back of the old wine cellar. I'm not sure how far back it goes."

They heard a scraping sound in the hallway.

Nikki picked up a hammer and handed another to Aubrey, mouthing, "Just in case."

Jasper pulled the metal door to the wine cellar open, cast his light inside, and beckoned to Aubrey and Nikki to join him. The arched tunnel was made of chiseled stone blocks. Most of the wine racks were empty, but a few dusty bottles remained and spiderwebs hung from every shelf.

Jasper wound one end of a stout rope around the inside door handle. Once he closed the door, absolute darkness descended. Aubrey fought the sensation of the walls closing in and tried to regulate her breathing. *A little claustrophobia is better than dying*, she repeated to herself in a strange little mantra.

He secured the other end to one of the wine racks lining the tunnel.

"Not sure how long that'll hold, but it's the best I can do," Jasper said quietly, hoisting the sledgehammer onto his shoulder. "Let's go."

They used their phones to light their way.

"He was right—it keeps going," Aubrey whispered, shining her light at an archway that led farther down the tunnel.

"Let's wait here for a moment, see if whoever that is goes away," suggested Jasper.

"We're probably overreacting, right?" said Aubrey. "It's likely a teenager. Or maybe Cameron, screwing around."

"Cameron Meroni?" Jasper asked.

Aubrey nodded. "Dimitri and I saw him here last time we heard the Victrola, and the elevator."

"Maybe—"

In the near distance they heard someone pounding on the outer door to the woodshop.

"Come on," said Aubrey, leading the way deeper into the tunnel.

The dark mouth of the tunnel seemed to lead on and on. A small trough in the center of the floor carried a trickle of water. Ancient oak barrels and wooden crates were stacked here and there, cobwebs festooned the ceiling, and they passed the desiccated body of a long-dead rat.

"What *is* this place?" Nikki whispered.

"I'm hoping it's an exterior supply entrance," said Jasper. "A lot of these old hotels had tunnels like this so goods could be brought in without the guests noticing. Either that, or it was built to smuggle in alcohol during Prohibition."

"That would mean the tunnel ends on the other side of the hotel walls, wouldn't it?" asked Aubrey. "Nikki and I saw something that looked like it might be a hatch earlier, when we were looking for the spring."

"I hope so," said Jasper. "If not . . . we may be screwed."

"Hate to jump on the 'screwed' bandwagon," said Nikki, "but that hatch was locked, Spencer, remember?"

They heard the metal door to the wine cellar clanging, suggesting that whoever was after them had gotten into the woodshop and was now trying to access the tunnel.

"Nikki, how many sets of footsteps did you hear?" Jasper asked.

"One, I think. I mean, I think they were footsteps. Maybe it was my imagination."

"If it's one guy, the three of us could probably take him."

"Unless he has a gun," muttered Nikki. "Also, assuming he's human. At this point, all bets are off. We don't know what we're dealing with, and I am beginning to seriously rethink my friendship with you, Spencer."

"As well you should. My sincere apologies to you both for getting you into this."

A piercing, crashing sound indicated the wine rack had fallen, meaning the metal door had been breached.

"*Run!*" Jasper whispered.

Their footsteps echoed off the stone walls, their phone lights jumping about wildly as they ran as fast as they dared through the pitch-black tunnel.

Finally, the tunnel came to an end. Narrow beams of light shone through the seams of a hatch in the ceiling. Several metal rungs had been screwed into the stone wall beside it, creating a ladder.

"Let me see if I can open that," Jasper said, climbing up and reaching out to throw the slide bolt locking the hatch. The rusty bolt held, and he grunted and struggled for a moment before it gave way with a loud scraping sound.

"*Yes!*" Jasper said in triumph. He threw open the metal hatch, looked around, then jumped back down.

"You first," he said to Nikki, who quickly climbed the ladder and scrambled up and out. Aubrey went next, with Jasper close behind her.

They found themselves by the service road, outside the hotel walls. It was indeed the hatch Aubrey and Nikki had seen earlier. Jasper slammed the door shut and the three of them dragged two heavy logs over and positioned them on top of the hatch to secure it.

"That ought to slow them down, at least," muttered Jasper. "Let's get the hell out of here."

They piled into Jasper's truck bruised, scratched, and winded. Jasper peeled out so quickly he sprayed gravel behind them.

"Were we actually being chased?" Aubrey asked after a moment, looking back at the hotel as it receded from sight. "Or could it have been our imagination? We were sort of freaked out, and it was so echoey in there—maybe we were hearing ourselves."

"We all just happened to hear the same imaginary person chasing us? And the wine rack falling over?" Nikki demanded, skeptical. "Nice try, Aubrey, but I'm afraid that was a real person busting through those doors."

"The chain on the front gates was no illusion, that's for sure," said Jasper with a grim tone. "I've got bolt cutters in the shop. We'll go back to the shop, grab the bolt cutters and my rifle and maybe a little more backup, and return to get your car. We also have to call the sheriff about the body we found in the attic."

"Don't remind me about the body," said Nikki from the back seat. "I mean, I know I said I like the idea of ghosts and all, but that was a bit much."

"I've got to call Sam," muttered Jasper, handing his phone to Aubrey. "Let me know when I get service?"

They fell silent as Jasper drove quickly and skillfully down the serpentine road, through forests and meadows. Aubrey kept turning what had happened over and over in her mind. They had found a body that had been hidden for decades and then were locked in and chased by an unknown person.

Who was the body they found, and why had she been living in the hotel's walls? And, assuming it was the same girl she had seen in her photograph . . . why had she shown herself to Aubrey? What did she want? Or need?

Eventually, they began to see welcome signs of civilization: a herd of sheep grazing, a neat farmhouse, a passing car. Aubrey released a breath she had not realized she had been holding in. She tried the phone again, and when service bars showed she handed it to Jasper. Keeping an eye on the rearview mirror, he pulled over to the shoulder and dialed.

"Sam? This is Jasper. Not sure how to tell you this, but we found a body up at the Hotel Seabrink."

What the hell were you doing up at the Seabrink?

"It's a long story." Jasper glanced at Aubrey. "The good news is, nobody's hurt and it's an *old* body. Like seriously old. Probably been there for decades. Also, someone tried to lock us in and may have chased us through a tunnel, but it's sort of hard to say."

Sam swore a blue streak, then said he was dealing with a possible drowning down in Jenner but would get to the Seabrink as soon as he could and in the meantime they were not to touch anything. Jasper explained that their cell phones weren't working up on the mountain, and that they were on the way into town to get bolt cutters because someone had locked the gates and trapped Aubrey's car inside, but that they would return to the Seabrink to give their statements.

This the same "Aubrey" who was with the jumper over at Dead Man's Bluff?

"The same."

I take it that's part of the "long story." Speaking of which, I
know you had your doubts, but the coroner signed off on
suicide so we're closing that case.

Jasper thanked him and hung up, tapping the steering
wheel as he stared out at the trees.

"So, the coroner went with suicide," said Aubrey.

Jasper gave a little shrug and pulled the truck back onto
the road. "I let them know what I thought, but I'm just a hardware guy. I've had some experience with this sort of thing, but
I'm not in law enforcement. I could be wrong. I'm *probably*
wrong."

"Interesting area you've got here in Mendonoma," said
Nikki. "Aubrey's been here all of a week, and already racked
up two bodies."

"At least this one's old," said Jasper. "And at least *we*
weren't added to the Seabrink's already impressive body
count."

Aubrey remained silent, thinking of what she had seen
while looking at the photograph she had taken on the attic
stairs.

The teenage girl in an apron. The Quiet Girl, she was sure.

Breathe me in before taking me out.

One thing Aubrey now knew for sure: that was no dream.

And with my last breath
I cursed him:
Breathe me in
before taking me out.

SIXTEEN

Stillman's Hardware and Lumber was busy, the parking lot full, people in work shirts and boots milling about and gathering supplies. Nikki and Aubrey trailed Jasper as he stopped at the main counter to give a quick explanation of why he had been gone for so long, and why he needed to leave again.

Jasper guided them to aisle four, where they found a man in front of the tool display, perusing a small selection of bolt cutters.

"Cameron?" Nikki said.

"What are you doing here?" Aubrey asked. "And why do you need bolt cutters?"

"Oh, hey! Went up to the Seabrink, and some asshat chained the gates closed. No idea why, but it's now my problem. These should do the trick." He gazed at Nikki with puppy dog eyes. "So, we meet again." Then, noticing their unkempt appearance, he frowned slightly and asked, "What have you guys been up to?"

"Um, we were at the Seabrink, as a matter of fact, and—" Aubrey began.

Cameron frowned. "You got a little problem understanding the 'No Trespassing' signs? Seriously, lady, that place is dangerous. You shouldn't go up there. Didn't you take enough pictures the other day?"

"Were you the one who locked the gates?" Jasper demanded.

Cameron rolled his eyes. "Yeah, sure, that's why I'm here looking for bolt cutters."

"Listen," said Aubrey. "Since you work with the developer, you might want to let her know that there's been a . . . development. As it were."

"What kind of development we talkin'?"

Aubrey met Jasper's eyes, and he shrugged. Then she glanced at Nikki, who nodded.

"We found something."

"Ah, geez. I'm afraid to ask. More witchy stuff on the front door? I already washed those off."

"Witchy stuff? Which witchy stuff?" asked Aubrey.

Cameron shrugged. "Somebody went up there and did occult-type stuff. Not the first time. Left a weird mark on the front door."

"This isn't that," said Nikki.

"Ah, *geez*, you're really scaring me here," Cameron said, running his hand through his scruffy hair. "What was it?"

"It's a body," said Nikki. "We already called the police."

Cameron looked stunned. "Are you serious?"

"It's an *old* body, though," said Nikki.

"How old we talkin'?"

"Decades, probably," said Aubrey. "She was wearing a really ancient apron."

"That's a relief. Still. This is gonna screw up my weekend."

"Also, someone chased us through the hotel."

"Someone *chased* you? What are you talking about? And hey—if you were inside when the gate was locked, how'd you get out?"

"We found a way," Nikki said.

Realization seemed to dawn. He nodded slowly. "The tunnel from the basement, am I right? Dude, that place is creepy. Ripe for a horror film. I think Obi's planning on turning the front part of it into a proper wine cellar and closing off the rest."

"What can you tell us about the Poor Farm days?" asked Aubrey.

Cameron's pale face went even ashier. "You know, I'm not really a history guy. You gotta talk to Obi."

"Hey, who was the man you were with at the bar earlier?" Aubrey asked. "He looked really familiar to me."

"You're full of questions today, aren't you?" Cameron said.

"Just answer the lady," Jasper growled.

Cameron glared at him. "How are *you* mixed up in this?"

"I'm the muscle. Speaking of which, I have to grab something from the back." He turned to Aubrey. "Wait for me here."

Aubrey nodded and watched as he headed through a door marked EMPLOYEES ONLY. Turning back to Cameron, she repeated: "So, who was the man you were with at the bar?"

"Some guy who wants access to the building," said Cameron.

"He's asking permission?"

"Some people do ask, you know. Plus, it's not easy to find, not on any map. How'd you manage it?"

"I have a sixth sense about these things."

"First the curse, now six senses . . . I don't go in for that woo-woo stuff. Anyway, this Stephen guy is proposing to do the place up, decorate the hotel with mannequins and whatnot. Real Halloween type deal. I go, 'Listen, dude, it's March. You're jumpin' the gun, there.'"

"Was he planning on holding a party or something?" Nikki asked.

"Nah. Wants to film it."

"He's making a movie?" Nikki asked.

"I think it's some online deal, I—"

"*That's* where I know him from!" Aubrey interrupted. "He's a YouTuber, Stephen something. He's one of the 'bro dudes' who explore abandoned buildings, but this guy's famous for using mannequins to up the creepy factor. Do you have his number, Cameron? I'd like to ask him some questions."

Cameron shrugged. "Sorry, can't help you. He found me, not the other way around."

"What did you tell him?" Nikki asked.

"I told him no, of course. That Halloween type stuff is off the table. No way do I want to attract more weirdos or satanists or whatever. I've got enough trouble already with folks sneaking in, drawings symbols on the door and whatever. We really should have round-the-clock security."

"That didn't turn out so well the last time," Aubrey said.

"Exactly."

"Let's go deal with the chain on the gates," Jasper said as he returned, carrying a navy-blue duffel bag. "And get your car back."

"I'll go up there with the ladies, snip the chain," said Cameron, hoisting the bolt cutters onto his bony shoulder like a bizarre lumberjack. "No problem. I probably gotta talk to the cops, anyway."

"We'll all go," Jasper replied.

"I've got this. No need to keep you away from your job any longer."

"Let me worry about that. Besides, we have to give statements to the deputies."

"Whatever," Cameron said with a shrug. He turned to Nikki and said, "Wanna ride with me?"

"Sure, why not?" Nikki smiled and patted her pocket. "I've got my Mace right here. Locked and loaded."

"No need for that," said Cameron. "I'm a gentleman, through and through."

Aubrey pulled Nikki aside. "You sure you're okay with this?" she asked in a low voice as Cameron and Jasper glared at each other.

"No worries, I can handle the wee lad. It's not like he's a phantom chasing us through a pitch-black tunnel, after all. I'll see if I can get any useful information out of him." She turned to the men. "Ready, gents?"

Jasper looked as if he wanted to object further, but then nodded. "Aubrey and I will follow, right behind you."

don't trust that guy," Jasper muttered as they trailed Cameron's Jeep down Highway One.

"And yet you're so subtle about it," said Aubrey.

"That obvious, huh? But I feel better with my rifle as backup." He had placed the duffel bag containing the weapon behind his seat.

"Well, I guess we can be sure about one thing: it wasn't Cameron chasing us through the tunnel. I just can't decide whether that's a good thing or a bad thing."

He nodded. "The facelessness of the threat is harder to deal with."

"You got that right." Aubrey was experiencing an adrenaline crash and wished heartily for a cup of coffee. She leaned her head back against the headrest. "I can't believe we found a *body*. A body in a hidden room, no less. I wonder who she was, and what happened to her. Poor thing."

"It's a historic building and has no doubt acquired numerous secrets over the years. Maybe . . . maybe she just got trapped in there, or something along those lines."

"And was never discovered? I mean, if she worked there, as the apron suggests, wouldn't someone have searched for her when she didn't show up for breakfast? And not to put too fine a point on it, but as I understand it, a decomposing body smells pretty rank. Surely the servants who lived in the attic would have noticed."

"Is it possible the sulfur stench from the mineral water masked the odor of death? Maybe they were used to bad smells." Jasper shrugged. "Or . . . maybe they assumed a rat died under the eaves."

"That would have to be a pretty big rat."

"True enough. I honestly don't know. But there's no point in speculating. Maybe the authorities will be able to tell us something after examining the remains."

"Maybe." Aubrey debated whether or not to tell him what she had seen in that haunting photograph. She tried to formulate the words to share it with Jasper, but the truth was she was not sure what she believed, herself, and did not want to sound like an idiot.

So she remained silent, gazing out across the fields fronting the ocean, again pondering the life of cows lucky enough to spend their days grazing on a bluff over the ocean. Did they enjoy the sea breezes, or was that purely a human thing? What about the kids who were raised out in this area; did they realize how beautiful it was? Or did they long for the excitement of the city?

"You've lived in this area your whole life?" Aubrey asked Jasper.

"Most of it," he said. "It's a great place to be a kid, but by the time I hit my teens I was itching for something different. Went back East, studied engineering at MIT, took a year off to bum around the world, then landed a job with an engineering firm in San Diego. I always vowed I'd never come back, but..."

"Life intervened?"

He nodded. "My dad got sick, and my uncle needed help running the family hardware store, so I agreed to come back for six months."

"How long ago was that?"

He gave her a rueful smile. "About five years. I was going through a divorce at the time, so I needed a change of scene anyway, and there's something about small-town life—after having seen a bit of the world, and sampling life as an adult, I guess its charms grew on me."

"How's your dad now?"

"He's fine but uses his heart condition as an excuse to play golf most days instead of working at the store. So, how about you? Ever been married?"

Aubrey nodded. "To my college boyfriend. It was not a good fit. We divorced a couple of years ago, which was best for all concerned."

"A mutual decision, then?"

"Yes, all three of us—he and his girlfriend and I—decided it was a good idea."

"Ouch."

Aubrey smiled. "It hurt, of course. But it wasn't exactly a surprise. He had his faults, but I also . . . I wasn't particularly emotionally available. I think I have a version of synesthesia; ever since I was a kid, I felt too much, and didn't really know how to handle it, so I just clammed up and kept it all inside. I spent a lot of time and energy trying to do everything right, but I wasn't really myself, if that makes sense. After the divorce, I vowed to be truer to my authentic self."

Jasper glanced over at her, sympathy and understanding in his hazel eyes.

"And now look at me, spilling my inner demons to a near stranger."

Jasper chuckled. "Well, that's progress, anyway."

"Hey, what do you know about the developer who's trying to buy the Hotel Seabrink?" Aubrey asked, feeling the need to change the subject. "Someone named Obeyesekere, they call her Obi?"

"I only know her by reputation. They've had a couple of public meetings to let folks know what the plans are and let them weigh in on it. It's not really my thing, so I haven't gone."

"You don't care if it's renovated or not?"

He hesitated for a moment. "Like I said, one of my best friends is Kashia. He used to tell me stories the tribal elders had told him about the place and the land it sits on. And then I went there on a dare as an idiot teenager, and . . ." He trailed off with a shrug.

"And? And what?"

He took his eyes off the highway for a moment to meet hers. "The friend I went with claimed to have seen the ghost in the attic window. He died the following day. Car accident."

"You're saying it was due to the curse?"

He shook his head, but seemed to be weighing his words,

keeping his eyes trained on the road. "I don't believe in curses, but . . . don't you find the place pretty damned disconcerting?"

"You mean before or after finding a skeleton and getting locked in and chased through a tunnel?"

He gave a humorless chuckle. "My nana always says that life throws enough trouble at us, no need to borrow more. On the other hand, folks around here need jobs, and the development would be paying taxes, so that's all good for the local economy. And maybe if the building was inhabited, the other issues would die down."

"'Die down' seems like a poor choice of words."

Jasper smiled. They reached Stewarts Point and Cameron turned left onto Asylum Point Road. They followed, and soon they started snaking up the mountain, engulfed by forest.

"I'm supposed to meet with Deborah Goldman in the morning to hear more about local history," Aubrey said. "I want to ask her about the Seabrink being a poor farm, of all things. This area is fascinating. I had no idea."

"How'd you hear about Deborah?"

"I met a woman in the bookstore, a Mrs. Harrison?"

"The Episcopalian?"

"I take it you've met?"

They shared a smile.

"Why does she introduce herself like that?"

"No idea. A sense of identity, I suppose."

"So, do you know Deborah Goldman?"

He paused, then said: "I do."

"And?"

"And what?"

"You hesitated, as if you wanted to say something more."

"You might want to take what she says with a grain of salt."

"I've heard that. Why?"

"Deborah has an axe to grind. Make that several axes to grind. And I don't trust her associates."

"She has 'associates'? What is she, a mafioso?"

"I just think that my grandmother might be a more reliable local historian. She's lived in the area her whole life, and even remembers when the Hollywood stars used to visit."

"Would she be willing to speak with us?"

"I don't see why not. Especially if I bribe her with Thai food. I'll give her a call and arrange something."

Soon enough they pulled up to the still-chained gates of the Hotel Seabrink, where Cameron and Nikki were waiting by the Jeep. There was no sign the deputies had arrived. The late afternoon light was softening, sifting in golden shafts through the canopy of trees.

"Wait here for a minute." Jasper got out and looked around, as if searching for something. He returned, brought his duffel bag out from behind the seat, extracted the rifle, and handed it to Aubrey.

"What am I supposed to do with this?" she asked.

He grabbed it, cocked it, and handed it back. "If you see someone coming for us, shoot first, ask questions later. I'm tired of this nonsense."

Jasper took the bolt cutters from the bed of the truck and marched up to the gates. He snipped the chain as if it were made of butter, and it clanked to the ground.

They heard an engine approach, and looked to see a sheriff's car pull up to park beside theirs. Kenny Jenkins climbed out and looked around with slightly squinting eyes, as if assessing the situation.

"I take it Sam couldn't get away," said Jasper.

"Empty kayak washed up in Jenner and they can't tell if it

used to have someone in it, so the search is ongoing. I hate drownings." Deputy Jenkins had a hard glint in his eye, and did not seem as goofy as he had before. "Audra, right? From Dead Man's Bluff."

"Aubrey."

"Right, like I said. You have a permit to carry that rifle?"

"She doesn't need one," said Jasper, taking back the rifle. "It's mine. For deer hunting."

"I was just holding it for him, briefly," added Aubrey inanely. "Deputy, is there a coroner, or . . . someone on their way? I mean, we probably need a forensic anthropologist. The body—she's really old."

"Yeah, sure, let me just call the forensic anthropologist we keep on staff," said Kenny, rolling his eyes. "Look, lady, what I really ought to be doing right now is citing you, *all* of you, for trespassing. It's clearly posted, plus I verbally told you to stay away."

"It's all right, Deputy," said Cameron, stepping forward. "I represent the developer, and we won't be pressing charges at this time."

Kenny sighed, looking annoyed, but nodded and asked for their statements, which didn't take long.

"Okay, so that's it, then?" he said. "You wanna show me where the whereabouts are of this particular individual?"

Aubrey opened her mouth to volunteer, but nothing came out. That poor girl seemed so vulnerable in her strange little hiding place behind the walls. Suddenly Aubrey wished they could have taken care of her themselves, maybe given her a proper burial somewhere here on the grounds. Were they disinterring her, after all these years, only to lie on a cold metal table in an uncaring coroner's examining room?

It felt like a violation.

"No freaking way I'm going back in that building," said Nikki emphatically, shaking her head. "I'm reconsidering my entire position on ghosts right now. I might even chuck my tarot cards."

Jasper had been leaning against his truck and pushed off with a resigned sigh. "I'll do it."

Cameron joined them. The three men walked up the long drive, Cameron opened the front door, and they disappeared into the old hotel.

Aubrey and Nikki waited in silence. The afternoon light cast an orange glow through the branches, and a chilly breeze wafted by. There was a rustling in the woods, a few birdcalls, a chattering squirrel atop the high stone walls.

"It's like it radiates something," murmured Nikki.

"What does?"

"The hotel. Don't you think?" Nikki gazed up at the building.

"I think it's your imagination. Although Dimitri said—"

"Shit shit shit!" Nikki started shaking her hands as though trying to rid herself of something. "I looked at the attic window! I saw her! I-I think I saw her? I think I peed myself!"

Aubrey gazed up at the window. Sunlight glinted off of the smudged panes, but otherwise she saw nothing but darkness behind the glass.

"I'm cursed!"

Just then Jasper and the deputy returned, crunching their way down the drive.

"What's *her* problem?" asked Deputy Jenkins.

"She's cursed," said Aubrey.

"Aren't we all," said Jasper under his breath.

"Look," the deputy said, "the sheriff's office will take it from here. But you guys stay away, will you? I see you here

again, I'll cite you for interfering with an official investigation."

They watched as he climbed into his car and slammed the
door shut.

"That's it?" Aubrey asked.

"Sam will follow up," said Jasper. "Not sure they have access to a forensic anthropologist, but you're right, she has to
be dealt with very delicately."

"Where's Cameron?"

"Stayed inside, said he needed to attend to a few things."
Jasper opened his truck door. "So, this has been fun, but I really need to get back to the store. You two take off first, and I'll
follow you as far as the highway."

"Thanks again for rescuing us," said Nikki.

He gave a little duck of his head. "It's what I do."

"Still . . . you've really gone above and beyond," said Aubrey.

"Do me a favor?" Jasper spoke softly. "Don't ask me again.
The burrito was good, but not that good."

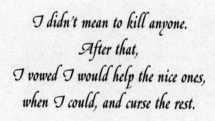

I didn't mean to kill anyone.
After that,
I vowed I would help the nice ones,
when I could, and curse the rest.

SEVENTEEN

'm serious, I think I peed myself. And I have cobwebs in my hair from that stupid tunnel, and God knows what else is on me at this point from falling down muddy slopes and crawling through haunted death wardrobes," said Nikki as they drove toward the highway. "I need a shower, big-time."

"As do I. And a drink."

"I thought you swore off drinking."

"A decision made in haste, and one I now regret."

"I can't believe we found a *body*. And a ghost! I swear I saw a face up in that window. How's that curse go?"

Aubrey gave her a sympathetic smile, but shook her head. "You didn't see a ghost. We're tired and scared and easily freaked out. It's been quite a day. Besides . . . I have the sense that the body we found is on our side, somehow."

"How's that?"

"I'm still piecing it all together. But do you remember I told you about the legend of the Quiet Girl? And in Effie Mae's letter, she mentioned a girl they called Dummy because she never spoke. And I saw a young girl in my photograph."

"Or in your dream."

"Or in my dream," Aubrey conceded. "But I think I might be changing my mind about that. I'm . . . pondering."

"Okay . . . but if I wind up dead, it'll be your fault. I just want to be clear about that."

"Understood. You would be well within your rights to come back and haunt me. Jasper's not the only one who's gone above and beyond."

"Speaking of whom," Nikki said, looking in the sideview mirror at Jasper's truck following closely behind. "I approve. I most definitely approve."

"Approve of what?"

"Your gentleman friend. Not only is he brave and strong, but he's also good with tools. Did you see the way he used those bolt cutters to snip that chain?" Nikki fanned herself. "*Hot.*"

Aubrey chuckled. "And what about your inamorato? Cameron seems smitten."

"He's not my type, as I'm sure you know."

"What did you two talk about on the drive back to town? Get any good info?"

"He said he grew up in Belvedere, near San Francisco."

Aubrey raised an eyebrow. "He must come from money, then. Belvedere's pretty swanky."

"Sounds like he's the black sheep of the family. He got in trouble in high school, flunked out of college, messed around with drugs, that sort of thing. He says his family cut him off."

"And now he's racking up gambling debts."

"I didn't ask about those."

"What about what the bartender said, that he was trying to pawn something?"

"I didn't ask about that, either. I was trapped in his Jeep with him, you know, didn't want to accuse him of anything directly. Besides, I know he's a bit weaselly, but—I feel sort of sorry for him. He strikes me as sad more than bad."

Aubrey smiled. "You always see the best in people."

"Happy childhood, remember? I wasn't raised to think everyone was up to no good."

"It's one of the things I love about you. It also scares the hell out of me. If you plan on seeing Cameron again, I'll act as chaperone."

Nikki chuckled. "That won't be necessary. I've sworn off men, remember? After what happened with Ty . . ."

"You're going to have to let that go someday."

"And I will. But today is not that day. Besides, you're one to talk: here you're hanging out with a perfectly handsome, not to mention extremely handy, gentleman and I'll bet you haven't even made a play for him."

"For Jasper?"

"Are there a lot of men in your orbit who fit that description?"

"I wouldn't say we're 'hanging out.' We've talked a bit, but it was mostly about my having slept with a stranger and then trying to figure out if that stranger was murdered. It sort of puts a damper on a new romance."

They reached the highway, where Aubrey turned south toward the Driftwood Cove Inn. Jasper tooted his horn and turned right, toward Gualala, waving out the window.

"He likes you, I'm telling you."

"Does not."

"Does too."

Aubrey made a snorting sound.

"Scoff all you want, missy, but I'm an expert on lunar love, now that I'm learning about tarot cards. Anyway, why else would he agree to go with you into a famously haunted, abandoned building?"

"*You* did," Aubrey pointed out.

"Yeah, well, I'm your sidekick, and your backup. I didn't have a choice. But the sexy hardware man? He had a choice." She leaned her head back and let out a long sigh. "I still can't believe we found a *body*."

Aubrey kept thinking of the image in the photograph, of the teenage girl on the stairs leading up to the attic. The smile, the shushing gesture. Her steady gaze right into the camera. She had worn an apron just like the shredded one that clung to the body. Of course, it could have been a different maid, but given where they found her . . .

The only things missing were the flute, and the bejeweled headband.

When they neared the Driftwood Cove Inn, they saw people milling about at the top of the cliffs. Curious, Aubrey pulled onto the side of the highway and parked behind several cars.

"What's *that* about?" asked Nikki.

"This is Dead Man's Bluff—where Dimitri jumped. Or was pushed. Or fell. Anyway, he was found at the bottom of that cliff."

"You don't think—did someone else fall? Or . . . get pushed?"

"I certainly hope not."

They got out. As they approached the cliff, Aubrey's heart started to pound. She had a metallic taste in her mouth and felt hot, then cold. *Trauma response*, she told herself, trying to regulate her breathing. She had learned all about the involuntary response to trauma in therapy, but learning about it intellectually was no guarantee of being able to fend it off.

Cautiously, Aubrey peered over the cliff to the jagged rocks below: no body.

The tide was in, and several flowers floated on the water, bright specks of color against the gray of the ocean, moving with the swells. The sun hunkered low in the sky, casting mellow golden sparkles on the surface of the ocean and lighting up thin streaks of clouds in shades of pink and orange.

"Did something happen?" Nikki asked the nearest on-looker, a young fellow with thick glasses and a vintage Oakland Warriors basketball T-shirt. He looked as though he might still be in high school.

"Do you know Dimitri Petroff?" he asked.

"No," said Nikki, tilting her head toward Aubrey, "But she does."

Aubrey nodded. "I . . . did. Briefly."

He shook his head in sorrow. "*Dude.* He died here. Jumped, apparently. His videos were *awesome.*"

"The *best,*" chimed in a young woman with bright blue hair gelled into a spiky do. "There are a lot of videos on YouTube, but his were special, you know? I can't believe he'd do this, but then artistic geniuses are always tortured, right? Like the painter who cut off his ear?"

Aubrey had to agree with her that Dimitri's videos were good, though "genius" seemed a bit much, as did comparing Dimitri to Vincent van Gogh. Still, their grief seemed genuine, and who was she to judge?

"So, are you all here to pay tribute to him?" Nikki asked.

"Yeah," said the blue-haired woman. "I mean, he was so inspiring, and his personal story was really awesome."

"What story?"

"Like, how his family came from Russia, and they were dirt poor. He had to overcome so much as an immigrant, even learning the language, and then he was on the verge of achieving the American Dream when . . ."

Aubrey and Nikki shared a glance.

"Anyway, I guess we all saw the memorial video," said the boy in the basketball jersey. "Couldn't believe it."

"What memorial video?" asked Nikki.

The young woman whipped her phone out of her jeans pocket, opened an app, then handed the phone to her. Nikki leaned in so they could watch it together.

It was Stephen Rex, the blond guy from the bar, the "bro" who filmed a lot of videos of abandoned buildings he had decorated with mannequins. But this video was different: he stood here, on Dead Man's Bluff, showing the Driftwood Cove Inn just to the south, the forests behind, but mostly focusing on the long drop over the cliff and the crashing waves below.

Stephen's voice sounded strained, and when he turned the camera on himself there were tears in his eyes.

"Dude. Dimitri just signed a huge deal with Netflix for an Abandoned special that would be a pilot for a new series. Me and him had talked about collaborating on the project. I really can't, like, believe . . ."

He shook his head and pinched the bridge of his nose, as if stemming the tears.

"I just can't believe he would do this, like, not now. I suppose one never knows what is in another dude's mind, right?"

"I heard he was living a lie," said a tall, willowy woman with long dark hair. She looked like a model. "Pretending to be someone he wasn't. Like that whole Russian thing was made up."

"Where did you hear that?" Aubrey asked.

She shrugged and gazed out at sea.

The blue-haired woman answered in her stead: "I take it you aren't into making videos?"

Aubrey shook her head.

"Well, let me tell you, there are a lot of rivalries online. It can get pretty vicious out there. You have no idea."

"I heard it was because he went to the Hotel Seabrink," said another young man, holding Aubrey's eyes. "There's a curse, you know. I'm from here, and my whole life, I've known about it. Someone I went to high school with went up there and saw the face of the ghost in the attic window. Sure enough, they next day he was dead."

"You think he died because of the curse?"

"I'm just saying," the young man said in a world-weary voice much older than his years: "You know what they say about the Seabrink around here? 'Screw around and find out.'"

EIGHTEEN

S o, seriously, am I marked for death now?" Nikki asked as they walked into the Driftwood Cove lobby. "I swear I saw something in that window. It gives me shivers just thinking about it."

A tall woman behind the reception desk called out to them, in a lilting Jamaican accent, "Ms. Spencer? Something came for you."

"Um, thanks," Aubrey said, her stomach clenching as she accepted the manila envelope. Her hands shook as she murmured, *"Not another one."*

"Let's have a seat over there," said Nikki, pointing to the lobby's raised fireplace hearth. "And give it to me. I'll open it."

Nikki opened the seal carefully, as though worried something might leap out at them. Inside was a smaller envelope, this one yellowed with age, accompanied by a handwritten note on the St. Ambrose Hotel's letterhead:

Found this under the bed in Dimitri Petroff's room. I assume you dropped it and would want it back.

Best, Miriam Conover
Manager, The St. Ambrose Hotel

"That was nice of her," Nikki said.

"I'm just glad it's not another threatening letter," Aubrey said with relief. "After the day we've had, I don't think I could deal with one more thing."

"The old envelope is addressed to Mrs. Gwen Peters, 125 Lenox Road, Bakersfield, California," read Nikki. "This must be the Bakersfield connection, right? And look, the return address is Seabrink Poor Farm and Asylum."

"In the letter I read, Effie Mae is writing to relatives in Bakersfield who are taking care of her daughter for her, and she mentions finding paper in the attic—maybe it was the old stationery. But . . . I have no idea what that tells us."

"Why don't we go upstairs, take showers, and order room service?"

"It's like you read my mind," said Aubrey.

On their way to the stairs Nikki stopped to grab a couple of vinyl albums to bring to the room: the Andrews Sisters and a compilation of hits from the 1930s.

"Why not something slightly more contemporary?" Aubrey asked. "Those records remind me of the eerie music we heard at the Seabrink."

"That's the point. I'm hoping the music might shake something loose, prod our subconscious to remember something we saw but didn't register," said Nikki. "Anyway, I'm in the mood for music from the past. Where else would we find a collection like this?"

"Okay, but if you start channeling spirits or anything of the kind, I'm leaving," Aubrey said, halfheartedly flipping through a few albums. "I'm taking Fleetwood Mac's 'Rumours.' That's about as far back as I want to go."

As they climbed the stairs, Aubrey tried to recall what she knew about the city of Bakersfield: It was in the Central Valley, closer to Los Angeles than to San Francisco, and she had a vague memory of having driven through once, but had not stopped. There were a lot of oil rigs pumping incessantly, if she remembered correctly, and vast agricultural fields on the outskirts of town. It was probably a nice place to grow up but was not the sort of place tourists flocked to.

Once in the hotel room, Aubrey made sure the door was double bolted and checked behind the shower curtain and inside the closet.

"Hey, did you arrange the pillows propped against the headrest like that?"

"Probably housekeeping," said Nikki as she placed the first record on the Crosley record player's turntable and gently set the needle in the first groove. A warbly voice singing about lost love filled the room. Even without the reminder of their adventures in the abandoned hotel, the song would have made Aubrey uncomfortable.

"I hung the 'Do Not Disturb' sign on the door," Aubrey said.

"They probably came in to replace the clock. I mentioned it to Monica, remember? And she's nothing if not attentive to details. Why? Are you spooked?"

"I guess I am," said Aubrey. "Anyway, how does the Russia story the women outside were telling us fit with the Bakersfield story? Why would a man born Roger Harmon in Bakersfield change his name to Dimitri Petroff?"

"Doesn't have to mean anything," Nikki asked. "Nothing

illegal about changing your name to whatever you prefer, as long as it's not for purposes of impersonation or fraud."

"Really?"

Nikki nodded. "It's 18 USC 1342, I think? Maybe 43 . . . anyway, it criminalizes the use of fictitious names or addresses with the intent of committing fraud or other criminal activities. Otherwise, you're allowed to call yourself Minnie Mouse if you want. Actually—wait. Disney would probably sue for copyright infringement. They're famously litigious."

Aubrey stared at Nikki in disbelief. "You memorized the federal statute?"

"I looked it up after you mentioned Dimitri having a second name," Nikki said with a shrug. "My mind works that way."

Aubrey perched on the side of the bed to pull off her boots. "A name change could mean Dimitri was hiding from something, or maybe running from something. I wish I knew what it was."

"A lot of people have something they want hidden, or would like to run away from. I know I do."

"Could be. So . . . if the maid, Effie Mae, sent her daughter, Victoria, to live with her extended family in Bakersfield, maybe Dimitri was connected somehow . . . but why change his name and pretend to be a child of Russian immigrants?" said Nikki.

"Good question. I do know a lot of Russians settled in this area, a long time ago. Fort Ross was established by Russian traders before California was even a state. They and their descendants were active in fishing and lumbering around here. It's common for adoptees to look into their biological genealogy. Maybe he was here not just to trespass at the Hotel Seabrink, but also to track down his biological grandparents, or *great*-grandparents, or something along those lines?"

There was a pause in conversation, and a jaunty, wavering tune blasted from the phonograph.

"So, what now?" asked Nikki.

"I say we change the music, take showers, and do some research online. Oh, and in the morning we have an appointment with Deborah Goldman and her 'associates' at nine a.m."

"Her 'associates'? What is she, a mafioso?"

"That's what *I* said," said Aubrey with a smile. "That's how Jasper referred to them."

While Nikki showered, Aubrey went online and looked up the phrase "Breathe me in before taking me out." She found several songs starting with "breathe me in," but nothing else.

"It sounds modern, though, doesn't it?" Aubrey told Nikki when she emerged from the bathroom. "I mean, 'taking me out' could refer to 'killing me,' I suppose, but isn't that a modern phrase?"

"Maybe it meant *out* out, like, on a date?" Nikki suggested, rooting through her small rolling suitcase.

"Maybe."

"And how is it significant?"

"I told you, it was written on that wall, on the stairwell leading up to the attic."

"Ah. Gotcha. I can't believe this," Nikki said, tossing clothes aside. "I forgot to pack underwear. How does a person forget to pack underwear?"

"You want to borrow some of mine? Or is that weird?"

"It's a little weird, but I appreciate the offer. I remember my tarot cards but forget the underwear. Typical." She laughed, then glanced over at Aubrey, who was scrutinizing a piece of paper with letters ripped from a magazine and glued onto it. "Is that another threatening note?"

"It's one of several I found in Dimitri's things."

"And you're thinking the same person who sent these notes to Dimitri sent yours as well? I mean, assuming it was a person and not a . . . you know."

"What? You're suggesting a ghost from the Seabrink is sending nasty letters?"

"At this point I'm feeling very open to ideas. Hey! Maybe the Seabrink is responsible for scrubbing the internet, too! Maybe it just wants to be left alone!"

"I say this in the kindest possible way, Nikki, but I think you're going 'round the bend a bit."

Nikki took the letter from Aubrey and studied it. "So, these letters are made of magazine cutouts, like yours, but the tone is different. Yours were telling you to back off, whereas his are more: 'You'd better talk to me! Who do you think you are?' Sounds to me like classic fixated behavior: feeling like you have a relationship with someone when you really don't, and unwilling or unable to understand when lines are crossed. Is it possible Dimitri's notes might be from an old girlfriend? They have nothing to do with the Seabrink at all?"

"What are you thinking?"

"Most people are killed by intimate partners. Could Dimitri have a wife tucked away somewhere? Maybe he changed his name to escape a wife and family."

"Ugh." Aubrey rested her head on her crossed arms. "I certainly hope not."

"A jealous wife or girlfriend might have followed his car here, or put a tracking device on it, or on his phone. It's not hard to do. I assume he didn't say anything to you about being involved with someone?"

Aubrey shook her head. "I told him I was divorced, and he mentioned a couple of old girlfriends, but certainly nothing current. But I only knew him for a few hours. We talked mostly about abandoned buildings. If only those threatening notes were more specific."

"Too much effort to cut and paste all those letters," said Nikki. "Here's another scenario: there *is* a wife or a girlfriend, but she didn't kill him, maybe doesn't even know he died until she finds Stephen Rex's memorial video. Speaking of which, I want to find that . . ." Nikki opened YouTube on her laptop.

"I already saw all I wanted to see," said Aubrey. "For starters, those were crocodile tears. Probably used eye drops."

"I'm not going to watch that maudlin memorial video. I want to read the comments."

"Why?"

"The comment section is where the cockroaches crawl out of the woodwork," Nikki said, staring at her laptop's screen. "Aha! Listen to this: 'You're a scammer and a cheat, and so was Petroff. Why don't you follow his example and take a swan dive off a cliff?'"

"Ouch." Aubrey grimaced. "That's pretty harsh."

"You ain't heard nothin' yet." Nikki went on to read aloud more of the posted comments. Some were heartfelt expressions of grief by people with screen names like GhostGirl96, ExploringLana, and Dontbekras. But most were hateful, casting aspersions on Dimitri's life and character, and hurling anti-Russian insults. Others went off on Stephen Rex, claiming he was a liar and a hypocrite. And several touted their own channels as better than either Dimitri's or Stephen's.

"What I'm getting from this is that social media brings out the worst in people, but I already knew that," Aubrey said. "I'm curious. I know Dimitri just signed a Netflix deal, which, I imagine, was lucrative. But can you really make money just by posting YouTube videos?"

"Most people don't," Nikki said. "But if you have enough

followers and enough people watch your videos, then you can make serious money. Attract advertisers and investors and everything. Which is part of why this memorial video is so irritating—it's trending, which means Stephen Rex's likely to make cash off it. I gotta say, this guy's obnoxious with a capital 'O.'"

"Yeah, he's a real 'dude bro.' That's why I liked Dimitri's channel so much, long before I met him: he had a true love of architecture and history, explained what he was seeing, and put it in its historical context. He even spoke in full sentences with proper grammar."

"You're so old-fashioned."

"I'm just saying. The bros don't impress me much."

As Nikki continued to read the comments on the memorial video, Aubrey spread a towel on the bed, placed the old poor farm ledger in the center, and carefully opened it. The old leather volume was crumbling, leaving a trail of reddish-yellow powder.

"This is fascinating," said Aubrey. "Listen to some of the supposed 'illnesses' suffered by the people who wound up at Seabrink Poor Farm and Asylum: defiance, masturbation, excessive reading of novels . . ."

"Uh-oh. I'm in trouble on all counts."

"Grief is listed here, as well. Mania, melancholia, being 'inbred.' Do you suppose that means the result of incest? And, of course, vagrancy."

Nikki joined Aubrey on the bed to look at the log. "Check out the list of 'inmates.' They called them inmates? Was it a home, or a prison?"

"Maybe a little of both," said Aubrey with a sigh. "It was a crime not to have any money."

"And, apparently, to grieve."

"And to read too many novels."

"Look, a Mrs. Harriet Stapleton was admitted for 'excessive melancholia.' Mr. Gordon Averin, for 'too much whiskey.' Here's one referred to as a 'raving maniac,' and a twelve-year-old boy who had epileptic fits."

"Look at this one," said Aubrey. "'Hazel, mute. Known as Dummy.'"

"Wow, they weren't terribly sensitive back then, were they?"

"Her name is Hazel," Aubrey said in a hushed tone.

"Whose name is Hazel?"

"I've been trying to figure out who I saw in my photograph, and whether she's the same one that we found today in the hidden chamber. Her story's beginning to come together. Look, Hazel arrived at Seabrink Poor Farm and Asylum at the age of two along with her father, who was described as 'feebleminded,'" Aubrey read. "There's a notation that he died six months later."

"And then she was raised there? At the poor farm?"

"At the bar at St. Ambrose, someone told me the Quiet Girl refused to leave even after the poor farm closed. So she must have stayed on, maybe hiding herself away during renovations, and then . . . in Effie Mae's letter, she mentioned a girl named Dummy working as a maid at the hotel."

"Until she died in the walls."

Aubrey grimaced.

"What was her diagnosis?" Nikki asked.

"Other than mute? I suppose it was being the child of a feebleminded poor man. Wait—there's something scribbled in the margin: 'Mania; Pyromania.' That's right, someone said she was suspected of having started a fire that killed several women. That's why the poor farm closed down."

"If this were a classic ghost tale then she would be trying to tell us something, or maybe wanting her side of the story to be told."

"I was thinking that, myself. The poor thing."

"Or else she's out to exact grisly revenge upon all living humans. Speaking of which, I'm on a twenty-four-hour deadline here, remember?"

"I'm taking my shower now," announced Aubrey. "If you're marked for imminent death, I should at least be presentable for it, right?"

Nikki threw her wet towel at her.

When she emerged from the bathroom, Nikki looked up from her computer.

"I've been thinking: Could Dimitri's death have to do with something valuable he found at the Seabrink? Something like a ferronnière?"

"You mean like the jeweled headband in Mia's 'instant ancestor' photos?"

"Exactly. Mia said her name was Colette, remember?"

"Interesting. I don't think you saw it, but there was a photo at the Seabrink of the same woman dressed as a fairy, and wearing a ferronnière." Aubrey scrolled through her photos until she found the image she had taken of the framed pictures in the library, and showed Nikki.

"Pretty," said Nikki. "So, what if she was Goffin's mistress, and he gave it to her, and it was worth a lot of money?"

"You think it might have been worth enough to kill over?"

"Just an idea. Trying to think outside the box, and all that."

"You know . . . I believe I also saw it on the ghost."

"I'm having a hard time adjusting to the idea that you now believe in ghosts. I mean, after all those years of crawling around abandoned places . . . why now?"

"I'm finding the Hotel Seabrink quite persuasive," Aubrey said, collapsing into the desk chair.

"So, just to be clear, you're talking about the ghost you saw in the photograph that disappeared."

"Right, the photograph which now looks like a black smudge. But why in the world would a poor young maid be wearing a bejeweled headband?"

"Maybe she stole it," Nikki suggested.

"Could be. And after all, if the jewel was worth enough, maybe it would inspire dastardly deeds."

"Such as murder?"

"Possibly? And maybe that's what Cameron was trying to pawn."

"So you're suggesting Cameron followed you and Dimitri back here that night, then somehow lured Dimitri out onto the bluff at four in the morning to steal the jewel from him and pushed him off the cliff? That only works if Dimitri had the jewel on him, doesn't it?"

"Or maybe Dimitri saw Cameron pocket the thing at the Seabrink, and Cameron wanted to shut him up?" Aubrey suggested.

"But then shouldn't he have killed you, as well? He couldn't be sure you didn't see him take it, too, or that Dimitri didn't tell you he saw Cameron taking it. All of which assumes the jewel would be worth killing for. Is it?"

"No idea. Not really a jewelry girl." Aubrey sighed and got up to put Fleetwood Mac on the record player. Stevie Nicks singing "I don't want to know" always reminded her of her mother, emotions that were . . . complicated. Still. Better to be haunted by her family history than by what happened to Dimitri, or to the poor Quiet Girl at the Hotel Seabrink.

"I wish it were easier to read Dimitri's handwriting," Aubrey said, flipping through the pages of his journal. "I keep thinking there must be something in here that might be a clue."

"You know, I saw that same symbol in Mia's shop," Nikki said, looking over Aubrey's shoulder.

"This one?" Aubrey pointed to a small sketch of a stylized cross, dissected by several crooked lines and circles. "It was in Mia's shop?"

"Yeah, it was on the jars of salve and salts she sells."

"Huh, the first time I went to the Seabrink it was on the front door, and then we saw it drawn on a stone when we went to the spring, remember? I have a couple of photos of it . . ."

"Send them to me," Nikki suggested. "I'll do an image search."

After a few minutes she shook her head. "I don't see anything, but it might not be reading it properly since it's handdrawn and sort of wonky. Anyway, I think I've had just about enough of murder talk for the evening," Nikki said, slamming shut her laptop. "I've got an idea! Let's read your tarot cards."

"No. *Freaking.* Way," said Aubrey. "We don't need any more conduits for spirits around here."

"Sheesh," Nikki said with a sigh. "One afternoon finding a dead body and being chased through a tunnel by unknown and possibly murderous individuals and you lose your moxie. I don't know what you're so worried about—*I'm* the one who was cursed, remember?"

Aubrey picked up the hotel phone and started dialing room

service. "How about I make it up to you by ordering us some dinner and a bottle of wine?"

"I knew there was a reason we're friends, Spencer."

Aubrey smiled and ordered room service.

But the image of Hazel lingered in her mind, and now, somehow, in her heart.

NINETEEN

Aubrey woke up the next morning at precisely 4:07 a.m.

Surely it was nothing more than her own mind playing tricks. She had noticed the time on the grandfather clock at the Seabrink, and then when Xavi confirmed that Dimitri had left the hotel shortly after four, her mind conflated the two and then her internal alarm clock roused her at that time.

Aubrey lay awake for a long time, listening to Nikki's steady, deep breathing. When she finally fell back asleep, she dreamed of glass raining down on her. And then she and Nikki were being chased through long, endless corridors and secret passages of the Hotel Seabrink. No matter where they turned, they ran into Hazel, wearing the ferronière along with her stained apron.

She danced and smiled, then held her finger to her lips in an eerie *Shhhhhhhh*.

Aubrey woke with a start, grabbed her computer, and started to scroll through the photographs she had transferred from her camera. She paid special attention to those she had taken on or near the attic stairs.

When she applied colored filters, images seemed to emerge, right before her eyes.

Just as before, she saw the girl's strangely distorted countenance looking directly into the camera, holding her finger to her lips, and smiling. She wore the ferronnière on her head, and held a little flageolet flute in her hand.

The flute that Aubrey kept hearing, emanating from behind the walls of the Hotel Seabrink.

Why don't you let me drive today?" Nikki offered over coffee later that morning, noting how tired Aubrey was. "You can take a catnap on the way to Sea Ranch."

"You've got yourself a deal," Aubrey said with a jaw-cracking yawn.

On the way, they stopped in at Twofish Baking, located in the Stewarts Point Store, which also boasted old-fashioned candies, handmade gifts, classic sodas, and local wines.

"Oh, I remember you!" said the teenage girl behind the counter upon spying Aubrey. She had huge brown eyes and a mass of mahogany curls. "I was afraid you were dead! My cousin said there was another body discovered there, just yesterday! He's a deputy with the sheriff's department. Kenny Jenkins."

"We've met," Aubrey said. "He's your cousin? Small world."

"I knew a guy in high school who went to the Seabrink and he, like, *died*. And my cousin knew someone else that happened to, too." She placed half a dozen sticky buns in a pink box. "So, I'm really glad you're not dead. I would feel so guilty for telling you about it."

"Thanks," Aubrey said. "Still alive, as you can see."

"Easy for you to say," Nikki mumbled as she placed a roll of Necco Wafers on the counter. "You're not the one who saw the ghost."

"You *saw* the *ghost*?" the girl asked, her eyes wide, her voice scaling up.

"No one saw anything," insisted Aubrey as they turned to leave. "Thanks for the sticky buns."

"Why am I not surprised you know the kid at the bakery, too?" Nikki asked as they carried the baked goods out to the car.

"As a matter of fact, she was the first local I met outside the Driftwood Cove Inn. She's the one who told me how to get to the Hotel Seabrink."

"She's Patient Zero, eh? Maybe *she's* the killer. She lures people up to the abandoned hotel, then follows them home and makes sure the curse comes true. Innocent-seeming teenager, gooey sticky buns, Dead Man's Bluff . . . classic B movie fodder."

Twenty minutes later they pulled into the Sea Ranch development and drove past a manicured golf course and a smattering of angular homes tucked beneath ancient, twisted cypress trees. In between houses and hiking trails were great swaths of lupine-filled meadows, twisting cypress groves, and Monterrey pine forests. Half a dozen deer grazed in a meadow, unfazed by the humans.

"We studied Sea Ranch in my architecture program," said Aubrey. "The founders established it in the seventies, envisioning a different kind of coastal development, one focusing on communal living and a continuous interaction with the natural world."

"Doesn't really give me seventies commune vibes, I gotta

say," said Nikki, craning her neck to check out a large, asymmetrical structure with two decks and a small tower that looked like a crow's nest.

"I get the sense the original mission mutated a bit in the intervening decades." Aubrey consulted her phone. "Deborah Goldman's house should be just up ahead."

"A house on the ocean," murmured Nikki with a little sigh as she parked in a small pullout designated for visitors.

"Right? Life goals."

Only the bluff trail and a small meadow stood between Goldman's house and the cliffs above the water. The early morning fog was just beginning to burn off and ghostly fingers of mist lingered along the bluff and the rock outcroppings. The air was damp, redolent of sage and brine, and the roar of the nearby crashing waves vied with the calls of seagulls.

Aubrey knocked on the solid wooden front door and a great kerfuffle ensued as two miniature bull terriers rushed to greet them, barking hysterically through the sidelight windows. The door opened a crack to reveal a smiling woman in her seventies, hale and hearty in the way of a lifelong hiker, wearing jeans and a red Patagonia vest over a long-sleeved, black T-shirt.

"Welcome! Don't mind the dogs. They're loud, but friendly," she said as she attempted, without success, to hold the dogs back with her leg. "Albert and Louise are their names. I'm Deborah Goldman. Call me Deb. You must be Aubrey."

"I am, yes. And this is my friend Nikki Politis," Aubrey said.

Nikki held up the TwoFish bag. "We brought sticky buns."

"Wonderful! I made scones, but TwoFish sticky buns are

the *best*. It's lovely to meet you both," Deborah gushed, waving them in. "Come in, come in. We're all ready for you. And hush, you two," she said in the dogs' general direction. "*Hush*, I say!"

Albert and Louise ignored her, barking excitedly and running around the main living area.

The home was fragrant with coffee and freshly baked scones. Skylights in the soaring cathedral ceilings and an ocean-facing wall of huge windows filled the space with light. Golden wood detailing reflected the light in a warm amber glow. The main room was separated from the kitchen only by a tall counter with stools, and a hallway at the end of the main room led to what Aubrey presumed were the bedrooms and baths. A set of sliding glass doors at the other end of the room opened onto an enclosed wooden porch overlooking the water. In an alcove near the kitchen was a large dining table covered in photograph albums, magazines, and scattered papers.

"What a lovely home," Nikki said.

"Oh, thank you! My late husband and I bought this place *years* ago, and I am so glad we did. Goodness knows, we could never afford it today. But isn't that always the way? Now, come, let me introduce you to a friend of mine."

A man in his seventies got up from a leather armchair, held out his hand, and introduced himself as Gideon Sims.

"Gideon, is it?" Nikki asked as she and Aubrey exchanged a glance.

"Please, have a seat, won't you?" said Deborah, gesturing to the sectional sofa surrounding a low coffee table laden with baked goods, cream and sugar, mugs and spoons. "I'll just put these delicious sticky buns on a platter. These are from TwoFish, Gideon! Such a treat."

"This really is so kind of you to talk with us," said Aubrey.

"Nonsense," Deborah said as she set the plate of sticky buns on the crowded coffee table, handed them each an earthenware mug of steaming coffee, and joined them on the sofa. "It's my favorite thing, speaking with young people such as yourselves. I spent years doing so—I was a university archivist, you know. Sometimes I miss those days."

Aubrey and Nikki smiled at being referred to as "young people," as if they were freshmen working on a research paper.

"Gideon, tell them who you are," Deborah urged. He opened his mouth, but before he could speak, she continued, "Gideon used to teach at Stanford. Tell them, Gideon."

"Theoretical geology," he blurted out.

"Oh, really? I never realized that geology could be theoretical," said Aubrey. "It seems so . . ."

"Rock-solid," said Nikki.

"Exactly," Aubrey said with a smile.

"A lot of people react that way," replied Gideon, apparently failing to see the humor.

There was an awkward pause.

"So," said Deborah as she offered them cream and sugar. "You have questions about the old Hotel Seabrink. It was still in use, you know, when some of the older locals were children—after the hotel itself closed, it was used briefly as a nursing home. Well into the late 1960s, I believe. But then it was left to rot."

"I tried researching it online," said Aubrey, "but found almost nothing."

"This is one of those subjects for which brick-and-mortar libraries are still the most useful. There's plenty that either never makes it onto the web, or—in the case of the Seabrink—gets taken down shortly after it's posted."

"Do you have any idea who's responsible for that, and why?" Nikki asked.

"The owners, of course," said Gideon emphatically, sitting forward on the couch. "They try to keep the bad news out of the public's view, and when it comes to the Seabrink, it's all bad news."

"Oh, I wanted to show you something," said Deborah, pulling an oversize album from the shelf under the coffee table and handing it to Aubrey. "It's my Seabrink scrapbook."

"You made this?" asked Nikki, touching the beautifully bound and intricately decorated album.

"I can't help myself," Deborah said with a chuckle. "I'm a scrapbooker of the first order. I began cutting out and painting paper dolls when I was a girl, and just never quit. Whenever I find photos or ephemera or the like, I turn it into a scrapbook. I started that one years ago. It doesn't have all that much, but I thought you'd be interested."

Within the album were a few old receipts for items such as laundry and kitchen supplies, similar to the ones they had found in the attic of the Seabrink yesterday. There was a matchbook and a napkin with HOTEL SEABRINK printed on one corner, and a picture of a frosted highball glass etched with the hotel's name. There were also several newspaper articles from over the years: an announcement that the hotel was closing, a mention of the nursing home opening. One old photograph showed a baseball game on the grounds.

"There was a baseball team?" Nikki asked. "Cool."

"Nikki's a jock," Aubrey explained to Deborah and Gideon.

"Do you play?" asked Deborah.

"I wouldn't say I'm a jock, though I *am* the star pitcher for my company softball team. I've got a wicked throwing arm."

Deborah smiled. "I believe that photo was taken back

during World War Two. Things were . . . different then. The Hotel Seabrink was very exclusive, but occasionally the public was invited to an event such as a baseball game. It was long before my time, of course, but I've heard stories."

Aubrey turned a page and recognized one of the photos: the French woman she had seen among Mia's "instant ancestors," and also among the framed photographs in the library at the Hotel Seabrink. The one with the headband and the jewel right in the middle of her forehead.

"I'm curious about this woman," Aubrey said. "Do you know anything about her?"

"Not much. She was what they called a starlet back in the day. Apparently she was French, a talented musician, and she was a favorite of T. Jefferson Goffin, the founder of the Hotel Seabrink." There was a pause. "According to legend, she died a tragic death."

"Did she see the ghost?" Nikki asked. Aubrey gazed at her friend, wondering if she were truly convinced she was now cursed and was soon bumping up against her twenty-four-hour time limit.

"Oh no, nothing like that. I always heard she jumped from the balcony, poor dear. Probably done in by the fickle whims of Hollywood, or some such."

"Here's something I was hoping you could clarify," said Aubrey. "The Seabrink was a luxury hotel—"

"*Very* luxurious, back in the day."

"But . . . it started out as a poor farm? Did I get that right?"

"Oh yes, originally. Goffin bought the old Seabrink Poor Farm and Asylum and transformed it into a luxury hotel, touting the miracle of its healing mineral water. Never should have kept the name, if you ask me. The road to the Seabrink is still called Asylum Point, after the poor farm."

"This is probably an ignorant question," said Nikki. "But what exactly is a poor farm?"

"It was a type of poorhouse, a place where destitute people lived and worked to pay for their support. Back in the nineteenth century, before things like social security and welfare, counties were legally responsible for their destitute citizens. Poorhouses and poor farms became popular as a way to economize on supporting those in need. Poor farms were actual working farms, the theory being that the agricultural life might help folks turn their fortune around, teach them skills, that sort of thing."

"Doesn't seem like the worst idea in the world," said Nikki, "to give people a place to live, and wholesome work."

"It's not a bad idea in theory, but in reality that's not always how it worked. Of course there are positive examples of such places, but often they were horrifically exploitive. More prosperous citizens often resented paying the poor tax, and so officials often cut corners and skimped wherever they could. In many cases the poor farm was less a refuge for those in need than a place of last resort, where desperate people with no other option than homelessness and starvation went to labor and die. At the Seabrink Poor Farm, the residents were required to give all their worldly goods to the superintendent upon entering. And unfortunately, the Seabrink superintendent, Gerald Cottrell, was not known for his kindness. A lot of inmates died during his tenure. According to rumor, the town would send charitable gifts of food and clothes and books and the like to the inmates, but the Cottrells diverted most of it to their own use and comfort."

"We saw some of the supposed 'diagnoses' of what ailed the inmates," said Aubrey. "Things like 'reading too much,' of all things?"

Deborah nodded. "It was not uncommon for men who tired of their wives to claim they were beyond help—too melancholy, that sort of thing—and dump them at poor farms."

"Seems a poor choice to turn such a place into a luxury hotel," Nikki said.

"It's not that odd, if you think about it. Nineteenth-century asylums were often good-sized and well-built, at times even beautiful, architecturally speaking. The poor farm finally closed after the building was severely damaged in a fire. Several of the inmates in the ladies' ward died."

"They were locked in, supposedly 'for their own safety,'" said Gideon. "Couldn't escape."

"How awful," said Nikki. "Was there an investigation?"

"They blamed it on a girl who lived there, but I don't think they did a real investigation," said Deborah. "Nobody cared enough to bother. After the fire, T. Jefferson Goffin tried to buy the poor farm for a bargain price, given that it was so heavily damaged. But the county decided instead to cede the land to a local grange, which is a kind of agricultural cooperative. The sense was that the building itself, which had seen so much misery, should no longer be inhabited. But once again, tragedy struck: the main advocate for the grange was gunned down on the property. Goffin made another offer, and this time the county accepted."

"What a lucky break for Goffin," Nikki said wryly.

"Did anyone suspect Goffin of being behind the murder?" Aubrey asked.

"Oh, there were rumors, of course, but nothing ever came of it. The man who died was a humble local fellow, a farmer and rancher, whereas Goffin . . ."

"Was a wildly wealthy capitalist," said Gideon. "The kind

who thinks he can get away with anything because, by and large, he can."

"After Goffin bought the Seabrink, he launched a grand renovation and added the Spanish Gothic flourishes," said Deborah. "He tried to rebrand the place, and went so far as to suppress news stories about it having once been an asylum—Goffin had plenty of money and connections, so he was able to bribe or pressure newspaper publishers into doing what he wanted."

"I understand that even now someone regularly monitors the internet and somehow manages to take down stories about the Seabrink," said Aubrey.

"Sounds like something the Goffin family would do," said Gideon. "True to form, their type think they can get away without consequences, just like their old patriarch."

"Well, I believe in karma," said Deborah. "And even the very rich are not immune from tragedy. T. Jefferson Goffin's young son was suffering from leukemia. It has been suggested that one reason Goffin wanted so badly to acquire the Seabrink is that he thought the waters might save his son."

"Did he live?"

She shook her head. "Sadly, no. He lingered for a while, but passed before his eighth birthday."

"Is he buried on the property?" Aubrey asked. "According to the poor farm documents, there used to be a cemetery in one corner of the grounds, but we didn't see it."

"No, I believe they paved right over those graves," said Deborah. "Anyway, supposedly the boy was Goffin's only direct heir."

"You have your doubts?"

"A man like Goffin . . ." Deborah trailed off with a shrug. "In addition to his wife, Goffin was known to keep several girl-friends and mistresses. Hard to believe there weren't other children, somewhere. There were even rumors that he impregnated a local girl, one of the maids at the Hotel Seabrink."

"Do you know her name?" asked Aubrey.

Deborah laughed. "Oh no, of course not. It's just a rumor."

"Did you happen to meet a man named Dimitri Petroff when he was in town?" Aubrey asked.

"Dimitri Petroff?" She and Gideon exchanged a look, and after a pause, she said: "Yes, he came asking about his biological grandmother, or great-grandmother, maybe? Supposedly she was born in this area, and he was adopted so he was investigating his genealogical line. One's bloodline is so important for one's sense of identity, isn't it? We couldn't believe it when we heard what happened. Suicide? Poor fellow."

"Listen," said Gideon, apparently bored with the direction of their conversation. "The Seabrink is special, and not only for historical reasons. There are pneumatic forces there, a kind of crossing over and coming together of energetic lines, and the power lines up there are—"

"I apologize for interrupting," said Aubrey. "But what do you mean by 'pneumatic' forces? As in tires? Or . . . drills?"

"No, no, no. Don't be silly," Gideon scoffed. "As in the 'pneuma,' or 'spirit.' The vital spirit, soul, or creative force. The word is Latin and relates to wind or breath. It has come to be used for machinery that uses forced air to work, like drills, but originally it referred to spirit—which also refers to breath."

Aubrey thought of the phrase "Breathe me in before taking me out."

"People find the concept hard to believe," Gideon continued. "But I know what I'm talking about. The reason the waters are so special is that there are ancient travertine and onyx deposits at the mouth of the spring. And I'm not the only one who thinks so. Why do you think the volunteer fire department and paramedics have their ritual initiations up there?"

"Now, Gideon," interrupted Deb. "I really don't think—"

"I know what I know. I saw the marking on the front door with my own eyes."

"Be that as it may . . ." Deb said and turned to Aubrey. "This is one reason Gideon is so determined to fight the developers in court, isn't it, Gideon?"

"Have you heard of the Suicide Club?" Gideon blurted out.

"The what?" Nikki said, confused.

"It began as a commentary on modern society," said Gideon pompously. "Like so many things, its original meaning was lost when it became more popular. Just like Burning Man; in the beginning it meant something. They were important, surreal commentaries on society, informed by the surrealist works of Dada and the Dadaists. Not everything is about money, you know. I—"

"Now, Gideon, we're getting off on tangents," Deb said. "It may seem like a rather quixotic quest to save the Seabrink from development, but after all, so was Sea Ranch, back in the day." She shook her head and let out a sigh. "We hippies were such idealists back then. It was a lovely time."

"But now we're where we are, aren't we?" Gideon said, glaring at her. "The point is, the old Hotel Seabrink should be left to those with an interest in history, not just making money. And we've gained traction lately, uniting our struggle with a group in Ukiah who are opposing a new spa in their area, too. Anyway, the actual title to the land on which Seabrink sits is murky, and so who has a legal claim to the land is in dispute. Since Goffin left no heirs—"

"—as far as we know." Deb cast a knowing glance at Nikki and Aubrey.

"Yes, as far as we know, there are no direct heirs," said Gideon. "The extended family feels they have the rightful claim but apparently the land deed was never transferred to them. Or perhaps it was, but if so there's no record of when that occurred, and that's a problem. As if the Goffin heirs need more money. This whole thing reminds me of what happened with the Bohemian Club on the Russian River. Have you heard of it? Their motto is 'Weaving spiders come not here.'"

"I saw that quote written on the walls of the hotel," said Aubrey.

"You see! It's all connected!" Gideon sounded triumphant, but Aubrey failed to follow his line of thinking.

"In any case," Deborah said, interrupting Gideon again. "That's the story of the Seabrink in a nutshell. It was built as a poor farm, was briefly ceded to the grange, but then Goffin moved in on it and established his hotel. Afterward, the family leased it to the nursing home for a short time, but they didn't renovate—much less maintain—the building. The nursing home closed after failing a state inspection, and the building was left to decay. The Goffin family had security guards there for a while, but one of them murdered a teenage girl in one of the mineral baths. Since then, it's mostly just gawkers and trespassers going up there."

"Those who are courageous enough, or stupid enough, to brave the curse," added Gideon.

"I have to admit that I was one of the trespassers," said Aubrey. "I didn't hurt anything, of course, but I did go in."

"I heard it through the grapevine," Deborah said with a wink. "We're all achatter about you around here, aren't we, Gideon?"

"One thing I don't understand: why hasn't the hotel been stripped of everything?" said Aubrey. "It's scarcely been touched. There are even old-fashioned skeleton keys behind the front desk."

"Not to mention an old-fashioned *skeleton*," muttered Nikki under her breath, taking a big bite out of a sticky bun.

Deborah froze. Gideon leaned forward, an eager glint in his eye.

"Did I say that out loud?" asked Nikki.

"A what, now?" said Deborah.

"A skeleton?" asked Gideon.

"We . . . we were there yesterday and happened upon a body," said Aubrey, and then clarified: "An *old* body, of a young woman or girl, it looked like."

"Oh, *my*," breathed Deborah. "There are so many rumors about starlets up there, do you think she was one of them?"

"More likely a maid, I think," said Aubrey. "She was wearing an apron."

Gideon sprang out of his chair. "They'd better not try to use this as yet another stalling tactic. I'm telling you, you have no idea what's going on up there. The pneuma, the absurdity of life . . . They'll be putting surveillance cameras up there, hooking it all up to the internet . . . All of this is more important than any tourist destination. Nice to meet you both, but I'm leaving. I need to make some phone calls."

The three of them watched as he stormed out of the house, the dogs barking happily and chasing him to the door.

"Pay him no mind," Deborah said. "Gideon feels his feelings, which is a good thing, and I thought you might want his perspective on the Seabrink—though I don't entirely agree with him, and some of his thinking is, admittedly, a bit hard to follow. Still, our fundraising efforts have been rather pathetic. And after all, perhaps it would be better to have it redeveloped by someone with deep pockets, especially if the local community has some input into the design. I mean . . . unless it's returned to the native people, the Kashia, of course."

"You don't share his thoughts on the existence of special energies?" asked Nikki.

"I do believe there are special energies there, probably due to the salts in the mineral water or something along those lines. But Gideon is also afraid that the power lines and the introduction of the internet, and that sort of thing, are going to be the end of civilization as we know it."

"What was all that about the paramedics having initiation rituals . . . ?"

Deb waved the air, as if shooing away a gnat. "Gideon says he went up there once and witnessed something suspicious. But you know, with all that talk of the Suicide Club and whatnot, I wouldn't take it too seriously. I mean, think about it: What do the Dadaists have to do with haunted hotels, for heaven's sake?"

TWENTY

"What do the Dadaists have to do with haunted hotels?'" intoned Nikki as they headed to the car. "I'm going to use that as a conversation starter the next time there's an awkward pause at a swanky cocktail party."

Aubrey chuckled. "It'll inspire either total silence, or a really interesting discussion."

"This is what I'm thinking. Where to now?" Nikki said, talking over the roof of the car as she started to open the driver's door. "According to my calculations, this might be my last afternoon."

"Nikki, I know we're joking, but do you really think you saw something?"

"I know I saw something. Seriously. On the other hand, I mean, I suppose it could have been my imagination. For some reason, I don't feel like that poor girl would try to curse me. I know it sounds weird, and I was more than a little freaked out when we first found her. But I get the strangest sensation that she's not afraid of us. Or angry with us."

Aubrey nodded. "You know . . . this doesn't pertain to murders, or hauntings for that matter, but while we're here, want to visit the rookery? It should be the season for baby harbor seals. According to my phone it's within walking distance."

"Baby seals? Sounds like the perfect antidote to the last couple of days."

They walked to the bluff trail that ran along the beach cliffs and followed it north. Before long they came across a turnout overlooking a small sand beach where a number of huge rocks emerged from the water, forming mini islands. The rocks were covered with what looked at first glance like light gray and beige driftwood, until the "logs," one by one, turned their heads toward Nikki and Aubrey watching them from the top of the cliff.

A large wooden sign reminded visitors to keep their voices down so as not to disturb the wildlife. Harbor seals have exquisite hearing.

"Check out the babies!" Nikki exclaimed in a whisper.

After the past few days, the reminder of new life was a balm to the soul. Aubrey had brought her camera and started snapping photos, zooming in on the seals' large black eyes and puppy-dog snouts. The pups lolled on their chubby tummies next to their equally plump mamas. Every once in a while, one would wiggle its way to the rock's edge and jump into the water with a splash.

Aubrey and Nikki lingered for a while, savoring the sight and enjoying the salty ocean air.

Next to the rookery was Shell Beach, so they decided to take a walk along the water. The day had turned sunny but was windy and cold, and they had the beach almost to themselves. Only one other couple was there, huddling under a blanket with a big black dog at their side. Nikki started pitching stones far into the water, demonstrating her famous soft-ball arm. The dog, excited to make a new friend and no doubt wondering why Nikki was wasting her energy on rocks, ran over to drop his slobbery ball at her feet.

She obliged, throwing it clear down the shoreline.

Aubrey perched on a large, sun-warmed rock and took a few photos of Nikki and the dog, the crashing waves, and several close-ups of the moss living in the cracks and fissures of the rocks. She had a visual of Dimitri showing her the guest room at the Seabrink, where moss was growing on the bed-covers.

Moss barely has any roots, yet it endures in the crevices, and flourishes in the broken parts.

Just then the dog, ball still in its mouth, came careening across the sand, splashing through the shallows and chasing after a flock of snow-white seabirds that had been pecking at the sand. The birds took flight as the dog neared, then landed on the other end of the beach. The dog spun around and gamely ran full tilt toward them, but the birds took off once again and returned to their original spot on the sand. The dog and the birds repeated this back-and-forth several times.

Aubrey took several shots of the joyful canine as Nikki came to join her on the rock.

"I'm beginning to feel like that dog," said Aubrey. "Chasing up and down and getting nowhere."

"I don't know about that," said Nikki, nudging Aubrey with her shoulder. "According to Gideon, there are mysterious oc-cult rituals at the Seabrink."

"Involving the volunteer emergency personnel? Why do I find that hard to believe?"

"What was all that Gideon was saying about the Suicide Club?"

"I remember reading about it, and he's right that it later became known as the Cacophony Society, and helped to found the Urbex movement."

"Which is . . . what?"

"'Urbex' refers to urban exploration, hence the name. Similar to how I like to explore abandoned places, but focused on cities. There's a philosophy attached to it, about searching out the unusual and the out of the ordinary and rising above the everyday. There's also a pretty strict code of conduct, as in not stealing from the places they explore. Not that everyone lives up to it."

"Interesting. So what does that tell us?"

"Exactly nothing, as far as I can tell," said Aubrey. "At the moment, I'm interested in speaking with the folks who want to develop the hotel, hear their side of things. Which reminds me, I need to follow up with the architect heading up the project." Aubrey scrounged around in her bag until she located the business card Cameron had given her and dialed the number. Aadarshini Obeyesekere seemed to be expecting the call, and invited Aubrey to her house in Gualala tomorrow morning.

"I've been thinking," said Nikki. "Dimitri had a deal with Netflix for a series based on his YouTube videos, right?"

"That's what he said."

"Why don't I put out some feelers, see if I can out find anything about him from that angle? Netflix might have an emergency contact, or something along those lines."

"That's brilliant. But how does a person get in touch with someone at Netflix?"

"If a person works in the industry, she makes a phone call. Also, if you're willing to part with Dimitri's thumb drive, I'll send it to that friend of mine to see if he's able to hack into it."

"I love knowing people who know people," said Aubrey as they started back to the car. "Makes me feel like I'm part of the 'in' crowd."

As they shook the sand from their shoes, Nikki gazed at Deborah Goldman's house. "Sooo, Deb's a scrapbooker."

"That she is," Aubrey said as Nikki pulled out of the spot and drove down the winding road, passing a small flock of sheep. The lambs gamboled in small groups, dashing around the staid adults in adorably fluffy ovine gangs. "What are we thinking? That Deborah Goldman is sending me threatening notes? I mean, would a woman like Deborah Goldman even use the term 'bitch'? That sounds like someone a lot younger."

"Older people can be just as nasty as younger people."

"True enough, but would a woman of her generation—she has to be at least in her mid-seventies—use that word?"

"Instead of what?"

"I don't know, 'wretch,' or 'floozy'?"

"'Floozy'? Did she used to frequent dime-a-dance dance halls, too?" Nikki said with a laugh as she slowed for a golf cart crossing the road. "She's not a hundred and ten."

"You know what I mean."

"She worked with college students until fairly recently. Odds are good she kept up with youthful slang, daddy-o. But I agree—it would seem to be very out of character for her. Maybe Gideon helped himself to Deborah's scrapbooking supplies."

"That's a little easier to believe. And yet . . . I mean, he's definitely on the offbeat side, but did he feel threatening to you?"

"No, but as we both know, I'm not always the best judge of character," Nikki said.

"If anything, Gideon would *want* us to dig up dirt on the

Seabrink, wouldn't he?" Aubrey asked. "It seems like it would make the sale that much less attractive."

"Good point. I have to say, though, it's pretty galling being lectured to about the unimportance of money by a Stanford professor living in Sea Ranch."

She pulled up to the stop sign at Highway One. "So, suppose there's a store in town that sells underwear?"

"I can't think of any place," said Aubrey. "Gourmet cheeses, fresh-caught salmon, and books, yes, but underwear? Not so much."

"In that case, I really should put in a few hours of work," Nikki said, checking the time. "I mean, I hate to shirk my detective responsibilities, but my other job pays the rent, and it comes with dental."

Aubrey chuckled. "Let's head back to the hotel. I want to go through that poor farm ledger more carefully and try to decipher more of Dimitri's journal."

"I've been thinking," said Nikki as they drove south, the ocean offering a magnificent vista on this sunny day. "Is it possible someone followed you and Dimitri after you left the Hotel Seabrink that night?"

"I don't think so," Aubrey said. "I left first, and Dimitri followed me back to Driftwood Cove. But I wasn't really paying attention, so it's possible. Why?"

"How would anyone know he was at the Driftwood Cove Inn? He wasn't an official guest; he was staying at the St. Ambrose."

"I was wondering about that, too. He did post a video about the Seabrink to his YouTube channel that night. Is there any way someone could find out where he was posting from?"

"Sure, through geotags. Or if someone had an in with the

sheriff's office. Or if someone had accessed his phone or his car and was tracking him that way."

"Still—if someone saw the video and figured out where he was, they would . . . what? Race to Driftwood Cove to kill him?"

"It would have to be someone local, then, someone he knew, right?" said Nikki. "They must have texted or called to lure him outside. Unless he had a prearranged four a.m. meeting on Dead Man's Bluff, which seems unlikely. Too bad you turned over his phone to Deputy Doofus. That might have answered a lot of these questions. I don't suppose you could get it back?"

"I could try, but I wouldn't bet on it. And even if I could lay my hands on it, I don't know his password—I just saw the one message because it popped up on his screen."

"If we had the phone, I could see if my techie friend in Emeryville could hack into it."

"Can't hurt to try," said Aubrey, already dialing Deputy Jenkins.

"Before you ask," Jenkins said upon answering, "it's gonna take a while to identify that body. You're not back at the old hotel, are you? 'Cause if you are, I'm gonna have to have a serious chat with you about disturbing a possible crime scene. I am not kidding."

"No, Deputy, I'm nowhere near the Seabrink," Aubrey said, annoyed. *It's not like* we *killed her,* she thought. *We just* found *her.* She could hear him muttering about out-of-towners making his life difficult. "I'm calling to ask if I could have Dimitri's phone back."

"'Fraid that's not possible. We located his family. Ran his fingerprints. Turns out this particular individual had a different name when he was younger."

"Roger Harmon?"

Deputy Jenkins was silent for a moment. "How did you know that?"

"Wild guess," she said, only then realizing that she should have shared that information with the authorities as soon as she discovered it. "Would it be possible to have the family's contact information? I'd love to meet them."

"Look: They seem like a real nice, normal family . . . you're not gonna harass them or anything, are you?"

"Of course not. I have some photos of Dimitri—"

"You mean Roger."

"Fine, Roger. I have some photos of him I thought they might like."

"Tell you what, I'll see if they're okay with me sharing their information and if so, I'll pass it along. One thing, though: don't go torturing them with ideas of Dimitri, or Roger, being murdered. Suicide is hard enough to cope with. The poor family doesn't need any more pain."

It was a surprisingly sensitive thing for Deputy Jenkins to say, so Aubrey responded gently: "Of course. I understand."

thought this was the offseason," Aubrey said to Xavi, the hotel desk clerk, as she and Nikki walked into the Driftwood Cove's suddenly crowded lobby.

Xavi hurriedly put down his phone and straightened, like a kid being called out by his teacher. "Oh, yeah, it totally is. That's why Monica, like, rents out the rooms for conferences and stuff? This place is real popular for business retreats. One starts today, so a lot of people are checking in."

"What kind of conference is it?" Nikki asked.

"Watchmakers and, like, watch repair people? I guess?"

"Really? I love that there are enough watchmakers to make a convention," said Nikki. "I never think about that sort of thing. Do people still wear watches? I mean, old-fashioned watches?"

"Some must," said Aubrey. "I just look at my phone."

"Speaking of phones," said Monica, approaching the reception desk. She glared at Xavi. "Where is your phone supposed to be, Xavi?"

"In the drawer, ma'am," he mumbled, opening a drawer and dropping his phone in.

"Thank you." Monica rolled her eyes as she turned back to Aubrey and Nikki. "Young people today don't know how to handle boredom. So yeah, a watchmaker convention. Kind of cool in a steampunk sort of way, right?"

"I'd say slightly more AARP than steampunk," murmured Aubrey. Most of the crowd sported gray hair and appeared to be in their sixties or seventies. "But definitely cool."

Monica dropped her voice and said: "Is it true what I heard? You found a body at the Hotel Seabrink?"

Nikki nodded. "It was an old one, though. She appears to have been deceased for many years."

"Oh, good, then," said Monica, though she seemed vaguely disappointed. "And you both survived, I see."

"Alive and kicking," Aubrey confirmed.

"So far," said Nikki.

"Sir, please be careful with those," Monica said as she hurried over to a conventioneer who was pretending to throw one of the records like a frisbee.

"Let the hijinks begin," Nikki said as she and Aubrey headed upstairs.

"You know, part of me finds small-town life really charming," Aubrey said. "But I'm not sure I could get used to everyone being all up in my business, all the time."

"Right? Word sure does spread quickly around here. I blame the sticky bun girl. She's a talker, and apparently has sources."

They worked in their room for the next few hours, Nikki on the bed with her laptop propped on a pillow and Aubrey at the desk, reading through the poor farm ledger and sorting through more of the photographs she had taken at the Seabrink. She paused at a photo of the big, algae-covered fountain in front of the hotel. It was in the style of a classic Renaissance sculpture, which seemed like an odd choice with which to welcome the fabulous Hollywood types to the Spanish Gothic–style Seabrink.

"Whatcha doing?" Nikki asked as she rubbed her eyes and stretched.

"I was just thinking about the Erinyes, otherwise known as the Furies."

"Oh, sure. Me too," snarked Nikki. "Remind me? I'm not up on my Greek legends."

"They went after those who commit atrocities, such as murder and betrayal. They're described as relentless, the personification of a guilty conscience in an era before modern psychology."

"Well, good for them. Sort of like karma."

"Did you notice? At the Seabrink, there's a sculpture of the Erinyes in the front fountain. It's a big one."

"And?"

"I'm thinking Goffin had a guilty conscience."

"Unless they're psychopaths, most wildly rich men back in the day had a guilty conscience. Probably do today, as well."

"Funny, Dimitri said something along those lines. Deb Goldman mentioned that Goffin wanted the hotel, but the county ceded the land to the grange instead."

"Until the grange guy was shot."

"Exactly. Suppose Goffin had the head of the grange killed so he could take over the building?"

"Not hard to believe. But what does that tell us?"

"Nothing, really. But I'm becoming increasingly curious about T. Jefferson Goffin. Everything I can find about him online is pretty unremarkable, standard 'scrappy white guy makes good' kind of stuff. I can't help thinking there's more, a *lot* more, to his story. Maybe I'm just frustrated because there's almost nothing about the Hotel Seabrink anywhere. None of this makes any sense, and I can't figure out how it would be related to what happened to Dimitri."

"You know, most murders are really just stupid. No deep motives at all."

Blowing out an exasperated breath, Aubrey turned back to her computer, distracting herself by flipping through today's photos. She smiled at the harbor seal babies and the big black dog running with joyous abandon after the birds.

She sat up: a man was standing on the bluff overlooking the beach. He was tall and well-built, probably in his thirties. He was too far away to be sure about his features, but he appeared to be holding a cigarette to his mouth, and there was something about the way he held himself . . .

"You okay?" Nikki asked. "You didn't see another ghost, did you?"

"No, but . . . Nikki, is this who I think it is?" She brought her computer over to Nikki to show her the photograph.

Nikki went pale.

TWENTY-ONE

"Maybe I didn't escape the Seabrink curse, after all."

"Don't say that," said Aubrey.

"But it's *Ty*, isn't it? This is from earlier today? At Shell Beach."

Aubrey nodded. "But how on earth did he know we were there?"

"He installed spyware on my last phone, remember? Maybe . . . maybe he somehow got to the new one, too. Or he could have put a tracking device on my car, he's done that before. I thought he had backed off."

"We *hoped* he had backed off. To tell the truth, it seemed too easy to be true."

"*Damn*." Nikki rubbed her temples, her voice tight with tears. "When will this be over?"

"I'll call Deputy Jenkins," Aubrey said, reaching for her phone.

"Wait—Ty hasn't actually violated the restraining order, at least as far as we know. He's more than one hundred feet away and didn't do anything overt."

"Still, we should let local authorities know about it, just in case."

"Do you think Ty was the one who locked us in, and chased us, at the Hotel Seabrink?"

"Good question. Could be."

"I mean . . . who knows how long he's been tracking me? Or us. Maybe he really is behind all this." She sniffed and straightened her shoulders. "Okay, I'm going to make a few phone calls."

Nikki first called Monica, who said she would alert the hotel staff and circulate Ty's picture. Then she called her contact at the San Francisco Police Department, to let them know Ty had followed her to this remote area of the north coast.

Meanwhile, Aubrey placed a call to Deputy Jenkins, informing him that Nikki had a protective order against a man who had unexpectedly arrived in town, and giving him the details.

"All right, I'll file a report so it's on the record in case he does do something. If I see him, I'll talk to him, but otherwise there's not much that I can do."

"We understand and appreciate your support."

"Ma'am? No offense, but you and your friend might think about heading back to the Bay Area," Deputy Jenkins said. "I'm not sure this is your kind of place. We're pretty quiet folks around here, and you seem to invite drama."

Aubrey awoke with a start.

With a sense of dread, she glanced at the glowing red numbers of the bedside alarm clock.

4:07.

She turned to check on her friend, just in case. Nikki was

breathing steadily; the twenty-four-hour time limit for the curse had expired. That was one thing, at least.

Aubrey fell back asleep, and dreamed of falling glass, and the long, seemingly endless corridors of the Seabrink—and Hazel, alive and dancing and playing the flute, a jewel twinkling on her forehead.

The next morning, slowly waking up over coffee, Nikki said, "Welp, I'm still alive. But apparently there's a minor crisis on our latest project at work."

"Oh, I'm sorry. Do you have to get back?"

Nikki waved it off. "Naw, it's just the usual crap that happens at this stage of a project. But I can't run around Gualala with you today—I need to meet with some colleagues via Zoom to make sure we're all on the same page. Will you be okay?"

"I'll be fine," Aubrey said. "I'm just meeting with the developer. We architects are not known for our violent dispositions."

"Funny. I mean . . . if Ty really did track me here, I'm probably safer hidden away in the hotel room than out and about, anyway. And . . . he's never actually been violent. I think he just wants to mess with my head."

"These things can ratchet up quickly, Nikki, as you know. I'll leave you Jenkins's number, for what it's worth—and Jasper's, which is probably more useful. Promise me you won't answer the door."

"I won't. Except for room service."

"Even then, please be careful. And keep the door bolted from the inside."

"I've got my Mace. And you: watch your back."

Aubrey drove to Gualala with one eye on the rearview mirror, just in case. Though the drive was nearly forty minutes, she had been traveling it so often the route was beginning to feel familiar: here, the big curve where a stone fireplace stood, the last remnant of a house that must have burned long ago. There, Fisk Mill Cove, and Salt Point State Park. The meadows studded with boulders and cows, and the deer grazing by the side of the highway. And then Stewarts Point, the rustic wooden fences of Sea Ranch, the big white barn, the stables, the fire department, the small chapel, and finally crossing the bridge over the river to arrive in the town of Gualala.

As far as Aubrey could see, she was the only car driving north on the highway. There was no sign anyone was following her. She proceeded through downtown Gualala and turned to the left, toward the ocean.

Aadarshini Obeyesekere's house would have frustrated even the most intrepid trick-or-treater. It was surrounded by tall, dense hedges and stone pillars marking the perimeter warned strangers to keep out. Aubrey stopped at the gates to ring the bell, then drove forward as the gate smoothly slid open. The house reminded her of Sea Ranch's angular buildings, except funkier: there were oxidized copper caps and flourishes here and there, and a series of metal figurines affixed to the exterior of the chimney like mini rock climbers. But most astonishing of all was the view: the house was perched on a cliff overlooking a demilune beach to the south, with dramatic outcroppings and rough rock formations to the north.

A tall, plump woman in her late fifties or early sixties opened the door. She wore a dramatic, asymmetrical tunic of fuchsia linen, chunky statement jewelry, and her eyes were lined with kohl. A tangle of dark hair, shot through with silver, was piled on her head in a messy bun.

"You must be Aubrey," she said in a deep, melodic voice.

"And you are Aadarshini Obeyesekere," Aubrey said, having practiced the pronunciation on the way to town. "It's nice to meet you."

"Call me Obi, everyone does, and I rather like the nickname. Do come in."

Aubrey followed Obi into a massive living room with cathedral ceilings and floor-to-ceiling windows overlooking the ocean. There was a leather sofa and chairs set up in a conversation pit around the fireplace and two walls were lined with crammed bookshelves. But the space was dominated by a huge drafting table covered with papers and blueprints scattered every which way, some spilling off the table onto the floor.

"Pardon the mess," said Obi as they took seats on the couch. "As you can see, I work from home, and these days I can't be bothered to clean up for anybody. But I feel sure you understand. You're the Aubrey Spencer who won the Gunderson Award a while back, aren't you?"

Aubrey nodded, surprised; even internationally famous architects are rarely recognized, and she was far from famous. "How did you know?"

"Don't be so shocked. Folks in the industry, like me, pay attention to such things."

"That was nearly ten years ago. You have an excellent memory."

"Only for certain things: names and architects."

"You've got me beat. I'm bad at names."

"Most people are. That's why I go by Obi, as in Obi-Wan Kenobi."

"I imagine you're sick of hearing the jokes."

She smiled and shrugged. "I don't actually meet many people face-to-face. I'm a bit of a recluse these days, and much prefer my own company. And that of my cats, of course."

Aubrey glanced around but didn't see any felines.

"They're hiding, but will probably peek out eventually."

"It's an amazing house. I assume you designed it?"

"I did. I bought three lots from longtime Gualala folks. Knocked down their old shacks and built this one from the ground up. My neighbors were none too pleased, I'll tell you that much. But I'm used to being an outsider. Like I said, I prefer my own company."

"I was just thinking, as I drove up here, that people must learn to love the solitude in this area. It's so remote."

"Most do, I think. I split my time between here and L.A., so I get my fill of city life there." Obi gestured to a couch and a coffee table fashioned from a large piece of driftwood. Obi handed Aubrey a bottle of sparkling water and took one for herself. "So, you're here about the Hotel Seabrink? It's been a long process, but it's very exciting."

"I hear there are some problems with the title."

Obi waved a bejeweled hand, the gems on her rings sparkling in the light streaming through the windows. "It's on hold for the moment, I'm afraid. There's an ongoing legal dispute over the title to the property. We can't proceed until the owner has a clear title."

"Who is the current owner?

"That depends on whose lawyer you ask, which is why the matter is in court. But it will be settled soon enough. Until then I really can't speak about details."

"I've met some of your people," said Aubrey. "One of your people, I should say."

"And who might that be?"

"Cameron?"

"Cameron Meroni, of course. He's done some preliminary work for me. Measurements, keeping an eye on the place, that sort of thing. Nothing too challenging because, frankly, he's not capable of it. He is good with computers, though, I'll give him that. They tend to confound me, I'm sorry to say."

"I must admit I'm the same way," said Aubrey.

"I use some architectural software, of course, but I much prefer to first draft plans by hand, the old-fashioned way."

"Me too. Or rather, I did, when I was still drawing."

"Tell me, Aubrey, would you be interested in working on the Seabrink renovation? I'll be handling the majority of the work myself, but I have a sense you might be someone I could work with. As a member of my team."

"That's very flattering." Aubrey's heart quickened at the idea. What would it be like, to be part of such a project? She had always designed new structures, not renovations or re-models. And to work on a building as historic as the Seabrink? "I've . . . I've stepped away from architecture for a little while."

Obi studied her, her intelligent eyes measuring and assessing. "Because of what happened with the Loyola Building in San Francisco?"

Aubrey's breath caught in her throat. Of course Obi would have heard about the Loyola Building; it was a big deal in architecture circles. One of those famous mistakes that would, no doubt, be included in architecture textbooks as an example of how not to build a skyscraper.

Obi held her gaze. Aubrey opened her mouth to speak, but nothing came out.

It had been a sunny day, a beautiful fall afternoon in San Francisco. A young mother was walking along the sidewalk with her child. Without warning, jagged glass shards rained down upon them, severely injuring both, scarring them for life. Aubrey did not actually witness the accident, of course, but the images were no less vivid in her imagination. Try as she might, the haunting vision would not leave her mind.

"I understand some of the building's windows failed, and people on the ground were hurt. A tragedy, to be sure. But think about it: Was it your fault? Did you miss something? These sorts of failures are usually the result of a series of mistakes, each compounding the other. Surely there were fail-safe measures in place. Was no one checking your numbers?"

"There were others in charge of those calculations, but . . . I should have double-checked. Triple-checked. I should have been on it, and normally would have been. But I was caught up in some personal issues and lost my focus."

"As I recall, the inquiry found you not responsible. Isn't that right?"

"How did you know that?" Aubrey said, surprised.

"I have my ways," Obi said with another wave of the hand. "Despite this, you hold yourself responsible, don't you? Is that why you're no longer designing buildings?"

"I needed some time," Aubrey managed. "A hiatus."

"A break can be rejuvenating. What have you been doing with your time?"

"Photography, mostly. I have a love of all things abandoned."

"Which is why you're interested in the Seabrink? Listen, Aubrey," Obi said, sitting back and fixing Aubrey with an assessing gaze. "I lost out on the Sea Ranch Lodge when it was for sale, and I have no intentions of losing out on this one. The Hotel Seabrink is tied up in some legal knots at the moment, but as I'm sure you know that's part and parcel of our business. That's also why I hired Cameron."

"What does Cameron have to do with the legal issues? Is he a lawyer?"

"Hardly," Obi said with a soft laugh. "His mother is a Goffin."

"As in T. Jefferson Goffin, who built the hotel?"

"The very one," Obi said.

"But Goffin left no direct heirs."

"True, no direct heirs. But plenty of indirect ones. Goffin had a large extended family, and they've done quite well for themselves over the years. Cameron, though, is not a trust fund baby. There was a falling out with his parents a number of years ago; he was accused of hacking in his college records to change his grades, or some such thing, so he works for a living like the rest of us. Still, as a member of the family, he stands to collect a pretty penny when—and, I suppose, *if*—the property sells. I hired him because I thought he might be motivated to see the matter settled, and because I might find his family connections useful. Not that it matters, particularly. The family is anxious to sell; the dispute over title has to do with the county, which built the old poor farm, and whether they had the rights to the land in the first place."

Aubrey debated telling Obi that Cameron might have taken something from the Hotel Seabrink but decided against it. She didn't have any proof, just a suspicion, and since Cameron was a Goffin, if he did take something, it might technically belong to him—or at least to his family. All in all, it wasn't a mess she wanted to wade into.

Obi's intelligent eyes studied her, then checked her phone. "I have the sense you were here to discuss something else. I'm sorry to say I can't give you more than another five minutes."

"Of course. Yesterday I met with Deborah Goldman and—"

"And Gideon Sims, am I right? That fellow's a pain in my ass. Pretends that it's all about the history, the environment, blah blah blah. Bet he failed to mention that he's part owner of the Driftwood Cove Inn and doesn't want the competition from a renovated Hotel Seabrink."

"He did not mention that."

Obi let out a loud snort. "Go on."

"And I . . . This is hard to explain, but I met Cameron when I was exploring the Hotel Seabrink. I was trespassing so I could take photos."

Obi's eyebrows rose and she gave a faint smile. "Do you expect me to arrest you?"

"No, nothing like that," Aubrey said with a smile. "I met a man there that day, a Dimitri Petroff."

She watched Obi's face closely to see if she would react, but if Dimitri's name meant anything to Obi, she revealed nothing. "He's well-known for making YouTube videos of abandoned buildings. Anyway, he died the next day."

Obi reared back. "*Please* tell me this isn't about the so-called Seabrink curse."

"No, nothing like that. He fell from a cliff and the coroner ruled it a suicide. Except . . ."

"You're not convinced."

Aubrey shook her head.

"Any particular reason why not? You said you just met him that day."

"That's true, but we really connected. We . . . well, not to put too fine a point on it, we spent the night together."

"And then he died?"

"Early the next morning. Very early. He left the hotel around four."

"And flung himself off a cliff?"

Aubrey twisted her mouth.

"Ouch, that's gotta hurt," said Obi. Aubrey wasn't sure whether Obi was referring to Dimitri falling off a cliff or leaving Aubrey's bed to fling himself off a cliff. "What I don't understand is why you're talking to me about it."

"I thought maybe you knew him. Or something. I'm just asking around, and your name came up."

"I'm sure it did. As I said, I'm not exactly well-liked here in Gualala. It's to the point that I do my shopping up in Manchester so I'm less likely to bump into my neighbors." Obi let out a long breath. "And now there was yet *another* body found up there yesterday. What is it with that place?"

"You heard about that?"

She nodded. "Cameron filled me in. Listen, Aubrey, you're an architect. If you've visited the Hotel Seabrink, you know that without intervention it won't be long before the building is beyond repair. Part of the roof has already caved in and it won't survive many more winters. It's now or never. It's such a storied building, a part of glamorous old Hollywood, and it could be again. It would be a shame to let nature reclaim it."

Aubrey climbed back into her car and drove slowly down Obi's long driveway and through the gates. She pulled over to the side of the road and called Nikki, who confirmed she was still alive, her meetings were going well, no one had come to the door, and room service was about to deliver a crab and avocado wrap for lunch.

Aubrey's stomach growled so she stopped at Trinks Cafe for a salad and a half sandwich. She ate her lunch gazing out at the ocean, searching for the subtle shift of color where she had been told whales were often spotted. There were plenty of seabirds, but squint as she might, she saw no sign of whales.

She was bussing her tray when her phone rang. It was an unknown number. Aubrey hesitated, wondering if everything was starting up again with Ty. She typically did not answer unknown numbers because of the barrage of phone calls, emails, and texts Ty had sent to both Nikki and Aubrey before the protective order was in place.

Still . . . she picked up. A tentative woman's voice came on the other end of the line:

Um, is this Aubrey Spencer?

"It is," said Aubrey. It wasn't Ty, but—remembering Nikki's words—she hoped it wasn't Dimitri's homicidal girlfriend or wife, either.

I'm . . . I'm Jo Simpson. Simpson's my married name. My maiden name is Harmon. I'm Roger's—I mean, Dimitri's—sister. Could we meet?

TWENTY-TWO

Aubrey pulled into in the small parking lot in front of the Sea Ranch Chapel, where Jo had suggested meeting.

Dimitri's sister looked nothing at all like him. She was as fair as he had been dark, and while he wasn't a particularly large man, she was very petite, almost pixie-like, with delicate features.

"Thank you for meeting me," said Aubrey. "I'm so very sorry for your loss."

"Thank you," said Jo. "Shall we go inside? It's a bit chilly out here."

They had the place to themselves. The nondenominational chapel was built with flowing, sinewy lines and would not have been out of place in Hobbiton, from *The Lord of the Rings*. Tall, free-form stained-glass windows splashed the stone floor with patches of deep blues, reds, and yellows. Carved redwood columns and snaking wrought metal formed the curvilinear structure. Even the doorknobs were hand-forged metal cages holding beautiful, polished stones. Shelves sprouted, mushroomlike, from one wall. And throughout were bits of inlaid shell and glass.

"This is stunning," said Aubrey, taking it all in.

"You haven't been here before?"

Aubrey shook her head. "I've driven past a few times, but never stopped."

"Rog—Dimitri—brought me here," said Jo softly. "I came to visit him once, when he was spending so much time in the area. He insisted I see it, said it was magical. I thought of having the—" Jo's voice caught, and she cleared her throat. "Excuse me. I thought of having his memorial service here, but as my husband pointed out, who would come? We'll hold it in Bakersfield so the whole family can be there, cousins and all."

Aubrey nodded, though it seemed a shame: the tiny chapel was a truly sacred space, and would have been perfect for a memorial service for Dimitri.

"Deputy Jenkins tells me you knew my brother," Jo said as she took a seat on a carved, polished wooden pew that almost beckoned to be touched.

"Not very well," said Aubrey. She had been anxious to speak with Dimitri's family but suddenly found herself at a loss for words. "Certainly not as well as I would have liked. The truth is, I met him the day before he died. We ran into each other while exploring an abandoned hotel."

Jo smiled. "Dimitri adored anything old and abandoned."

Aubrey nodded. "For some reason, we really hit it off. We didn't have a lot of time together, but . . . it was clear he was very special."

"He was." Jo nodded. "Special, and troubled."

"How so?"

She gazed at the stained glass, then at the arched ceiling, a soft smile of remembrance on her face. "Even as a little boy my brother was adorable, inquisitive, always exploring places he shouldn't and getting into trouble for it. He was smart as a whip and so sweet, never mean or cruel. It was as if he were living in his own world, separate from the rest of us. My parents doted on him, and he was polite, good to them, good to everyone—and yet . . ."

"And yet?"

"He was always looking for something more. For something different. Something *else*. As a child he would get up and leave the classroom whenever he felt like it—but he was always a straight-A student. When he got a little older, he ran away a couple of times and when the cops located him and asked if he was unhappy at home, he said, 'The Harmons are good people. I just need something different.' You believe that? He was just twelve years old when he said that." Jo shook her head. "I thought Mom was going to keel over from worrying about him. As soon as he became an adult, he left, and we had no choice but to let him go and hope for the best. I guess we all knew that it was inevitable."

"Did he stay in touch?"

"Not often, but in his own way, he was very thoughtful. A phone call on birthdays and holidays. Roses for Mom on Mother's Day, and chocolates for Dad on Father's Day. When each of my babies was born, he sent a huge bouquet of peonies to the hospital. My favorite flower. Do you know how much peonies cost in California, out of season?"

"A lot, I would imagine."

She nodded. "He was so loving, in his way. Just always . . . different. Like a man out of time, somehow."

Aubrey thought back to the portrait she had taken of him sitting on the shoeshine stand; he had looked as if he belonged there. "I have some photos of him I took the day I met him. I thought your family might like to have them."

"Oh, that would be wonderful! Thank you, that's very kind."

"Jo, if it's not too intrusive, would you allow me to look at his phone?"

"I'm afraid I don't have it. I put it in his casket with him, which is on its way to Bakersfield. Was there something you needed?"

"I was hoping his texts or call history might provide some insight into what happened that evening."

"I see. The phone won't help you, then. I deleted his texts and calls."

"May I ask why?"

"It's hard to describe, but my parents are already so heart-broken, I couldn't bear for them to be exposed to anything more."

"More, like what?"

"It was just a feeling I had. I'm not sure how to explain it," Jo said. "My brother was always so secretive, almost obsessively private, and I wanted to honor that. Respect his wishes, even after his death. I guess that sounds silly, doesn't it?"

"Not at all. It sounds very thoughtful." Aubrey paused and considered her words. "The thing is, Dimitri didn't seem suicidal that night. At all. He was excited about what he was doing, what he had planned, the Netflix deal he had just signed. I mean, I'm no expert but he just seemed . . . happy."

"I mean no offense, Aubrey, but you didn't know him well—no one did, not really. That was his thing, he was a man of mystery and happy to remain so."

"I understand. I am curious about something, though. His given name was Roger. Where did 'Dimitri' come from?"

Jo laughed. "The family has discussed that a lot. The best we can come up with is that he was searching for an identity more interesting than being a member of an average suburban family in Bakersfield. And once he learned that his biological grandmother had family in this area, I think he enjoyed the idea that he had some Russian heritage. It seemed more exotic than Bakersfield."

"Here's a question: Was Dimitri a night owl?"

"Yes! Even as a little kid he used to get up at night, an infant insomniac. He preferred the nighttime, and if he was allowed to, he'd go to sleep at five in the morning and sleep until the afternoon."

"So he liked to take walks at night?"

"*All* the time. My mother was so worried about it that she took him to a doctor, and then a psychiatrist, thinking maybe something was wrong with him. They said he would probably grow out of it, but he never did. Listen, Aubrey . . ." Jo paused, as if searching for the right words. "Dimitri was a complicated man. I wasn't there, so I don't know what happened, but I do believe it is possible that Dimitri might have taken his own life. Not out of despair or pain, exactly, but just because . . . as I said, my brother was always searching, always looking for something more than what this life has to offer, if that makes sense. He was excited about the next step, convinced that this life was just Act One of an eternal existence. The last time I saw him, he told me that he knew, he *knew*, there was more out there, that there was an existence after death. And I don't mean some saccharine version of a milk-and-honey heaven. He thought there were more adventures awaiting each of us, and he was impatient to get on with them."

Aubrey listened intently, gazing at the stained glass, fighting the burn of tears at the back of her eyes.

"That being said . . ." Jo frowned, looking troubled. "While I can imagine him taking his own life, on his own terms, he wouldn't get out of bed with you to do so. He wouldn't be that rude. That probably sounds really odd, but you're right . . . it makes me wonder about exactly how he died."

"You mentioned he spent a lot of time in this area," said Aubrey. "Do you know what he was doing here?"

"He was looking for information on his biological genealogy. Supposedly his grandmother was from a family with deep roots in the Russian community."

"Does the name Effie Mae sound familiar?"

She nodded. "Dimitri thought she was his biological grandmother, or great-grandmother, maybe? He told me she was a maid at a very fancy hotel. I guess she was an unwed mother, back when that wasn't looked upon with kindness, so she sent her daughter to live with relatives in Bakersfield. Sadly, she died of tuberculosis before they were reunited. Roger found a few of her old letters at a historical society in Bakersfield when he was researching his bio family, and left them with me for safekeeping."

"Have you read through any of them?"

She shook her head. "I have kids, and frankly I always felt too busy—and too happy, I guess—to get caught up in my brother's dramas. We were both adopted, but I always felt as though I fit in. Roger did not—and as 'Dimitri,' even less so. Last time I saw him he was speaking with a slight accent—I think he honestly wanted to stand out, or maybe he was part alien." She laughed, then teared up. "We used to joke about that."

Aubrey gave her a sad smile. "A lot of us feel like aliens. Do you know anything more about his biological family?"

"Not much. Dimitri told me his birth mother's name was Christine, I think, and he discovered she died young. By suicide, as a matter of fact."

"What happened?"

"She had come here years ago looking into her own family history," Jo said, running her hand along the smooth wood of the back of the pew, her finger over a piece of inlaid abalone shell. "I'm sorry to say, she must have been despondent, and took her own life. Apparently, she jumped off a cliff."

Before Jo left, she and Aubrey exchanged contact information. Aubrey promised to send the photos she had taken of Dimitri, and asked Jo if she would be willing to scan Effie May's letters and send them to her.

"Sure, but . . . why?"

"I really don't know. Just in case they might shed some more light on . . . everything." Aubrey decided to keep her reasons vague. "By the way, I have his suitcase back at my hotel, along with some of his papers. Do you want to come by the Driftwood Cove Inn to pick them up?"

Jo hesitated and checked her phone. "I'm actually running really late, and to tell you the truth . . . I'm not sure I can handle any more, emotionally, at the moment. Would it be too much to ask you to hold on to those things, for the time being?"

"I'd be happy to. I'll keep everything for now and when you're ready, we can arrange to send them to you or your family in Bakersfield. And please let your parents know that I'm happy to speak with them, in case they have any questions or . . . for any reason at all."

"I will. But if you talk with them, please don't mention that you and Dimitri slept together. They're pretty old-fashioned."

"I'll leave it at 'We had a meeting of minds,'" said Aubrey. "I didn't have enough time to get to know your brother well, Jo, but I truly liked him. He was very special, and I wish . . . Well. I understand what it is to grieve. I am truly sorry for your loss."

Jo nodded, tears in her eyes. "Goodbye, Aubrey."

When Jo slipped out the door, a harsh shaft of daylight sliced into the mellow light of the space like a blade. The door closed and Aubrey was once again immersed in the peace of the small chapel. Loath to leave its beauty, she wandered about, studying the overlapping wood slats that formed the undulating ceiling, the splashes of colored sunlight on the stone floor, the bits of shell and gleaming abalone inlaid in the smooth wood. Every detail honed by human hands, rendered by human design.

The chapel reminded her of the St. Ambrose: handmade, exultant, joyful.

She could only imagine what the blueprints must have looked like. These were the sort of places she had dreamed of building when she first became an architect. She had imagined herself creating spaces that celebrated and rejoiced in the human spirit but somehow ended up designing more efficient ways to cram more workers into ever smaller cubicles in skyscrapers and office buildings. How had that happened? The lure of money and security, she supposed. And then . . . the disaster with the Loyola Building. The windows failing, falling twenty stories to the sidewalk below.

And then her father had died. Her already screwed-up childhood now seemed even more so, in retrospect.

Was this why she was so obsessed with Dimitri? Because

he had kept his true self hidden, just as she always had? As a child, Aubrey tried to be the perfect daughter, perfect sister, perfect student. She went to UC Berkeley, got a good degree, landed a well-paying job, married the perfect husband. But it had all fallen apart because she had been playing a role, not being true to herself.

Had Dimitri made himself into who he wanted to be, a successful man of mystery, and the price he paid was to leave his family behind? She liked to think he would have gone back to them in time, had he lived.

His birth mother . . . took her own life . . . had come here years ago . . . She jumped off a cliff.

Had she jumped from Dead Man's Bluff? Had Dimitri felt compelled to repeat his birth mother's final moments?

Aubrey startled when the chapel door opened. Again, a shaft of bright daylight sluiced in, almost blinding her.

A man stood in the doorway. Tall, broad-shouldered. He was backlit, so it took Aubrey a moment to recognize him.

Ty?

TWENTY-THREE

No, it was Stephen Rex, the YouTuber.

Her first reaction was relief that it wasn't Ty, but then Stephen fixed her with a menacing look. Her heart sped up.

Aubrey was on the far side of the chapel, but it was a small space. She felt cornered. There were several pews between them, but there was nothing she might use as a defensive weapon, not even a Bible. She cursed herself for having left her pepper spray in the car. She should keep it on her at all times, especially lately.

"Oh, hi," she said after a beat. "Stephen, right? From the bar the other day, with Cameron."

"Look, lady," he said in a low voice, slowly walking around the apse at the front of the chapel while she rounded the back. "I don't know what you think you're—"

The chapel door opened again, and a portly, middle-aged man entered. A carefully coiffed blonde woman and three preteens crowded in behind him.

"Oh, sorry, folks!" the man said with a big smile. "Were

you two enjoying the solitude? The wife and kids and I just drove all the way up from Vallejo. Phew! That's some twisty-turny road, isn't it? Hate to drive that after a night with the boys in the bar, you get my meaning?"

"It sure is beautiful around here," the woman said. "The kids spied this little chapel from the highway and insisted we stop, 'cause they said it looked like something from 'Lord of the Rings.' You ever see that movie?"

"I had that very thought myself," said Aubrey, edging toward the door. Stephen had been slowly circling the sanctuary toward her and was now on the far side of the pews. "And no, you're not interrupting, not at all. Please, come in and enjoy yourselves—it's a beautiful sanctuary."

Aubrey hurried toward the door and slipped out before Stephen could get past the pews and the family. She ran to her car, hopped in, gunned the engine, and swiftly sped away from the chapel and down the long lane to the highway, glancing in the rearview mirror. The only vehicles besides hers in the parking lot were an RV and a red sports car.

In her rearview mirror she saw Stephen by the chapel doors, watching her flee, but he did not follow. At least, not yet. If he was after her, the last thing she wanted to do was lead him back to Nikki. She racked her brain, wondering where she should go. When things were at their worst with Ty, she and Nikki knew the location of every police station in Oakland and San Francisco. Nothing like driving up to the door of law enforcement to get a stalker to back off.

Aubrey had not thought to ask Deputy Jenkins where he was stationed. This part of the coast was in Sonoma County, which meant his office must be . . . where? Guerneville? Santa Rosa? Too far to be of immediate help, anyway.

She had not driven far when she spotted a firehouse. Was

this the headquarters of the volunteer firefighters and para-medics? Strong, brave people, in any case. She pulled in.

Neither Jasper nor Mia was there, so Aubrey spoke with a large, bearded man named Rusty, explaining that she had been spooked by a suspicious man at the chapel. Rusty walked outside with her to take a look, but only the RV remained in the chapel's parking lot. They spotted a red sports car pulling onto the highway and heading north, toward Gualala, away from them.

"Looks like he's headed into town," Rusty said. "You want me to call it in? Did he threaten you in any way?"

She shook her head. "Not really. He scared me, but I may have overreacted. I've had some bad experiences in the past."

"Listen to your gut, ma'am," Rusty said. "It won't never steer you wrong."

"Good advice. Why don't I think about it, and if I'm still worried, I'll call it in myself." Aubrey tried to imagine how Deputy Jenkins would react if she reported Stephen Rex simply for trying to talk to her—in a public space, no less. He was likely to suggest, again, that she go back to Oakland. "Thanks for your help, Rusty."

"Anytime, ma'am. Come back inside with me, and I'll give you my card. You feel free to call if you need anything, or if you see him again."

They returned to the firehouse, and while Rusty retrieved a business card, she paused to peruse the framed photos on the wall. Most featured parties and promotion ceremonies. One large photo reminded her of a modern version of the costume-party photo she had seen at the Hotel Seabrink.

"That was from last Halloween," said Rusty. "Good group we've got here. We all work together."

"I've met Jasper and Mia," Aubrey said.

"Yep, they're good people."

Jasper was dressed as Indiana Jones, wearing a hat and carrying a bullwhip. She also recognized Rusty, clad in a toga with a laurel wreath on his head. Mia was in full 1920s regalia, with a flapper dress and carrying a long cigarette. But what caught Aubrey's attention was the ferronière she was wearing, with a large jewel in the center of her forehead. Could it be the same one? She brought out her phone and snapped a quick photo of it, and looked up to find Rusty's eyes on her.

"Um, cool costume ideas," said Aubrey. "Here's a weird question: Have you ever been up to the old Hotel Seabrink?

He frowned. "A few of us checked out a suspected fire the other night, false alarms happen a lot up there. But otherwise I keep my distance. Why?"

"Just wondering. Also, is there a sheriff's station anywhere around here?"

He shook his head. "The main Sonoma County sheriff's office is in Santa Rosa."

"That's, what? Two hours from here?"

"Maybe an hour forty-five, depending on traffic."

"You're really remote out here, then."

"There's a sheriff's substation in Guerneville, and three deputies cover the coast and the unincorporated areas along the river and around Guerneville, up to Gualala. Once you cross into Mendocino County, the sheriff's office is in Ukiah, with a substation in Fort Bragg, so it's just about as far in the other direction. The California Highway Patrol has jurisdiction over the highway, mostly. But yeah, we're remote, which is why we have to rely on ourselves. Neighbors helping neighbors, that sort of thing. In the rest of my life, I'm a cobbler."

"As in shoes?"

"Yep," he said, handing her his business card. "Shoe repair, and even custom shoes. They're coming back into vogue."

"Nice." Aubrey tucked his card in her pocket and thanked Rusty for his help.

"How about I walk you back to your car," he suggested, puffing out his chest a little. "And if he circles back, me and him could have a little chat."

"That's very kind of you," Aubrey said. "But I imagine he's in Gualala by now."

"If you need me, you know where to find me," Rusty said, and walked her out, making a show of scoping out the highway.

Aubrey sped back to Driftwood Cove, keeping one eye on her rearview mirror, just in case. No red sports car in sight.

Why was she so spooked? He hadn't really done anything... but as Nikki had said: *Most murders are really just stupid. No deep motives at all.* Still... if Stephen really had been involved in Dimitri's death, he knew where Aubrey was staying. In which case he could come after her anytime.

She raced through the lobby and up the stairs, breathless as she burst into the room. Nikki was sprawled on the bed, laptop on her knees, music playing on the record player.

"Are you okay?" Nikki asked, alarmed.

"I'm fine, but remember that guy, Stephen Rex ?" Locking the door behind her, Aubrey's eyes fell on a tray with the remnants of a room service lunch. "I thought you weren't going to open the door."

"Only for room service. I checked the peephole and had my Mace at the ready."

"You also forgot to bolt the door from inside."

"I was expecting you. And anyway, Monica's shown Ty's photo to everyone on staff and told them to call the police if he tries to sweet-talk his way in here. Besides, after surviving the curse I have a whole new lease on life. Tell me what happened."

Aubrey stashed her things, grabbed a bottle of water from the room's small refrigerator, and took a long drink.

"First off, I met with Dimitri's sister, Jo."

"Really? How did you meet her? What did she say? Shed any light on her mysterious brother?"

Aubrey told Nikki that Deputy Jenkins had actually come through and given Aubrey's contact information to Jo, and that they met at the Sea Ranch Chapel.

"According to Jo, Dimitri tried on new identities the way an author might write different kinds of stories under different pen names. Also, he was a night owl who loved to go for walks in the middle of the night. And he wasn't afraid of death. She did, however, take pains to assure me that he probably wouldn't be so rude as to kill himself right after sleeping with me."

"Well, that's something. Now, what about a guy named Stephen?"

Aubrey told Nikki about their encounter at the Sea Ranch Chapel, but as she described her response, it sounded like an overreaction to her own ears.

"I think I might just be spooked lately. And anyway, would it make any sense for him to kill me, or Dimitri?" Aubrey asked aloud. "And how would Stephen have known that Dimitri was here at Driftwood Cove Inn?"

"You said Dimitri posted a video that night, teasing the Seabrink story."

"True."

"He might have used geotags, and a tech-savvy person

would be able to figure out where it was shot, more or less. Is this guy a techie?"

"He's at least good enough with computers to have his own YouTube channel."

"It doesn't take much know-how to do that," Nikki said. "Or maybe Stephen followed you two here from the Seabrink. You said someone, or something, scared you and Dimitri and Cameron at the Hotel Seabrink that first day—maybe it was him."

"Seriously?" Aubrey blew out a long breath, kicked off her shoes, and joined Nikki on the bed. "We think this guy was so hungry for more subscribers that he, what? Offed his rival, Dimitri?"

"There's also the Netflix deal. That might inspire a murderous rage." Nikki started typing on her laptop. "Yada yada yada . . . Let's see, wow, there have been a surprising number of deaths of YouTubers. Crazy stalkers, coming to kill their favorite YouTube star, rivalries . . . But of course none of this has anything directly to do with the Seabrink."

"In the teaser he posted, Dimitri mentioned that he hoped the first episode of his Netflix show would feature the Seabrink," mused Aubrey. "Maybe that's the connection."

"Oooh, check out this video, though," said Nikki. "'Old house near Bohemian Grove, inhabited only by mannequins.'"

"Ugh. Mannequins creep me out."

"Mannequin phobia? That's a thing?"

"To me it is." Aubrey nodded. "When I was a kid, I watched a rerun of an old show called 'The Night Stalker' featuring some spooky mannequins, and haven't trusted them since. Especially when they're in abandoned, and allegedly haunted, buildings."

"I imagine that's the point. Wait—" Nikki sat up. "Isn't that your hot hardware man?"

"What? Where?"

Nikki turned her laptop to face Aubrey and paused the video. "Is that, or is that not, your very own Jasper?"

TWENTY-FOUR

"He's hardly 'my' Jasper," Aubrey said, her voice hollow as she studied the grainy image.

"Maybe it isn't him," Nikki said. "Let me back the video up, see if we can get a better look."

They examined the image at several different angles.

"It's him," Aubrey said. "It's definitely him."

Nikki was silent.

"I told Jasper about Dimitri's YouTube channel. He didn't say a word, not a single word, about being in one of Stephen Rex's videos," Aubrey continued, stunned.

"Even hot hardware guys have secrets," said Nikki with a sigh. "And to think we bought that man a burrito."

"His nice-guy persona certainly fooled me," Aubrey said with disgust as she collapsed back into the pillows. "Good thing you're here, Nikki, or I wouldn't know who to trust."

"Maybe there's an innocent explanation."

"Like what? He has amnesia? Multiple personalities? An evil twin, perhaps?"

"I'm just saying, until very recently you were a total stranger to Jasper. Maybe he intended to tell you later, when he got to know you a little better, but what with cliffside rescues and escorting us through haunted hotels, he never found the right time."

"Maybe," Aubrey said, staring at the ceiling and thinking about the time she spent talking with Jasper at the St. Ambrose, and their conversation in his truck on the way to cut the chain at the Seabrink. "Or maybe he's a big ol' liar who lies."

"Another puzzle: How did Stephen Rex know you were at the Sea Ranch Chapel? Could he have followed you?"

"He drives a bright red sports car, and I was keeping an eye out for a tail because of Ty, so I don't think I would have missed it."

"According to Xavi at the front desk, 'Everyone should go see the Sea Ranch Chapel,'" said Nikki. "Maybe Stephen was just sightseeing and happened upon you. So, did Jo tell you anything useful? Did Dimitri have an ex? It's almost always the ex. The problem with that theory is, if that's what happened then I'm not sure how we proceed. Accompanying you to Bakersfield to track down former girlfriends isn't an option for me, I'm afraid. Our Best Friend Backup Agreement is geographically limited."

Aubrey smiled. "Fair enough."

"Oh, by the way," Nikki continued. "I talked to someone in development at Netflix who was stunned to hear about Dimitri's death. After a little prodding, I got them to confirm they were working on a new series with him. And get this: according to this source, someone had been trying to horn in on his deal, even threatened to file suit against him for copyright infringement."

"Who?"

She shook her head. "Wouldn't tell me. Claimed it was confidential."

Aubrey got up and looked out the window, watching the waves crash on the rocks in the cove, the seabirds playing in the spray. "Something else I learned: Cameron has computer skills."

"As in serious hacking skills, to scrub the internet?"

"Maybe. Also, he's a Goffin."

"A what?"

"Remember you said Cameron came from wealth? Turns out, he's a descendant of T. Jefferson Goffin, the original owner of the Hotel Seabrink. The Goffin family stands to make a pretty penny if this development deal goes through."

"Where did you hear that?"

"From Obi, the architect Cameron referred me to."

"Oh right! But wait—Cameron told me he was on the outs with his family."

"His parents cut him off, but that might not matter. As a descendant of T. Jefferson Goffin, he might stand to inherit a portion of the proceeds from the sale of the hotel and its land if a court case decides the extended family as a group are the rightful heirs. Or maybe he and his parents have kissed and made up."

"I can see someone going to great lengths to protect an inheritance. But murder? Cameron just doesn't seem the homicidal type to me. And even if he is, why would he go after Dimitri? How was he a threat?"

"I don't know. One other, seemingly unrelated but weird thing: when I was at the firehouse, I saw a photo of Mia wearing a ferronnière at a Halloween party."

"When did you go to the firehouse?"

"After the chapel, in case Stephen Rex was chasing me. Let me see something . . ." Aubrey compared the photo she had taken at the fire department to the one she had taken of the French flautist in the Seabrink library. "The headbands look similar, but it's hard to tell for sure. The old photo is sepia-toned, and this one of Mia is tiny."

Nikki started tapping on her keyboard, then turned the laptop to show Aubrey the painting of *La Belle Ferronnière*.

"Beautiful. By da Vinci?"

"Not exactly. Says here it's attributed to the *school* of Leonardo da Vinci, which means it might have been painted by one of his apprentices. Does it matter?"

"Not to me. Beauty is beauty. That's the origin of the ferronnière fad?"

"Apparently," said Nikki. "You know, we should totally bring that back."

"Because I'm such a fashion icon that if I started wearing one, the world would follow?"

Nikki chuckled. "Hard to believe that Dimitri's death, and our being chased through the Hotel Seabrink, all have something to do with a bejeweled headband."

"When you say it like that, it doesn't sound likely," Aubrey said. "And anything found at the Hotel Seabrink would by default belong to the Goffin family anyway, wouldn't it?"

"Or to whoever holds the legal title to the Hotel Seabrink."

Aubrey groaned. "It's like I'm looking through a kaleidoscope. Every time I turn it, I see new patterns, but none of them amount to anything. I don't think I'm cut out to be a homicide detective."

"Okay, let's spitball here, maybe our subconscious minds will come up with something," Nikki said, stretching her arms and legs to refresh herself. "Albert Einstein once said, 'A little knowledge is a dangerous thing. So is a lot.' Maybe Dimitri's research turned up some damaging information about the Seabrink. Maybe even some criminally damaging information."

"Like what? Even with the scrubbing of the internet, all the locals seem to know about the mysterious deaths up there, not to mention the curse," said Aubrey. "What else could Dimitri have learned that someone would be desperate to cover up?"

"You're an architect: What puts the kibosh on a big project?"

"A lot of proposed developments are delayed or even canceled by a bad environmental review. Maybe Cameron and whoever else might be involved is trying to quash a disastrous Environmental Impact Report. If the place was a toxic dump of some sort, they'd never be able to unload it."

"Good idea, though hotels and nursing homes aren't usually the locations for toxic materials," Nikki said. "What about radon?"

"Radon's not much of an issue in California, especially not Northern California."

"What else might cause a negative Environmental Impact Report?"

"Asbestos is a possibility. The best way to avoid problems with asbestos is to leave it alone or to encapsulate it. But this is all standard stuff that is investigated before starting any project, much less a large-scale one."

"Hold on." Nikki was again typing furiously on her computer. "According to this map, there are potential asbestos deposits in the Seabrink area. What if Dimitri figured that out, and then Obi somehow found out he knew, and then, what? Sent Cameron to kill him?"

Aubrey gave her a look.

"Okay, you're right," said Nikki. "Far-fetched. What other reasons would force a development project to shut down?"

"Earthquake and fire insurance might prove prohibitively expensive. The whole West Coast is in a seismic hot zone, and we all know about the growing threat of wildfires. But if insurance is the stumbling block, then it would make sense to kill the insurance executives, not a videographer."

"True. What else?" said Nikki.

"Water and sewer."

"Okay! Now we're talking. The hotel clearly has water from that spring."

"Assuming the water's safe to drink," said Aubrey. "Standards have changed in the past hundred years. And supposing... what if someone poisoned the well?"

"Isn't 'poisoning the well' sort of a medieval thing?"

"The Germans did it in France during the First World War."

"All right. Say someone poisoned the Seabrink's famous mineral water," said Nikki. "But the water isn't from a well, it's from a spring, which is continually flowing. How long could the water possibly *stay* poisoned?"

"Good point. Scratch the poison angle. Still, even if the Seabrink's spring water is pure as the driven snow, that spring couldn't possibly provide enough water to service a big hotel," Aubrey mused. "We're not just talking drinking water, but also bath and toilet water, cooking water, dishwater, and water to clean, garden, and do the laundry. That's a lot of water. Maybe ... maybe the wells on the property have dried up, and they're too remote to tap into the city water supply?"

"And therefore ... ? I mean, that might close the project down, but murdering a man to keep it secret doesn't make sense."

"The problem is that none of these are obscure issues,"

said Aubrey with a nod. "Any developer worth their salt would have done their due diligence and uncovered these problems long before investing any money."

Nikki was scrolling through sites about sewage disposal and disputes. She shook her head. "Imagine being killed over a sewer issue."

"Hey, don't underestimate the power of human waste. In the course of history, it has led to some very crappy behavior."

"You don't have to tell me how shitty people can be," Nikki murmured.

Aubrey chuckled.

"Hey," said Nikki. "Cameron said something about people drawing occult symbols on the front door? And didn't Gideon insist he saw some spooky initiations going on up there? Maybe there's a coven in town and the sweet little old ladies are using their scrapbooking club as a cover."

Aubrey smiled. "Which little old ladies might those be?"

"Deb Goldman, and the other one—the Episcopalian. Surely there are others. And they meet over scones and sticky buns, and it's just like in 'Rosemary's Baby,' they're the last people you'd suspect of evil intent."

"You watch too many old horror movies, my friend."

"No doubt. But I'm still suspicious of Deborah and her 'associates,'" mumbled Nikki, her eyes glued to the videos now streaming on her screen.

"You think Deborah and Gideon somehow lured Dimitri outside at four in the morning and killed him? Why?"

"They both acted squirrelly when you mentioned Dimitri's biological mother. And Gideon was a bit . . . wackadoo, don't you think? The Episcopalian warned us about him, remember?"

"That was the bookseller. The Episcopalian was the one who gave us Deborah's contact info."

"I'm getting our cast of characters mixed up," Nikki said.

"Well, there are quite a few," Aubrey replied. "Kind of undermines my faith in the virtues of small-town life, I must say."

"Including the hardware hottie?"

"Yeah, bite me, Hardware Boy. We were supposed to meet him tomorrow for lunch, to go talk with his nana, remember?"

"You want to cancel?"

Aubrey shook her head. "No. I want to talk to him face-to-face and hear what he has to say. The fact that Jasper's in Stephen's video is bizarre, but it doesn't actually link him to anything. Besides, he's been trying to help us figure out how Dimitri died."

"That's classic criminal behavior. A murderer pretends to help solve a case in order to throw detectives off the scent. Psychopaths are famous for that sort of thing."

"What possible motive would Jasper have to kill Dimitri?"

"You've got me there . . ." Nikki played with a lock of her long black hair. "It could be something personal. Maybe they were both in love with the same woman. They both went for you, after all."

"But I didn't even meet Jasper until after Dimitri died."

"So maybe they share a type. But I see what you mean. Or . . . suppose Jasper makes his own videos. Maybe they were competitors?"

"That would make sense if there were any evidence that Jasper had a YouTube channel or any such aspirations. He seems about as clueless about the internet as I am. And I hardly think him showing up—briefly—in a video makes him a YouTuber. I appear briefly in Dimitri's video but *I'm* neither a suspect in his death nor a YouTuber."

"That's the video that was taken down?"

Aubrey nodded.

"Are we thinking Cameron deleted it?"

"I suppose, if he's the one doing the scrubbing, though we don't know that for sure, and I'm not sure why—or whether—it matters."

"This is discouraging."

"You can say that again. Are there any possible motives or suspects we've overlooked?"

"Here's something," said Nikki. "I started reading the comments Dimitri's subscribers posted to his channel. There are an awful lot from someone who goes by Dontbekras, and they seem a little unbalanced and stalkery. 'Why don't you respond to me,' that sort of thing. Oh, and check this out: Dontbekras has their own channel."

Nikki brought up the channel and they watched several videos of poor quality: shaky camera work, lots of ambient noise, and the narrator's strangely droning voice, sounding as if they were mimicking someone telling ghost stories.

"Why is the voice so weird?" asked Aubrey.

"They're using a voice synthesizer."

"Why?"

"Could be someone with an obvious accent, or a hard time with English. Or . . . as cruel as the internet can be for men, it's much, *much* worse for women. I've read that some women use a voice synthesizer to disguise their gender."

"Any way to find out who Dontbekras is?"

"Probably, but a subpoena would be involved. There may be another way, but it's beyond my skill level. And anyway, I could be wrong. The video's script sounds like a real bro," said Nikki. *"Totally, dude."*

"You think he's cool enough to be a bro? Sounds more like a bro wannabe. Or a . . . what's the female version? A real sis?"

"I don't think there is an equivalent," said Nikki. "Besides, whoever Dontbekras is, nobody seems to care. They have only a handful of followers, not many views, and plenty of vicious comments."

"I think you've fallen down an internet rabbit hole."

The concept of Alice falling down the rabbit hole made Aubrey think about the upside-down view of the Seabrink she saw when gazing through the crystal ball at the bottom of the attic stairs.

"And the question remains: How might any of this be connected to the Seabrink?"

Early that morning, once again, Aubrey woke with a start at 4:07 a.m. This time she felt more weary than surprised or fearful when she gazed at the clock.

Humans can get used to just about anything, she thought, remembering an old cartoon she used to keep taped above her desk at work. The first frame showed a terrified man and woman and cat falling down a bottomless pit. The second frame showed the same trio six months later, now perfectly relaxed: the woman knitting, the man reading, the cat curled up and napping. With the passage of time, the terrifying had become an everyday reality, the new normal.

She fell back into a blessedly dream-free sleep.

TWENTY-FIVE

"What are you going to say to Jasper?" asked Nikki the next day as they drove to Gualala to meet up with him.

"I'm going to ask him how he knows Stephen Rex." Aubrey ticked the items off on her fingers. "What he knows about Stephen, why Stephen is threatening me, and whether Stephen killed Dimitri. Though depending on how this goes, I might need to be a bit cagey about that last one."

"This should be fun," Nikki said wryly.

When they got to Gualala, Jasper was waiting for them in the parking lot of the hardware store. Aubrey had volunteered to drive them in her car, since it was more comfortable for three than his truck.

He reached for the door handle, but paused when Aubrey got out and said, "Hold on there just one minute, Sparky. I have a few questions for you."

"What's up?" If Jasper had a guilty conscience, it didn't show.

"How do you know Stephen Rex?"

Jasper looked surprised. "Stephen? How do *you* know Stephen Rex?"

"He threatened me."

"He *threatened* you?"

"In the Sea Ranch Chapel."

"The Sea Ranch *Chapel*?"

"Eventually you're going to have to stop repeating every word I say and answer my questions," Aubrey snapped, wondering if he were stalling for time to make up a story. "Why were you in his video?"

"What video are you talking about?"

"Old house, full of mannequins, you lurking in the background. Ring a bell?"

"Is that what's got your knickers in a twist?"

"My knickers are none of your business. Answer the question, please. How do you know Stephen Rex?"

Jasper relaxed. "We were in a paramedic training program together a few years ago."

"That guy's a paramedic?"

"No. He started the program but was asked to leave."

"Why? What'd he do?"

He blew out a breath. "It'll sound like gossip if I tell you, but it's no secret. He was busted for drugs. It's not uncommon for people in the field. Lots of pressure and easy access to meds is a risky combination."

"And why were you in his video?"

"I didn't realize I was until you told me just now. I went with him not long ago to an old place down in Guerneville, on the Russian River. He'd just come to town and got in touch. I . . . We're not close, but I get the sense that he needs all the friends he can get. I've been trying to encourage him to go to meetings and stay sober."

"What's with all those mannequins in his video?" Nikki asked, getting out to join them.

"Stephen said the old guy who owned the place lost his wife, became lonely, and filled his rather creepy house with even creepier mannequins. I believe Stephen added a few more."

"Mannequins made that poor man feel less lonely?" Aubrey asked with a shiver, trying to wrap her head around the idea of mannequins as companions.

"Mannequin phobia," said Nikki, gesturing to Aubrey with her head.

"I don't blame her. Mannequins are like clowns, in my book," said Jasper. "Just plain creepy."

"That would be the word," said Aubrey with a sigh. "And you wouldn't happen to be performing some sort of satanic rituals up at the Seabrink with your volunteer rescue buddies, would you?"

He burst out laughing. "I told you not to listen to Deborah Goldman and her associates. Gideon said that?"

She nodded.

"Just FYI, Aubrey," Nikki said in a stage whisper. "You're not supposed to challenge the suspected satanic ritual folks to their face. In the movies you'd be marked for death, right there and then."

"There you have it," said Jasper. "Now, if I don't kill you, you'll know I'm innocent of all charges. But in all seriousness, it's like I told you: until I went there with you, I haven't been to the Seabrink since my teenage years."

"So why does Gideon think otherwise?" asked Aubrey.

"I have no idea how that man's mind works," Jasper said, a little impatiently. "I know he's suspicious about the power lines, or something like that. And he's had an ongoing feud with one of the lead volunteer firefighters for years over a long-ago quarrel about some fire-threat assessment. I think in Gideon's mind it all sort of converges. He's an interesting guy if you can keep him talking about geology, but on other topics he's more than a little out there."

Aubrey leaned back against the car, mulling this over.

"You said Stephen threatened you?" Jasper asked. "He's a little socially awkward, and as I say he's had troubles with addiction. But I've never known him to be violent."

"He wasn't violent, exactly," said Aubrey. Again, she wondered: Had she misjudged Rex's intentions at the chapel? She'd been consumed with thoughts of murder, and the threat posed by Ty. "We were alone in the chapel, and I felt . . . vulnerable. I suppose I might have gotten it wrong."

"Did he seem under the influence?"

"Not that I could tell."

"I'll talk to him."

"Please don't," said Aubrey, shaking her head. "I'll handle it."

"It's your call." Jasper glanced at his watch. "We'd best get a move on, or we'll be late. Nana's expecting us. We're having rice ball salad, which is much better than it sounds. I called in a double order to the Thai place in Anchor Bay, which is on the way to my nana's house in Point Arena."

The drive, as was typical all along the Northern California coast, was gorgeous: they passed verdant forests, grassy meadows, and stunning ocean vistas. Aubrey and Nikki filled Jasper in on the possibility that Ty was in town and what Deputy Jenkins had said.

"I'm sorry to hear that, Nikki," Jasper said. "That must be incredibly stressful."

She nodded. "That's a good word for it."

"And those protective orders only go so far, right? There's usually nothing that can be done until it gets really scary."

"He's been a creep to Aubrey, too, by the way," Nikki said. "He's fixated on me but sees Aubrey as standing in his way."

"Do me a favor: if either of you see him, or suspect he's around, give me a call. I'll light a fire under the deputy sheriff. We've known each other for years. One of the advantages of small-town life."

They stopped at the Anchor Bay Thai Kitchen to pick up Jasper's order and soon the car filled with the mouthwatering aromas of lemongrass and ginger. Another twenty minutes and they arrived in the town of Point Arena, whose charming main street was filled with bars and restaurants and even a movie theater.

"Point Arena is smaller than Gualala, but it has a fun nightlife. And here's an interesting fact: the Point Arena lighthouse is the tallest in California," Jasper said, gesturing toward a slender white tower rising in the distance. "And if you set sail from here, the next stop is Japan."

"I love lighthouses," said Aubrey.

"It's open for tours most days, and there's a nice museum and beautiful hiking trails. As soon as you track down your murderer and shake your stalker, you should check it out."

"We will. You can come along as our bodyguard."

"Only if there's another burrito in the offing."

Jasper's grandmother—"Call me Nana Joyce"—lived in a modest bungalow with a well-tended garden full of bird feeders and wind chimes. She was a small woman and slightly hunched over with advanced age, but her dark eyes were lively and intelligent.

She greeted them warmly, told Jasper he needed a haircut, and ushered them into a small dining area off the kitchen, where a stack of plates and a pile of silverware awaited them. Jasper opened the take-out cartons and assembled them in the center of the table. They all took seats and filled their plates with appreciative oohs and aahs.

"Oh, this is such a treat! My handsome grandson, his two lovely new friends, and a Thai feast, all at once!" said Nana Joyce with a smile.

No wonder Jasper's so sweet, thought Aubrey. He must have had a happy childhood, if his nana was any indicator.

"Jasper tells me you're interested in the Hotel Seabrink, is that right?" Nana Joyce said. "Of course, I was only a tot when it was in its heyday, but I've heard plenty of stories from other locals through the years. I grew up in Gualala, moved here to Point Arena as a young bride. I *do* remember when Dorothy came into town, and Toto, too!"

"Judy Garland came to the Hotel Seabrink?" Nikki asked.

"She did! And she brought a little dog with her, though now that I think of it, it may not have been the original Toto. Hard to say. But it was quite an event for us children."

"I can imagine," said Aubrey.

"There were other stars, too, though they didn't usually come to town but kept to themselves up on the hill, at the hotel. Let's see. . . . there was Gene Tierney . . . Hedy Lamarr—did you know she was a genius? She holds a patent for something high-tech, I can never remember what. But just imagine, being a famous sex symbol and a genius at the same time!"

"I read about that," said Nikki. "It was a radio guidance system for torpedoes, something about the frequency used to guide them."

"That sounds about right," said Nana Joyce. "Anyway, only the townsfolk who did work at the hotel ever went up there.

But one time I was on a hike through the hills and forests with a church youth group . . . oh, I couldn't have been more than eight or nine. I wandered off the trail and had a good view of the hotel. That's when I saw a woman pushed to her death off a grand balcony."

They all froze, their forks halfway to their mouths.

"Wait. Nana, you saw a woman *pushed* to her *death*?" Jasper clarified.

"I told you that."

"You said you saw someone fall, but not that she was pushed."

She shrugged. "You were never interested in hearing my stories about the Seabrink."

"That'll teach me to pay attention," Jasper said. "When was this?"

"Like I said, I was very young. No one else saw it, and no one believed me, not even my parents, when I told them. They said I was an imaginative child. Which I was, but I didn't imagine *that*. Later, the authorities said she jumped, that it was a suicide. But I know what I saw. A man was on that balcony with her, and the two were arguing."

"Did you recognize him?"

"No, but of course I didn't run in those circles."

"Was this the starlet we've heard stories about?" Aubrey asked.

"I think so. I remember they said she was French."

"What can you tell us about the Quiet Girl?" Nikki asked.

"What I heard was that when the Seabrink was still an asylum, there was a fire that killed several women. Afterward, the remaining residents were relocated—except for a girl of ten or so, maybe a little older. She was a mute, who refused to leave. They called her the Quiet Girl. She was accused of starting the fire, apparently because she had set a couple of fires before, but there was no actual proof she was guilty of starting this one. If she did start the fire the poor thing must have been racked with guilt at having killed those people, don't you think? And you'd think she'd be glad to leave that place, wouldn't you? I mean, if she tried to burn it down, why would she stay? But she did. I suppose she had nowhere to go."

"She had no family, nothing like that?" Aubrey asked.

Nana Joyce shook her head. "She arrived at the poor farm as an infant-in-arms, and her father died not long after, and when no relatives could be located, she stayed and grew up there. I would imagine she ran rather wild, but it was the only world she knew. After the asylum closed, the officials weren't able to find her. When T. Jefferson Goffin began to renovate the asylum and build his hotel, it was assumed she had escaped into the forest. But what I heard was that she had a hiding place in the attic, where she lived for years. In fact . . ."

Nana Joyce paused and refilled her plate.

"In fact . . . ?" Nikki prompted.

"Some say she's still there. And . . . from time to time, when the music plays, she can be seen dancing. A pale young woman, dressed in a dirty apron, her hair wild. Smiling. Dancing. Haunting . . . I do remember hearing flute music whenever we were near the hotel." Nana began to hum a few bars. "La di da, dum dum dum da . . ."

A chill rushed over Aubrey. It was the same haunting melody she had heard both times she had stepped over the threshold of the Hotel Seabrink.

"You still remember the tune?" Aubrey asked, her voice sounding breathless to her own ears.

"Can you imagine, after all these years?" Nana Joyce

smiled as she served herself more rice ball salad. "It's quite poignant, rather plaintive, isn't it? But for some reason it went right in and stuck there, in my brain. I can recite every word of my Girl Scouts pledge, as well. More iced tea, anyone?"

Outside, as if on cue, a melancholy foghorn sounded.

"Would you listen to that? The fog's moving in," said Nana Joyce. "One thing I love about living in this area is that the climate is so much a part of daily life. It has its own mind, and we're just along for the ride. Now enough talk about death: How did you all meet my Jasper?"

"This rice ball salad is amazing," said Nikki in a blatant ploy to change the topic. "Despite the confusing name. I mean, there are no balls, it's not a salad, and the rice is sort of hidden . . ."

"The pad thai is delicious, too," said Aubrey. "Nikki and I met years ago in a Thai cooking class, but we could take some pointers from this place."

Nana Joyce was undeterred. "Jasper?" she said, waiting for an answer.

"More talk of death, I'm afraid," Jasper said with obvious reluctance. "Aubrey and I met at the scene of a tragedy. A friend of hers died at Dead Man's Bluff."

"Oh," said Nana Joyce, looking at Aubrey with sympathy. "I'm so sorry to hear that. Were you two close, honey?"

"We were just getting to know each other," said Aubrey. "I met him at the Hotel Seabrink, where I was taking photographs. He died very early the next day. That's why I have so many questions, which Jasper has been kind enough to help me try to answer."

"Of course you do. I'm so glad that our dear Jasper was there to help. He's such a good boy, now that he's stopped drinking."

"Thanks, Nana," said Jasper with a ghost of a smile. "No need to air my dirty laundry."

"Nothing to be ashamed of, my dear. You're facing your demons. That's something to be proud of."

He gave a subtle nod.

"And I'd prefer either of these lovely ladies to that so-called wife of yours," she said, pressing her lips together in anger.

"*Ex*-wife," said Jasper, noting Aubrey's look of surprise. "And that's all in the past now. We're here to talk about local legends, not my love life. Such as it is—or *was*."

"Of course. Did I answer your questions? Let me see, what else can I tell you . . . ?"

"We saw some logbooks from the old poor farm/asylum days," said Aubrey. "There was something in there about a cemetery on the grounds where residents were buried?"

"Oh, yes. There was a paupers' cemetery in a rear corner of the grounds, but again, that was before my time. Some say Mr. Goffin had the old stone grave markers torn out and used them as building materials in the renovation which, if you ask me, was profane in the extreme. There were no names on the markers, only numbers, but still. They meant something."

"What about the bodies?" asked Nikki.

"I believe he paved right over them. They say the formal rose garden was planted in that corner."

Nikki glanced at Aubrey and mouthed, "Poltergeist."

"They say Goffin was an unhappy, tortured man, and it's no wonder."

"Because his son died so young?" Nikki asked.

"That, and for other reasons. He returned to the Seabrink when it was a nursing home, you know. He was quite elderly then, in his nineties. A friend of mine was an attendant there and said Goffin was very strange: he never socialized, never even spoke to anyone, occasionally played a tune on the grand piano and ran his hand along the polished wood, even up and down the legs. Then one day he climbed all the way up to the attic, sat down on the very top step, and killed himself."

"He killed himself in the attic?" asked Aubrey. "I hadn't heard that."

"Few people have. The family hushed it up, of course. They've done that for years. But the locals know the real story."

"How'd he do it?" Nikki asked.

"He drank a vial of cyanide. They say it's a very painful way to die. Afterward, no one went back into the attic, they just left everything as it was. My friend told me that one of the staff members was so afraid of what might be lingering up there that she placed a crystal ball at the base of the old servants' stairs leading up to it."

"That crystal ball is still there," said Aubrey. "You're saying it wards off spirits?"

Nana Joyce laughed. "Supposedly it works as a prism, or something? It separates and reflects the light, which she said dispelled spirits, or captured evil, or something along those lines. I didn't say it was logical, but it made the staff feel better. And do you know, apparently after all of that, and his advanced age, Goffin died intestate. He left no will, nothing at all. Just a mess for his family to inherit."

"Have you ever heard of a ferronnière associated with the Hotel?" asked Aubrey.

"A what, now?"

"It's a headband, with a jewel in the middle."

Nana Joyce looked surprised. "I do remember hearing

about a ruby, a family heirloom that a local woman inherited from her grandmother, who had immigrated from Russia. This was way back when, before my time. When her husband had her admitted to the poor farm—he was tired of being married and saw no reason to pay for a divorce—she was supposed to turn over all her possessions to the superintendent. Later, of course, the superintendent denied he'd ever seen it and claimed she must have squirreled it away somewhere. There were lots of rumors about him, though, including that he beat his wife. But again, this was all before my time, so it's just hearsay. Just like the ghost sightings. That's what most people ask me about."

"Have you ever seen anything ghostly up there?"

She shook her head. "I heard the flute music, and I saw the woman pushed from the balcony. That was enough for me; I didn't go back. But if it's the spirits that interest you, you might want to talk to Mia Ramirez, Jasper's friend. Do you know her? She has a sweet consignment shop in Gualala."

"I've met Mia," said Aubrey. "She didn't tell me anything in particular about the spirits of the Hotel Seabrink, though."

"Well, I believe she has a gift. Oh, she tries to fight it, but I know her grandmother, who is a talented *curandera*—that means 'healer' in Spanish. The talent skipped her mother, went straight to her. I heard she went up to the Seabrink not long ago, and tried to shut the portals, but it didn't work."

"These are the portals represented by the spring with the special mineral water?"

Nana nodded. "The native peoples knew about it, and gave it a wide berth, even way back when. And then when the structure was built, and the tragedies occurred there, they magnified the negative powers. Or so they say."

Aubrey and Nikki both looked at Jasper, who held his hands up in surrender. "Once again, I know nothing. Apparently I don't ask enough questions."

The foghorn sounded again, and Nana Joyce glanced at her watch. "Oh, I do hate to say goodbye, but my neighbor's son is coming over soon. I'm helping him with his algebra. I was a math teacher, way back when."

As she walked them to the door Aubrey heard Nana Joyce humming that same haunting melody under her breath.

"Catchy tune," said Aubrey.

"I swear, once I think about it, it gets stuck in my head."

She gave Aubrey and Nikki each a lavender-scented hug. "Come see me again. My door is always open to Jasper's friends." She turned to kiss her grandson. "And you, sweetie. Get a haircut! And promise me you won't let these ladies go back to that hotel alone. It's not safe."

"I promise, Nana," Jasper said.

As Aubrey turned to leave, Nana Joyce reached out and grabbed her arm with surprising strength.

"Aubrey, I can say this one thing for sure: it was wrong for the Seabrink to be abandoned. Profoundly wrong. One doesn't leave corpses behind. They should be taken care of. The dead deserve a proper burial, or they'll never rest in peace."

Your Nana is lovely, Jasper," Aubrey said. on the drive back to Gualala. "But she kind of spooked me at the end there."

"If the Seabrink isn't rife with poltergeists, I want to know why not," Nikki said. "I mean, how can someone just rip up grave markers and pave over the bodies like that?"

"Happens all the time with paupers' graves, I'm sorry to say," said Jasper. "Folks whom society didn't think mattered much in life matter even less in death."

"And they used the stones in the renovation? Definitely bad juju there."

"What was all that about Mia?" asked Aubrey.

"I really don't know, to tell you the truth," said Jasper. "I've known Mia for years through our work, but she's never spoken to me about anything . . . otherworldly. Quite the opposite, as a matter of fact. I know her grandmother has a reputation as a talented natural healer, but Mia never seemed to take an interest in that sort of thing, at least not that she told me about. Do you want me to give her a call?"

"I'd rather see if we could talk to her face-to-face," said Aubrey. "Check out her body language, and all that. Right now I'm more interested in what your nana told us about the woman being pushed from the balcony. Nikki, remember the old letter I found in Dimitri's things, the one written by a hotel maid who was waiting for her child's father to come back and marry her?"

"Effie Mae?" Nikki said.

"Yes, Effie Mae. Remember how Deborah Goldman said there were rumors of affairs between the Seabrink's guests and the staff? What if the man Effie Mae was referring to was none other than T. Jefferson Goffin himself?"

"And rather than marry her, Goffin pushed her off the balcony?" Nikki asked. "That tracks, except that everyone says the victim was a French starlet."

"True. I guess I'm getting my women—and my murders—mixed up. And I just remembered that Jo—that's Dimitri's sister—told me that Effie Mae died of tuberculosis. But she had sent her daughter, whom she named Victoria, to live with

extended family in Bakersfield. So, let's think this through:
What if Effie's daughter, Victoria, grew up in Bakersfield and
had a daughter, Christine, and Christine was the one who put
Dimitri up for adoption?"

"Didn't you say Cameron is a Goffin?" Jasper asked.

"Yes, that we know for a fact. Why?" Aubrey said.

"What if Cameron somehow figured out that Dimitri was
also a Goffin, biologically speaking?" Jasper suggested.

"Hold on—if Aubrey is right, and Dimitri was biologically
a Goffin, he wouldn't just be a member of the extended family," Nikki said. "He'd be a *direct descendant* of the big guy.
Grandson? Great-grandson?"

"Could you explain the family tree to me again?" Jasper
said. "I think I missed a step."

"Okay. Effie Mae was a maid at the Hotel Seabrink, where
she met T. Jefferson Goffin. They had an affair, she got preg-
nant, and she gave birth to a daughter whom she named Victoria. Effie Mae sent Victoria to live with relatives in
Bakersfield, which is where Victoria grew up and later had a
daughter, whom Dimitri's sister, Jo, said was named Christine," Aubrey explained. "Christine, in turn, had a son whom
she put up for adoption. That child was adopted by the Harmon family in Bakersfield and named Roger. Roger grew up
and started going by the name of Dimitri Petroff . . ."

"And he then came back to the Hotel Seabrink," said Nikki.
"Where it all began."

"So Dimitri Petroff would be T. Jefferson Goffin's one and
only direct descendant and thus Goffin's heir," said Jasper, his
tone thoughtful. "Would this mean Cameron and his relatives
have no claim on the Seabrink?"

"Says here that until the 1960s, illegitimate children did
not have inheritance rights," said Nikki, tapping on her phone

and reading aloud. "But apparently today's law is pretty murky on this sort of thing."

"Maybe that's what Obi meant when she said title to the Seabrink was tied up in court," Aubrey said. "If Goffin died without a will, and Cameron and his family found out Dimitri was Goffin's heir, they might have . . ."

"Killed him to get him out of the way," Nikki said.

TWENTY-SIX

After saying goodbye to Jasper in the Stillman's Hardware and Lumber parking lot, Aubrey started driving down Gualala's main drag, but turned left into the parking lot of the Cypress Village shops.

"Oh good, back to the bookstore?" Nikki asked. "I could use a comfort read."

"No, I want to go speak with Mia directly. It's not late, her shop should still be open."

But as they approached the store, they saw Deputy Jenkins, a small bag in his hands, standing outside the consignment shop's closed door.

Aubrey's heart fell. "Is everything okay?"

"What?" The deputy blushed a deep red. "Yeah, sure, why?"

"I assumed Mia would be in her shop."

"Yeah, um, me too. But the note says she had to close early today."

"Oh, okay, then," Aubrey said. "At first, when I saw you here, I thought maybe something had happened to her."

"Nothing that I know of. I was just, um, gonna ask her about something. Oh, by the way," he addressed Nikki. "You have any more run-ins with your stalker type? You know where his current whereabouts might be?"

Nikki shook her head.

"We in law enforcement take protective orders seriously," he insisted. "You be sure to let us know if you see him."

"Thank you, Deputy," said Nikki. "I truly appreciate that."

"Any word from the coroner about the body we found?" Aubrey asked.

"Realistically, it's gonna take a while. This isn't like on TV, you know." Jenkins hesitated, then added: "I mean, the official COD—that's cause of death—could be a lot of things. We'll have to wait a while for the report from the forensic investigator. And, you know, we in law enforcement aren't supposed to reach conclusions. Our job is to collect evidence and investigate suspects."

"But you have your suspicions?"

Jenkins nodded and seemed to be searching for words. "The thing is, when I was examining the body in the attic, I had a hunch."

"What was it?" Nikki asked.

"Have you heard of the hyoid bone? It's a U-shaped bone in the neck, sort of near the base of the skull."

"I know where you're going with this," Nikki said. "The hyoid bone is often broken in cases of strangulation."

"In about a third of all strangulation cases," Jenkins confirmed with a nod. "The forensic report won't be back for a while, but since there were no obvious broken bones or a bashed-in head or whatever, I asked a buddy in the coroner's office to x-ray her hyoid bone. This girl's was broken. I thought you'd want to know. I mean, I know it's kind of weird, but I felt sorry for her, just left like that, abandoned for all those years under that pile of blankets. No wonder she's a little pissed off."

"Pissed off?"

"I mean, like, haunting the place, I guess? I tried to gather up a few things from her room, and . . . well, I don't mind saying, I hightailed it out of there."

"Did you see something?" Aubrey asked.

"More felt something. Like I wasn't welcome, like, at *all*."

They all sat with that for a moment.

"So." Aubrey changed the subject. "Do you know Mia Ramirez well?"

"Most of us locals know each other."

"Have you heard anything about her having supernatural abilities?"

He blushed again. "She sells tonics, that kind of thing, that her grandmother makes. To tell you the truth, that's what this is." He held up the bag. Aubrey recognized the logo as the symbol she had seen on the front door of the hotel, and also scratched into the stone at the mouth of the spring. "I bought it last week for my hair, 'cause I'm already losing it, believe it or not, but I stopped by 'cause I wanted to ask Mia exactly how I'm supposed to apply it. Anyway, they say it's natural, but I wouldn't say '*super*natural.' Anyway, ladies, I've got to get back to work. Stay safe out there."

By the time Aubrey and Nikki pulled into the Driftwood Cove parking lot, the afternoon sun cast an orangey glow on a thick bank of fog approaching from the west.

"You know, some watchmakers are also jewelers," Nikki said, as they passed through small groups of jovial conventioneers gathered in the hotel lobby. "Maybe one of them could tell us something about the ferronnière."

One older man was holding court, telling three enthralled listeners about the internal workings of the famous astronomical clock, or "horologium," in Prague. He had a thin face and a bulbous nose and wore a three-piece tweed suit with an honest-to-God pocket watch, its golden chain dangling from his vest pocket.

"That fellow seems like a good candidate," said Nikki. "He looks like he was sent from central casting to play the role of an expert watchmaker."

"Worth a shot." Aubrey approached the group, apologized for interrupting them, and introduced herself and Nikki.

"May I ask you a question?" she said to the man with the pocket watch.

"I would be honored," he said in a gallant tone, and introduced himself as Mr. Ronaldo Tomassi.

Aubrey held up her phone to show him the photograph of the starlet wearing a ferronnière. "Would it be possible for you to estimate the value of this antique headband? Assuming the central ruby is genuine."

The man studied the digital photo, then nodded. "Unless a jewel is associated with something or someone of historical importance, the fact that it's an antique doesn't affect the market value. But assuming the jewel is a genuine ruby? It would be valuable. *Very* valuable indeed. Most folks don't realize that rubies and emeralds are worth far more than diamonds."

"How much are we talking?" Nikki asked. "Ballpark figure."

"A number of factors affect the market value. But assuming

it is a high-quality genuine ruby, then a conservative estimate would be between ten thousand to one hundred thousand per carat, depending on the color, cut, and clarity. Possibly even more. Judging from the photo, that jewel is quite large, so a small fortune, certainly. Why do you ask?"

"We're wondering if something like this could be a motive to kill someone," Nikki said.

Mr. Tomassi passed his rheumy eyes over them. "I have to tell you, young ladies, I've lived a long time and unfortunately one of the things I've learned is that it doesn't take much to inspire some people to violence. Sadly, some will kill for what amounts to petty, even inconsequential amounts of money. Or for no reason at all."

"That's what I've been saying," said Nikki.

"And to acquire a ruby like this? A very likely motive for murder among unscrupulous types."

They thanked him and started up the stairs to their room.

"Okay, so maybe someone found out that Dimitri had a claim on the Goffin fortune and pushed him off the cliff," said Aubrey. "Or someone was after the ruby, thought Dimitri had it or knew where it was, and pushed him off the cliff. Or . . ."

"Or a stalker ex-girlfriend decided if she couldn't have him then no one could and pushed him off the cliff, in which case his death had nothing to do with the Seabrink or lost jewelry," noted Nikki. "And let's not forget that Gideon thinks the emergency responders are having strange rituals up at the Seabrink to tap into the supernatural energy there. Maybe it has to do with the rocks, or the salts in the water . . ."

"Jasper said there was nothing going on up there."

"Maybe it's like in a horror movie, and the whole town is in on it."

"Even Nana Joyce?"

"Especially Nana Joyce. She'd be the ringleader. Think about it."

"I'm going to give that suggestion every bit of consideration it's due," Aubrey said, unlocking their room's door and following Nikki inside.

She kicked off her shoes and collapsed on the bed while Nikki took a seat at the desk and opened her laptop.

"So T. Jefferson Goffin took his own life in the attic," Aubrey mused. "Drinking cyanide of all things. That sounds awful. I wonder if he died near where we found the body."

"You think he killed that girl?"

"Maybe. What if she found the ruby and Goffin somehow learned she had it? A man like Goffin was accustomed to getting what he wanted when he wanted it. And then he gave it to his mistress, which is why it's in those photographs."

"But then why did he kill himself? That suggests a consciousness of guilt."

"Remember, his son died, despite all his efforts," Aubrey said. "He might have seen that as a form of divine punishment for his many sins against others. Maybe as he neared his own death, he was haunted by everything he'd done so he returned to the scene of the crime to take his own life. That would explain why I smelled almonds when we were up there."

"What do almonds have to do with anything?"

"Cyanide smells like bitter almonds. Or so they say."

"Okay, but would the smell linger for, what, fifty years? Or more?"

"Not normally, but I'm going to go out on a limb and say the Hotel Seabrink isn't normal."

"You don't have to convince me. I saw someone or some *thing* in the attic window there."

"But there was a twenty-four-hour time limit on the curse,

remember? It's been longer than that. And I have a feeling . . . about Hazel, the Quiet Girl. I think she's angry with men, not at women."

"I had that sense, too," Nikki said in a low voice, rifling through her computer bag. "Dammit, now I can't find my favorite pen. As my mama used to say, if my head weren't screwed on I'd lose it, too."

While Nikki checked in with her colleagues at work, Aubrey turned to Dimitri's handwritten journal. As before, decoding Dimitri's messy script and numerous cross-outs, arrows, and insertions made it slow going. But after slogging through a meandering discussion of various legal issues, a list of dimensions for unnamed spaces, and suggestions for good camera angles, she came across a notation in one margin:

But the quiet one remained, losing herself in the attic's secret passages.

The Quiet Girl.
Hazel.

I t was a Saturday night, but after a half-hearted debate about whether or not to venture into town in search of nightlife, and whether or not Ty might be lurking somewhere, and whether or not they should allow Ty to dictate their lives, they agreed to order room service and watch classic movies on television.

Nikki fell asleep by nine, in the middle of *Casablanca*. Aubrey's body was tired, but her mind was wide awake and she knew she wouldn't be able to fall asleep anytime soon. Loath to wake Nikki, she grabbed her jacket, pepper spray, and flashlight and slipped out of the room.

Downstairs, she noticed that the watchmaker convention had held some kind of event in the restaurant, which had recently concluded. Several guests were having a nightcap at the bar, while others were looking through the record collection. Four people sat around a game table playing Monopoly. From behind the reception desk, the woman with the Jamaican accent greeted Aubrey with a smile.

"Looks like there was some kind of party here," Aubrey commented.

"Tonight was their big gala. They're leaving tomorrow," she said of the watchmakers. "I wish all our conferences were this fun."

Outside, the ocean air was fresh and invigorating, and a number of people were out and about. A few were smoking, others were checking out the Bufano peace sculpture, and several were walking along the bluff trail. With so many people around, Aubrey relaxed but kept her pepper spray in her jacket pocket, just in case.

It was a beautiful night: blustery up on the cliffs, but warmer than it had been recently. Overhead, an unbelievable number of stars shone against the ebony sky.

When she reached Dead Man's Bluff, she found a small crowd milling around. These were not young YouTube fans but older folks, whom Aubrey assumed were attending the watchmakers' conference. She spotted Mr. Tomassi, who had answered her questions about the ferronière, and they exchanged a few words, appreciating the natural beauty of the area and the astonishing canopy of stars.

Aubrey lingered near the bluff, lulled by the roar of the

waves far below as she thought about everything that had happened the past few days.

She sighed and reluctantly tore her gaze from the ocean. Time to go back to the inn. She turned and found herself face-to-face with Stephen Rex.

TWENTY-SEVEN

Aubrey reached for her pepper spray, her mind racing.

There are so many people here. Surely he wouldn't . . . ?

"Take it easy," Stephen said, holding his hands up in surrender. "I'm not here to hurt you. Would you just listen to me for a minute?"

"Everything okay over there?" Mr. Tomassi called out from a few yards away, apparently sensing her unease.

"I think so," she said, recalling what Jasper had said about Stephen. Maybe he was one of those people who was not great at picking up on social cues. Maybe he wasn't a threat. She just wished they were speaking anywhere but here, on Dead Man's Bluff.

"We'll be right over here if you need anything," the chivalrous Mr. Tomassi said, as the group of watchmakers shot stern looks at Stephen.

"Look, if it'll make you feel better, I'll stand next to the edge of the cliff, okay?" said Stephen, walking around her. "That way, if anyone's going over the side, it's me, not you."

"I don't want anyone falling off the cliff," Aubrey replied. "What do you want, Stephen?"

"I'm just—okay. Here's the thing. I sent Dimitri the threatening texts. I'd been trying to talk with him about collaborating on the Netflix deal. It was a stupid thing to do, okay? I may have misjudged the situation, probably came off like an asshole. I do that sometimes, and I don't even mean to."

Aubrey wanted to believe him but wasn't yet sure if she should. "Go on."

"I mean, I really admired Dimitri. I'm honestly sad he's gone. Even if Netflix offered me the series now, I'm not sure I could handle it on my own. I was thinking a collaboration with Dimitri would be good for both of us. Give me exposure and boost his ratings because I would bring in a younger demographic. Dimitri's work was great, but his target audience skewed older and more educated. Younger and more ignorant is where the money is these days, you know what I mean?"

"Unfortunately, I do. But why are you telling me all this?"

"Because I know some things you don't." Stephen paused and looked around, as though afraid of being overheard. The watchmaking contingent were still glaring at him, and Aubrey smiled to herself that she had her very own protection detail.

"Like what? Spill it, Stephen. It's now or never."

"Dimitri found a suicide note by the guy who used to own the Seabrink," Stephen said, the words pouring out of him. "Goffin somebody? In the note he admitted he had murdered a girl there—"

Suddenly there was a flash of headlights, and the loud

screeching of wheels. Stephen's gaze shifted over Aubrey's shoulder, and he suddenly reached out and grabbed her arm.

He's going to push me off the cliff, just like he did Dimitri!

One of the watchmakers yelled "Watch out!" and Aubrey unleashed her pepper spray on Stephen, but the wind gusting off the ocean blew some of the pepper spray back toward her, stinging her eyes and filling them with tears. She was flung to the ground just as a car clipped Stephen, tossing him into the air like a rag doll before speeding off.

Gravel dug into her knee and thigh, and her eyes were streaming tears, but Aubrey was more shocked than hurt. Stephen had pushed her out of harm's way and borne the brunt of the attack. She crawled over to his side.

Mr. Tomassi and several others came running over. "Are you all right? We saw everything! Oh, the poor man!"

"I'm calling 911!" one of the watchmakers cried out, a cell phone to her ear.

Aubrey knelt next to the injured man. "Stephen? Can you speak?"

He groaned and mumbled something, but she couldn't make out the words. His head had struck one of the small boulders that dotted the bluff and was bleeding profusely, and one leg was twisted in an unnatural position. Aubrey took off her jacket and, as gently as she could, pressed it against his head wound to staunch the bleeding.

"My . . . leg . . ."

"Don't try to move. Just lie still. We've got you. Help will be here soon," Aubrey said, hoping she was right. She heard the woman on the phone to emergency services trying to describe where they were.

"Tell them we're at Dead Man's Bluff," Aubrey called out. "They'll know where it is."

thought Stephen was trying to kill me," Aubrey told Nikki much later that night, after giving a statement to the sheriff's deputy. Fortunately, Jasper's friend, Sam, had shown up this time. He had calmly and efficiently taken statements from everyone on the cliff, but it was dark and no one had seen who was driving, or noted the license plate number. The most the eyewitnesses could say was that the car was gray or silver and possibly a late-model Honda sedan. It all happened so fast.

"Did he say anything helpful before he was struck by the car?"

"He admitted that he sent the threatening text messages to Dimitri, trying to spook him, I guess. He wanted a piece of Dimitri's Netflix deal."

"I knew it! He'll probably go after it now."

"Maybe. But if he does, it won't be for a while," said Aubrey, trying to wash the blood out of her jacket at the bathroom sink. "His head wound looked serious and one of his legs was pretty messed up. He was taken by helicopter to the hospital in Santa Rosa."

"So, he wasn't a bad guy, after all," Nikki said. "Did he say anything else?"

"Get this: according to Stephen, Dimitri found a suicide note in which Goffin admitted to murdering someone."

"The Quiet Girl?"

"Could be. Or the starlet? Or maybe someone else."

"He's starting to sound like a serial killer," said Nikki.

"Or an unscrupulous rich man who wants what he wants and is willing to kill for it."

"Are we thinking Dimitri was murdered—and now Stephen was almost killed—to keep Goffin's suicide note a secret?

I mean, Goffin died a very long time ago. Why would someone kill to keep the note a secret now?"

"Maybe for the same reasons they're willing to break the law to scrub the internet? Some people care a lot about things like family reputation."

Nikki yawned and headed for the bathroom. "I don't suppose you took a photo of the car as it sped off?"

"Are you kidding?" Aubrey said. "I had pepper spray in my eyes and was still thinking Stephen wanted to shove me off the cliff."

"Yeah, that could be distracting. No one else did, either?"

"Turns out watchmakers tend to be old-fashioned—not one of them thought to whip out their phone and film it. The YouTube crowd would be appalled."

"You know, the driver could have been a woman," mused Nikki, brushing her hair. "What kind of car does Obi drive?"

"I would imagine a Mercedes or a Jaguar of some type, judging by her upscale home. But why would you suspect Obi?"

She shrugged. "Some of those developers are pretty ruthless. Or . . . how about Mia? Nana Joyce said she went up there to do a cleansing, and her shop was suspiciously closed during regular retail hours."

"But why would Mia kill Dimitri, and then try to kill Stephen?"

"You saw that picture at the firehouse. Maybe it's the actual priceless headband. She stole it and Dimitri found out about it, so she had to shut him up. Then Stephen found out about *that*, so she had to shut *him* up."

"That photo was taken last Halloween. Why would she kill over it now, if she already has it?"

"*Hmm*. Important detail. I still think it would be interesting to see if she drives a gray sedan."

"Lots of people drive gray sedans," Aubrey said, applying salve to the scrapes she had incurred when she fell on the gravel. "*I* drive a gray sedan."

"I'm not sure of much these days, Spencer," Nikki said as she climbed back into bed and pulled up the covers. "But I do believe we can cross *you* off the suspect list."

TWENTY-EIGHT

called the hospital to see how Stephen's doing," Aubrey said when Nikki came out of the bathroom the next morning, her long hair wet from her shower. "He's stable but is in serious condition. He hasn't been able to give a statement to the police."

"I've been thinking," Nikki said, toweling her hair dry. "What makes us think Stephen was the intended target? Maybe the driver was after you, instead."

"That thought kept me awake for quite a while last night." After she woke, as usual, at 4:07 a.m.

"You did get those threatening notes, after all," said Nikki.

"True. And according to the notes, someone wants me to back off for some reason. Could be reason enough to try to run me off the cliff." She blew out a breath. "I'm going to call Jasper and let him know about Stephen, since they're sort of friends. Assuming the small-town grapevine hasn't informed him already. And then I propose we go downstairs and linger over a well-deserved Sunday brunch."

"With mimosas?"

"Oh, definitely with mimosas."

Twenty minutes later they found Monica behind the reception desk.

"On front desk duty this morning, eh?" asked Nikki.

"I'm a jill of all trades around here. Hey, did you hear what happened last night, on Dead Man's Bluff?"

"We sure did," Nikki said. "Aubrey was there."

"You *were*?" Monica said with a little gasp. "I have to hand it to you, Aubrey. Our guests don't usually encounter so much drama during their stay."

"That's what Deputy Jenkins tells me."

"You are all right, I take it?"

Aubrey nodded. "A few scrapes and bruises, but nothing serious. And the hospital says that the man who was hit is stable, so that's good news."

"That is indeed," said Monica.

"You've met Mia, the woman with the consignment shop in Gualala, haven't you?" Nikki asked Monica.

"Sure. I love that shop," said Monica.

"What kind of car does Mia drive?"

"I have no idea. Why?"

"Just curious."

The magazine Monica had been flipping through lay splayed on the counter, and Aubrey noticed the pages had been cut up.

"Looks like you need some new magazines," Aubrey said.

Monica smiled. "Right? We had a Valentine's party last month for the guests, just some arts and crafts. Cut up a bunch of magazines to make cards. It's funny, print magazines aren't as easy to come by as they used to be. When I was a kid there was always a big stack of magazines on the coffee table. They sort of fit with the midcentury vibe here, don't they?"

"They do. Last night it was fun to see people playing board games."

"That's part of our whole schtick here." Monica let out a sigh and checked her phone. "Now, if Breanna would just show up for her shift, I could get ready for the storm that's headed our way later today. I tell you what, these young people call in at the last minute, claiming they're 'sick' when they're probably all on social media. Well, enjoy your breakfast, ladies."

Aubrey and Nikki had started for the restaurant when Nikki stopped and turned back.

"I noticed you're pretty active on social media these days," she said to Monica. "Seems like Driftwood Cove is all over the socials lately."

"I've done a few promo pieces for the inn, sure. Just short videos, or memes. It's a good way to get the word out about us."

"You didn't . . . I mean, you didn't post anything showing me or Aubrey, did you?"

Monica looked guilty. "I . . . I may have. I didn't mean anything by it, just posting happy clients. I got a really cute shot of the two of you looking through the record albums. But I didn't give your names or anything. This was before you told me Ty might be in town, of course. Oh no . . . it wasn't a problem, was it?"

"I'm sure it's fine," said Nikki, her expression troubled. "But no more photos, okay?"

After a luxurious breakfast, Aubrey received a phone call from Deborah Goldman, asking her to stop by her house in

Sea Ranch because she had something important that she wanted Aubrey to have. Nikki begged off and stayed in the hotel room to work.

"Be sure to get back before the storm hits," said Monica as Aubrey left. "You have two or three hours, tops, before it starts to move in for real. The weather can get serious in these parts. I just hope our generator is up to the challenge. Do you have any idea what it's like to run a hotel when the power goes out and the phones go down and the internet stops working?"

"I can only imagine," Aubrey said. "Thanks for the heads-up. I'll make it quick."

As she drove to Sea Ranch, Aubrey answered a call from Obi.

"Aubrey, have you seen Cameron Meroni?" Obi asked.

"I saw him a few days ago, but not lately. Why?"

"Someone's been stealing things from the Seabrink."

"And you suspect Cameron?"

"I do. After all these years of being left alone, the Seabrink's suddenly being looted and Cameron—who I know has gambling debts and no money—drops out of sight? I knew he had problems, but I wanted to give him an opportunity. But an addict's an addict, I suppose."

"What did he steal?" Aubrey asked.

"Not sure yet, but the old Victrola's missing. That was worth a pretty penny. Hey, by the way, we got some good news from our lawyers today. It looks like the legal dispute over the title to the Seabrink might finally be coming to a close. Which means I have a hell of a lot of work to do to even have a prayer of staying on schedule. This might seem sudden, but I know your reputation, Aubrey. I was hoping you might seriously consider coming to work with me on this. You could work remotely from Oakland most of the time if you'd prefer. This is going to be a spectacular project. Great for your portfolio, and I'll make it worth your while."

"That's very tempting," Aubrey said. *But what about the Quiet Girl? What would she make of such renovations?* "I promise I'll think about it."

By the time Aubrey reached Sea Ranch's bucolic grounds, she could see dark clouds hovering in the distance over the ocean. The skies overhead were still blue, but the wind was picking up.

Just like last time, her knock on Deborah Goldman's door was greeted with wild barking. Deborah opened the door, fruitlessly hushed the dogs, and asked Aubrey inside.

"Aubrey! I'm sorry, I didn't realize the storm was moving in so quickly," she said as they went into the living room. "I'll make this fast. I started a scrapbook for you."

"For me? That's so kind of you."

"I felt as if I owed you an apology for Gideon's behavior; he's really not a bad fellow, but he does get carried away. Anyway, the scrapbook isn't much, just bits and pieces about the history of the area and the Hotel Seabrink. There are even a few references to when it was a poor farm and asylum. I left spaces for you to add your own photographs, see? I know you take a million digital photos, but you really should print the best ones. And now, if you do, you can add them to your scrapbook, and you'll always remember your time spent here with us."

Aubrey sincerely doubted she would ever forget her time in Mendonoma, scrapbook or no. But it was such a sweet, old-fashioned memento, she was touched.

"I tried to buy you some sticky buns this morning, but

they'd already run out," Deborah continued. "So I bought you some Necco Wafers. Anya said you liked them."

"Anya?"

"She works at Twofish Baking. Her cousin is a deputy, so she's a font of information about the goings-on around here."

"Oh, thank you. That's so thoughtful of you. And the scrapbook is a lovely souvenir. You're quite the artist."

"Well, I must confess, it wasn't just me. Our group got together yesterday, and all the gals contributed."

"Who do you scrapbook with?"

"It depends. Sometimes it's just a couple of us, sometimes more. It's mostly an excuse to get together to gossip and eat snacks. Yesterday it was just Gideon's wife, Laurie, and my old friend Claudia Krasniewski. She's not a Sea Rancher, but she has a sweet little house on the little hill that sits over the Cypress Village parking lot."

"Krasniewski? That name sounds familiar."

"You've probably met her son, Xavi, who works at the Driftwood Cove Inn. Xavi was a troubled boy, but he's been doing better recently—at least he's been able to hold on to that job! He still lives with his mother, and he joins in our scrapbooking get-togethers when we meet at her house. It's rare to have a young man sit with us, but he seems to enjoy it."

Deborah's living room began to dim as threatening black clouds rolled in.

"Oh my, would you look at that," said Deborah. "They say this storm's going to be a bad one. They're already warning people to stay off the roads. You're welcome to stay here if you'd rather not risk driving back. I have an extra bedroom. We could do some scrapbooking!"

"That's very kind, but I'd prefer to get back to the hotel while I still can. Thanks again for this lovely memento."

Aubrey drove as fast as she dared down Highway One, Xavi on her mind. Could he have been the one who sent her threatening notes? What possible motivation would he have?

The sun had disappeared behind clouds an ominous shade of slate gray, and gusts of wind buffeted her car. Aubrey gripped the steering wheel so tightly her knuckles were white. As she neared Driftwood Cove, the clouds opened and great sheets of rain began to pour down on her windshield. Her windshield wipers struggled to keep up.

Aubrey turned into the inn's parking lot with relief. She hadn't realized until then that she had been holding her breath.

She ran inside, shaking off the rain. The lobby was crowded with people from the watchmaker's convention milling about, and she overheard one saying a tree was down, blocking the highway to the south. They were supposed to check out today but were now realizing they might be stuck here for days.

"We'll be lucky if we don't lose power," she heard the bartender say. "But we've got a backup generator, at least."

Aubrey asked for Xavi at the front desk, but the young woman said he had called in sick.

Aubrey had started up the stairs when she heard Monica calling her name. She swore under her breath; all she wanted to do was go upstairs, peel off her wet clothes, and jump into the shower in case the power did go out and there was no more hot water. But Monica was hurrying across the lobby toward her, looking on the verge of panic.

"I'm sure it will be okay, Monica," said Aubrey. "It's not that cold, and if you have a generator—"

"What? No, it's not that. *Aubrey*," she clutched her arm. "I saw it from the lobby. They were in the parking lot, and I couldn't get to them in time. She was taken."

"Taken? What are you talking about? *Who* are you talking about?"

"*Nikki.* She's been taken."

TWENTY-NINE

She was in the parking lot arguing with someone, and then the guy shoved her into the trunk and slammed it closed! I think it was Ty from the photos, but I can't be sure. In this rain—"

"When?"

"Just now! A few minutes ago! I called 911 but everything's a mess, and I couldn't tell them much."

"What kind of car?"

"A gray four-door sedan of some sort. I don't really know cars. I got a partial plate, though, JGL 9 . . . something. They headed south on the highway, but there's a tree down, blocking the route, so they'll have to turn around, I think, and come back by here. There are no other through roads between here and there."

Aubrey's mind was a blur. *Think.* Was it Ty? It must be, right? *What should I do?* Should she chase them to the south? How fast did she dare drive on the winding coastal highway, in a storm?

She ran out to her car, pointed it toward the highway, and waited at the parking lot entrance. She called 911 and reported what Monica had seen, including the partial plate. The harried operator said they had already registered Monica's complaint and would send someone out as soon as they could.

Frustrated, Aubrey hung up and stared out the car window, stunned by how quickly the weather had turned ferocious. Rain drummed on the roof and wind gusts slammed against the car. Aubrey waited anxiously, her heart pounding, her mind racing. She shivered in her wet clothes, and her leg was stinging from yesterday's mishap on the cliff. What had Stephen been trying to tell her? Did it matter?

She held her phone up and watched the road through her viewfinder, trying to regulate her breathing. As always, looking at the world through a lens helped to calm her.

A gray car approached from the south, driving faster than was safe. She snapped photos, including of the license plate. The rain obscured the face of the driver, but she could see there was not one, but two people in the front seat.

Was it the wrong car? There were a lot of gray sedans on the road.

Aubrey quickly reviewed one of the photos of the license plate: it began JGL. Then, as the car sped past her, Aubrey saw a hand reaching out through a broken right taillight and waving.

Nikki.

Aubrey gunned the engine and pulled onto the highway, following the gray sedan as closely as possible, determined not to lose sight of it. She dialed 911 again but the circuits were jammed, and the call did not go through. She gripped the steering wheel with one hand and used the other to text Jasper and Deputy Jenkins, hoping that even if calls weren't going through, the texts might.

When they approached Stewarts Point, the gray car slowed slightly and turned right onto Asylum Point Road. *What are they doing?* In a storm like this Asylum Point Road was the last place a car should go. The road eventually led to Cazadero, but only after miles through heavily wooded, tightly twisting mountains. If Highway One was already blocked by fallen trees, she imagined Asylum Point Road would be the same, soon enough.

Surely they weren't heading to the Hotel Seabrink?

But the gray car turned off onto the overgrown, semi-paved road she knew well by this point. The unmarked road to the Hotel Seabrink. Runoff from the relentless rain gushed down the lane, digging gullies into the soft dirt.

The gray sedan had pulled in through the tall gates and was parked in front of the hotel's main entrance. Aubrey maneuvered her car into a sideways position in front of the gates to block the car from exiting. Her phone calls were still not connecting so she tried resending the texts. Hoping, *praying* they would reach someone.

The only weapon she had with her was her pepper spray. She tried to remember if there was a tire iron in her trunk. But even if there was, did she trust herself with such a weapon? Nikki was the jock, not Aubrey. More likely their assailant would wrestle it away and use it on her, or on Nikki, or on both of them. She decided to just take the pepper spray.

Surely they had seen her car following them. Aubrey had not dared lag too far behind, for fear she would lose sight of their vehicle. They were probably waiting for her inside.

But she had to do *something*. Even assuming help would eventually arrive, it was too risky to wait. Aubrey jumped out of her car and ran up the drive, ignoring the torrential downpour and the wind gusts buffeting her about.

She glanced into the front seat of the gray sedan, and spied a crumpled pack of unfiltered Pall Malls on the front seat.

Ty.

Aubrey reminded herself she had one advantage: she knew the Seabrink layout better than Ty. But who was the second person in the front seat of the car with him? She trotted around the corner and climbed through the broken atrium window, as she had the first time she had come to explore. That was only about a week ago, but it felt like years.

She would not have thought the Hotel Seabrink could be even eerier than before, but in a raging storm, with no lights, the hotel's interior was dark and forbidding. Rainwater dripped through spots in the ceiling, and she could hear water trickling somewhere in the building. The wind howled so hard the windowpanes shook, and tree branches lashed the walls. She heard her own harsh breathing, wiped the rain from her eyes, and tried to calm her pounding heart.

Why would Ty bring Nikki here? As far as Aubrey knew, he had no connection to the Hotel Seabrink. She wasn't sure if he'd even heard of it—unless, of course, he had followed them here the last time, and was the one who had locked them in. And what could Aubrey possibly say to convince him to let Nikki go and leave them in peace?

But first things first: Where were they?

Aubrey thought quickly. Attics and basements were the creepiest parts of any building, Nikki had said. Knowing Ty, if he learned that a murder had taken place in the basement decades ago, he would take Nikki there. If only for the shock value.

Aubrey ran to the rear of the building and, as quietly as she could, opened the doors to the basement baths and crept slowly down the enclosed stairs. The stench of the mineral water enveloped her. She listened intently, but the only sound was the constant trickling of the spring water through the baths and the roar of the storm outside.

She stopped at the landing, still hidden from view, and carefully peeked around the wall to the baths below.

Nikki.

Bound, with a burlap bag over her head, her friend was sitting on the dirty floor with her back against a stone bath.

But . . . where was Ty? Or whoever had been with him in the car?

Aubrey crept down the rest of the stairs, casting her gaze around the cavernous space, straining to hear anything above the sound of the storm outside and the constant trickle of water through the baths.

As she reached the bottom of the stairs, she winced as her sodden boots made a loud squeaking sound on the stones.

Nikki started to squirm and grunt at the sound of the footsteps as Aubrey approached.

And finally . . . Aubrey spotted Ty.

The stalker was sprawled on the floor behind a pillar, in a pool of blood. He was unmoving, with a knife sticking out of his abdomen, and there was a corona of blood marring the stones beneath him. Aubrey let out a breath she hadn't even realized she was holding.

Still, she gave Ty a wide berth as she passed him. Knowing Ty, this could be some sort of sick trick.

There was no sign of his accomplice.

As Aubrey approached Nikki, her friend grew increasingly agitated, making a high-pitched noise that sounded like a muffled scream.

Aubrey held the pepper spray aloft, crouched down, and spun around, searching for Ty's accomplice. There weren't a lot of hiding places down in the baths, besides the massive columns. She put her back to one, then jumped around to the other side, spraying her pepper spray, in case someone stood behind it. There was no one.

Had she been less panicked, Aubrey might have laughed at herself for acting like a parody of an action movie heroine, but her heart was pounding so hard and fast, all she could think of was getting Nikki loose and getting the hell out before Bad Guy #2 came back from wherever he was hiding.

Still crouching and pivoting her head this way and that, Aubrey hurried over to Nikki's side and snatched the hood off her head. One of Nikki's eyes was red and swollen, but Aubrey read first panic, then relief, in her friend's gaze.

Aubrey swore under her breath as she undid the gag.

"They *hit* you? Are you all right?"

"I'm okay. I think the other guy left. Let's get the hell out before he comes back."

"Who left? Who is the other guy?" Aubrey asked, working on the tight knot in the rope.

"In case you didn't notice, I had a *sack* over my head."

"You didn't recognize his voice?"

Nikki shook her head. "It sounded sort of familiar, maybe, but he whispered, and I couldn't place it."

"I didn't think Ty *had* any friends," muttered Aubrey.

"You and me both, sister," Nikki muttered, wincing as Aubrey pulled on the rope. She glanced over at where Ty lay motionless on the floor. "Is he dead?"

"I don't know. And I don't actually care. Are you sure you're all right?" Aubrey asked as she finally freed her friend's arms, realizing that one of Nikki's wrists was sticky with blood. "What happened to your wrist?"

"I cut it, punching out the taillight."

"Oh! That was clever! That's how I knew it was you."

"I told you all that true crime stuff would come in handy one day. But otherwise I'm okay."

"Are you sure?"

"Yeah, I'm fine. I mean . . . I was punched and kidnapped by my stalker, and taken to the haunted mansion I swore I would never return to, and brought into the baths where it *stinks*, and where a girl was murdered on prom night, apparently, and then heard someone stab my stalker to death—about which I am of two minds, if I'm being honest—but otherwise I'm . . . just dandy."

Aubrey gave Nikki a quick hug and helped her to her feet. "Let's get out of here."

Nikki stared at Ty. "Is he really dead?"

"I think so. Do you care?"

"W-will you check?"

Pressing her lips together, Aubrey held her pepper spray up as she neared him, trying to stifle the image of a bloodied and enraged Ty surging up and assaulting her. She crouched beside him and gingerly placed two fingers on his neck, just under his chin. His skin was slick with blood.

"I can't feel a pulse. And . . . he's lost an awful lot of blood," she whispered. "But I'm no professional. Maybe if they can get to him in time, but in this storm . . . I don't know. Let's get the hell out of here. If we can."

"What do you mean, *if* we can?"

"With that storm outside . . ." Aubrey shook her head. "I barely made it up here. Not sure how easy it will be to get back to civilization."

"What is the alternative?" Nikki's voice scaled up. "You're telling me we have to *stay* in this place? In the haunted mansion with a dead body, and his murderous accomplice running around?"

"Haunted hotel, to be precise. But you're right, there's no telling what the other guy might be up to, and I've already spent more time with Ty than I ever wanted to, so let's go. Maybe we'll catch a break and the storm will let up."

They both jumped as a crack of lightning brightened the basement, followed by a boom of thunder.

"Or not. But listen, this place is big enough that we can hide, if we have to. Wait it out. No one knows about Hazel's hiding place; we can hunker down in there for a while."

"You're not serious."

"I have Necco Wafers in my backpack," said Aubrey.

"Well, that makes all the difference, then. Seriously, Aubrey, I'd rather take our chances on the road than stay here one more minute."

"Okay, then," Aubrey said, blowing out a breath. "Let's try our luck on the road."

Nikki nodded, and they quietly rushed up the stairs to the corridor that led to the main floor, hurried past the library, the sitting room, and the dining room, then out to the atrium, now flooded with water. They climbed through the broken window and jogged down the driveway.

The rain was coming at them sideways, and the trees were whipping and bending dramatically in the fierce winds. A large branch had fallen atop the stone wall.

"I'm not sure we can walk in this, much less drive," yelled Aubrey to be heard over the storm.

"Let's try," Nikki shouted in reply. "I want *out* of here!"

They ran toward the iron gates, which were swinging wildly this way and that in the wind. Aubrey's car, parked across the road, beckoned to them like a sanctuary.

But as they neared the gates they heard a thunderous crack as a massive tree branch came crashing down over the road, blocking their exit.

"Great! That's just great!" Nikki yelled. "What's next? A bunch of flying monkeys?"

An ear-piercing shriek rose above the storm's fury. The distinctive scream of a mountain lion.

Nikki and Aubrey stopped short, looked at each other, and, ignoring the advice not to run away from big cats, raced back to the dubious shelter of the Hotel Seabrink. Soaked to the bone and shivering, they climbed through the atrium window.

"What now?" Nikki whispered. "And *please* don't say creepy attic closet."

Aubrey checked her phone again, hoping for some good news. Nothing but failure messages on the texts, and no bars indicating a call would go through.

"I don't know . . . we could try one of the guest rooms. There are so many. I mean, how could he find us?"

"We're leaving a trail of wet footprints."

"Half of this place is already wet. With luck he won't be that clever, or that eager to hunt us down. Probably he's hiding, too. I mean, he just killed someone."

"That makes me feel so much better."

"Follow me," Aubrey said, checking the hallway before scurrying through the kitchens to the servants' stairs. They climbed to the second floor, and ventured down the corridor to the first guest room door. Aubrey opened it cautiously, then waved Nikki in before shutting it. She went to throw the lock, but the device had been unscrewed and was lying uselessly on the floor.

"*Shit!*" Aubrey exclaimed. "Let's find another—"

A man's voice called out: "Who's there? Is . . . is someone there?"

"*Shit!*" echoed Nikki in a fierce whisper.

"This way," said Aubrey, running to the valet pass-through. The voice had sounded fairly far away, but that might have been due to the overwhelming noise of the storm—but whoever it was, he was not nearly far away enough for comfort. After all, the man had already proved himself capable of killing.

"I don't think I can fit through that thing," said Nikki, after Aubrey had struggled through the opening and beckoned to her from the other side.

"You can make it. A few bruises are no big deal at this point."

It took some effort, but Nikki finally made it through and tumbled out the other side.

They stood silently for a moment, listening intently, but heard nothing but the storm. Until Aubrey thought she could make out . . . was that flute music playing?

Rubbing one shoulder, Nikki looked around and asked: "What is this place?"

"The staff working area. Guests would put their clothes in the closet to be pressed and darned and the like. This whole hotel is riddled with secret passages like these, but . . . Do you hear that?"

"What? You hear him again?"

"No, not that. A flute?"

Nikki shook her head.

"I think we need to make our way back to Hazel's closet," Aubrey said.

"Maybe we're safe enough here. I mean, how many people

know about this area? And a grown man couldn't make it through that valet thingee, could he?"

"I don't know, but I don't want to find out. And . . . I don't know why, but it's almost like I'm hearing Hazel's voice in my head."

"I thought she was the Quiet Girl."

"I can hear her flute. And yes, I know how that sounds, but that closet hid Hazel's body for what? Fifty years? Seventy? More?"

Nikki blew out a loud breath. "I suppose if it's good enough for a corpse, it's good enough to keep us from *becoming* corpses."

"That's the spirit. Let's go. Maybe the attic will give us some cell reception since it's up so high."

"I'm not sure that's how cell towers work," said Nikki. "But sure, can't hurt to try. And I think I need those Necco Wafers, too."

"Even the licorice ones?"

"Even those."

Their inane banter helped to keep them calm as they crept up the servants' stairs to the third floor. From there, it was but a few short steps across the landing to the narrow attic stairs, which would lead them to what Aubrey now thought of as Hazel's closet.

But as they emerged on the third-floor landing, they skidded to a halt.

They weren't alone.

THIRTY

Xavi Krasniewski was leaning over the banister, gazing down the center of the stairwell to the stone floor three flights below.

He had a messy noose around his neck; the other end of the rope was tied to the marble plinth holding the crystal ball.

Aubrey and Nikki tried to turn back before being spotted, but Xavi heard them and whirled around.

"What—what are you doing?" he stammered.

"We're just . . . um, nothing," said Aubrey. "What are *you* doing?"

"What does it look like I'm doing?"

"It looks like you're considering hanging yourself."

Xavi leaned over the banister and looked up at the stained-glass cupola overhead. Rain had pooled on the glass, and water was dripping through the failing lead seams.

"Be careful there, Xavi," said Aubrey. "The banister's old; it might not be secure."

"Is Ty dead? He's dead, right?"

"It's hard to tell. He needs a doctor, that much is true."

Xavi again looked at the marble floor three stories down and made a whimpering sound. He had tears in his eyes.

"Xavi?" Aubrey said. "What's going on? What happened?"

"I didn't mean to hurt him."

"I'm sure you didn't," she said, speaking slowly and trying to convey empathy. "But he's a bad guy, right? He didn't give you a choice. You did what you had to do."

"Exactly." Xavi sniffed loudly. "I didn't mean for Ty to hurt anybody. It's just . . . he said he could help me with my You-Tube channel and maybe even with that Netflix deal. He said he knew important people in the industry."

"I didn't know you have a YouTube channel," said Aubrey.

He nodded. "It's called Dontbekras. I don't have a lot of followers yet."

"Well, that takes time, right?" Aubrey said. "So . . . what happened?"

"You mean, like with Ty? Or before?"

"Um . . ." Aubrey thought about the pool of blood around Ty. "How about before. What happened with Dimitri?"

"I didn't mean to. He just . . . he wouldn't *listen* to me. I had to make him listen to me. I kept trying, and it was like the more I tried, the less he listened to me. It was his fault. He forced me to."

"You followed him out to the bluff that night?"

"I just wanted him to listen to me," Xavi said, his voice petulant like a sullen teen. "At first, Dimitri seemed nice, but then when I followed him out there, he told me he couldn't help me and to please leave me alone, and . . . I dunno. My mind went blank. I didn't even realize what happened at first. And I guess . . . I guess Ty was out there, watching the hotel, and he saw what happened. He threatened to tell the sheriff unless I helped him. So I did, but I didn't know he wanted to hurt Nikki, I swear. Nikki seems nice. I tried to talk him out of it, but he, like, totally laughed at me and called me a nerd and a loser. So I stabbed him. Is he dead?"

"I don't know. If he is still alive, we should get him some help, don't you think?"

"Why? You're right, he's a bad guy. Monica told the staff he was after you two. He had your room's key card, you know."

Aubrey's stomach clenched. "He did? Did you give it to him?"

"What? No! I wouldn't do that."

Xavi's outrage at her suggestion that he had helped Ty gain access to their hotel room seemed more than a little absurd considering he had helped Ty kidnap Nikki, Aubrey thought. But maybe she could use that to their advantage.

"Of course you wouldn't," she said. "You're not that kind of guy."

"I'm not! My mother raised me right," Xavi said. "Ty found it at Dead Man's Bluff. I guess Dimitri must have dropped it when . . . Anyway, Ty said he was gonna use it, was gonna hide in your room, maybe, and scare you. He even showed me some panties he stole. He's been following you two for a while, said he followed you up here once and chased you around, and had plans to—"

"No, please don't tell us," said Aubrey, cutting him off. The last thing any of them needed to hear right now were Ty's maniacal plans. "But I'd like to help *you*. If we get Ty some help, that would go a long way with the judge."

"What judge?"

"Xavi, listen to me. You didn't mean to kill Dimitri, right? It was a crime of passion. Maybe even an accident! He wouldn't listen to you, you lost your temper, maybe shoved him a little, but he slipped . . ."

Xavi nodded. "He was holding on to the edge, though, and I . . . maybe I stepped on his hands so he'd let go."

"Okay," Aubrey said, feeling ill and trying to hold her mounting rage in check. Xavi had murdered Dimitri, plain and simple. Not because Dimitri had threatened him or caused him any harm, but simply because he envied Dimitri and wanted what he had. She forced herself to concentrate on extricating the two of them from this dangerous situation; the authorities would deal with Xavi later. "But still, what I'm saying is that it wasn't premeditated. The judge will take that into account. And now, if we get Ty some help, they'll take that into account, as well. Mitigating circumstances, it's called."

Xavi started crying, his sobs amplified by the acoustics of the stairwell. He looked so young, all of the sudden, like a twelve-year-old who still hadn't quite grown into his own skin.

"It doesn't matter anymore," he said, wiping his face with his sleeve. "Ty told me . . . I mean, right before . . . he told me I was a sn-sniveling worm and I should just k-kill myself. It's not like I haven't thought about it before. I mean . . ."

"Listen to me, Xavi," Aubrey began. "You don't need to do this. There are alternatives."

"Ty said I should have done it a long time ago, and, let's admit it, he's prob'ly right."

"Hey, I have a question," said Aubrey, trying to stall him. "Why did you hit Stephen with a car?"

"That guy's a jerk."

"I think you might be right, but—"

"And it wasn't me! It was Ty. He borrowed my car, and said he was trying to hit *you*, not Stephen. I don't even think he knew who Stephen *was*."

"Ah, well that answers—"

"Look, I . . . I'm really sorry. For everything. Sorry about those notes, too. I just wanted you to back off, and my mom's part of a scrapbooking group, so I used her stuff. I figured you'd get scared off. But . . . I don't know what I was thinking." Xavi shook his head. "Could you do me a favor? Tell my mom I'm sorry. I left a note for her by the crystal ball. This . . . I never meant to be this guy. I had dreams, you know? Ideas of what my life would be like. But now—"

"Xavi, please step away from there, and we'll talk this out, find a way forward. There's always a way forward."

He gave a scoffing laugh, looked up to the dripping skylight, and when he looked back a hard glint came into his eye, as though he was transformed. Possessed.

"You know what? You're right," he said. "I mean, why do *I* have to die? I could just kill you both, and then run away. Leave no witnesses. Everyone would blame it on the Seabrink curse, and no one would ever know."

He pulled from his pocket a small pistol, no bigger than his hand, and aimed it in their direction.

Suddenly they heard the sound of a flute playing, the muffled tune emanating from somewhere in the walls.

"What *is* that?" Xavi asked. "I thought I heard it down in the baths, too. So creepy."

Then they heard the warbly voice of a record on the Victrola, despite the fact that Obi had said it was no longer there. The clanking of the elevator, the smell of smoke, the notes of the grand piano from the lobby.

Xavi's gaze shifted over their shoulders and a look of horror crossed his face.

Aubrey and Nikki turned around to see her dancing at the bottom of the attic stairs. The Quiet Girl. As if it were a camera trick, she whirled round, blending into the darkness behind her, leaving trails of herself behind, tendrils of a distorted face. She smiled at Aubrey and Nikki, held her finger to her mouth, uttered, "*Shhhhhhhh!*"

Then she turned to Xavi. Smiled. And rushed at him.

Xavi led out a bloodcurdling scream. He dropped the gun, which skittered along the stone steps, falling down half the flight of stairs.

The banister gave way with a loud *crack*.

Xavi dropped into the stairwell. He gagged and jerked and danced for a moment, then fell silent forever.

Nikki let out something between a yell and a scream. She closed her eyes and turned away, not wanting to see something she would not be able to unsee. Aubrey put the camera between herself and reality, and started snapping photos of the crystal ball, the landing, and the attic stairs.

But the Quiet Girl was no longer visible.

Nikki edged over to Aubrey's side and clutched her arm.

"What in the *hell* just happened?" Nikki asked in a fierce whisper, barely audible above the sound of the storm raging. The wind rattled the windows while the driving rain found its way inside, causing a small stream of water to start cascading down the attic stairs.

The rope creaked as Xavi's body swung.

Lowering the camera, Aubrey dared herself to look at things without the buffer of the camera lens. Her breathing was harsh; her eyes darted toward the attic stairs. The crystal ball seemed to glow, and the black rectangle of the open door appeared to pulse with energy.

She scrolled through her last photos. There, on the stairs, was a young teenager in an apron and a bejeweled headband. She was looking straight at the camera and smiling.

Behind her, easily legible on the wall, was: **BREATHE ME IN BEFORE TAKING ME OUT . . .**

"If I'm not mistaken, the Quiet Girl just saved our lives."

"I'm, um . . . I don't know how to respond to that. I mean, a simple 'Thank you' doesn't seem quite sufficient, does it?" Nikki said in a hollow voice. "I don't suppose you have cell reception yet?"

Aubrey shook her head. "We barely had reception when the weather was beautiful, so I'm guessing it's not going to work. I tried sending texts on my way here, maybe one of them will get through. Maybe help is on the way, even now."

"Maybe. So, now that all the resident murderers are taken care of, does this mean we don't have to hide in the creepy closet?"

Aubrey smiled. "We do seem to be the last two standing. And there's a library downstairs, we could look for—what is it?"

Nikki's gaze was fixed on the stairs below them. *"You've got to be shitting me."*

THIRTY-ONE

A bloodied Ty was mounting the steps. He was deathly pale, one hand pressed against his bloody abdomen. He was sweating profusely, his breathing labored. With a peculiar, crooked smile on his face, he grunted in pain as he leaned over and picked up the gun Xavi had dropped.

"Can you believe this guy?" Ty said, sneering at Xavi's body dangling in the stairwell. "What a loser! At least he solved one little problem for me. Unless you two did that?"

Nikki just shook her head.

"Nikki, listen to me. I'm sorry about your eye, baby, really I am. But why do you make me do these things? I love you so much it hurts, you know that. No one will ever love you like I do. I just want us to be like we were. Remember? Remember how it used to be? All our talks? I just want to *talk* to you."

"So talk," said Nikki. She squeezed Aubrey's arm. "You've got a captive audience."

Aubrey stood glued to her friend's side, her hand on the can of pepper spray at her waist.

"You and I have always had something special." Ty's smile dropped and he glared at Aubrey. "Your so-called friend here has poisoned your mind against me. If it weren't for her, we'd be together. Don't you see? She's no friend of ours."

They had heard all of this before. Ty's moods were erratic, ping-ponging from romantic and sweet, to angry and vengeful, to mournful and sad.

The flute music began piping again. Emanating from behind the walls. First from one direction, then the other.

"What is that?" Ty demanded, cocking his head. "Is someone here?"

"The ghost," said Aubrey. "Her name is Hazel. She has a thing against men, violent men in particular."

He scoffed. "Sure she does. You believe in ghosts, then?"

"I didn't used to," said Aubrey. "But you should spend a little time here at the Hotel Seabrink, and see how you feel. Maybe, you know, spend an eternity."

Ty flinched, and pressed harder on his wound. When he turned his attention back to Nikki, he sounded weepy. "Baby, I'm hurt real bad. And I really didn't want to do this, but you leave me no choice. We'll go together. Her first, then you and me, together. It'll be like Romeo and Juliet."

Ty raised the gun and aimed it at Aubrey, but Nikki jumped in front of her. "*No!* If you're going to shoot Aubrey, you'll have to go through me."

"Aw, don't be like that, baby! But if—"

A loud crack rang out and in a flash the ornate stained-glass cupola caved in, sending a torrent of water down the stairwell and over Xavi's still-swinging body. Shards of glass rained down, much as they did, night after night, in Aubrey's nightmares.

But this time the glass fell on Xavi's swinging body, colored slivers clinging to his wet skin and clothes in a preposterous, sparkly mosaic.

Ty laughed out loud at the macabre sight, then turned back to them. But the smile dropped from his face as his attention shifted to the attic stairs, his eyes widening in terror.

In one smooth move, Nikki grabbed the crystal ball from the marble plinth, whirled around, and hurled it at Ty with deadly aim. The heavy quartz orb struck his forehead with a sickening *thunk,* knocking him off his feet, and he tumbled like a rag doll down the stairs.

The gun flew out of his hand and skittered through the stair rails, landing with a clatter on the marble foyer two floors below.

The crystal ball continued rolling slowly down the stairs: *thump,* roll, *thump,* roll, *thump.*

That crystal ball really did ward off the bad juju this time, Aubrey thought.

Ty sprawled face up on the stairs, motionless.

"How many lives does that guy have?" Nikki cried.

"At least two."

"Is he dead *now*?" Nikki asked.

Aubrey took a few steps toward Ty. His forehead had caved in, and his eyes were wide open and staring.

"Pretty sure he is, this time."

"Good." Nikki sniffed loudly, squared her shoulders, turned on her heel, and headed toward the narrow stairwell that led to the attics. "I'm going to my creepy closet now. Let me know when the cavalry arrives, will you?"

THIRTY-TWO

S o, the Hotel Seabrink has claimed two more souls," said Jasper.

"At least they were the right two, as opposed to Aubrey and me," said Nikki.

Mia, Nikki, Aubrey, and Jasper sat at a high café table at St. Ambrose. The bar was mellow this evening, only half a dozen people, mostly locals, lingering over drinks and garlic bread. When she first walked in, Aubrey had been greeted by Rusty from the firehouse, and Sheila Harrison, the Episcopalian. Nikki was right, she thought: if she stayed around much longer, she'd know half the town.

Nikki had a black eye and sported a bulky white bandage on her wrist, and Aubrey still felt bruised and stunned, but they had survived.

As soon as Deputy Jenkins received one of Aubrey's text messages—"It was almost like an ESP-type deal, I knew in my bones there was something wrong," he insisted excitedly in the retelling—he got in touch with Jasper, who recruited two other friends, and they had managed to use four-wheel-drive vehicles to reach the Hotel Seabrink.

It was only when Nikki and Aubrey heard the men calling out for them that they emerged from the safety of the Quiet Girl's snug hidden closet, up under the eaves. The secret chamber had been surprisingly welcoming. And there, under the blankets, they found the old flageolet. Hazel's wooden flute.

"I can't believe you went to the Hotel Seabrink alone," muttered Jasper. "I promised my nana you wouldn't go without me."

"You're going to have to get over that," said Aubrey. "I tried calling and texting. There was no time to run to Gualala to look for you. I didn't have a lot of options."

When Lucia came to take their order, Aubrey asked for an herbal martini.

"None today, not enough fresh herbs. But I have a new one, called a Spicy Dead Lady. You like spicy? And mezcal? You'll like it."

"Considering our recent experiences, I should hate the name on principle, and yet I cannot resist," Nikki said. She turned to Aubrey. "How about you?"

"Make it two," said Aubrey.

"Three," said Mia.

"Club soda with lime for me," said Jasper. "So, Mia, ready to tell us what the deal was with you doing some kind of occult ritual up at the Hotel Seabrink? You've got Gideon pretty freaked out."

Mia gave a laugh and play-punched him in the arm.

"It was hardly an 'occult ritual.' My grandmother keeps a lot of the old ways, and that includes performing cleansings

on troubled homes. It's not that out there—a lot of people believe in it. It isn't really my thing, but the last time we were
called to Hotel Seabrink on a report about a suspicious fire—
there's never any fire, but we get called up there pretty
frequently—I decided maybe I could help. I wanted to bring
my grandmother up there to do it, but she hates the windy
roads, so she just told me what to draw, and the words to say,
and to pour the salt across the threshold . . ."

"When we first spoke about it in your shop, I got the sense
that you weren't comfortable with the supernatural," said
Aubrey.

Mia hesitated, pushing a few spilled grains of salt into a
triangle shape. "I don't know how to say this, but when I was
up there, I felt something. Heard something . . . not normal.
There was a flute playing, maybe? It sounded like it was in the
walls, but it kept shifting from one area to another. And then
the record player came on, some kind of warbly old song from
the 1920s or '30s, it sounded like."

"We're familiar with those sounds," said Aubrey.

"In any case, I'm not my grandmother. I gave it a whirl, and
I failed, and I swore I'd never go back. There's something . . .
chilling about that place. Something off. Like it's been a witness
to horror and it was irreparably damaged, sort of like how people who grow up in terror can grow up to terrorize others."

"Not always," said Jasper in a quiet voice.

Mia trailed off with a shrug. "I think I'll stick to science
from now on. Performing CPR I can handle, delivering babies
is great, but . . . ghosts? I'm not great at ghosts." She shivered
and shook her head. "I mean, not that I believe in ghosts, of
course. But I wouldn't want to push it."

Aubrey thought of the spirit who had helped them not

once, but twice during the storm. She even had the photos to prove it . . . not that she would share them with the world. Hazel deserved respect, and if the world found out that she actually inhabited the Hotel Seabrink, it wouldn't be long before the building was overrun by obnoxious ghost hunters. Aubrey would honor her secret.

"Oh, look, here he comes," said Mia.

Cameron entered the bar, scanning the area for a moment before joining them at the high table. As usual, his attention was on Nikki.

"Well, hello, gorgeous," he said, his expression turning grim at the sight of Nikki's black eye. "Ah, geez. What happened? Are you okay?"

"We had a problem," said Nikki. "We took care of it."

"Did they ever," Jasper said.

"She's got a great pitching arm," said Aubrey. "As in major leagues great."

"I really do," Nikki agreed. "So, Mr. I'm-A-Goffin, start talking. What did you steal from the Hotel Seabrink?"

"Geez, offer a man a drink, why dontcha?" He gestured at Lucia for a draft beer and took a seat. "Honestly, before, maybe I took some little things, a couple small paintings, a few old books I thought might be worth something. But once you talked about the jeweled headband, I started thinking maybe it was still in the hotel somewhere. And after you found that old body I figured maybe she had squirreled it away, but I tore that place apart and couldn't find it. Then I was getting my hair cut, and my phone ran out of juice, so I was reading this old magazine they had there, and there was this article about where people hide things in old houses? And one of the places was a piano leg. A *piano* leg, of all things.

That grand piano has been sitting right there at the Seabrink, right in the middle of everything, for ages. I tried the legs, and lo and behold, there it was, along with a bunch of old stocks and a big wad of cash. Couldn't get the leg back on right, though, there was this little latch, like, and—"

"And what happened to the headband?" Aubrey interrupted.

He blushed. "I wound up handing everything over to Obi. She was willing to let the other stuff I'd taken go, but that was too big, and she was talking about involving law enforcement. Besides, it's too much for a pawn shop to handle, you get my drift. That jewel's worth a small fortune, sure, but you gotta get it into the right pair of hands, not some yahoo down in a dusty shop in Santa Rosa. The cash I found only added up to a few thousand dollars, but I guess that was worth a lot more back then. I was thinking maybe the bills were old enough to be worth something as antiques, like, but again, I wasn't sure how to fence them."

"Sometimes it just doesn't pay to be a thief," Nikki said dryly.

"Dude, so true!" Cameron agreed.

"So the headband ultimately had nothing to do with anything?" said Mia.

"According to the letters from Effie Mae that Dimitri's sister sent to me," Aubrey explained, "Goffin found the ruby that had been hidden back when the place was a poor farm, and had it put into a headband which he gifted to his mistress, the beautiful French starlet named Colette Badeaux. She, in turn, later gave the headband to Hazel, because she was angry with Goffin for not leaving his wife—which was Effie Mae's heartbreak, as well. Effie Mae gave birth to his child, after all.

Colette also gave Hazel her little flute, the flageolet. Colette spoke broken English, and when teaching Hazel a special breathing technique she would say: 'Breathe me in before taking me out.'"

"So, ultimately the ruby didn't have anything to do with Dimitri's death," said Nikki. "That was due to a troubled young man, acting on impulse."

"Poor Dimitri," said Mia.

"Poor everybody," said Nikki.

"Don't tell me you're feeling sorry for Xavi?" Cameron asked.

"For his family, mostly. But also for him. That he would let himself be driven by such jealousy and stupidity. That he threw away his own life, and Dimitri's, for no reason."

"I've reached out to Xavi's mother," said Mia. "She's devastated, of course, but seemed somewhat comforted by the note he left. He had been troubled for a long time; I don't think it was entirely a surprise that he would take his own life."

Nikki and Aubrey had discussed how much of Xavi's final horrifying death scene to share with their friends, and with the authorities. It was easier, and seemed gentler for everyone, to leave it at suicide. He had left a note, after all.

"What about Ty?" Jasper asked Nikki, his tone gentle.

"I know it probably sounds strange, but I feel sorry for his parents, as well," said Nikki. "They doted on him."

"Maybe that was part of the problem," Aubrey muttered.

"So," said Mia as the drinks arrived and Lucia set frosty glasses in front of each of them, "the police are making inquiries?"

Nikki nodded. "They asked me not to leave the country or anything while they carry out their investigation, but said it looks like a clear case of self-defense. I had already informed them of the protective order, and warned them about Ty. Also, the bartender at Driftwood Cove stepped forward to say they thought they recognized him from the hit-and-run with Stephen Rex."

"Rex is on the mend, by the way," said Jasper. "I spoke with him yesterday. He's still in the hospital but he's in good spirits and is already talking about approaching Netflix to pitch his own series about abandoned buildings."

"Well, that's him sorted, then," said Mia.

"In other exciting news, my hacker friend was able to access Dimitri's thumb drive," said Nikki. "According to his notes, Dimitri had learned that a young mute girl named Hazel—also known as the Quiet Girl—started the deadly fire that closed down the poor farm. She wasn't trying to hurt anyone, she just liked the cleansing properties of fire, apparently. She had grown up in the asylum, and refused to leave even after it was sold. She was probably also beset by guilt, I would imagine—several women died in that fire."

"How did she live there, all alone?" Mia asked.

"She squirreled away canned goods and lived up in the attic walls, undetected," said Aubrey. "She was so small, I imagine she was able to slip through the pipe access vents, which led to every corner of the building. She grew up there; she must have known every inch of that place."

"After the Seabrink became a hotel," Nikki said, "Hazel worked as a scullery maid for a while, and she was befriended by the visiting French actress and musician, Colette Badeaux. But Goffin and the actress had a fight, and he wound up pushing her off the balcony. But of course he claimed it was a suicide."

"*Dude*," said Cameron. "That's . . . a lot."

"Like I said, Goffin was a real class act," Nikki said.

"But why did he kill Hazel?" Mia asked.

"Hazel might have witnessed the murder," said Aubrey. "Or maybe she knew about the maid, Effie Mae, giving birth to his baby? I'm sure she overheard all sorts of things, moving around silently through the walls."

"Or maybe Goffin killed her to get the ferronnière back," said Nikki. "I wouldn't put it past him."

"I just hope the Furies did their jobs," said Aubrey, thinking of that incongruous sculpture in front of the hotel.

"Goffin lived to be in his nineties," said Jasper. "That's a lot of hounding."

"I, for one, am glad he was tormented by his conscience," said Cameron. "I don't go for this killing little girls thing."

"Way to take a stand, there, Cameron," said Nikki.

"And we're thinking that Hazel's ghost has remained?" asked Mia in a quiet voice.

"If we believe in ghosts, we are," said Jasper. "If anyone has a right to haunt the Seabrink, I'd say it's the Quiet Girl."

"I'll drink to that," said Cameron.

"I sort of like the idea that she stayed," said Aubrey in a soft voice. "Although according to what I hear about ghosts, she'll be disturbed by the upcoming renovations."

"Maybe she'll play a few pranks," said Nikki. "But she let us hide in her closet without bothering us, didn't she? I don't think she's a harbinger of death so much as trying to warn people, maybe. Poor thing's been misunderstood all her life. And afterlife."

"Poor thing is likely a figment of our imaginations," said Jasper.

Or not, thought Aubrey. She had not yet confided in Jasper as to everything she and Nikki had seen, much less photographed. It was a lot to process.

Silence descended on the table as all were lost to their thoughts.

"Aubrey, Nikki, how much longer will you be in town?" Mia asked after a moment. "Your time hasn't been very relaxing so far. I hope you have a chance to enjoy our beautiful stretch of the California coast."

"I'm staying a little while longer—taking a few days off of work," said Nikki. "Paramedic's orders."

Mia smiled and nodded her approval.

"Actually, it looks like I might be spending a lot more time in the area," Aubrey said, glancing at Jasper. "Obi thinks the title to the Seabrink will soon be clear and asked if I'd be willing to work on the architectural plans for the renovations."

"Of the Hotel Seabrink?" asked Jasper with an inquisitive smile. "We'll make you a Gualalan yet."

"Also, it's a bit unorthodox, but Obi is looking into the possibility of laying Hazel's remains to rest there on the grounds of the Seabrink. With a proper memorial to her."

"You think that will help her rest?" asked Mia.

"It will help *me* rest," said Aubrey. "The Quiet Girl deserves a little recognition and respect, after all these years."

"Good reason to stay and work on the project, then," said Jasper, holding her gaze across the table.

"That's not the only reason to stick around," said Aubrey.

Jasper gave her a slow smile.

"I also have unfinished business with the whales," she added.

"Whales?" Mia asked.

"When I checked in to the Driftwood Cove Inn, I was promised migrating whales, and dammit, I want to see migrating whales."

"Then whales you shall see," said Jasper, holding up his glass in a toast. "To the whales."

"To Gualalans, old and new," Mia said.

"To renovating the creepy old Hotel Seabrink," said Nikki.

"To Hazel," said Aubrey, and they all clinked glasses. "To the Quiet Girl."

EPILOGUE

The grounds of the Hotel Seabrink are bustling this misty morning. Construction sounds—hammers and compressors and power saws—vibrate from the building, supply trucks rumble up and down the drive, gardeners clip hedges, and caterers are setting up tables and chairs out on the south lawn for this afternoon's inauguration of the historic marker and plaque.

But for the moment Aubrey stands alone, breathing deeply of the pine-scented air, gazing around at the newly sculpted landscaping, and reveling in a rare moment of privacy while on the Seabrink premises.

Aubrey had designed this little grotto—reminiscent of the source of the spring—to honor Hazel and the many others who had fallen at the Seabrink. As far as anyone knows, Hazel's are the only actual remains that are currently interred on the hotel grounds; during the renovation they had excavated and disinterred the remains of those buried during the old poor farm days, which were then laid to rest in a cemetery north of Gualala.

But Hazel is still here on the grounds of the Seabrink, where she always has been.

The plaque in the grotto offers a brief history of the Seabrink Poor Farm and Asylum, including a list of the deceased that had been gleaned from the old leather-bound ledger. It goes on to describe the glittering heyday of the Hotel Seabrink, including several names of its most famous Hollywood visitors. The marker lists other names, as well: the teenager who was murdered in the baths, and the young man who had been found on the stairs, and the French actress, Colette Badeaux, who had fallen—or been pushed—from the balcony.

Aubrey and Obi had worked long and hard on the wording for the plaque, and finally decided to include references to the alleged Seabrink curse and suggestions about the spirits that might still roam the halls of the grand hotel.

As Obi likes to point out, a lot of people *like* the idea of vacationing amid ghosts.

As they finished up the renovation of the attics, Aubrey had taken the little flute back into Hazel's closet and played a few notes, thinking to herself: *Breathe me in before taking me out.*

Afterward, they had decided to shut up the room, and keep it as is.

Now, Aubrey glances up at the attic window and her breath catches. Is that just the morning light glinting off the now-sparkling windowpanes?

Or could it be Hazel's ashen face, gazing down at her? Does

the Quiet Girl remain ever watchful over those who enter the Seabrink and wander its labyrinthine halls?

As Aubrey lingers in the little grotto, she thinks to herself that had she known about the Seabrink curse, she might never have come.

But she would have missed out on so much.

ACKNOWLEDGMENTS

As always, thanks are due to so many—too many to list here.

First, to my editor, Kerry Donovan, and my agent, Jim McCarthy. The book business can be perplexing at the best of times, and yet you help make it a pleasure.

Thank you to the wonderful staff of Four-Eyed Frog Books, especially Jill Blew. A bookstore brings such vitality to any town, and Four-Eyed Frog enriches Gualala immeasurably by surviving, and thriving.

Many thanks to Jayson Rackerby for invaluable stories about San Francisco's Suicide Club and the Cacophony Society, and insights into synesthesia and the strange sacredness of abandoned spaces. And as always to Xe Sands, for introducing us—and for sharing with me her own take on photography, visual storytelling, and the grace of the camera lens.

To our amazing Sea Ranch neighbors, especially Dan and Denise Skinner, Scott and Linda Nevin, and Linda and John Harrel.

As always, I have so much gratitude for my brilliant sister, Carolyn, for all the rewrites and suggestions and historical knowledge. Thanks to Susan for fostering my love of reading as a youngster, and for reading everything I write as an adult. Much, much, much love for my wonderfully patient, ever-supportive fella, Eric Stauffenegger . . . *toujours et encore.*

Please note that while Gualala is a real town, there is not, and as far as I know never was, a hotel like the Hotel Seabrink in the hills along that stretch of coast. The Driftwood Cove Inn is loosely based on a lovely midcentury jewel called the Timber Cove Inn; the St. Ambrose is based on the beautiful St. Orres, just north of Gualala.

Four-Eyed Frog Books is real, though, and awaits your visit!

Continue reading for a preview of

OFF THE WILD COAST OF BRITTANY

available now!

Natalie

And we're off, to continue our adventure on the Île de Feme,
renovating a historic guesthouse and opening a gourmet restaurant!
Because when you grab life with both hands and hold on tight,
you never know where it might lead:
perhaps even to a rocky island off the Wild Coast of Brittany.
Stay tuned . . . This tale is not over.

—last line of the international bestseller *Pourquoi Pas?*
A Memoir of Life, Love, and Food by Natalie Morgen

T hings are not going according to plan.

Natalie Morgen sat at a little metal café table on the
stone terrace outside her guesthouse, watching the latest herd
of tourists surge off the ferry.

An aroma of anise rose from her glass, melding with the
smoke from her cigarette and the scent of the sea: a mélange
of dead things and salt, of the abundant seaweed and muck
that marred the shallows during low tide. Island sounds
wafted over on the ocean breezes: the histrionic seagulls
squabbling over a bucket of scraps Loïc had tossed out the
back door of Pouce Café, the rhythmic lapping of the waves in
the snug harbor, the murmurs of visitors enjoying lunch at

outdoor tables, the occasional clacking of a *pétanque* ball hitting its mark.

Natalie imagined the newly arrived tourists mistook her for a native sipping her glass of pastis—though most of the actual natives preferred beer or hard cider—and enjoying a sunny day on the beautiful island.

And sitting here like this, Natalie could almost convince *herself* that life was good. That everything was going according to her carefully thought-out plan. Lounging on the terrace of her ancient guesthouse, its rusted iron gates still secured with a heavy steel chain because the Bag-Noz was not yet open to guests even though accommodations were well-nigh impossible to come by on the Île de Feme during tourist season.

Bobox strutted by, clucking in contentment. The fluffy white hen had come with the house and had made herself a little nest in the shed. Ridiculously long snowy white feathers on the top of her head quivered and swayed with every confident step, reminding Natalie of stylish Parisian ladies in photographs of yore, parading along the Champs-Élysées in their feathered chapeaux.

Paris. What had Audrey Hepburn said? "Paris is always a good idea"? *Maybe for Audrey—she was rich and beautiful*. Absentmindedly scratching at a mosquito bite, Natalie realized she was clenching her jaw, willed herself to relax, took another sip of pastis, and turned her attention back to the ferry passengers.

Trying to get their bearings, the newcomers weren't talking much as they staggered along the walkway that hugged the thick stone seawall. Some carried inflatables and beach toys; others clutched scraps of paper with instructions directing them to their rented guesthouses or to the Ar-Men, the only hotel on the island. It must have been a rough crossing:

most of the children and more than a few of the adults were decidedly green around the gills. A storm had thrashed the region yesterday, and though to the unpracticed eye the sea today appeared calm, Natalie had lived on the island long enough to have learned a few things from the locals, such as how to read the water.

Or, at the very least, when to ask a local to read the water for her.

Even after a storm appeared to have passed, waves lingered and surged. The swells rippled out and down, the awesome energy of the sea needing time to settle, to balance, to find its footing once again, lulling sailors and landlubbers alike into a false sense of security only to slam them with choppy water if they dared venture too soon onto open sea.

Sounds like a metaphor for life. Natalie made a mental note to post this, or some poetic version of it, on her social media accounts. She should post some photos as well. It had been a while. Too long. She had a lot of followers to keep happy.

Her readers loved the snapshots of Natalie's life on an island off Brittany's Côte Sauvage, or "Wild Coast," where she was renovating an ancient guesthouse with the proceeds from her bestselling memoir. In fact, some of the new arrivals lurching off the ferry might well be women of a certain age who had read Natalie's inspirational tome about finding love and self-fulfillment through the art of French cooking, and had decided to come to the Île de Feme in search of love and self-fulfillment themselves.

But as Natalie had learned, in a most painful way, the Île de Feme was still an *île*—an island—which meant that if you didn't bring it with you, you weren't likely to find it here.

How could she explain that her Prince Charming—*le prince charmant*—the man she had fallen head over heels for, the reason she had come to Brittany in the first place, had turned out to be a lying, cheating, spendthrift schmuck who left her high and dry in the middle of their guesthouse renovation?

Even his name was annoying. *François-Xavier.* Being French, he insisted she say his entire name, every time: *Franswah Ex-ah-vee-ay.* A full six syllables. *Six.* She once made the mistake of addressing him simply as François and he accused her of calling him by another man's name. *A classic case of psychological transference,* she thought with grim humor, knowing what she now knew.

François-Xavier claimed it was an American thing to give people nicknames. He was forever blaming her quirks on Natalie's being American, but in this case it might have been true. In college Natalie's roommate had introduced herself as Anastasia—a mere four syllables—and everyone on their hall immediately shortened it to Ana. Natalie had fought her entire childhood against being called Nat because it sounded like the bug, which her sister Alex insisted she was: Nat-the-Gnat, small and annoying, bouncing around ineffectually, her head in the clouds, endlessly searching for some unspecified thing. Natalie had tried to retaliate by calling Alex "Al," but in that irksome way of smug elder sisters, Alex had embraced the name, stomping around the family compound, singing at the top of her lungs, loudly and proudly, the old Paul Simon song "You Can Call Me Al."

Which wasn't fair. Nobody wrote songs about gnats.

Natalie never managed to outmaneuver her four older sisters, and Alex, the closest to her in age, had been by far the most difficult.

Anyway. François-Xavier. She supposed two names suited a man with two faces. Still . . . that gorgeous face flashed in her mind: the sloping, intensely blue eyes; the sensual, full lips; the hint of dark golden whiskers glistening along his strong jaw. The way he looked at her as if she were not merely desirable but that he had waited a lifetime to meet her, that he was ready to share his life with her, wanted to create a family with her right here on his native island, where they would play *pétanque* in the sunshine, drink *apéro* curled up in front of the hearth, and cook together, transforming classic ingredients into sumptuous dinners through the dedicated application of traditional French techniques. And then they would linger for hours over elaborate meals with friends and extended family and guesthouse visitors.

That was the plan.

At the moment her cupboard contained half a box of crackers, an open bag of dry-roasted peanuts, and a single fragrant cantaloupe well on its way to rotten. Natalie had forgotten to put an order in with the mainland store that shipped to the island, so today's ferry brought no bundle of supplies with her name on it. She supposed she could buy something from the island's small but well-stocked "general store" that primarily served the tourists, but if she did, then the shop's owner, Severine Menou, would know Natalie's business, which meant soon *everyone* on the island would know Natalie's business.

Better to do what she usually did these days: eat the ample *menu du jour* at Milo's café, blaming it on her torn-up kitchen, and stick to peanuts and stale crackers—and plenty of pastis—the rest of the time.

François-Xavier would be appalled.

What was she going to *do*?

Keep your head down and the pretense up. At least until she figured out her next steps. She had told everyone that François-Xavier was on a business trip to Paris, scouting for kitchen help for the gourmet restaurant they were supposed to be opening in the large dining room of the Bag-Noz Guesthouse. No one was surprised; he traveled to Paris frequently, after all.

This time, though, François-Xavier had no intention of coming back. How long would it be until people started asking questions? Also, the construction workers hadn't shown up this week and Natalie was afraid to ask why. It might be because today was *le quinze août*, a national holiday. Or just because it was August, and a lot of French people took the entire month off for vacation.

Or maybe the workers hadn't shown up because Natalie hadn't paid her latest round of bills. When he left, François-Xavier siphoned off the majority of their shared bank account, leaving her to get by on a few hundred euros and maxed-out credit cards until she received a check from her publisher for the book under contract, a follow-up to *Pourquoi Pas?*

Her jaw tightened again. Her current work in progress was meant to be all about her perfect life with her perfect French chef fiancé, and to be accompanied by a liberal smattering of recipes and mouthwatering photos of the meals she and François-Xavier prepared—what her agent referred to as "French food porn."

Natalie took a deep quaff of her pastis, let out a long sigh, and watched as Bobox scratched the ground in her incessant search for something appetizing in the sandy soil of the weed-strewn courtyard.

François-Xavier was supposed to run the kitchen, and Natalie was supposed to run the guesthouse, and it was all supposed to be beautiful.

But things had not gone according to plan.

Alex

Why in the world did Nat move to such a godforsaken island?

The Île de Feme revealed itself coquettishly, first appearing through the ocean mist like a vague mirage, the kind that shimmered along the highways on the hottest days in the remote Northern California mountains where they had grown up.

Alex squinted as she tried to make out the strip of low gray land. On the map the distance between the island and the mainland didn't look that great, but she and her fellow passengers had left the dock at Audierne more than an hour ago. The bobbing ferry had headed north at first, turning to the west only as they passed the Pointe du Raz, no doubt fighting the channel's famous currents and avoiding the perilous reefs that lurked just below the surface, a vast underwater maze protecting the island. According to the travel guide—Alex always did her homework before beginning something new—the jagged rocks had brought catastrophe to legions of sailors and ships over the years. There had been 127 documented shipwrecks in this strait, and that was only since they'd started keeping track, back in the seventeenth century.

The danger of shipwreck explained the multitude of lighthouses on the islands and along the coastline of the channel. Perched on rocky outcroppings, the towers appeared lonely and stoic. And hauntingly beautiful.

Alex had also read in the travel guide that the French had two words for lighthouses: A *phare* was a true lighthouse, usually home to a keeper in the days before the lights were automated, while a *feu*—which meant "fire"—was a smaller tower with a smaller light. The mile-and-a-half-long Île de Feme was equipped with one true lighthouse on its western tip, a large *feu* on the easternmost point, and two smaller *feux* dotting the southern coast.

Clearly, this region was well acquainted with maritime disasters. Alex found that oddly comforting. She was a bit of a shipwreck herself, these days.

Alex climbed the steep set of steps, clinging to the cold metal handrails as the boat pitched sharply. She would be windblown on the open upper deck, but breathing fresh air was preferable to being stuck in the crowded, too-warm cabin below.

Upon boarding the ferry, Alex had needed to harness every bit of self-control not to climb onto one of the seats and order everyone to don one of the bright orange life vests stacked in a cupboard. *Don't be weird,* she reminded herself for the thousandth time. *Act like the others.* Besides, her very limited French didn't include the vocabulary for "Safety first, folks!" She had contented herself with grabbing a dozen seasickness bags from a little stand next to the first aid cabinet and making a mental note of the location of an inflatable life raft.

Just in case.

As soon as they left the shelter of the harbor, the sea had become choppy and the boat was tossed about like a child's toy, heaving this way and that, leaving its human inhabitants retching and grasping onto their molded plastic seats for dear life.

Alex dug through her backpack for a package of wet wipes and handed them, along with a couple of the seasickness bags, to a young father whose little girl had lost her lunch all over the front of his sweater vest and jacket.

She wasn't feeling all that chipper herself, but keeping busy helped. It always had.

Father and child taken care of for the moment, Alex made her way to a seat and kept her eyes on the horizon, gazing at a fixed point to quell the nausea.

But seriously. Setting aside the "why" for the moment, how had Nat even *found* this place?

Her little sister was forever bragging on social media, posting photos of herself dancing in the clubs of Budapest or shopping the open-air markets of Marrakech as she traipsed around the world "looking for herself." On her blog she posted rambling descriptions of how she spent her days learning classic French cooking, and her nights hobnobbing with chic Parisians in cinematic wine cellars and cabarets. And if all that weren't galling enough, irresponsible, carefree Nat had hit the jackpot when her memoir of finding herself and food—and *love*—became an international sensation, lingering at the top of the bestseller list week after exasperating week.

Even the title annoyed Alex. *Pourquoi Pas?* Seriously? There were always plenty of reasons why *not*.

But readers hadn't agreed. Which just went to show you that people today were pathetic, casting about for direction in their sad little lives.

Was *she* now doing the very same thing? Alex's stomach heaved at that thought more than the seasickness. An island off the coast of Brittany had sounded so fantastical somehow when the thought first occurred to her back in dusty Albuquerque. It had seemed as if destiny had intervened. Anyway, she didn't need forever. Just a little while, time to regroup, to make a plan. A respite from the convoluted joke that her life had become.

Alex was out of options; she would swallow her pride. She had swallowed worse in her time.

The island slowly came into focus. A small lighthouse had "Ar-Men" painted on it in tall black letters. The harbor was full of boats, varying in size from small dinghies to good-size sailboats to large commercial fishing vessels. A sweeping curve of three-story houses with crenellated rooflines fronted the harbor, gazing to the east as though longing for the mainland. Built of native stone, the houses were covered in stucco in cheerful shades of chalky blue, pale apricot, and butter yellow, their steeply pitched slate roofs studded with redbrick chimneys.

A charming fishing village, read the caption under Nat's bio at the end of *Pourquoi Pas?* Alex had stared at that bio for a very long time before making her decision to come.

The rocking of the ferry subsided as the engines slowed and they navigated the entrance to the harbor. As they chugged toward the dock, a large silver tail broke the surface of the water. *The Little Mermaid!* Alex thought, then chided herself. It was probably some kind of huge fish, the likes of which she would no doubt soon be dining on.

Alex hadn't let Nat know she was coming. Her sister might not be thrilled to see her, but Nat wouldn't turn her away.

If there was one thing they had learned from their survivalist childhood, it was the imperative of helping one another when the chips were down. As their father, who insisted on being addressed as The Commander, liked to say as he stomped around their remote mountain compound, barking orders and checking the contents of their bug-out bags, "Nothing brings a family together like Armageddon."

It won't be forever, Alex thought, blowing out a long breath. Just until she figured out her next steps. If there *were* any next steps.

Or until her own personal Armageddon arrived.